Margreete's Harbor

ALSO BY ELEANOR MORSE

White Dog Fell from the Sky

Chopin's Garden

An Unexpected Forest

Margreete's Harbor

A NOVEL

WITHDRAWN

ELEANOR MORSE

ST. MARTIN'S PRESS
NEW YORK

First published in the United States by St. Martin's Press, an imprint of St. Martin's Publishing Group

MARGREETE'S HARBOR. Copyright © 2021 by Eleanor Morse. All rights reserved. Printed in the United States of America. For information, address St. Martin's Publishing Group, 120 Broadway, New York, NY 10271.

www.stmartins.com

Designed by Omar Chapa

Library of Congress Cataloging-in-Publication Data

Names: Morse, Eleanor Lincoln, author.
Title: Margreete's Harbor : a novel / Eleanor Morse.
Description: First edition. | New York : St. Martin's Press, 2021.
Identifiers: LCCN 2020048590 | ISBN 9781250271549 (hardcover) |
    ISBN 9781250271556 (ebook)
Subjects: LCSH: Domestic fiction.
Classification: LCC PS3613.O77855 M37 2021 | DDC 813/.6—dc23
LC record available at https://lccn.loc.gov/2020048590

Our books may be purchased in bulk for promotional, educational, or business use. Please contact your local bookseller or the Macmillan Corporate and Premium Sales Department at 1-800-221-7945, extension 5442, or by email at MacmillanSpecial Markets@macmillan.com.

First Edition: 2021

10 9 8 7 6 5 4 3 2 1

For the young ones

Alden, Wyatt, and
Tenzin Dekyi

The world begins at a kitchen table.

—JOY HARJO

PART I

I

Burnt Harbor, Maine

1955

Margreete walked barefoot down the hallway to the stairs as the floor-boards muttered. "Move," she said to the cat. Downstairs in the kitchen, she rummaged around in the refrigerator for his food and spooned some bacon drippings into a frying pan to fortify the bread crusts she'd saved for the crows.

As the flames licked around the edges of the pan, she went back upstairs and shuffled into her slippers. On the landing was a mouse that Romeo had partially eaten in the night. She bent over the head-less body, the gory truncated neck, the tiny pink feet shriveled up like dried weeds. The cat joined her and nudged the carcass with a paw. "Why did you kill it?" she said. "It just wanted to live its life."

Her feet were still cold, and she turned on the hot-water faucet in the bathroom and watched the steam rise and the small bubbles gather on the bottom of the tub. Scooping water into her palm, she wet her lips and was about to undress and climb in when she smelled something burning.

She ran downstairs and found a sheet of flames engulfing the stove. Before she knew it, her sweater was burning, and fire was leaping to the wallpaper to the ceiling to the beams holding up the roof. She filled a saucepan with water and dumped it across the top of the stove and threw what remained at the wall. Then ran out into the yard, stripped off her sweater, and rolled in the snow.

Across the field, Mr. Wootton, who'd just finished milking his cows, saw smoke, jumped into his car, and hurried down the road and into the driveway. "I'm all right, I'm all right," Margreete said, pushing him away.

Black smoke billowed out the open door, and Mr. Wootton ran inside and called the volunteer fire department while Margreete dragged a hose out of the garden shed through the mudroom and into the kitchen. The flames leapt higher, but the hose didn't work—she'd brought both ends inside. She didn't know how the firemen got there, but now they were everywhere. "Who are you?" she asked. More and more men came, nudging her out of the way into the living room. She stood in the doorway while the avalanche of water from the hoses knocked pictures off the walls.

By the time the blaze was brought under control, the kitchen was pretty much gone.

She watched as two of the volunteer firemen climbed into the town fire truck; the rest—all but one—got into their pickup trucks and sped away. Margreete stood in her singed nightgown and slippers, leaning heavily against the doorjamb. The kitchen window was clouded with soot, the stove was a sludge of water and grease, and the wallpaper, with its cheery red and yellow teapots, hung down in black strips. Two cupboards had fallen, bringing down most of her crockery and glasses and teacups. The clock had smashed on the floor.

"I didn't mean to do it," she said, looking at the fireman who'd stayed behind.

"No, ma'am, I know that. I'm sorry. . . . Do you remember me? I played basketball with your son Peter in school."

She shook her head.

"You burned your hair," he said.

Her hand reached up and came away with threads of black carbon. "My sweater burned, too. Synthetic crap. Wool wouldn't have gone up like that. I threw it in the bushes. Who'd you say you were?"

"Terry. Terry Leroux."

"Who did you say you were?"

He told her again, and offered to take her out to breakfast.

His forehead had streaks of ash across it. She saw that his eyes were very blue. Wide open, as though he still had his boy-eyes. He was wearing big black rubber galoshes.

"You have big boots."

He turned his feet out slightly. "Regulation equipment."

"I have to tell Liddie. You know Liddie? I'm not looking forward to calling her, I can tell you that. I have to clean up this mess before we go."

"Your daughter would want you to get something to eat, Mrs. Hocking. I wouldn't bother to tidy up in here. You'll need a wrecking crew. How about if I get some clothes for you?"

"Not underwear. I don't allow men in my underwear drawer."

He went upstairs and came down with a pair of pants, a shirt, and a sweater draped over one arm. "There's a dead mouse up there."

She remembered now. Romeo had woken her, yowling like a jungle cat. She'd been dreaming, rocked in the bottom of a boat someone was rowing.

She took the clothes he offered and went into the living room and took off her nightgown next to the upright piano. "Don't look!" she called. The fireman was picking up wreckage from the kitchen floor. "You brought me a pair of pants with a hole in the knee. Never mind. No one looks at old ladies." When she was dressed, she reappeared in the doorway to the kitchen, weeping quietly.

"Don't touch anything in here," he said. "Everything's hot. Are you hurt?"

"Only this." She held out her arm and pointed to the inside of her wrist.

With a gloved hand, he opened the refrigerator door and dabbed butter on the burn.

"Shall I take you to the clinic?"

"No."

"Someone will come and rebuild your kitchen, Mrs. Hocking. It'll all come right in the end."

"That's what you think. You're still young."

He brought her coat and held it for her.

"I'm not a klepto . . . kleptomaniac. I didn't mean to do that."

He helped her into her boots. "Pyromaniac? I know you're not."

"Not one of those types."

He took her elbow and led her toward his pickup. A sentinel crow clung to a branch and waited for its morning scraps, its black feathers lifting in a wind that coursed up from the bay. Small flecks of snow drifted down. The ground was already covered with a foot, blue tinges in the shadows where it had drifted.

He helped her up into the truck, closed the door for her, and came around the other side. As he turned the key and the engine started, she opened the passenger door and started to climb out. "My cat!"

"Don't worry. Cats are good at taking care of themselves. Better shut the door now."

She pulled it closed, and he backed out. She took in the smell of cigarettes and man stuff. She liked the litter. She liked men, period. She remembered once in New York City being on the arm of someone in the rain, a warm rain, and the lights shining through the water, fogged with beauty, like how she'd always imagined Paris.

The road was plowed smooth, heaped on the edges with fresh snow. The heater in the truck rattled, and she looked over at the fireman's face, trying to place him.

"It's March," he said. "Almost spring."

"Are you making conversation, or do you really believe that?"

He laughed. "Making conversation, I guess." He glanced over at her, still smiling. "March always has its own ideas."

Inside the café they sat in a booth, and Lillian, the owner, came out from the kitchen and said she'd already heard about the fire and was awful sorry. She had a large, kind face, a big bosom, short arms. Her grandson ran around, ducking under tables, racing in and out of the kitchen. Lillian poured coffee, and Margreete and the fireman both ordered the he-man breakfast: three eggs, home fries, sausages, bacon, toast.

"You're not from around here, are you," she said to the fireman.

"Five generations."

"I'm only two."

There was a clatter of dishes and buzz of voices, mostly male: ironworkers, fishermen, grandfathers needing to get out of the house.

"How's your arm now?" he asked.

"Are you a doctor?"

He smiled. "An electrician."

"Do you fix lightbulbs? I've got one out in the basement. It's creepy down there, and I don't dare fix it with the light out."

"I could do that for you."

The food arrived, and they began in silence. "That's pretty spicy, you know," he said as she picked up the hot sauce.

"I like hot." She shook some on her eggs, pushed her hair behind her ears, and dug in.

"You're doing yourself proud on that plate, Mrs. Hocking."

"Mr. Hocking died. I'm Mrs. Bright again. I went back to Mrs. Bright."

"I remember Mr. Bright. Irving was a good man. Do you have anyone to help you around your place now?"

"I miss Irving Bright. My daughter thinks I need help. She lives in the Midwest, I forget just where. I need to tell her what happened. I'm dreading it, I can tell you that."

"You know, I used to be sweet on Liddie in high school, but she wasn't interested."

Margreete looked up from her plate at him. "She always was picky. You have nice eyes, but they're kind of close together. Liddie thought close-together eyes were a sign of someone who wasn't all that bright. Maybe that was why. She was looking for someone su-persmart."

He laughed. "That wouldn't be me."

"She's married to a nice fellow. I don't know how smart he is."

"What's your son Peter doing now?"

"He lives out of state." She polished off the sausage and had a couple more bites of toast. "Liddie's married now." She finished the rest of her toast and smiled.

"You've got a healthy appetite."

"You'd think I'd be fat I eat so much, but I'm not plump like I used to be. Pretty soon I'll be like an old rooster."

"No, you won't. You're good and strong. Not like a lot of old ladies—I don't mean you're an old lady. But they get kind of scrawny, you know what I mean?"

"Well, you're a handsome young fellow yourself."

"I could do with losing a few pounds."

Lillian's grandson came back, popping up behind a booth. Lillian pulled him out, held him by his shirt to slow him down, and laid a check on the table. Looking at Margreete, she said, "You'll need food, honey, until you get your kitchen up and running."

"I've got shredded wheat. I've always liked shredded wheat."

"I'll bring something by."

Terry Leroux put some bills down on top of the check. "Fine breakfast as always, Lillian." He reached a hand across to Margreete. "Ready to roll?"

"You're paying?"

"For old times' sake."

"I knew you before? My brain isn't what it once was. My son Willard says . . . He thinks I should be in a home for old people."

They climbed back into the truck and traveled down the peninsula toward her house, passing Wilbur Crockett's old boat, which had been sitting in his yard for forty years. "That boat's not going anywhere," said Terry.

"He could use it for a planter. Sunflowers."

"I remember you had a real nice garden once." He drove into the driveway and asked, "You want me to wait while you call your daughter?"

"No, it's okay. But I'm not looking forward to it. I can tell you that."

"How about that lightbulb down in the basement?"

"Not right now. I've got things to do."

"You'll be okay?" He wrote down his name and number and gave it to her. "Just in case. Let me help you into the house."

"I'm all right. Thank you." She opened the door and got out.

"I'm just a phone call away if you need anything. You won't forget?"

"I've got to call my daughter now. I'm dreading it."

She waved to the truck, watched it disappear, climbed the porch steps, and went to open the door to the mudroom. Her hand reached up for the handle, but she couldn't make herself go inside. Not yet. She sat down on the steps, where the firemen had trampled the snow. It was cold on her bottom, and flakes fell into her hair.

"Mrs. Bright is in a mess," she said. She brushed the snow off her boots and brushed again as more fell. No flowers anywhere these days. The garden with Irving had been wild with blue bachelor's buttons mixed with carrots, sunflowers, beets and cabbages, morning glories, delphinium and forget-me-nots, red geraniums and peas, roses, buttercups, daffodils, sweet alyssum. After Irving died, she couldn't get anything to grow in Mr. Hocking's garden, not even pansies.

She hugged her arms around her shoulders and called Romeo. She called and called, but he didn't come. She bounced her knees together for warmth. Cats never do what you want them to. That was a basic truth about cats. They had their opinions, and if they decided to hide, you could look right at them and not see them.

Light snow settled into the crook of her arm where the creases of her green coat were deepest. One single snowflake landed on her boot, and she doubled over to look at it and squashed it before it could melt. She moved her toes inside her boots to keep them warm. "You went away," she said to Irving, "and you didn't tell me where you were going. You always told me when you'd be back, but it's been two weeks. It's not like you. I called the police, but they told me they couldn't help me. They told me not to keep calling them, that I mustn't call them again. Liddie said that you died and we buried you. I find that hard to believe."

She stood and went to her car, got the broom out of the backseat, swept off the snow, and got in. She opened the glove compartment, took out the key, and started up the engine. Her hands were cold on the steering wheel, and she put them in her pockets while the wipers swept back and forth. She cranked down the window on the driver's side, backed out, headed up the driveway, and turned right toward the end of the peninsula.

A wide boat of a car moved unsteadily down the road, a head out the driver's side, a voice calling "Romeo!" over and over.

2

Liddie read in the paper that twelve inches of snow had fallen in Maine, with more expected. She imagined her mother rising from her pillow, a question mark in her gray eyes, hair askew, a rakish bun driven to one side by sleep. She thought of her opening the door to all that snow and sweeping at it with an old wedge of a broom, most of its bristles gone.

She needed to call Mr. Dickie and make sure he'd dug her out. Harry was still asleep beside her, with one hand holding on to the covers. In the innocent way he was clutching the blanket, it reminded her of a child. His hand was pale in the predawn light, fine dark hairs from his wrist to his fingers, one fingernail blue where he'd hit it with a hammer fixing a piece of siding that had come loose from the house.

She tucked the quilt around Harry and closed her eyes. After eight years in Michigan, she still missed Maine and the ocean: gray one moment, green the next, rough and troubled with waves, then serene. The chuckling eider ducks, the cormorants standing on a rock drying their wings. The smell of salt and moldering seaweed, the call of gulls, the winter loons, the peninsula that ended at Barrow's Point and looked straight out to Bull Head Rock. And beyond, Tinker's Island, which in certain lights and tides appeared to be floating on air.

Burnt Harbor, where her mother still lived, was the tiniest eyelash compared to the great eye of ocean beyond. There was no movie theater where she'd grown up, no library, no bowling alley, no Laundromat, no hardware store, no bar. But you could get gas and a few groceries at Shirley's Shop 'n Drop; there was Lillian's Café, and a book barn sitting in the middle of a field halfway down the peninsula, an inn owned by a German couple, and Lola's Hair Salon, where her mother had her hair done. One tiny Congregational church. She still knew people from her high school days, but Nan was the only close friend she kept in touch with.

Normally, Harry was awake before now, but he'd been up grading papers until after midnight. She folded back the covers on her side of the bed and lowered her feet to the floor. The sky was light gray now, shot through with a glow of brightness. She grabbed her robe off the back of a chair, crept downstairs, and turned up the heat. Fred thumped his tail and stood over his food bowl, looked at her, looked at the bowl, then gobbled the food she gave him, his tag dingdinging against the metal bowl. She started a school lunch for Bernie, put an English muffin in the toaster and coffee in the percolator.

Harry was dressed for work when he came downstairs. His blue tie with the airplanes was crooked, and she straightened it.

"Did you finish?" she asked.

"Not yet."

She handed him a cup of coffee. "Lot going on today?"

"Not too bad." He ate fast—Wheaties, the Breakfast of Champions, orange juice, coffee—then gave Liddie a kiss and started for the door.

"Darling, wait!" she called out. "You're wearing two different shoes." He ran upstairs, back down again, and gave her another kiss. She heard the car door open and slam shut, then the sound of the car disappearing as he rounded the corner.

Liddie went outside with both their children to wait with Bernie for the school bus. And also to wait for their neighbor, who babysat Eva three mornings a week while Liddie practiced the cello. Both kids were frightened of the school bus, and the best mornings were when the neighbor turned up before the bus. That didn't happen today, and by the time Bernie was on the bus and Julia, the neighbor, had turned up, Eva was screaming.

"She'll be all right," said Julia, grabbing up Eva in her arms. "Wave goodbye to your mom. We're going to have loads of fun this morning. Just wait till you see what I have planned."

"What?" asked Eva.

"It's a surprise."

Liddie returned to the house, feeling like a bad mother, and found Fred sitting sentry duty at his food bowl. She gave him a little more breakfast, and he chewed the last of his crunchies, followed her into her studio, and settled himself on the floor.

She opened the blinds to the early light of the Michigan day and snapped open the latches of her cello case. A spiderweb over the window shifted gently in the heat from the radiator. She felt uneasy this morning in the sudden stillness of the house. Somehow it felt like a tiny act of courage to rosin her bow and begin, but as soon as the Bach Sarabande sang out of the strings, the music carried her: tension, resolution. Every morning, she began with Johann Sebastian Bach, who still had the power to set the world straight these two hundred years after his death.

Because she didn't go to an office every day, or teach at a school, some people who hadn't heard her play thought of her music as a leisure pursuit, as in, *How lovely to have something to occupy you when your children are at school.* This was so far off the mark, she didn't know where to begin to explain. Music was her lifeblood, as necessary as food and water and air. It was her anchor and solace; it gave meaning to the meaningless. And it was also her financial contribution to the family: teaching, giving concerts, and playing as first cellist in the Ann Arbor Symphony.

She tightened her bow, gave it a bit more rosin, and took out Schubert's Piano Trio in E Flat. She and her trio partners, Ross and Claude, would be playing this piece in the university chapel that coming Sunday night. They'd performed it last winter in a small town in Indiana, with the audience clapping in ignorance and delight after each movement and the steam pipes in the concert hall gurgling and clanking and snorting. Ross, the violinist, had a temper tantrum, stopping in the middle of the second movement and demanding that someone do something about the racket. There was scurrying in the back of the hall, the slamming of a door, and then a groan and hiss as the radiators died down and the music began again.

It would be different this coming Sunday.

She heard the ghost sound of the piano playing rhythmic, staccato chords in her ear, and then her cello began a melody so lovely, it seemed to play itself.

When the phone rang, Liddie almost let it go but then thought, *Something with the kids,* and dashed for it, nearly tripping over Fred.

"I burned down the kitchen," her mother said. "I forgot something on the stove. The fire went up to the ceiling and then I caught fire, and a bunch of men came with hoses, and the fireman who used to be in love with you cleaned up some of the mess and took me to breakfast at Lillian's and the whole house smells like smoke."

"Wait. What?"

"My old red sweater and part of my nightgown went up. I rolled in the snow and put out the fire on me. And Romeo hasn't come back. I put a blanket outside to keep him warm."

"Is someone with you?"

"The firemen came, but they all went home."

"Where are you?"

"In the living room."

"Are you hurt?"

"One place on my arm. A little of my hair burned." Her mother's voice quavered and grew small. "It's nothing. The fireman put butter on it."

"It's not nothing, Mom. It's certainly not nothing. I can try to come for a day or two and come straight back. I have a concert Sunday."

"Don't come."

"I can figure it out."

"No. Don't come."

"Nan can stop by until I can get there."

"I don't want her to see me like this. And I don't want you to come."

"It doesn't matter how you look, Mom. Where will you sleep tonight?"

"Here."

"How will you cook?"

"I don't like cooking."

Liddie heard a sound as though her mother was kicking bits of broken crockery around the floor, then quiet.

"They dumped a lot of water everywhere. You wouldn't think they'd need to flood the house."

"I'll pay for a motel for you."

"I don't want a motel."

They were quiet for a moment.

"You can't live in the house like that."

"I didn't want to tell you what happened."

"I'm not mad. You didn't need to worry about telling me. You could come out here for a few weeks. I'll send you an airline ticket. They can rebuild the kitchen while you're here. You can hear the concert. We're playing Schubert. You'd like this piece."

"I'm not leaving. Romeo is missing."

"It would be temporary. Just a visit. Romeo will come back. Someone can look after him while you're here."

"I don't want to. Don't boss."

"I'm not bossing. I'm worried."

"I'm going now."

"Wait."

The line went dead.

Liddie stood there with the bow still in her hand. She tried calling back and got a busy signal, then placed the cello and bow back in their case, did up the latches, and set the case upright in the corner by the piano.

The last phone call like this, her mother had forgotten to turn off the outside water faucets before winter hit. The pipes had frozen and cracked, and during a January thaw, a geyser spouted up the side of the house and rose in a giant monument to forgetfulness. Her mother didn't realize anything was wrong until she heard a ripping sound when the glacier pulled down half the siding.

Liddie called her old friend Nan, then Jonny, the carpenter who'd replaced the siding, then Lillian, who said she could arrange to get meals delivered. She called her brothers, Peter and Willard, but she could only reach Willard, who said their mother was getting worse and shouldn't be living alone and why not put her in a home?

"*You* put her there, then," she said, knowing he wouldn't. He was a coward.

She tried her brother Peter again and then recalled that he was in Mexico with his good friend, Tom.

It felt worse than wrong, being so far away. The last time she visited Maine, she'd kissed her mother goodbye and backed out of the driveway, and her mother had stood on the porch in the rain, her arm lifted in a wave, wearing a red sweater that Liddie had given her. She could still picture that splash of red against the gray shingles of the house, still feel the way her throat had caught, knowing that someday her mother would not be there to wave.

Fred looked sideways into her face, pushed up on her elbow, and went to the door, just the tip of his tail wagging. She followed him out into the yard and stood on the back step while he dashed around, returned out of breath, and leaned into her legs the way her cello had been leaning into her before her mother's call.

Harry came home from work late that afternoon while Liddie was teaching. She heard him in the other room and knew he'd be setting his briefcase down, opening the refrigerator door and staring inside, greeting Bernie and Eva, then piling them into the car while he drove the babysitter home. She wanted to go to him, but she had three more lessons before she was free. At last, she said goodbye to her final student, a boy with sticking-up-straight black hair and cheeks that went pink when he played fast. She was very fond of this boy and hoped he'd continue on with music.

She came into the kitchen, dog-tired, and by then Eva and Bernie were already eating at the table.

"Hungry?" Harry asked her. "Spaghetti and meatballs. Blue plate special. Two ninety-nine."

"Something happened to my mother," she said, sitting down. "She forgot something on the stove this morning and burned down the kitchen."

"Jesus."

"What happened to Grandma?" asked Bernie.

"Grandma's okay. Her sweater was on fire, but she was smart. If your clothes are on fire, you shouldn't scream and run around. You should do what Grandma did—roll on the ground."

"Like this?" Eva got off the chair and rolled under the table.

"Get up, now," Harry said. "Finish your meatball."

"I spoke with her this morning," said Liddie. "She doesn't want me going there, and she won't come here. I've called various people— the insurance man, carpenters, my brothers, Nan. Lillian who runs the café is bringing her food."

"What about you?" asked Harry.

"What *about* me? She's losing it. Last week she couldn't even remember what the thing was called that flies in the sky."

"It's Superman," said Bernie. "Faster than a speeding—"

"Stop," Liddie said. "I need to talk with your father. Go upstairs and get ready for bed—you, too, Eva—and pick out a book you want to read. I'll be there soon."

They left the table and lingered in the doorway. "Go," said Harry. "Now." He dished up the blue plate special for the two of them and sat down. "What about your brothers?"

"Peter's in Mexico. Willard, well . . ."

"There must be nursing homes in Maine," said Harry. "Isn't that the obvious solution?"

"I told you before, she won't hear of it."

"She'd have to be moved against her will—"

"No."

"I haven't finished. Or we find someone to stay with her."

"Her insurance won't cover that."

"Meaning what?"

Liddie said that she'd already talked to someone in geriatric care services and the government would only pay if her mother was incapacitated. And even if they covered the cost of someone to stay with her, she'd throw them out of the house, the way she had when she'd broken her arm.

"So what are you saying?"

She cast her eyes away from him. "I don't know."

She thought they shouldn't have moved so far away. Looking back, her mother had been fine when they'd made the decision, but a certain vagueness had been creeping in, now all too clear. She recalled her mother as a young woman, hanging laundry on the line, burning dinner, running the vacuum to bagpipe music. She was Rubenesque, with arms big enough for everyone, her laugh like an explosion. She blew into a room like wind, hooked rugs with large, splashy flowers, turning the wool in her plump hands. That brave, outspoken, mischief-loving, no-nonsense mother had become an ant in a high wind, her mind clinging to a straw.

3

Harry woke in the middle of the night and found Liddie sitting up in bed, looking straight ahead into the darkness.

"It's late, honey," he said.

"I can't sleep."

"What are you thinking?"

"Nothing."

"You might as well tell me."

"About what it would be like if we moved back."

"To Maine?"

"If it were your mother . . ."

"If it were my mother, she'd do what she already did—have a stroke and get it over with."

"Well, in that case, why not just go bop Mom over the head?"

"For godsakes."

"I'm sorry. You didn't say that."

"Do you want a back rub?" he asked.

"No." But she lay down again.

"We're settled here," he said.

"She has a big house."

"What? *Live* with her?"

"Five bedrooms, counting the third floor. We could fix it up, insulate it better."

"She's going to get worse," he said.

"That's the whole point."

"What would we do for work?"

"We'd find something."

"You're serious, aren't you."

"If you didn't want to come, I could go with the kids and see how it works out."

He turned on the light and narrowed his eyes. "What are you talking about? Why on earth would you say such a thing? They're my kids, too. We're married. . . . Unless you don't want to be married."

"I want to be married."

"I don't want to move there," he said.

She squinted. "Do we have to have that light on?"

"I think better with it on."

She was turned sideways to him, her arm folded under the pillow, one hip jutted out, hair backlit by a lamp. Fatigue had sculpted her face into something ravished and strangely beautiful.

"I always liked your mother," he said.

"But you didn't sign up for a package that included her."

"No. And I like it here. There's our friends, the house, the garden. I like where I'm teaching—the kids are bright, the other teachers are decent. I bet the schools are crappy there."

"Maybe."

"On the positive side, there's the ocean."

"And a field where the kids can run around."

"Plus, they'd get to see what it's like to lose your mind," he said.

"Turn out the light, would you please?"

"But why would we have to live in the same house?"

"Isn't it obvious?" she said. "We can't afford anything else."

He turned out the light.

"It's one thing for her to burn down the house with herself in it. It's another thing with our kids in it."

"She'd have to stay away from the stove."

"And the woodstove," he said.

"Are you saying you might be open to going?"

"I guess I need to be, don't I."

"I was thinking I'd go to Maine after the concert and talk with her. Maybe she'd be up for an old-age home here."

"How long will you be gone?"

"I don't know."

He moved toward her and put his hand softly on her throat. "It's not your fault. And if it hadn't been for your mother, there'd be no Liddie."

Making love, he'd never bitten her before, never dreamed of it. It was her shoulder, smooth, curved toward him. She yelped like a colt, and he stopped, surprised at himself, at this primal act that felt, somehow, like the redressing of some imbalance. Afterward, he wanted to apologize, to say he hadn't meant to hurt her, but that wasn't exactly true, so he didn't say it. It felt as though they'd crossed over into new territory—a balance shifting, a foot in the unknown.

Sometimes he wanted to ask if he was still a good-enough lover. He hated thinking she'd just go through with it to please him, a kind of condescension. Visible through the window behind her head, Orion was slightly tilted; Betelgeuse on the left shoulder shone bright, a red supergiant, supposedly nearing the end of its life. By the time it exploded, none of this would matter: Liddie, Margreete, their children, Harry, whether they lived in Ann Arbor or Burnt Harbor.

"Burnt Harbor," he mumbled as they were headed back to sleep. "Kind of ironic."

"Years ago," Liddie said, "someone had the bright idea to light a cigarette and refuel an old outboard motor at the same time. The white pines along the shore went up like fireworks. But Mom renamed the harbor. She thinks it's Margreete's Harbor now."

She turned toward him and reached for his hand. "I'm tired. Are you?"

"Yes."

"Good night, my love."

4

Liddie found herself facing the trip with dread. If their family ended up moving, it would mean giving up everything. This was the trio's eighth year together, and she loved both of her partners. Ross, the violinist, was a musical scholar, on the volatile side; Claude, the pianist, could be stubborn, as could Liddie. As strongly as they each held to their opinions, though, the disagreements among them were almost always edged with good humor and mutual regard.

Thinking about what might lie ahead, Liddie left quickly after the Sunday concert, before either of her partners could ask about the tears in her eyes. She mumbled something about Schubert getting to her every time (which was true), packed up her cello, and almost ran to the car.

Early on Monday, she set off by bus to Detroit, then Detroit to Boston, and up the coast to Maine. Her friend Nan picked her up in Portland the following morning. "You're skinny," Liddie said, hugging her.

"Stress," said Nan. "Did you sleep on the bus?"

"Only about three hours. The girl next to me from Boston had a hamster sitting on her lap, running around a wheel. Probably powering the bus."

They found a café in Portland and ate scrambled eggs and talked about Nan's marriage, which had recently ended.

"You didn't know it was coming?"

"Completely sideswiped," said Nan. "He came home one day and said, 'It's over.' 'What do you mean?' I asked. 'I mean, it's over. You and me.' The last time we made love, I said to him, 'We're so lucky.' Looking back on it, I don't think he replied. Or maybe he said something noncommittal. It makes me feel like a fool."

"You know," said Liddie, "I never quite trusted him."

"Why didn't you say something?"

"Because I figured you knew him a lot better than I did. Besides, you seemed happy, and that trumped everything."

"I'd have more self-respect if I could be vengeful. But I pleaded with him and ran down the road after his car. So pathetic. And now I just feel sad. And ashamed of myself. I finally understand, he was a classic narcissist."

"You haven't a thing to be ashamed of," said Liddie.

"How does love just disappear? And where in the world does it go when it dies?"

"A big garbage dump in the sky," said Liddie. "Used condoms, old valentines and roses . . ."

Nan dropped a bit of scrambled egg on her sweater, dipped her napkin in her water glass, and dabbed at it. "Can't take me anywhere . . ."

"It's fine now."

"Anyway, your mom told me yesterday you were coming back to live here."

"I never told her that."

"That's what she thinks."

"I don't know. It's complicated."

"In other words, Harry doesn't want to."

"There's a lot we'd both be leaving behind. He's teaching at a really good junior high—I've never seen him this happy in a job. And I can't even imagine leaving the trio. It would break my heart."

Nan drove her down the peninsula, and Liddie waved goodbye to her from her mother's porch. One of the steps needed mending, and from here she could see black on the siding outside the kitchen window where the glass had cracked.

"Mom?" She opened the door and heard the washing machine in its spin cycle. She stepped inside and shouted again. She found her mother with her hand on the washer, feeling the vibration of the machine. She wondered how long she'd been standing there. "Mom?" she said softly, not wanting to scare her.

Her mother jumped, and a smile of recognition softened her face. "Where have you been?"

Liddie wrapped her arms around her—she smelled as though she hadn't taken a bath in a few days. "Are you okay?"

"Where have you been?"

"I just took the bus from Michigan. Nan drove me from Portland."

"That's nice. What took you so long?"

"You didn't want me to come."

"I did want you to come. Nan who?"

"You know Nan. My old friend."

"That's nice."

"How's your arm?"

"It's fine."

"Can I see it? Remember you got a burn on your arm?"

Her mother raised and lowered the sleeve of her sweater. "It's fine."

"What about the kitchen? Have they started work?"

"Oh, you don't want to go in there. I get meals from the government now."

"Lillian's the one bringing food, right?"

"I thought it was the government behind that."

"I don't think so. It's Lillian." Liddie unpacked an electric kettle from her suitcase. "This is for you, Mom. So you can make coffee without the stove. The switch turns off automatically. I'll put it upstairs in the bathroom. The water's shut off down here, right?"

"Where have you been, anyway?"

She hugged her again. "It's so good to see you, Mom. I missed you."

That night, in the living room, Liddie said, "Harry and I have been talking about the kitchen. About what happened."

"You don't want to go in there."

"That's why I'm here, Mom. You could have died in that fire. It's not safe for you to be here alone anymore."

"I'm all right. I didn't die."

"You're not all right."

"I just said, I'm all right."

"We could hire someone to live here with you, Mom, do the cooking, make sure you're okay."

"Who?"

"We'd have to find someone. But you couldn't keep firing them the way you did before, when you broke your arm."

"I don't like strangers in the house. They open my drawers. Poke around."

"If you don't want someone here, you could move to a facility where they cook your meals."

"I'm not staying with a bunch of old people." She pushed herself up out of her chair and paced the floor. "You'd have to shoot me first."

"Mom? Could you sit down?"

"I want to stand up." She did a turn around the room and sat down on a round piano stool.

"What do you want to do, then?"

"Stay here. I already told you."

"You just burned down the kitchen."

"I didn't mean to. Where's Peter?"

"Peter's in Mexico. I can't reach him right now. Willard thinks something has to change."

"Willard is an old busybody. Don't listen to Willard. And I told you, I didn't mean to start that fire. You don't have to get all huffy."

"I'm not huffy. What if you moved out to Michigan?"

"Without the ocean? I honestly don't know how you stand it out there."

They were quiet awhile, and Margreete got up and paced around the room again.

"How about some tea?" Liddie said.

"How about some gin rummy?"

Liddie laughed. "That's a game."

"I mean straight gin."

She stayed another two days, took her mother out for dinner, talked to Lillian about continuing the food deliveries, met the contractors who'd promised to start on the kitchen the week before but hadn't, and spoke with her brother Willard about her mother's insurance company.

Over the phone with Harry, she told him her mother didn't want a caretaker, didn't want to move into an old-age home, and definitely wasn't coming to Michigan.

"Did you ask her what she thought about us moving there?"

"I thought that was pretty much off the table."

"It's not."

"You'd do that?"

"I think you should bring it up."

"Our conversations aren't exactly what you might think of as conversations. I tell her something has to change, and she wanders around the room, sits down, gets up again, and tells me what she won't do."

Her last full day there, Mrs. Powers, an old friend of her mother, arrived unexpectedly. Liddie offered her a cup of tea, excused herself for a moment, opened the door to the blackened kitchen, and found a box of Lipton tea in the pantry. Upstairs in the bathroom, she washed three cups and set them on the edge of the bathtub. She waited for the water to boil and thought of a day, long ago, when Mrs. Powers had come home from the hospital after gallstone surgery and Liddie's mother had gone to visit her and brought Liddie along. Mrs. Powers was sitting up in bed in a strange state of exultation; beside her on her bedside table was her gallstone. She picked it up and held it out to them. The thing was whitish, about a half inch across, perfectly round except for a small indentation like a belly button. Later, Mrs. Powers took her gallstone to Goodman's Jewelers and asked them to polish it and set it in silver.

Liddie brought the tea downstairs as Mrs. Powers was telling her mother about the minister of the Congregational church and how he'd left town under a cloud. She stayed two and a half hours, filled them with gossip, and finally left.

Liddie's mother said, "I thought she'd never go."

"She sure knows everyone's business."

"Everyone but her own. I wish I was never her friend. But once you start, you can't stop."

"Being a friend?"

"That's right."

That night, Liddie asked, "How would you feel if Harry and I and the kids moved here?"

"Not them. But you could come."

"I could only come if everyone else came."

"You can come, but not the others."

"Mom, listen. You can't stay here by yourself anymore."

"I said you can come but not the others."

"I won't leave my family behind."

"Why not?"

"Because I love them."

"Fine, then."

"Fine, what?"

"Fine, then. Let them come. But I'm not leaving this house."

"It would have to be all of us."

"Yes, all right. Just don't talk to me about it anymore. And they can't have my bedroom."

5

Liddie arrived home, and that night Harry said, "There's no real alternative, is there? Other than wrestle her kicking and screaming into a van and drop her off at an old persons' home like a lost kitten."

"You have such a way with words," Liddie said.

"I can't stomach the thought. You can't, either. But we can make a life there, I guess. Can't we?"

"Do you mean it?"

"I mean it."

"She won't be easy to live with."

"Harder for you than me," he said.

They told the kids the next day that they were going to move, that they'd be living with Grandmother Margreete. Bernie said he wouldn't go, not for a million dollars. And then Eva said she wouldn't, either, that she was scared of her grandmother.

"Oh," said Harry, "so when the moving van comes, the two of you will stay right here and cook your own meals? Fred might as well stay, too, and you can feed him. We'll leave your beds for you, and the stove and refrigerator."

Eva started to cry, and Liddie hugged her and said, "Daddy's just kidding, honey. We're all going. No one's going to get left behind. Not you, not Bernie, not Fred. And not Valentine." She was speaking of the two-and-a-half-foot avocado tree that Liddie had grown from a pit when she and Harry were first together.

Harry's school threw a going-away party for him. Their good

friends next door said they wanted to have a party, too, but Liddie pleaded for them not to. She could barely hold herself together during the last concert she played with Ross and Claude, and she cried outright when her favorite cello student left for the last time. It felt as though she'd exploded the ground out from under her feet.

They hired a Mayflower moving van to take their goods from Michigan to Maine. Four men stampeded through the house, packing cardboard boxes, carrying furniture out to the truck parked in front. Fred lay in the dirt by the wheel, smiling ingratiatingly, his tail wagging with the hope of not being left behind, the brow of his black-and-white head wrinkled, as though he'd already been abandoned. He wandered in and out of the house in agitation, and when he found his dog dish gone from its usual place in the kitchen, his eyes filmed over with grief. Bernie, who'd given up his one-boy resistance campaign, called him outdoors, sat beside him on the curb, and put his arm around him.

Harry dug up a few of his favorite peonies in the backyard to take along. And that last day, he walked the perimeter of their small vegetable garden, saying goodbye to the vegetables they'd asked their friends to harvest before the new people moved in.

It was June of 1955. Harry had finished out the school year, and Liddie had played her final concerts and said goodbye, one by one, to her cello students. Liddie felt a low-grade, floating panic in her bones. It was hard to pinpoint—it was, well, everything, including the country. The United States had exploded two more atomic bombs at the Nevada test site. Test houses incinerated and collapsed, test mannequins melted into blackened, twisted heaps of plastic.

The moving van left in the evening, bulging with the contents of their lives. The family drove a short distance, long enough for Fred to fill the car with his gassy anxieties. Then they checked in to a Howard Johnson's motel with its orange roof and cupola like a horse barn, and smuggled Fred into the bathroom with his food and water before going into the dining room for their own dinner. They sat at a Formica table on Naugahyde seats, grumpy and tired, except for Eva, who was excited about the plastic menu. Harry had pulled a muscle in his back that afternoon, moving the stove out from the wall to clean. Not until he was drinking a martini did he mention the pain.

"Why didn't you tell me?" asked Liddie.

"What was the point?"

"Well, I expect we're through the worst of it."

"Not really. There's unpacking. And work starts next week."

Bernie looked up from the menu. "Where, Dad?"

"Bath Iron Works. They build warships."

"Cool."

"Not cool. It was the only job I could find this summer." Harry gestured to the waitress for a second martini, while on her placemat Eva drew a picture of the Ann Arbor house they'd just left. She made herself and Bernie large, her mother and father smaller, and Fred sitting under a large tree—a tree Eva would always remember as her favorite, although there'd never been a tree there.

"I'm sorry," Liddie said.

"What good does that do?" said Harry. "We've left now. And what are you sorry about—that you have a mother you care about?"

Bernie gulped his ice water. "You didn't want to go, Dad? Why didn't you say so?"

"Because it was inevitable," said Harry. "Because this was the right thing to do. What do you want for dinner, kiddos? Hamburgers and french-fried potatoes?"

"And Coca-Cola," said Bernie. They were not allowed to drink Coke. Liddie always said it would rot their teeth.

"All right," she said. "Have whatever you want."

"And ice cream for dessert?"

"Yes, whatever you want," said Harry.

In the middle of the hamburgers, they heard singing through the wall. *Jesus loves me, this I know. For the Bible tells me so.*

The waitress told them there was a religious convention that weekend. The kids were next door while the parents prayed in the ballroom. *I'm H-A-P-P-Y, oh, I'm H-A-P-P-Y, I know I am, I'm sure I am.*

Liddie took another swallow of wine. "Brainwashing those poor kids."

"What does that mean?" asked Bernie.

"Never mind."

After dinner, Bernie threw up in the bathroom from too much fat and sugar and emotion and ice water. Fred stood next to him, wagging his tail and taking note of the additions to the toilet bowl. Eva cried that she missed Bobo, her bear, who'd been packed in a box by mistake and was God knows where, rumbling across Pennsylvania. Liddie finally got into bed with her and held her until they both slept.

The next morning, they climbed into their 1952 Plymouth station wagon—the Old Gray Mare—and made their way through Toledo and Cleveland and Erie. The backseat was divided down the middle: Bernie's half, Eva's half, Fred at their feet. Bernie scowled at Eva; Eva scowled back. He made faces, mocked her. "Mom, he's doing it!" Eva kicked wildly and flailed her arms to get him to move his feet back on his side. He moved his foot an inch, moved it back. Their hate was pure, running clear as water. "Mom! *Mom!*" But their mother ignored them, looking straight through the front windshield at squashed bugs.

Harry wanted to take a detour through Johnstown, Pennsylvania, where his mother had been born. Liddie wanted to take the fastest route to Maine, straight through New York State. She saw it was important to Harry, though, and gave in. They arrived in Johnstown in the middle of the afternoon and checked into another Howard Johnson's, which looked the same as the one before, and smuggled Fred into the bathroom. Harry sat down on one of the beds and turned to Liddie. "Thanks, honey, for humoring me. I know you didn't want to come here." Turning to Bernie, he said, "Do you know what happened in Johnstown back in 1889?"

"What?" asked Bernie.

"Please," Liddie said. "You'll give him bad dreams."

"I want to know," said Bernie.

"One of the worst floods in the history of the United States," said Harry. "And do you know who was in it? My mother, and her mother and father."

"What's a flood?" asked Eva.

"I'll take you out and show you. Then you'll understand."

"I'm not coming," said Liddie. "I've got a headache."

Years later, Eva would recall the chocolate ice cream cones her father had bought them that afternoon, hers dripping down her leg. And she would remember how scared she'd been, thinking she needed to get back to her mother, that the water could come rumbling down the mountainside at any moment.

Bernie would recall an old brick building with the white flood marks six or eight feet up the wall, way higher than he could reach. He would also remember the passion with which his father said that this disaster, which killed more than two thousand people, was not caused by an act of God but by greedy men. His father pointed to the mountains above Johnstown and said, "See up there? A bunch of rich men thought they'd have a fishing-and-hunting club up the mountain. People like Andrew Carnegie. They dammed up the river to make a lake, and even though a few people said the dam wasn't strong enough, they didn't pay any attention. At first the lake wasn't that deep, but it got deeper and deeper, and still no one fixed the dam and still the rich guys weren't worried, because what harm would come to them if it broke? They weren't thinking of the people down below who worked their lives away, making steel and locomotives. One day, the rains came, and more rains and more rains, and the water went over the top and the dam burst, and four billion gallons of water rushed down that mountainside like a tidal wave, faster than a car can go." He pointed upward, to the path the flood had taken. "There were no phones to warn the people, and there was no time for anyone to get out of the way. A few people ran to higher ground and escaped, but most everything was swept away. Horses, babies, houses, even a train. My mother, who you never met, was born in Johnstown in 1889, two months before the dam burst."

"Did she get out of the way of the water?" asked Eva.

"If she hadn't, honey, I wouldn't be here, and you and Bernie wouldn't be, either."

"But children died?" said Eva.

"Yes."

"My grandmother held on to the baby, and they went shooting down the river on a mattress and were saved. But my grandfather was working that day at the Cambria Iron Works, and he was swept away and never found."

"I want Mommy," Eva said.

"You scared her, Daddy."

Harry grabbed his daughter's hand. "You know," he said with sudden cheerfulness, "all that happened a long time ago. There are rules about building dams now, not like the olden days. How about an ice cream cone for you two?" Both kids were crying when they came back to the motel, and Eva was still scared the next morning.

On the way out of Howard Johnson's, Liddie said, "You might have spared them the gruesome details." She pulled Fred away from a spot on the carpet out in the hallway, where his nose quivered. "Fred, get away from that."

"What?" Harry asked, closing the door to their room.

"You have no off switch."

"This is an important part of their heritage. My own mother survived that flood. How else are they supposed to learn?"

They got into the car, and Bernie and Eva staked out their territories in the backseat. "Noah's ark is also a part of our heritage," said Liddie, "but who wants to hear that story? The only thing that holds a candle to the brutality of it is Abraham and Isaac." She drove out of the motel and turned right, trying to find her way out of Johnstown. "Which road do I take?"

"Left at the next light."

"I mean, if you were God, why wouldn't you just tell the people to shape up? But don't drown them all. And what did the animals ever do to deserve that? Retribution for what, in their case? And what about the children? What did they ever do? God can't be all that great if he goes around drowning animals and children."

"Watch the road, darling."

"I'm watching."

"You didn't see that truck until the last minute."

"I didn't hit it, did I?"

"We're all tired," Harry said. The kids were quiet in the backseat, cowed by all the talk of drowning.

Her tone softened. "What do you think it did to your mother?"

"I imagine she'd have stayed here if it hadn't happened. As it turned out, she just wanted to get out. She didn't really belong anywhere—didn't you feel that about her?"

"I didn't really know her. She held herself at a distance."

"That's what I mean."

They passed through Elmira, stayed overnight in Schenectady within sight of the huge General Electric sign that lit up the sky, continued on to Concord, New Hampshire, then to Portland, Bath, and down the long peninsula to Burnt Harbor.

Burnt Harbor Road had once been paved but was now equal parts dirt and asphalt. On one side were tumbled-down stone walls and on the other side a wild tangle of grass and field flowers spilling into the thoroughfare and waving with the passage of their car. Lupines, blue and white and pink, blanketed a field just before Margreete's driveway.

From the porch steps, Romeo watched the car drive in, hid in the bushes as people spilled out, and then made his move. With his yellow eyes gleaming and black tail twitching, he stalked Fred until the enemy jumped back into the car and cowered in the well between the front and back seats.

"That's one mean cat," said Bernie. "Does he live here?"

"He's a good boy," said Liddie. "Just a little wild."

Margreete came out onto the porch. "We finally made it," said Liddie. "It took us three days." She put her arms around her mother, almost weeping with relief.

"Where did you come from?" asked Margreete.

"Michigan."

"How long are you staying?"

"We're going to live with you now."

"Who said?"

"We talked about it, remember?"

"I don't recall that."

6

They were a herd of locusts. Worse. An occupying army. The girl cried. She was scared at night. She was a silly little thing. And the two children fought by day, slammed doors, thundered through the house.

It appeared to be more than a visit. A moving van came with boxes. And more boxes. The bedrooms were full. This wasn't her idea. When you're old, you need quiet; you need the shadows of the day to fall over you softly.

The wild geese had returned and settled down by the harbor. Margreete heard them after dark through her open bedroom window. Their voices were urgent, the way the world began. They honked across the sky, barking like flying dogs. They brought tears to her eyes, remembering her mother's tears when the geese would return in the spring.

What remained in her, Margreete, were memories that no one cared about, except her and maybe the boy who was living here now, with the large, dark eyes. Her daughter's boy—at least that's who Liddie said he was. He asked her questions and she told him. "I was born in Saskatchewan. And my mother was born there. And my father, Pearl Crowe, was born there, too. Saskatchewan is in Canada, a long way from here."

"Pearl is a girl's name," the boy with the dark eyes said.

"I ought to know the name of my own father," she said. "That was his name. Men were named Pearl in those days. Hush, now. After my parents married, my father couldn't find work. They had baby

Margreete—me—and they moved to the United States, to Upstate New York, where winters were dark and you could smell the cold coming over the Adirondacks. My mother said it was a pure smell, like a mountain spring. My father worked in the woods, and my mother worked at home, and when her work was done, she walked to the lending library with me and brought back armloads of the great classics in a rucksack. She read Shakespeare to me; she expected great things, but there was no money for great things. When I was seven years old, my parents moved to Bath, Maine, where my father found a job working as a sternman on a lobster boat. He built most of this house with his own two hands and with the help of his brother, who lived with us for a time. It was no bigger than a shed when we moved here."

"Why did you burn down the kitchen?"

"Did you think I meant to do that?"

"So we'd have to move here."

"You thought I wanted that?"

"Because you were all by yourself and you were losing your brains."

"I like being by myself."

"And do you like being *not* all by yourself now?"

"No."

They were sitting in the living room, Bernie on the round piano stool with the wrought-iron legs, and she next to him. He twirled around on the stool, and the stool did a heavy little gallop.

"Do you want us to go away?"

"Why? Do you want to go back home?" she asked.

"We can't. We sold the house. Some other people are living there now." He looked at her. "Why are your teeth all scraggly, like a witch?"

"I used to like to chew ice, but I don't do it anymore. It got expensive. Let me give you a piece of advice. Never start the habit. It's a hard one to break. Worse than a smoking habit. Don't ever start that, either."

"So they broke, just like that?"

"Just like that. Crack. Crunch."

"Did you ever have a husband?"

"Three of them. The first one died. He fell off a tall building, although some people say he jumped. I'll never know. The second one was Mr. Irving Bright. Irving grew up in the Bronx. Do you know where that is?"

"It's in New York."

"You're a smart boy."

"Yes, I am."

"Irving was a smart boy, too, but he was very impractical, growing up in New York. He knew nothing about cars. He didn't even know how to drive when I first met him. I had to drive him everywhere. I did the tune-ups and oil changes, and when winter set in, I lay flat on the frozen ground in the shed out there with my head beside the tire of the car and wrestled the chains onto the bald tires so the car could climb the hill to the main road. Traction is a very important thing." She said it again, for emphasis.

"What's traction? Like a tractor?"

"Don't interrupt, I'm telling you something. I was good behind a wheel. Irving was lousy with cars, but he was a fine man anyway, and we loved each other."

"Where is he now?"

"Under the ground. He was seventeen years older than me. He worked in a shoe factory. Then he was a day laborer. The work took a lot out of him. He was a handsome man. An amorous man. I'm not telling you what that means."

"I know what it means."

"What does it mean?"

"I don't know."

"Irving was a good father. Liddie was fifteen when he died, Peter was thirteen, and Willard was eleven years old."

"My mother Liddie?"

"Are you Liddie's boy?" She peered at him and went on. "I didn't know what to do after Irving died, I was so sad." She was quiet a moment. "I didn't know what to do. When you kids were in school . . ."

"I wasn't with you, Grandma. You're talking about someone else."

"When you kids were in school after your father died, I used to drive a long ways and come home before the bus dropped you off. Sometimes I didn't make it home in time. One day I almost thought I wouldn't come home at all. While I was driving, I sang songs that Irving and I used to sing together. 'Pistol Packin' Mama.' 'Some Enchanted Evening,' you know that one?"

"No."

"Some enchanted evening," she sang. "You may see a stranger . . ."

"You don't know how to sing, do you, Grandma."

"I used to sing just fine, but it's the breath, boy. And I'm not your grandma. The breath gets thinner. Like mountain air. But that doesn't matter. It's the thought that counts. You mustn't be afraid of sentimental, romantic things."

Bernie did another couple of fast rotations on the piano stool. As it jumped toward the wall, he put his foot out to keep from hitting it and left a footprint in the middle of the lilac wallpaper. He put his hands on either side of the bench and made one slow twirl. "So that was two husbands."

"Then there was Everett Hocking, who worked at the bank, and he said he'd like to marry me. And he did marry me, and Mrs. Bright became Mrs. Hocking. Mrs. Hocking had more money than Mrs. Bright, but if Mrs. Bright had been standing at the top of the stairs of happiness, she tumbled right down to the bottom with Mr. Hocking."

"Where is Mr. Hocking? Did you get a divorce?"

"He died just in time. Shoveling snow. He must have had a heart condition. He looked strong with his big chest, but he wasn't. He was a clumsy, rumbling man. An old goat. He cleared his throat a lot. As though he was about to say something important. But he never did. We had nine years together. He belched after dinner and pontificated. Do you know what *pontificated* means?"

"No."

"He was boring, but he didn't know how boring he was. Like a show-off."

"I know some show-offs," said Bernie. "Sometimes I'm a show-off."

"It's hard to love a show-off. I couldn't bear to look at Mr. Hocking after a couple of years. I asked Liddie what I should do and she told me to leave him, but I didn't. But then he left me all of a sudden. Heart attack. My name is Mrs. Bright again. I didn't feel bad about losing Mr. Hocking, but I felt bad for other reasons, and I said to Liddie that maybe I killed him by not loving him enough, and Liddie told me I was crazy. She said he was an impossible man to love and he just died, that was all."

"If you don't love someone enough, you can kill them?"

"Some people would say no, but I think you can. What do you think?"

"I think you can. But it doesn't work that way with your sister, only someone you're supposed to love."

"You're not supposed to love your sister?"

"Not really."

"Well, let me tell you one thing. When you grow up, don't ever try to love someone you don't love. And don't ever try to *not* love someone you do love. Don't ever forget that, you hear me?"

7

1955 − 56

Eva had no idea what that noise was. She thought it had come from the kitchen. Her mother said not to go near there. The men weren't finished working. But one afternoon after the men had left for the day, she crept toward the doorway and peeked around the corner. There were tools all over the floor, and everything was a mess. Then suddenly it started up. Like something groaning. The pots and pans on top of the refrigerator rattled and moved on their own, and then it stopped again.

"What are you doing?" her grandmother asked behind her. Eva jumped.

"There's a monster in the refrigerator."

Her grandmother laughed, a snorty kind of laugh, and her top teeth slipped off her gums. Her glasses were crooked on her nose and smudged with grease from her cheeks.

"Did you see the monster, Grandma?"

"I'm not your grandma."

Eva ran upstairs to the room she shared with Bernie. She heard her mother's cello from the other side of the house. Bernie was drawing with crayons.

"Grandma is scary."

"No, she's not." Bernie bent over the paper.

"What are you making?"

"A tidal wave. When the ocean rises up so high it sweeps every-thing away."

"Even this house?"

Bernie paused for a moment and looked at her. "Yes."

She went to the window and stood on tiptoe and looked out at the water. "It's not doing anything."

"You can't tell from this far away."

She ran downstairs. "Mama! Where are you?"

The cello stopped. "Don't listen to him," her mother said. "There's no way the water could ever get up the hill; plus there's never been a tidal wave in Maine. Never. Leave me alone now. I have to practice. I told you, I'm auditioning for the symphony next week. You go tell Bernie that I told him to stop tormenting you."

The house was alive with mice and squirrels running up and down inside the walls. When the lights went out, there were scratch-ings on wood and plaster. They made Eva think of eyes in the dark. She pictured creatures coming out of their holes, across her bed, over her hair, dragging things they'd hidden in the wall, little claws, little teeth.

Before bed one night, Eva's father told her a story about a rabbit with wings who heard a strange bump in the night. Her long ears quivered with fear and she folded her wings tight around her and put her nose under the covers.

"Is that me? That rabbit?"

"There's nothing to be afraid of, sweetheart," her father said. "What you hear at night are just the noises of small animals living their lives."

But there *was* something to be afraid of. After her father left, after the sun went down and her mother came and kissed her and Bernie good night, she thought of the refrigerator monster. At night, after the sun went down, she imagined the monster pressing his big lips against the glass of the windows. His hands were huge and hairy, and she had to watch out or he would carry her off down the road. The monster's laughter would rumble in her bones. She would be so scared she couldn't even scream.

She sat in bed and looked out the window. The birds were finding their night nesting places as the grass turned dark. Down the hill was the harbor. She could just see Mr. Wootton's house and barn across the field. In the other direction was the Uffords' house, with the muffin-shaped bushes in the front yard. And up the road beyond the Uffords, the Beasleys' two trailers sat end to end.

Rays of moonlight passed through the old, wavy glass and spilled onto the painted floorboards. She couldn't see Bernie's face, but she knew his eyes were open, too.

"Bernie?"

"What."

"Do you think we'll always be brother and sister?"

"Why wouldn't we?"

"I mean, will we always know each other?"

"Of course."

"When we're grown up, can we get married?"

"Brothers and sisters don't marry each other."

"Why not?"

"They just don't."

"What's that noise?"

"The wind rattling the window."

"It's the monster."

"Don't be silly."

There were three ways to their bedroom: climbing up the side of the house, climbing the front stairs, or climbing the narrow, dim stairs at the back of the house, where slabs of plaster had fallen onto the treads. If you took the front stairs, her parents' room was on the right. Next to it was the only bathroom and a small sewing room; her grandmother's room was on the left, and beyond it was Bernie's and her room. As long as she could keep Bernie talking, she was safe, but he told her to be quiet and turned over, and then there was just the lumpy, still outline of him in his bed and the sound of his breathing.

Later, she heard her grandmother's feet pausing on each stair tread as she rose from downstairs. Then sounds of water and the toilet flushing, and a clink as her grandmother popped her teeth into a glass that sat on a shelf next to her foot powder. Finally, her snores through the wall, like a big hoofy animal.

And then, without realizing it, Eva slept.

That first summer, the birds sang late, and the golden light beckoned, and the flies twirled their buzzy dances of death on the window-sill and joined the other carcasses there. Sometimes, Eva heard the sounds of the seven children who lived up the road beyond the Uffords' house, playing into the twilight and even after dark, running around screaming and laughing. The Beasley family.

Her father had applied for teaching jobs all over the place during the summer. He finally got a job at the junior high school in Bath and quit Bath Iron Works and came home looking happier than he had since they came to Maine. Her mother took on private cello students and taught them in a room off the kitchen, with a separate entrance to the outdoors. She was a member of the Portland Symphony Orchestra now, and when she practiced at night, music filled every corner of the house.

Bernie started school and came home the first day saying that another kid had called him weird. "That's a compliment, right? What is weird, anyway?"

Eva went three days a week to Sprouts, a nursery school where she had to take naps and every Wednesday share "a little happiness." "What if I don't have a little happiness?" she asked her mother.

"Just say, 'I don't have one.'"

"Miss Ducette might be mad."

"It's okay. You can still say, 'I don't have one today. Maybe next week.'"

"Do you like Miss Ducette?"

"I don't really know her. What do you think of her?"

"She doesn't like to hug. She says she's afraid of germs."

"You'll just have to have that many more hugs at home—like right now. Come here, Evie Peevie."

When winter came, Eva's mother made her wear a head-to-toe snowsuit and rubber galoshes that slapped against her ankles. After school, she and Bernie climbed Woottons' hill and slid down on a Flexible Flyer sled, Eva in front, her legs scrunched up, screaming all the way down, Bernie behind, steering with his feet. On the way back home, Eva pulled lumps of ice off her woolen mittens with her teeth, and with every step, her socks slipped down farther into her galoshes until they were all balled up. Her legs were so cold and chapped, she had to walk with her feet wide apart.

"You look like a penguin," said Bernie.

"You look like a . . ."

"Like a boy."

"Like a chicken," she said.

In early spring, the Woottons' cows came out of the barn, and they watched Bernie and Eva with their great black-and-white hulks pushed up to the fence and their placid eyes unblinking. The pussy willows opened into their softness. Skunk cabbages melted their way through the snow, red-veined and throbbing, a rotten, meaty-smelling yellow flower springing up inside the hood of each one. Eva collected pollywogs in Mason jars with Bernie and dumped them back in the pond when the buds of frog legs appeared. In the early evenings they heard the spring peepers, like sleigh bells in the marsh.

Across the road, Eva and Bernie discovered an old car in the field. They rode to Michigan in it, fighting over who got to drive. Its windows were all punched out, but three out of four of the doors still opened. The backseat smelled of vinyl, and the sun-baked wheels were flat and hidden under grass and clover and crickets.

The field behind her grandmother's house stretched down to Dyer's Cove. The tides came in and out over the black seaweed-covered rocks; at night, the lights of ships moored off the coast pierced the darkness. When clouds settled onto the ocean, the foghorns sounded from three directions. Like cows mooing.

And meanwhile, surrounded by the busy din of that summer, there was the silence of a new being who made no noise. Their mother told Eva and Bernie that she was pregnant. Eva didn't know what that meant, although her mother tried to explain. What she saw was her mother's tummy getting bigger, but she didn't see the baby that was supposed to be there. Her mother said, "Give me your hand, honey," and she took Eva's hand and laid it on her stomach. "Here, feel." What Eva felt first was her mother's flesh, warm and firm, then something rolled against her palm, filling her with its strangeness.

8

FALL 1956

Toward the end of her pregnancy, Liddie went on leave from the symphony and stopped teaching; she could no longer get her arms around a cello. She and her friend Nan had seen each other often that summer. Nan had moved into a new apartment near the Bowdoin College campus, where she taught, and kept herself company by adopting a large cat named Zeus, whose vainglorious personality was oddly like her former husband's. Nan was singing with a choir, learning Arabic, and full of plans for a sabbatical.

That fall, a couple of weeks before the baby arrived, Bernie came home from second grade with a rash. Liddie felt his forehead and put him to bed. His fever spiked, and he climbed out of bed and ran around the room, flailing, battering her with his fists, terrified of something. She held him tight but couldn't lift him. She urged him over to the bathroom sink and tried to lay cool compresses on his forehead, but he escaped and ran down the stairs and out onto the front porch, then up the stairs and down again. Fred clattered down the stairs after him, back up, back down, skittering around corners. Bernie finally fell onto the floor in exhaustion, and Liddie got him onto the couch and bathed his forehead with wet washcloths.

Fred sat by him while he cooled down, and when Bernie woke, Fred's snout was up close to his face. Bernie peered at his mother and mumbled something incoherent.

"What, darling?"

"About that picture," he said. "You know the one?"

"Which picture?"

"The magnified fly. You know, its eye with big black swirls. That's Fred's nose."

Bernie reached out and touched Fred's head; the tail slapped the leg of the couch. "Do you think he's a white dog with black spots, or do you think he's a black dog with white spots?"

"I don't know. How do you feel?"

"My head hurts."

She brought him some ginger ale. "You were a scary wild man," she said. He didn't know what she was talking about.

He stayed in bed for a week, and when he got up, he held his hand in front of his face and it looked like someone else's hand. All pale and thin. He still had scabs everywhere. By the time they disappeared and he was allowed back in school, the chicken pox had moved on to Eva.

The baby was born, and the nurses wouldn't let Eva into the hospital. She stood on the grass while, up above, her mother held the new baby up to the window for her to see. Years later, Eva thought that her father must have been beside her, but she didn't remember him being there. She just remembered being alone, a small girl standing on the wet grass staring upward at her sister in her mother's arms. Her throat had a sad lump in it, too big to cry through. She was four years old.

Because of the chicken pox, her mother had to stay in the hospital longer than usual, and when baby Gretchen came home at last, Eva stood next to the old mahogany piano in the room with the lilac wallpaper and sobbed in her mother's arms.

"Are you crying because of your new sister?"

"No." She didn't have the words to explain. She hadn't known whether her mother would ever come back. No one had said one way or the other.

"Did you miss me?"

Eva cried harder.

"Do you want to see the baby?"

Underneath the soft blankets, Gretchen's tiny hands were balled up into tight fists, and her face was clenched. Eva felt protective of her from the moment she stood on tiptoe and peered into the nest of blankets. Her sister had dark hair and dark-blue eyes, and she looked out at the world as though being born was some sort of disaster.

"Why is she so sad?" Eva asked.

"Do you think she looks sad? Maybe it's because she was all cozy in a warm, dark place, and suddenly she's out in the world and it's too bright and she doesn't know anything."

Her mother boiled the bottles and nipples in a big kettle, mixed the formula, warmed the milk, and tested the temperature on the inside of her wrist. Every so often, Bernie and Eva were allowed to feed Gretchen. Sometimes they fought and weren't allowed near her. When they were calm, they sat on the couch and held her, one at a time. Much later, Eva read that as many as one in eight people start out life as a twin. One baby spontaneously aborts, and the one left behind feels the loss of that close beating heart. It fit Gretchen, who looked like someone who'd lost someone important, her arms flapping out from her body as though she were falling through space.

9

Late autumn fell like a cloak around the house. One November afternoon, two months after Gretchen was born, Harry came home from school with Bernie, and a short time later he heard the other car drive in, then a door slam. Liddie helped Eva from the backseat, lifted out the baby, and struggled into the house with a bag of groceries in the other hand. Harry took Gretchen from Liddie and tried to kiss her, but she moved away from him.

As he lay a sleeping Gretchen down in the bassinet, he asked, "So, what did the doctor say?"

"That I'm suffering from the baby blues. Anyway, I'm supposed to cheer myself up taking nice long baths, and reading joke books. Joke books, for godsakes? And what's the baby going to do while I'm lolling around in the bathtub?"

"What did you say to him?"

"I told him he was right, I was depressed, but I didn't have time to be taking long baths. Who does he think I am, some Southern belle?" She opened the refrigerator, brought out an onion to chop, and slammed the door. "Where did Bernie get to?"

"Playing upstairs."

"I think he's alone too much."

"He seems all right to me."

"Is my mother up there?"

"I think she went for a walk." He turned to Eva. "Why don't you go upstairs, honey, and see what your brother is doing?" He wanted two minutes alone with his wife, with his own Liddie. Just two minutes.

Eva stayed put. "Go ahead," said Harry again. "Go see what he's up to. That's a good girl."

Liddie pulled out a chopping board and moved a skillet next to it. "Sometimes I worry about Mom finding her way back home."

"I can go look for her if you want."

"No."

"It's probably lack of sleep that's getting you down, honey. You're up all night. Days, you have no time for yourself, for music, for anything but nursing and washing poopy diapers. Of course you'd be depressed. I don't remember it like this with Bernie and Eva."

"You've forgotten." She tried to move out of his arms, but he held on tight.

"Let me go."

"I want to hold you a moment."

"I don't want—"

"Please let me." He held her tighter and tried to stroke her hair.

"What are you doing?"

He held on, and they grappled together by the sink.

From Liddie, a cry began low in her belly and exploded out of her like a beast. "Don't patronize me," she cried. "Can't you see I'm hanging on by my fingernails?" She was wailing now, bent over at the waist, her shoulders shaking, her breath coming in terrible staggers.

"I was just trying to help. You feel so far away."

"I don't want to be helped. Jesus, Harry. You just make things worse."

He let go and stared at her. "Well, then, stew in your own juice." It was a horrible thing to say, something he'd heard his own father say. He backed away from her, put on his green hat, and shrugged into his jacket. On his way out, he said, "You know, you don't have to do what you're doing."

"And what do you think I'm doing?"

"Making a habit of discontent."

"Oh, really. Well, maybe I can't help it right now. Maybe—Where are you going?"

"Out to plant garlic before the ground freezes solid."

"Now?"

He didn't answer and passed Margreete in the doorway on her way back in. Once outdoors, he realized he'd forgotten the garlic he'd stored in the refrigerator, but he didn't want to go back in after making such a point of going out.

It reminded him of his first job interview, way back before he knew Liddie. He thought he'd answered all the questions pretty well. At the end of the interview, he'd picked up his file folder. With his hand on the doorknob, he said his goodbyes, thanked the interviewing committee, and walked out, closing the door behind him. He found himself in a supply closet. There he was and there they were on the other side of the door, waiting to see what he'd do.

He stood on the porch, looking into the empty branches of the old maple tree. When he went back into the house to get the garlic, Eva was whining at Liddie's knee in the kitchen, the baby was crying, and Margreete had turned the radio up. He went to the refrigerator, stuffed three heads of garlic into his jacket pocket, and went out again without saying a word.

The light was low in the sky, and the clouds were thin over the palest blue. The first snow had already fallen and melted, and various stalks were sticking up in the raised beds: the dill, which would seed itself everywhere and be a nuisance in the spring; ruined cosmos, one zinnia hanging its head where the stem had thinned and gone limp. The huge rhubarb leaves were nipped by frost and plastered against the ground like amoebic cytoplasm; the peonies were brown, the raspberry stalks brown, everything brown, brown—except that one almost-pink zinnia.

He went to the garden shed and opened the door. Liddie had thrown some stuff in there at the end of the summer, all higgledy-piggledy. Lawn chairs and flowerpots and the cat carrier, one gardening glove here, another there, birdseed. He'd asked her not to leave birdseed in the shed. The mice tore into the bags and helped themselves, and then Romeo climbed into the shed and brought their bloody, seed-stuffed carcasses into the kitchen. And once to their bed.

When he tried to organize their lives, Liddie accused him of being overly scrupulous, bordering on neurotic. He didn't believe he went overboard. There was just more chaos than he could take: Margreete's smear of peanut butter on the cupboards, Fred's drool on his pillow. Sometimes he tried to recall their lives in Michigan. Did he regret this move? Some days, yes, but what was the point of that? Sometimes you just couldn't control your fate. Once Margreete had burned down the kitchen, the whole thing was set in motion. What didn't seem inevitable, though, was how snappy and quick to blame Liddie had become. He missed her. It wasn't that he didn't still love her. He did. Or at least he was pretty sure he did, but these days he felt like a moon circling an angry planet.

He picked up a hoe that was leaning against the wall in the shed. His father had once said to him, "You'll fall in love with the things in a woman that will later drive you crazy." What had fascinated him about Liddie when they'd met fourteen or fifteen years ago was her semi-feral nature, her unpredictability. Some days, there was laughter and her warm body so close, the next day a stinging nettle: *Come this close and no closer.* Her hair had been wild, light brown, standing out from her head like a great cloud. She carried her cello case like a shield-maiden, plunging down the streets of Boston in a purple moth-eaten cape that had been someone's half-mad great-aunt's. Big high ankle boots, and passionately for or against anything you could name, like a crazy, volatile Russian, without any Russian blood in her.

He stepped out of the shed, carrying the hoe, and took the heads of garlic out of his coat pocket, separating them. Twenty-nine cloves in all, some with their reddish papers intact, some a buttery yellow. He thought he'd plant them next to the kale, which hadn't been killed yet. He might even pick some kale for dinner if he could swallow his pride by then. A hard little wind whistled through the hedge and around his ears and nosed its way between the buttons of his jacket. It was almost too late to plant garlic, and then he thought of the early brave greenery that would come up next spring, alongside the unseemly pink phallic strivings of the rhubarb. The garlic scapes would twist into circus-like shapes, shouting spring at the pasty-faced humans who'd lost every hope by then.

He dug the trenches for the cloves and felt in his arms the way she'd struggled against him. Like a falcon in a net. He didn't know why he'd done what he had. Maybe he'd needed her to cry. For herself, for her life.

He set nine cloves upright in the trench and covered them over, then tamped them down with the flat of the hoe.

They hadn't meant to have Gretchen. She'd knocked the wind right out of Liddie, waking up every two hours day and night, a ferocious little starveling. Once he'd read a book written by a lighthouse keeper in England who said that it wasn't one gale, two gales, ten gales one after the other that frighten you. It's what comes after several days, when the wind has had a chance to put thousands of miles of ocean into motion and it turns and hurls itself at the land: the sea coughing up boulders and launching them toward the base of the lighthouse like an angry giant. If he could speak the truth to Liddie, he'd say he could feel their lighthouse shaking.

Why couldn't he speak? He didn't know, but he guessed it was for the same reason that she couldn't be comforted. They were parents. They couldn't afford to fall apart the way she'd just now bent over double in the kitchen from grief and exhaustion and anger, weeping and fighting for her breath.

He wondered if Bernie really was alone too much, and he stopped digging for a moment. He put down the hoe, walked back to the house, and opened the front door a crack. He heard a metallic clattering on the landing halfway up the stairs, where Bernie was assembling a crane from an Erector set. "Bernie," he called softly, "come on outside."

"I'm busy," Bernie said.

"Come on. Put your jacket on."

He heard the pad, pad of Bernie's slippers against the wooden floor and then his voice telling his mother he was going outside with Dad. He appeared at the door in his winter coat and slippers.

"Where are your shoes?" Harry asked.

"I don't know."

"Well, never mind."

Months later, Harry would think about how that *never mind* began a chain reaction like one he'd once set off in a high school chemistry class: the filling of a balloon with hydrogen, the striking of a match. Boom.

"Are you warm enough?" Harry asked.

"Yup." Bernie's hand was cold and the top of his head warm.

"You know what I'm doing out here?"

"Getting away from Mom."

Harry laughed. "And planting garlic."

"I don't like garlic."

"You will when you're older. In the spring, after all the snow goes away, each one of these little cloves will send out a green shoot and it will push its way up, and when it gets to the air, it'll keep growing taller as it gets food from the sun. Underneath the soil, this one clove will turn into a whole head of garlic. It grows slowly, and it needs the whole winter in the cold and dark to think before it starts growing."

"Wouldn't it be weird if dead people did that when you planted them?"

"Whoa." They stood together in front of the turned soil. "Who were you thinking about? Grandpa?"

"I guess."

"What do you remember about him?"

"His teeth smelled funny."

"When did you smell his teeth?"

"You know. When he laughed."

"How did they smell?"

"Like the cornflakes box."

So that's how his father would be remembered.

"So, do you want to help me plant the garlic?"

"I'm going to look for the ball I lost."

Harry bent down to tuck ten more cloves into the trench he'd dug. He suddenly felt happy. He'd pick some kale, he'd make dinner, peace would be restored. He dug another trench and sat on his haunches.

The sun had lit up the sky on its way down and illumined the gray trees and fields with slanted gold. A chickadee sang once in the dimming air, again, and flew. He looked up and realized he could no longer see Bernie. He got up off his knees, and as he approached one side of the shed, he heard a muffled sound. Around the other side, Bernie was sitting on the ground, whimpering, tears rolling down his cheeks. One slipper was off, and he was holding his foot like a baby doll.

Harry knelt down beside him.

"What happened?"

"I stepped on a nail. It was sticking out of a piece of wood."

Harry bent over in the dim light and saw the puncture wound, hardly bleeding. "Does it hurt?"

Bernie nodded.

"Where's the nail? Did you pull it out by yourself?"

Bernie nodded again.

"Jesus." Harry had a sick feeling in his throat that went all the way down to his knees.

"Why didn't you call me?"

"You were busy."

"Don't you know you're more important than anything I'm doing?"

Bernie cried harder. Harry carried him back to the house, and Liddie blew up.

"It happened fast," said Harry.

"Things *happen* fast. He'll need a tetanus booster."

"Not a shot!" Bernie yelled. "Not a shot!"

"What happened?" asked Margreete.

"Bernie stepped on a nail."

"What happened?"

"I just told you," Harry said.

He carried Bernie out to the car. There was a coral-colored glow still visible in one small part of the sky. The headlights on the Plymouth weren't as bright as they ought to be, and a few cars passed in the other direction, momentarily blinding him. Didn't anyone use their dimmers anymore? Harry had forgotten to bring any food, and his head felt awash. He looked straight into the oncoming lights, unable to stop himself, and realized then that the road was blurred with his tears, crying for his son, his marriage, all of it.

The emergency room was quiet. Only one old man coughed into his handkerchief, accompanied by a younger woman, probably his daughter. The nurse was in her thirties, with dark hair and long limbs. "I can see you've been a brave boy," she said to Bernie, and Harry felt she was talking to both of them. She went to the cafeteria and bought food with her own money. "For the wounded boy," she said, giving Bernie a Dixie cup of ice cream and Harry a packet of salted peanuts. "I'm not supposed to do this. Don't tell anyone." She said that Dr. Greenleaf was on that night and whispered to Harry that he gave clumsy shots; she'd find a way to do it herself.

She kept her word. She bathed the wound and gave the tetanus shot, and since no one else needed her, she sat for a bit.

"Do you live in Bath?" asked Harry.

"Close to Bath, in Woolwich, on the Kennebec River. My husband and I have been there fifteen years. How about you?" She seemed aching to talk. Long night, no patients, bored out of her mind. Something racehorse-y in her.

"We live in Burnt Harbor," said Harry. "We were in Michigan before that."

"I could never live inland. I'm like a seal. I need to smell salt water." He could see that. Liquid movements. And curiosity, the way a seal will pop out of the water when she sees a boat.

"I sink in water," he said. "If I had a boat, I'd probably sink that, too."

Bernie was swinging his legs off the edge of the examining table, looking at them.

She asked Harry what he did for work, and he told her he was a junior high schoolteacher. And he told her about the kitchen fire and why they'd moved, and about Gretchen's sleepless nights, and his wife's wonderful music, and his brief stint at Bath Iron Works, and he noticed that he couldn't stop talking, as though he'd been living like the Count of Monte Cristo, in a dungeon. He apologized.

"What are you sorry for?" She had bright, amused eyes.

Was she flirting? No one had flirted with him in years, unless he hadn't noticed. It made him nervous. He turned to Bernie and said, "Well, buckaroo, what do you say we hit the road?" He lifted him off the table and thanked her for her kindness—he wanted to thank her for more than that, to bathe in the brightness of her eyes.

"You have a very brave boy here. Most kids would have screamed."

"He's a good kid. Aren't you?"

"Sometimes," said Bernie.

"Are you on all night?" asked Harry.

"Just till eleven. It's good you came when it was slow. How's that foot feeling?"

"Okay," said Bernie. "But I still wish it didn't happen."

"No running around for a few days, and then it'll be good as new. You never found the ball, right?"

"No."

"Well, you stay away from those nails."

They got back in the car and made their way down the peninsula, mile by mile, with Bernie sleeping in the backseat wrapped in Harry's coat, a gibbous moon shining over fields. Harry felt renewed, as though she'd fixed his foot, too. And grateful for this night, for his boy, for the moon, for their house lit from within when they pulled in the driveway.

10
1956 – 57

The next day, Bernie went off to school hobbling and leaning dramatically on a tree branch as the bus came down the road. The rest of the house emptied out—Eva on her way to nursery school, Harry on his way to teach, Margreete at her old friend Betty's house for the morning. Liddie sat down in a rocking chair by the living room window with Gretchen. The baby latched on to her breast while Fred lay at her feet, licking his paw.

She and Harry had been wary of each other when they'd woken.

What ties bound them together, other than three children? The weight of familiarity? That was pathetic. Was it even a good idea to ask what kept them together? Or better to pretend the question didn't exist? A long, long time ago, when they were getting to know each other, Harry put his palm on her ilium—is that what it's called? The bone that sticks out in front of your hip. He put his palm there and said, "I'm home." It was a sweet moment.

She couldn't feel that sweetness today, though. Self-pity—something she abhorred in herself—poured over her thick as fog: sore breasts, her nonexistent musical life, the wind blowing so strongly that the door on the north side of the house had slammed open while everyone was out and frozen poor Valentine, the avocado tree she and Harry had started from seed, which now—bad metaphor—was dead. The approaching winter felt darker, more vengeful and unappeasable than any she could remember, and Valentine was sitting in a pot in the back hall with her flaccid, blackened, unrevivable branches. No one had the heart to throw her out. The woodstove smoked, the car needed a new clutch, and Bernie came home from school saying the boys had made fun of him at recess and thrown pinecones at his head.

"What for?" Liddie asked.

"I don't know. They don't like me."

She knew, before being told by that doctor to take nice long baths, that her mind had darkened, but she didn't know what to do about it. In the grocery store, leafing through the *Ladies' Home Journal,* she'd read that the solution for feeling blue was forcing yourself to be cheerful, even if you didn't feel it. But it didn't feel like good advice to run around being a phony.

Liddie had once known a woman at the Unitarian church in Ann Arbor named Joy, a skinny, intense woman with two kids, married to a nice but ineffectual physical therapist. Joy "worked in the home," which was to say she fell apart out of sight of others. This Joy was barely coping, and then she and her husband had another baby. Liddie had never cared for Joy all that much, and why she went over to help her, she couldn't remember now, but when she walked in the door and sized up the scene, it was too late to back out. All three kids were crying and the dishes were piled up in the sink, like a domestic horror movie. She set to work on the dishes so she wouldn't have to deal with the emotional wreckage. An hour later, she hadn't reached the bottom of the sink.

After that, she stayed away, feeling guilty but not bad enough to go back. Four months later, Joy disappeared, leaving even the baby behind. Months later, she was located in California at some creepy intentional community, and she sent word to her husband that she would not be coming back. At the time, Liddie could not imagine anyone doing such a thing. Some days now she *could* imagine it, except for the intentional community. She wouldn't go to a place like that. She'd drive and drive and finally stop in front of an out-of-the-way motel. There would be a woman behind the counter with a beehive hairdo and a cigarette hanging from her lower lip; Liddie would check in with her cello and a false name and shut the door behind her.

Gretchen pounded a small fist against her chest, trying to get the milk going faster, and Liddie switched her to the other breast. "Little greedy one," she said, laying her hand on the soft head. It was snowing, the flakes small, huddled, compacting out there in the cold, piling up on each other one by one, overtaking the porch, blanketing the apple tree and the scrawny peach tree beside it. Down the hill the ocean looked dark and sulky. The sky was gunmetal gray. The birds were fleeing south. Old Mrs. Powers would be visiting her mother again tomorrow or the next day, maybe wearing her gallstone.

She stroked Gretchen's head with her fingertips. The baby was nearly asleep but still hanging on, the milk dribbling out the side of her mouth; every so often, she woke enough to suck a little more. "How about a nap, little one?"

Liddie rocked her and thought about yesterday when Harry had held her in the kitchen and wouldn't let go. She'd felt like a wild animal trying to pull its leg from a trap. Music had always been her escape valve, but with no music, the dark night of the soul had crept in. Harry was right about habits of discontent. But it didn't feel as though she was doing it. It was being done to her. Passive voice.

The chair squeaked rhythmically as she rocked. Harry didn't understand her, not deep down. And she didn't understand him, either, not really. That didn't seem so terrible. Not even necessarily marriage-imperiling. Who really understands anyone else? But if she stretched out the years and looked ahead, shouldn't there be gladness? He wasn't a wife beater; he often cooked meals and did the dishes; he was kind to the kids. He had a job. It seemed the problem was hers, the weight she carried was her own.

Her parents had wanted a large life for her. When she'd practiced the cello as a child, her father would pretend he was reading the paper, but he'd close his eyes and listen. Her mother had named her Lydia Marian Bright in honor of Marian Anderson. Long after Liddie's birth, in April 1939, Marian Anderson had opened her mouth on the steps of the Lincoln Memorial, and a celestial power had poured forth over a crowd of seventy-five thousand stunned listeners.

Her mother had wished she could have been there. She had lived a large life herself, pushing a baby carriage to the library and dragging the great classics home. She told the church ladies that she didn't have time to bake cakes for their cake sales. She taught Liddie about Margaret Sanger and Eleanor Roosevelt. And about Bessie Coleman. "She died in a plane crash," her mother said, "but that wasn't the most important thing about her. The important thing was that she didn't understand the word *no*. She only understood *yes*."

Which made this kind of self-pity close to a mortal sin.

Liddie found a butterscotch-colored leak around the edge of Gretchen's diaper, unlatched her, burped her, and took her to the changing table. Gretchen's face creased into a smile, and Liddie's heart melted. She washed her soft bottom, smoothed Vaseline over it, sprinkled talcum powder into the diaper, dressed her in a clean romper suit.

What would the world bring to this small, ferocious one? There was an urgency in Gretchen, an inability to rest, as though she'd landed behind enemy lines and needed to stay vigilant. Liddie and Harry hadn't intended to have another baby—they just got sloppy about birth control one night. She would never regret this child, even though she felt today how much courage it would take to raise three children, perhaps more than she possessed. Not courage like a soldier planting a flag on a hilltop or a fireman saving a trembling dog. Not what anyone else would even call courage.

Lying next to Harry that night, Liddie moved over to him and laid her head on his shoulder. He seemed surprised. She touched his head, the hair on his chest, kissed his ear, then his lips. First softly, then hard. His lips shook a little when hers touched them, like an old man's, oh. Like her father's before he'd died. She placed her hand on his lips to calm them. She felt sad for him, felt he deserved someone who loved him all the way. She did her best that night, but she was watching herself, the way people who return from the dead describe seeing their bodies down below.

Toward morning, she dreamed that she was in a ballroom. Her feet hardly touched the floor, and then they didn't touch the floor at all. She rose in her filmy gown upward toward the high ceiling and glided around weightlessly, her arms outstretched. It made her utterly happy. She waved to Harry, but he hadn't seen where she'd gone. She called to him. "Harry! Up here!" He heard her voice and looked all around but couldn't find her up there.

II

SPRING 1957

Harry had not fully understood why April was called the cruelest month until he entered this one, working at a school with a little turkey cock of a principal drunk on his own power. And just when he thought winter was over and done, along came another splat of snow. Soon the black flies would be out, biting behind the ears, feasting on the corners of the eyes.

He forced himself to remember that the ground would thaw, the leaves would unfurl, improbable things would spring from the ground: The garlic he'd planted that night last fall. Rhubarb. Strawberries. Not only that, but Liddie had just returned to teaching and was playing in the symphony again.

After a day of teaching, with hope in his heart, he drove to the hardware store, where he found a handsome spade and a rake with a tapering wooden handle that reminded him of his grandfather's. He nosed around the store, set the tools down for a moment, and filled a small paper bag with yellow onion sets. He was standing in front of the seed display, pondering, when an arm reached in front of him and grabbed a packet of seeds, and then another. It was a female arm. A rude arm. When he glanced at the face, he saw the nurse with the bright eyes.

She looked at him, startled, and laughed. "It's one of those movie moments."

He didn't know what she meant.

"Woman meets nice man in the hardware store after thinking she'll never see him again."

He snorted. "I bet you never gave me a second thought."

"How do *you* know what I thought?"

"I don't."

"You happen to be wrong. I liked the way you were with your son."

He'd thought of her, too. He'd even thought, while shoveling snow off the roof of the house in March, that he might accidentally lose his footing, break a leg, and have a reason to go back to the hospital. And then on the way into the house, he'd banged his head on a coat hook but not badly enough to need stitches.

She asked about Bernie, how he was.

"He still remembers you."

"Please tell him I said hi."

"I will. What are you planting?"

She reached for a few more seed packets. "Beans, peas, corn, lettuce, carrots, the usual. I should leave out the bush beans, but I can't. Every year I end up with this huge mound of them on the kitchen table, waiting to be canned, and I look at them and ask why I do this to myself. But every spring, I'm so excited, I just pop the seeds into the ground."

"I forget what a pain it is to mow the grass every year. And I forget the black flies are coming and the mosquitoes. It's probably a good thing people forget all sorts of things. If we didn't, there'd never be a second child after the first one, or a third after the second."

She looked at him. "I'm glad to see you again."

"I'm glad to see you, too."

"Are you in a hurry?" she asked.

"What? Now?"

"Yes, now. I was just wondering if you'd like to have a cup of coffee. Maybe at the café?" She gestured with her chin toward the main road.

He hesitated. "I don't drink coffee after two or I'm up all night."

"Is that a *no* for coffee or a *no* for I don't talk to strange women?"

"No, no, you're fine."

"Well, would you like to go somewhere?"

"Just to talk?"

She laughed. "You do still talk?"

"I do." But he could think of nothing to say.

"Look, I'm sorry I asked. I just liked the way you were with your kid that night, and I enjoyed our conversation. I'm not proposition-ing you, if that's what you're thinking. It was just a silly thought. But suddenly it got over-complicated."

"No, wait a minute. I'm just befuddled. I was planning to detour by the dam on the way home. See if the ice has gone out. Want to check it out with me?"

"Near the power station?"

He nodded.

"You're sure?"

He nodded again.

She looked in her shopping basket. "I've got two packets of beans. You want one?"

"You're not a good advertisement for them." He took the packet from her and put it back, picked out a packet each of carrots and let-tuce and gathered up his spade and rake and started toward the cash register. "So meet you there in ten minutes or so?"

She smiled. "Your tools are clanking."

"I like the clanking."

He was aware, getting into the car, of his silent voice like a man-tra: *I'm only human, I'm only human.* But they were just going to look at a dam. And who suggested this? Not him. Anyway, fifty–fifty she wouldn't be there. Or maybe he wouldn't be there.

He slowed the car and drew over to the side, scuffing the tires against the gray heaps of melting snow, trying to decide whether to just head home. He imagined Gretchen's wailing, Fred's happy snout greeting him. But then he looked in the rearview mirror, pulled back onto the road, and continued on his way. She was already there when he pulled up. He climbed into the passenger seat of her car and said, "Hi, it's me again."

"Hello, you again."

"I hope you're not about to say, 'This was meant to happen.' I hate it when people say stuff like that."

"I wasn't about to say that," she said.

"I don't even know your name."

"Molly," she said. "I know yours."

Next to them, the dam had collected a tangle of logs and branches, plastic bottles, the remnants of a children's wading pool; the snowmelt spilled over the top of the debris. Downriver were the hulking stone remains of a nineteenth-century insane asylum, the roof half caved in on one side. The windows were flat and grimy and lackluster, and under them, the gray granite was stained dark, as if with the tears of elephants. He'd forgotten about this view and wished they were looking at just about anything else.

She had two children, she said, both in elementary school; her husband was involved in international law. She worked part-time at the hospital. She'd started out to be a doctor but ran out of money for school and became a nurse. "It's not what I'd hoped. . . . What about you?"

He told her he taught junior high school history. "I've always loved history. I was a conscientious objector during the war. I couldn't make myself shoot German boys who probably didn't even know what they were fighting for. I first met Liddie, my wife, in 1941. We have three children."

"Did they put you in prison for being a CO?"

"They sent me to work in an asylum in Oklahoma—one reason I wish we weren't looking at that wreck of a building over there. Then I fought forest fires in the Southwest. After that . . ." But he stopped, because what he was about to tell her would sound like bragging.

"My older brother was killed in the war," she said. "In the Philippines."

"I'm sorry."

"Your decision to be a conscientious objector had nothing to do with Rick dying. I could dislike you for it, but I don't."

He looked at the crumbling granite building downriver, half collapsed under the weight of its history. Turning back toward her, he said, "I have a decent marriage. We've been going through kind of a bad patch—a new baby, my wife's mother living with us—but I think we'll make it through." His voice was husky, and he cleared his throat. "I'm not in a very steady place right now. I just thought I'd let you know. You know, it's probably better if I get home."

Her hair had fallen forward. "I imagine you're right." There was a soft appeal in her face, and she said it again. "I'm sure you're right."

"Thank you." He kissed her on the cheek, meaning goodbye, although it could just as well have meant the opposite. "And thanks for looking after Bernie the way you did. As I said, he still remembers you."

Driving down the peninsula in the dim slanted light of April, Harry passed only one car going in the other direction. The road, like a funnel, passed through blue, wind-disturbed water on the right and, farther away, on the left. As he entered the driveway, he thought of his family inside. The porch roofline was not straight, something he'd have to see to this summer. The house seemed to wobble slightly as he drew closer and with it the walls that sheltered the people he loved. But nothing had really happened except that Molly's number was in his wallet.

12

"Can I have some, Grandma?" Eva asked, touching Margreete's sleeve.

"No." It was that little one with the braids, hair falling into her eyes. "This is my Jell-O." She preferred the red Jell-O to the green. She remembered once being invited to a garden party where they'd served green Jell-O mixed with cottage cheese so it looked like a pale vegetable, like a celery stalk. You had to raise your little finger when you held your teacup or you were considered uncouth. Which people probably thought she was. She didn't know why she was asked, and she never was again.

The little one was staring.

"What are you looking at?"

"Your bowl."

"This is *my* Jell-O, do you understand?"

"Did you make it?"

"I found it. Finding establishes ownership."

"What does that mean?"

"It means it's mine."

"What's that on top?"

"Whipped cream."

"Can I have some whipped cream?"

"It's in the refrigerator, but sometimes the squirt can explodes."

"I don't want any."

She looked at Eva. "How old are you?"

"Five."

"Do you go to school?"

"Nursery school."

"How old are you?" she asked again.

"Five. I have a loose tooth." Eva opened her mouth wide. "See my loose tooth?"

"Someday you'll be toothless like me."

"You have some teeth, Grandma." She looked at her hard. "When you're very old, your heart stops, right? . . . Is your heart still beating?"

Margreete laid her palm against her chest. "I can't feel anything."

"You'd be dead if it wasn't going, right, Grandma?"

"That's enough now. I'm going outside."

"Can I come with you?"

"No. Sometimes people just want to be alone."

"What are you going to do out there?"

"That's my business."

"Can I finish your Jell-O?"

"Why not?" She slid the bowl across the table, went out to the entryway, grabbed Irving's old lumberjack coat, and pulled a hat over her ears. The sound of cello music was coming from the other side of the house, and she paused to listen. She wrapped herself in the coat, stepped out onto the porch into the late April afternoon, remembering Irving's smell and how she had fallen in love with him. With his whiskers, with his breath that smelled of tobacco, with his eyes of deep brown and his laugh like blue water. She remembered it was after her first husband had fallen or jumped off the building and she and her parents had taken the bus down to Methuen, Massachusetts. They were going to her mother's niece's wedding. She did not want to go to the wedding, but her mother insisted. Said it would be good for her.

Margreete's cousin Esther married a man with sparkly eyes and sparkly teeth; after saying their vows, Esther and Sparkle Man danced the first dance, a waltz. She could still remember the floor with its dark stains of beer from other weddings, its scuffs from boots and high-heeled shoes. The ceiling was low and draped with white streamers, which wound around the posts that held the roof up, and there were white and pink flowers made from tissue paper, some of them already fallen to the floor and trampled.

Tables were set up on either side of the dance floor, and waitresses in white-and-black uniforms hurried here and there with drinks and food. Margreete was not accustomed to wine and drank it too fast— and when Irving stepped across the floor to ask her to dance, his face seemed to shimmer like a reflection in water, and then his features grew still and she saw that he was serious about getting her to her feet. She stood, and her head whirled as he took her into his arms and held her at a respectful distance from his body. She could feel the heat through his navy blue jacket, through his dress shirt, through his undershirt, across the small gap between them, through the cotton of her light blue dress with the daisy flowers. He was a good dancer, and she liked the way he steered her firmly, finding his way through the crowd of other dancers, the way a cardinal flies through dense branches. There was a bit of the cardinal in him. Not a dandy, but he had style. She'd never met a man from New York before.

He was up in Massachusetts just for the wedding, he said, urging her out onto the porch with a hand on the small of her back, away from the other guests. She shuddered when he touched her there, and he asked if she was cold. She told him no, she was not cold.

It was not cold she felt.

"I came up on the train this morning," he said. "Nearly missed the wedding. A tree fell onto the tracks."

"I'm glad you didn't miss it," she told him, the boldest thing she had ever said to a man in her life. And then bolder yet, she told him where she lived, and he said he would be seeing her again.

But she did not see him, not for almost a year. When he did knock on her door that day in April, on an afternoon like this one, with the winter still in the air and the spring grappling the cold rawness aside and promising sweetness, she didn't remember his face looking so serious before. His mother had died, he said, and his father had gone to Milwaukee for a job, and he had been working in a shoe factory and looking after his younger sister. She had moved in with an aunt, and only now had he been able to come. "Did you think I wouldn't?" he asked.

"I thought you were stringing me along," she said, "that's what I thought. I thought you'd given me one big load of malarkey; that's what I thought boys from New York do."

"Not this boy," he said.

He was right. It wasn't a load of malarkey.

Now these forty years later, she stepped off the porch and went into the shed for birdseed. He was gone, and she was gone haywire. Some days she could think almost like normal, and other days everything was so mixed up—the jumble inside her, what happened yesterday, what did she eat for breakfast, who was that man who cooked in the kitchen and called everything a blue plate special. Words came from her mouth that she knew weren't right the minute she said them, but the words she searched for fell down holes. She could see her blunders on the faces lifted to hers. The way strangers called her *honey* as though she was seven years old. The way they spoke loud to her as though she were deaf. She wasn't deaf, she was haywire. If she could open her brain for them, they'd see. They would see the circuits floundering for their snaps. They would see the mess in there and know she was doing damn well considering what she had to work with.

There was no point being sad, but some days she had to go upstairs and get into bed. They thought she was napping, but on those days she was a child crying for her mama, who would have known what to do, who had always known what to do.

You stand on the edge of the ocean and your feet are cushioned in sand and the tide goes out. The waves break and draw back into the sea. Each time the waves pull back a little farther, they take a little more sand with them, grain by grain, until your feet are rocking. She did not so much mind that she could not remember what she had for breakfast, but she would mind if the memory of Irving went swirling down into that blank whiteness, not even his bones left behind. She wanted to die before that happened. Or before her mother grew dim and disappeared. *Please let me die before then.*

She stood in the shed, trying to think what she was doing there, and then she spotted the garbage can where the bird food was stored. She took off the cover and carried it out to the feeder. A chickadee was waiting with its black watch cap and its black triangle of beard and its blush of gold under its wings, hopping from branch to branch, jabbering at her. *Seed, seed, seed, give me seed!* She put a small pile of sunflower seeds in her palm and held her arm out straight. The chickadee flew over her head, landed on a nearby branch, flew a little nearer and nearer still, until it landed on her outstretched hand. The feathers on top of its head fluffed out and lifted, flattened and lifted again. Its body was almost weightless except for the small pressure of its claws on her fingers. It grabbed a seed and flew up to a branch to open it, and she closed her hand on the seeds and brought her arm down to rest. She stretched it out again, and here came a second chickadee, this one picking over the seeds in her hand to find the plumpest.

She filled the feeder and took the seed back into the shed but forgot to put the cover on the garbage can and forgot to close the door. Harry would find it later when he came home and scold her, but by then she would have forgotten the seed, the chickadees, the garbage can, the shed door, all of it.

13

That night, Harry lay in bed next to Liddie, listening to her breathing and the settling of the house: a creak of the roof, the soft footfalls of Romeo as he came upstairs to Margreete's room, the clickety-clack of Fred's toenails as he climbed the wooden stairs to the second-floor hall and stationed himself as sentry for the night. Harry closed his eyes and saw deep blue and opened them again to the room shadowed with the light of a half-moon. He lay his hand on Liddie's shoulder. She stirred, and he took his hand away again. He felt, even in that brief touch, her bone-deep fatigue. He couldn't think of anyone he respected more, but respect wasn't necessarily the same as love. Love's bedfellow, his body's desire, was alive and well, but it made him feel beggarly and contemptible. She had enough on her plate without him wanting her breast—and everything else. He knew this without being able to stop the wanting. He was further ashamed that a telephone number written on a scrap of paper had been burning a hole in his pants. What was he? Nothing more than a disorganized bundle of randomly firing impulses?

He felt restless, got out of bed and walked downstairs, with Fred toenailing after him. There were still embers in the woodstove, and Harry sank down beside the warmth in the red wingback chair that had been his father's. Fred lay across his feet. Eva was now at the age when Harry's memories began. He wondered sometimes what his children would remember. He hoped no one would remember him smelling like a cornflakes box.

He thought there must be hundreds of thousands of memories in his head, each of them waiting patiently to be triggered; many would just sit there until he went to his grave. People wondered where souls go after death, but what about the memories? At this very moment, someone in the world was newly born and someone else was newly dead; that dead person's memories were suddenly released like a murmuration of starlings. What must it be like for Margreete, watching her precious ones flying out behind her, like scraps out a car window? She didn't seem to mind, but if she could speak about it, he was pretty sure she *would* mind.

Harry could picture his father, James Furber, sitting in the very chair he sat in tonight, his lips set in a thin line, his ruined hand in a pocket, where it was used to hiding. His father had been a shy, remote man who sat stiff, all angles and bones. He was never called to serve in World War I because of the hand, mangled as a boy when he was helping his mother feed clothes through the hand wringer of a washing machine.

His mother had told Harry that most of the men in their town disappeared into the war; those who returned were changed forever. Like Mr. Wilkins, the owner of the grocery store, with his pinched-together mouth and a crazy laugh that roared out of him like a lion living inside a rabbit costume. Some of the wives changed forever, too. Mrs. Pelletier, who lived next door, had been a jolly woman before the war, and only weeks before the fighting ceased, she had gone to the front door and taken an envelope from a Western Union man. She knew what was on that single yellow sheet of paper without opening it and went into the backyard under the umbrella-shaped clothes dryer that Mr. Pelletier had mounted on a hollow metal pipe for her, pulled it out of the ground, and screamed to the heavens as she stamped it flat.

Harry's mother hadn't needed to worry about whether her husband would come back. But when Harry thought of his parents' marriage, he saw a nest of frozen twigs.

After Liddie had met Harry's father for the second time, she said to Harry, "Promise me you won't turn out like that."

"It's not my plan," Harry said.

"People do, you know."

His father had built himself a greenhouse, where he grew a giant crown of thorns with blood-red flowers, plus dozens of other plants and orchids and creeping vines. During Harry's boyhood, long after the evening star appeared, long after old Mr. Kingstone down the road had set his book and reading glasses down and turned off his bedside lamp, after the rowdy Gowdy twins had thrown their empty bottles off the railroad trestle and called it a night, a muted light shone through the trees behind the Furber house, a light filtered twice through green, once from inside his father's greenhouse and once outside, through high leaves, on its way to the sky. Even without the words for it, Harry knew that plants were his father's life, his solace, more important to him than his younger son.

Harry wasn't especially welcome in the greenhouse, although sometimes his father would let him play among the old clay pots or look for Mosey, the box turtle who hid under the wooden shelves and slept in the sun. As a boy, sitting outside the door of the greenhouse, his back to the wall and hands around his knees, Harry could sometimes hear the low rumble of his father's voice, a pause, his voice again, and the spray of the hose.

Once, he asked his mother, "Who's he talking to?"

"That turtle," she said. "He tells him everything."

Now Harry rose from his father's chair and went to his desk to find a tiny snapshot he kept there, then settled back in the chair, next to Fred. The date on the back of the photo was 1924. In it, Harry is four years old; his father is dressed in a white shirt and striped tie, a dark vest, and dark suit. A small leather notebook sticks out of the pocket of his father's vest. His head is small and compact, with ears tucked in close, his hair already thinning but still black, his forehead firm and intelligent, his mouth straight across. Young Harry is sitting on his knee in the garden. He's wearing a shirt and shorts. His father's injured hand rests on his son's back. His other hand is holding a shard of ice, which pierces the leaves of a shrub behind them with a bright shaft of light.

Before Harry was born, his father had become a partner in a business with his brother. Furber Brothers Coal and Ice: WE WARM YOU IN WINTER AND COOL YOU IN SUMMER.

He remembered a trip with his father up into the mountains to see a man about a shipment of coal. The road home passed in and out of a number of small towns, went down a steep grade, and at the bottom crossed a railroad track. It was early spring, with the windows wide open, the wind blowing in. Harry's father wore his driving cap—a small flat tweed one with a snap in front—at a tilt. He was singing off-key in his foghorn tenor voice, and over his blatting, they heard the train from a long way off.

Because of the angle of the road, they could see the locomotive and cars as they came down into the valley; it looked as though their car was about the same distance from the crossing as the train. Harry's father put his foot to the floor, and the car shot forward down the hill. They would probably have made it before the train with plenty of room to spare, except for the boy at the bottom of the hill, wobbling across the road on his bicycle.

"Out of the way, boy!" Harry's father roared out the window at the same time as he hit the horn. In his confusion, the boy got off his bike and stood in the middle of the road.

Harry's father braked at the last moment, swerved to the left, shifted up into high gear, and gunned it. Harry could hear the rumble of the train as the car raced toward the crossing, could almost smell the breath of it bearing down. He expected his father to stop and laugh at the last moment, and when he saw he wasn't going to, he yelled. They hit the track with their front tires. It seemed impossible that the rest would clear in time. The whistle was in their ears, screaming through their bones, and then they were through, the thud of each train car in their veins.

His father's hat was on the floor, his eyes shining. He geared the car down to second and puttered along the road, up the other side of the mountain. He looked over at Harry. "Don't ever tell your mother."

Harry put the photograph back in the drawer and sat down in the chair again. Fred wasn't allowed up on the furniture, but Harry patted his knee and Fred put a tentative foot up, then another, and climbed into Harry's lap.

"He just about killed us both," Harry whispered. "I never told anyone." Fred looked at him. Harry stroked Fred's fur absentmindedly, thinking what a lifelong labor it was to make sense of what his two parents had given him. What remained in his memory was the smell of coal and the smell of the greenhouse, black and green equally weighted. "I loved that old bastard," he said. "And for better or worse, he's still right here." He patted his chest, and Fred sniffed where he'd patted. "Don't ever let me come that close to hurting someone I love."

14

SUMMER 1957

Liddie didn't want a television in the house. "A work of the devil," she said, mocking herself, but she half-meant it. On Friday nights, they watched *The Adventures of Superman,* and Liddie said Lois Lane was as dumb as a pike, always falling into traps and needing to be saved by guess who. And how could that silly woman not put two and two together and notice that Clark Kent was never around when Superman was?

"He has a nice big chest," said Margreete. "But look at that double chin."

"That's not a double chin, Grandma," said Bernie. "Those are his neck muscles."

One night, Bernie watched the news with his family and saw a girl named Elizabeth Eckford clutch her notebook and schoolbooks to her chest, hiding as much of herself as she could behind dark glasses while a mob poured hate over her head and spat in her face.

Bernie's father explained that nine students had been selected to attend an all-white school in Little Rock, Arkansas—something called "integration." He said there was hardly anyone in the world braver than these nine students. They were supposed to get to the school together, but Mr. and Mrs. Eckford, Elizabeth's parents, didn't have a telephone and never learned about a change of plans. So Elizabeth ended up at the school alone. She tried to walk through the front door, but the National Guard crossed their rifles in front of the door, and she had to walk back through the crowd she'd just faced.

"Lynch her!" they screamed.

"What are they saying?" asked Bernie.

"Okay," said his mother, turning to his father, "that's enough. Turn off the TV."

"He's old enough to understand."

"It's too much."

"No, it isn't," said Bernie. But that night, he lay in bed with his eyes open to the darkness. He listened to the late-summer crickets outdoors, and inside to the quieting of Eva's breath, and downstairs to Gretchen crying and finally stilling, and his parents' voices talking to each other, and then to his grandmother's tread on the stairs, uneven on one side, where she favored her sore knee. And all the time in his mind, he thought about the way Elizabeth Eckford had moved forward, like a fire walker, with her thin, straight body entering the crowd. And the way her shoulders had slumped a little as she retraced her steps through the mob toward the city bus. And the white girl behind her, wearing the dress with the big ugly triangular collar and her face scrunched up, wild with hate, and the grown women and grown men there to do her harm, and who were those people who couldn't see how young and frightened she was?

It worried him what his father said when he came to kiss him good night, about the things you couldn't see right up here in the North. "You know, son, don't think just because those kids manage to integrate Little Rock High School that this country is making such great strides. And don't you ever get smug about the North. It's harder to see the hate up here, but it's here just the same." Bernie didn't know what he meant, but he wondered whether it was anything like the boys at school, the way they sometimes tripped him and called him a sissy. He wanted to be able to walk past them as bravely as Elizabeth Eckford.

He didn't tell anyone that one of the worst things about school was Red Rover. Two teams stood in a long line on either side of the field, like soldiers in a war, with a big space between them. Each team held hands to keep the enemy from busting through. One team yelled, "Red Rover, Red Rover, send so-and-so right over." Bernie prayed that his name wouldn't be called, but he was almost always the first they called, because the enemy team knew he couldn't bust through. He had to run as fast as he could and try to break through the opposing line, but he always bounced off and got captured. Once, when he was running across no-man's-land, he tripped and fell down even before he got to the enemy team.

Charles Hicks was the slowest boy in Bernie's third-grade class. One of his ears stuck out and was folded over itself. When he was nervous, his neck went red. Charles had not yet learned to read, and each day since the beginning of school, he'd worn a faded red T-shirt that was stretched out around his neck and hung from his torso like a scarecrow. He smelled of lobster bait and cigarettes and unwashed dog. The desks were screwed to the floor, and if you were unlucky enough to land where you did in Miss Hatlee's seating plan, you sat next to him for the year. That fall, Bernie was assigned to sit on one side of him, with Dennis Szwedko behind Charles.

Imitating birds and animals was what Charles did best. He could make a sound like a crow or a sheep or a flock of disturbed chickens, but his favorite was a snorting bull. He chuffed out his nose and grunted, pawed the wooden floor of the classroom with one sneaker. His breath came in spurts, a rhythmic *haw . . . haw . . . hawhaw.* Out on the playground, Dennis Szwedko said, "Do it again. Do it again."

On the second week of school, Charles went *haw . . . haw . . . hawhaw* from his seat and Miss Hatlee said, "Settle down now, Charles Hicks. That honking has no place in here."

Haw . . . haw . . . hawhaw. He couldn't stop.

"I'm warning you."

Haw . . . haw . . . hawhaw. Haw . . .

"Stop it, I tell you!"

Bernie reached over to Charles, opened his clenched fists and flattened them out onto the wooden desk, whispered for him to breathe the way his mother told him to breathe when he became overexcited, and Charles stopped. The only other kid who didn't laugh was Noah, the new boy.

At recess, Noah was leaning against a chain-link fence when Bernie came up to him. He'd never talked to this new boy, and he'd never met a Negro before. "I moved here from Michigan," he said, scuffing the toe of his sneaker into the dirt and digging a small trench. "Where did you come from?"

"Maryland."

"Where's that?"

"Near Washington, D.C. My father got a job up here designing destroyers at Bath Iron Works." He turned to grasp the metal fence with both hands.

"My father worked there, too, but now he teaches junior high school. Do you like it here?"

"No," Noah said.

"I have a picture of a meteorite in my pocket," said Bernie. "It fell out of the sky in Russia, and the Russians just issued a stamp for the tenth anniversary." He unfolded a piece of newspaper, and they looked at the photograph: a few small houses, a wooden fence, a fire in the sky. "Do you want the picture? You can have it if you want it."

"I guess not. How come you have it in your pocket?"

"I like meteorites. Someday I'm going to dig one up. They have them out in Ohio. In farmland out there."

"My mom says the stars are brighter in Maine. That's the best thing about being here."

"We had to move because my grandmother was losing her mind. Are you smart?"

Noah said, "Yes. But my dad says being smart is only part of it."

"What's the other part?"

"He didn't tell me."

When he got home from school, Bernie sat down with his *Boy*

Mechanic book, opened to the page that laid out the Morse code. He puzzled out the words he wanted to say and wrote the code out on lined paper. Like an international spy, he dropped the folded piece of paper on Noah's desk the next day, looking the other way. As he walked to his seat, he felt his ears redden. At recess, he escaped behind the school, but Noah found him there and asked, "Did that paper say SOS?"

"No."

"What did it say?"

"I don't know." But he did.

15

Eva didn't have any special friends. Privately, she thought maybe it was the way her hair stuck up in back. Or that her last name was Furber, which was funny-sounding. Like the word *squirrel* or *nincompoop*. That fall, when she told her mother that she wanted to play the piano, her mom said she could start with "Twinkle, Twinkle, Little Star" or with "Mary Had a Little Lamb." "You choose."

"I don't want to play baby songs."

"Well, that's where you start."

Eva kicked the piano with her Buster Brown shoes.

"Stop that. You have to start with easy things first."

Eva said she wasn't going to start that way, and if she had to, she wasn't going to play at all. They stood looking at each other a moment.

"Okay, you win," her mother said. "Let me see what I can find."

She dug around in the bookcase that was full of music for piano, for cello, for trios. "Ah!" she said. "This one is called the *Notebook for Anna Magdalena*. Johann Sebastian Bach gave it to his second wife. . . ." She leafed through and stopped. "This one's lovely." She told Eva it was written in the key of D minor. "Every piece is written in a particular key. You could play the whole thing exactly the way it's written—like this—or you could play it a note higher. Or here . . ." She played it mostly on the black notes. "You hear how it sounds different wherever you play it? It's hard to say what feels different, but it's almost like a mood, like a feeling you can't quite talk about but it's there. You understand? Bach chose to write it so that it would be played right here. . . . And you know the other thing he decided?"

"What?" Eva could hardly wait to put her fingers on the keys.

"He chose between a major and a minor key. Listen to the difference." She played it in the key of D minor, and then she played D major.

"I like the minor one."

"I do, too, and that's the one he chose. Minor is a little quieter. Some people say it's sadder, but I don't think of it that way. It's like when you get up in the morning and you don't feel like talking to anyone, you just want to be quiet. Major is more like when you get up and you run down the stairs, and you eat your cereal as fast as you can and you run out the door, excited about the day. They're both good."

"How do I play it, Mom?"

"I'll show you in just a minute. But I want to say one more thing. The great thing about playing the piano is that you have two hands, and those two hands can talk to each other. Some pianists think that the right hand—this one—is the most important one because it almost always carries the melody. You know what a melody is?"

"Yes . . . No."

"If you're singing a song, it's the part that's easiest to remember, like in 'Frère Jacques.'" She sang a bit. "Because you have two hands, you can add something more on the bottom that makes the melody even more interesting. Like this . . ." She added an accompaniment in the left hand.

"But don't ever think that the left hand doesn't matter. In Bach, especially, the left hand is really important, just about as important as the right hand. And sometimes it decides it wants to have the melody, and it grabs it from the right hand. Let me show you."

Her mother's eyes were moist, she was so happy. She played the right hand, and then she played the left hand. "I know you want to play the whole thing, but to start with, you'll learn one hand and then the other hand, and then you'll put them together. Okay?"

"Yes."

"Which hand do you want to start with?"

"The left one."

Her mother played the whole thing, and then one phrase at a time. "Try this first phrase. And when you put your fingers on the keys, try to keep them nice and round. And if you ever lose your place, you know how you can find where you are?"

"How?"

"Here's the belly button of the piano. It's called middle C. There are two black notes right beside it. You always know where you are if you can find the belly button. . . . I'm going to play this first phrase again. . . . Now you try it."

Eva pressed down on a key, and another. She had made noise on the piano before and knew how to do it. The phrase that her mother had played was already in her head, like a path that someone else's feet had made, waiting for her. She played it.

Her mother seemed surprised. "Yes. Wonderful. Let's do it again." She played the phrase, and Eva played it after her.

"The next one," said Eva. "I want to do the next one."

Her mother played it, and Eva repeated it.

She learned the left hand and then the right, and then a few days later she was able to put them together. She played the piece over and over, and every now and then, Margreete sat in a chair and listened.

"You already played that."

"I'm practicing."

Her mother showed her how to make the accompaniment softer than the melody and how, when you pause just a tiny bit, the next note becomes more important.

Years later, she remembered her mother's joy. And hers. Her mother told her that practicing helps your fingers be ready to do whatever you want them to do. That after many years of practicing, you no longer have to think about what your fingers are doing. You can pay attention not to the notes, which aren't all that important by themselves, but to what matters: the feeling of the music. "There is nothing greater than music," her mother said, "for expressing what words can't express."

She said that Eva probably wouldn't understand one other thing until she was older but she would say it anyway. "Some people think that playing is all about themselves. They roar through a piece thinking, *Look at me! Look how fast my fingers are going, listen to how much noise I'm making!* If you're thinking like that, you're not making music. You have to make yourself small enough to disappear inside it. Then you can make music that makes other people feel something."

Eva thought about this at night in bed. Outside the window, the moon shone and the stars shone. She could feel the bigness of the night and she was very small but also inside that bigness. She thought that might be what her mother was talking about. She wasn't the one who was important. She was inside everything that's important.

16

Harry lathered his face with a shaving brush and stopped. He stretched his mouth to one side and scraped the razor down one cheek. There was a gentle rasping sound, and the short bristles fell into the pillow of shaving cream. He finished, patted his face with water, and buried his head in a towel. He opened his eyes and there he was, always older than he expected, a deepening crease between his eyes, a kind of puzzlement, dark, slightly curly hair thinning at the temples, rampant eyebrows, one white hair wildly jutting out above one eye, as though foretelling the future like a tiny, pointing god. And in his cheeks the gaunt remnants of those starvation months in 1944 and 1945.

As a conscientious objector, he'd volunteered along with thirty-five other COs to let himself be brought to the brink of starvation so that researchers could discover the best ways to bring the many thousands of people starving in Europe back to life after the war. It was the hardest thing Harry had ever done, but it was probably also the most important thing.

Except for his kids. He wanted each of them to grow up with a strong moral compass, an understanding of the world's oppression, a sense of their own power to change things. That was his hope, at least. But Liddie said he was heavy-handed, had no off switch, and that his haranguing made her tired. She didn't say it in so many words, but what she meant was that he could be bullheaded and tedious when he was on the right side of justice.

Things were looking up between them, though. The day before, Liddie had said that she wanted to be done with breastfeeding. Gretchen was beginning to bite, and she wanted her body back. They hadn't been anywhere together since Gretchen was born, and he suggested they go away for a weekend together. They'd get a babysitter. Maybe two babysitters, one for the kids and one for Margreete.

"Where would we go?" she asked. The TV was on. The kids were in bed. The two of them lay with their heads on opposite sides of the couch, their feet touching.

Harry switched off *The Thin Man* just at the moment that Nora asked Nick how many martinis he'd had. "Six," Nick said.

"Where do *you* want to go, sugar?"

She smiled. He never called her that. "New York? Quebec City? Vancouver? Paris?" Her eyes flashed the way they used to when she'd worn that ratty cape and high boots and sang in the streets.

"Train? Car? Plane? Limo?"

"Train. Let's take a train," she said.

"New York? We'll stay at the Algonquin. Do it up."

"When?"

"Tonight," he said, smiling.

"No, really."

The regular sitter wasn't available on Columbus Day weekend when they wanted to go, but the sitter's friend, Patty, said she could come then, and her mother could also help out between dinner and bedtime. Patty was twenty years old and the kids already knew her. The few times she'd filled in for her friend, she'd been responsible, calm, uncontroversial, knew how to handle a baby, and the older kids liked her well enough. Liddie had heard her say *no* once or twice without getting shrill about it. As an added bonus, she could make macaroni and cheese.

Patty came over one afternoon, learned where Fred's and Romeo's provisions were, located Gretchen's diapers and bottles and baby food, met Margreete, and wrote down bedtimes.

Liddie drove out of the driveway on Friday afternoon to the sound of Gretchen wailing. She nearly turned around, but faster and faster she drove toward Harry's school, his suitcase in the backseat, hers beside his, her eyes brimming—*it's okay, it's okay*—thinking she didn't want to be one of those women who went away for a weekend with her husband and all she could think about were the children, as though her thinking slate had been wiped clean by winter colds and ear infections and diapers and squabbles and remembering the permission slip for Bernie's field trip and making sure the door was shut so Fred wouldn't chase the neighbors' chickens. Her breasts were full and aching, still producing milk and weeping through her shirt, and she thought with sadness about how after this trip she would never breastfeed again.

Harry was waiting for her in the school parking lot, where Liddie had dropped him off that morning. His hair blew over his eyes in the wind; he squinted into the sun and bounded toward the car when he saw her. They drove to Portland, boarded a bus to Boston, ate the egg salad sandwiches Liddie had packed, and got on a train at South Station headed to New York. As they moved down the Connecticut coast, Harry slept while Liddie looked out the window. The moon was three-quarters full, and she could just make out the rim of water breaking against sand, a single heron, the leaves of trees red and yellow in the train's light, houses mostly dark, with a few bright windows where people were still awake. She was aware she hadn't traveled since they'd moved east from Ann Arbor. She'd been out of synch with Harry then. They were still out of synch, but differently now.

The dark landscape flashed by, poles zigging one after another in a jerky, silent rhythm. She thought she and Harry had never been a particularly great match. He was more idealistic than she'd ever be. In her bedrock self, she believed nothing really large in the world could be fixed—you just had to wait for the pendulum to swing back. Believing that he could make a difference was a kind of innocence in Harry; sometimes it made her impatient, but more often she loved him for it. She glanced over at him. His mouth was slightly open and he breathed lightly, speeding up momentarily as though he were being chased. He wore a suit jacket over a sleeveless sweater vest: an old-man look, but on him it was earnest and teacherly and sort of sweet.

She doubted that she would ever fully understand what made his heart tick, or vice versa. When they went to a concert, he bobbed his head to the beat. He was an easy mark, responding to just about anything. Music, for him, was entertainment, relaxation. For her, as she'd told him the other day, it was beyond necessary. How do you describe that feeling to someone who can't feel it for himself? It was like explaining the smell of the ocean.

Their marriage bore pockets of solitude and incomprehension; it sounded bad when she thought of it like that, but mostly it was all right. More than all right many days. To her, a parallel life was preferable to sharing every tiny thing. And she was glad that Harry wasn't the sort of man who required constant adulation or who chewed up a wife with his raw ambition.

The train jostled down a rough piece of track and threw the two of them together. Harry startled in his sleep, and she put her hand on his chest to steady him. She remembered the day he'd returned to the East Coast after being discharged from the Minnesota Starvation Experiment. It was December 1945. They hadn't seen each other in over a year. When she'd put her arms around him, his scapulae were like the blades of wooden oars in a sinking boat. His skinny neck held his head like the stem of a barely supported tulip; his arms were sticks, his chest caved in, his clothes hung from his body. He weighed 99 pounds, down from 152.

"Oh, darling, what have they done to you?" Liddie asked. She didn't know back then if he'd ever recover. He seemed breakable, and if recovery meant becoming who he was before the war, Harry was never that person again.

The train pulled into New London, and Harry opened his eyes and closed them again. A few people got off, a few got on, and the train started again. She laid her head against his shoulder and slept.

They arrived in the city after midnight, grabbed a taxi to West 44th, and fell into bed.

Liddie woke first the next morning, tiptoed out of the room, down to the lobby, and called home. Bernie picked up the phone, and she asked how things were.

"Grandma told Patty this wasn't her house and she needed to get out."

"And what did Patty say?"

"She explained about being our babysitter."

"Can I talk to Grandma?"

"She went out for a walk."

"Well, will you tell her I said it's okay for Patty to be there?"

"Eva couldn't get to sleep last night. . . . Mom? When are you coming home?"

"The day after tomorrow. You be a helpful big brother. I'm not going to talk to anyone else right now. We'll be home by dinnertime on Monday, okay?"

"Okay."

"Bye-bye."

"Yup." The line went dead.

"Where have you been?" Harry asked when she returned, rummaging in their joint suitcase for a clean pair of socks.

"Calling home." She hadn't wanted him to know.

"And?"

"It's okay. More or less."

"So you can be here now?" He said it half accusingly, half playfully.

Her breasts were painfully full, and she went into the bathroom and milked herself into the avocado-green sink, tears dropping beside the blue-white milk. She heard the television go on, then the voice of Daffy Duck, his antic cheerfulness. She dried her breasts, dried her tears, showered, brushed her teeth.

"Do you remember," she said, coming out of the bathroom, wrapped in a towel, "that time just after we were married when we were up at that lake in New Hampshire and it rained and rained and you'd forgotten your sneakers and only had the pair of leather shoes you were married in?"

"And you were helpful and wifely and put them on the floor grate to dry—"

"And the toes curled up like a sultan's shoes."

"And after that, I didn't wear any shoes, just went around like a savage for a week, and we swam across the lake and found a shirt that someone had abandoned—"

"That denim one you still have, the one you wear when you clean out the gutters."

"The week Bernie began," he said.

"Your savage week."

"I'm feeling a little savage right now."

"What are you going to do about it?"

"Ho," he chuffed. He looked at her, nuzzled her like a frisky horse.

"I have one request," she said. "Don't touch my breasts. I'm sorry."

"I'm not really a breast kind of guy anyhow."

"Oh, really?"

"So what kind of guy am I, then?"

"An everything guy." She pulled him onto the bed. It was the first time in as long as she could remember that one ear wasn't listening for a kid.

When they emerged from the rumpled bed, she asked, "Do you think we're old marrieds yet?"

"What's the definition?"

"I don't know. When farting is no longer an embarrassment."

"I'm still embarrassed," he said.

"What for?"

"I don't know."

She stopped for a moment and sat down on the bed again. "Do you think we should have moved?"

"From Michigan? It's too late to wonder that."

"But do you think we should have?"

"Why are you asking?"

"Some days I feel I can't do this anymore."

"What? Us?"

She reached for his hand and pulled him down beside her again. "Honey. Not us. I'm talking about my mother. It's like watching a picture in a darkroom going backward in a developing tray—every day is blurrier, less contrast, heading toward blank. I want to scream at her sometimes, tell her to wake up. She can't, and sometimes . . ." She rubbed her thumb over the webbing between his thumb and first finger. "Sometimes it's all I can do not to run down the road. I wonder what it does to the kids."

"I think it's probably good for them. They have to figure out how to be patient with someone who's not all there."

"You're patient. It amazes me some days."

"I like her. I like that she tells me when I'm full of baloney. But if she were my mother, I'd want to run screaming down the road, too."

She squeezed his hand and stood up, feeling relieved for speaking. And a kind of giddiness: *I'm still alive, Harry's still alive, we still remember how to love.* They bought coffee and pastries and wandered with the paper bags up to Central Park, sat on a bench and drank tepid coffee and ate Danishes while watching a crowd that looked nothing like Maine. They rented a rowboat and lazed over the green water while the October sun warmed them. Harry rowed, and a Tareyton dangled rakishly out one side of his mouth, with smoke streaming out behind him. For lunch, they visited a Horn & Hardart: FIRST DROP YOUR NICKELS IN THE SLOT. THEN TURN THE KNOB. THE GLASS DOOR CLICKS OPEN. LIFT THE DOOR AND HELP YOURSELF. "How about that?" said Harry, peering in a tiny window, then pulling out a slab of cube steak with mashed potatoes.

Years later, Liddie still held certain images in her mind: the rowboat, five mallard ducks scooting here and there, Harry's hands on the oars, his favorite green baseball hat askew on his head. The ropy calves of a stranger in shorts ahead of her as she climbed a spiral staircase round and round and round, leading to the crown on the Statue of Liberty. A woman up in the crown by herself, gazing out over the water, wearing black leather shoes with thick heels and tie-up laces, a white nylon blouse, and a navy-blue skirt, her hair gathered in a snood. In Battery Park, a shoeshine man on his knees, his son beside him watching his father polish a white man's shoes. Three young greasers in black leather jackets, high poufed hair, dangling cigarettes. A man charging people fifty cents a photo for the privilege of posing with a python around their neck, a policeman coming down the path with his club, saying, "Move along, buddy. This ain't no place for rattlesnakes." A photo booth, four poses for twenty-five cents, portraits of happiness she'd never throw away.

17

Patty lost the name of the hotel in New York. It was written on a slip of paper that had been on her kitchen table back home, but she couldn't find it anywhere now. Her mother brought their trash bin over to the Furbers' house, and they laid newspapers out on the kitchen floor, dumped out the contents, and pawed through banana peels and coffee grounds and junk mail while Bernie and Eva looked on. "What are you looking for?" Bernie asked.

"A phone number," Patty said.

"The number for what?" asked Eva.

"Just something."

"Where's Grandma?"

Neither Patty nor her mother wanted to say they didn't know where Margreete was. They'd only realized she was missing a couple of hours after Bernie's phone conversation with his mother.

Patty asked, "Do you remember, Bernie, where your dad and mom said they'd be staying?"

"How come you want to know?"

"I need to tell them something."

"What?"

Patty didn't answer. Gretchen was crying, and Mrs. Huber, Patty's mother, was getting a bottle ready.

"Are you going to ask them to come back?" Bernie asked. "I think you should ask them to come home now."

"I don't know where they're staying."

"I don't, either," said Bernie.

"Where's Grandma?" Eva asked again.

"I don't know," said Patty.

Bernie went up to her room and came back down. "She's not up there."

"Where *is* she?" asked Eva, louder now.

Bernie started for the door.

"Oh, no, you don't," said Mrs. Huber. "You're not leaving this house!"

"But I know the places she goes," said Bernie.

Eva began to cry, and Patty told her to be quiet, there was nothing to cry about.

Bernie looked at her. "She can cry if she wants to."

"Shut up."

"We're not allowed to say that," said Bernie.

"I can say what I want," said Patty.

"Was it the Biltmore?" asked Mrs. Huber. "That's a famous hotel in New York. Or the Park Sheraton?"

"That doesn't sound right," said Patty. Her ponytail was halfway out of its rubber band. "Anyway, what good would it do? They're all the way down there. And they're not coming back until Monday."

"If the police have to conduct a search," said Mrs. Huber, "you'll never get another babysitting job."

"I don't care."

"You haven't got the sense you were born with," said her mother.

"You can leave now, Mom, if you're going to make it worse."

"I'm not making it worse, and I'm not leaving. I'm going to feed this baby. And then I'm going to do a load of laundry, and you can do what you want. Call the police. Call out the National Guard."

Bernie slipped out the door while they were fussing at each other and took off down the road. Fred tried to nose his way out the door, but Bernie whispered for him to stay.

"Grandma!" he shouted when he was out of earshot. He raced down to the stream. "Grandma!" he yelled again, and listened for her splashing. Sometimes she sat on the shore and threw pebbles.

And sometimes she waded across into the woods. Often she let him come with her, but then she might say, "Get along home with you. I want to be alone." Once, she told him that Greta Garbo had said those words.

A pair of crows screaked overhead in a sky overhung with sullen clouds. Bernie took off his shoes, crossed the stream, and plunged into the woods, down a path his grandmother called the Holy Grail Trail, which ended at a circle of birch trees surrounding a hummock of moss. He expected she'd be there, sitting out the commotion at home. But the circle was empty.

That's when he got worried. He retraced his steps, crossed the stream, put his shoes back on, and headed home. As he was walking, he called and called. In the field, dried Queen Anne's lace clacked in the breeze like tiny skeletons. The sky had a funny greenish cast, the way it sometimes did before thunder and lightning.

When he came in the door, Mrs. Huber yelled, "Didn't you hear me say no one leaves this house?" She cuffed him on one ear.

"Yes, I heard that."

"And you decided you knew best and suddenly we've lost two people, not just one. Was that a smart thing for you to do?"

He wanted to say yes, but he said nothing and went to his room without being told.

Eva was lying on her bed with her head buried in her pillow, stifling sobs. "Grandma might never come back."

"Don't be silly. She just went for a walk. Hasn't she always come back?"

"I guess."

"Well, she'll come back this time, too."

"But maybe she went to look for Mom and Dad."

"She knows better than that. She knows they left town."

"But maybe she forgot."

"Anyway, Patty called the police, and they're going to search for her."

"Now?"

"I think so."

"Mom should never have gone away. She didn't even ask us, she just told us."

"That's because we're kids." Then he remembered. "Mrs. Huber hit me."

"She has a wart on her nose like a witch."

The police sergeant asked Bernie to find a photo of his grandma that the TV station could use, and Bernie dug through a drawer in the kitchen and gave them one from the previous summer, when the whole family had gone to Pemaquid Beach. His grandmother was wearing a sagging black bathing costume with a large-brimmed sun hat, smiling broadly and holding aloft a long, fat ribbon of kelp.

Volunteers fanned out from the Furber house; the local TV station said the story would be broadcast live on the six o'clock news. The TV van pulled into their driveway, and Bernie watched from the window while two men unloaded the camera and equipment. He hoped they would knock on the door and ask him questions and he could tell them about his grandmother and how he'd gone to look for her but couldn't find her in the usual places. He'd leave out the part about Mrs. Huber boxing his ear, and he might mention that he had two sisters, one named Eva and the other Gretchen, who was still a baby, and his parents had gone to New York City on a special trip because . . . well, he didn't know exactly why but they were coming back Monday. And he might also say that they moved here from Michigan and he'd just started the third grade and his grandmother had burned down the kitchen because she'd grown forgetful and that's why they were worried about her—because it got dark pretty early now that it was fall and the nights were cold. He rehearsed it all in his head, but no one knocked on the door, and Mrs. Huber said once more that he was not to go outside, did he understand?

It was the first time that anything this important had happened to his family, and he hated Mrs. Huber so intensely that his ears throbbed. He wouldn't let the tears happen, though, in case he did get interviewed, because by third grade you didn't cry unless you broke your leg or your dog died. He thought about ducking out the back door. It would have been an easy thing to do, but he couldn't even imagine what Mrs. Huber would do if he disobeyed her again. And it occurred to him that he was the oldest one of his family here now, and it was his responsibility to look after Eva, since no one else was thinking about her.

Bernie and Eva stood by the front window and watched the search party. There was Mr. Leroux the firefighter, his grandmother's friend. And Mr. and Mrs. Beasley and their seven children from the double-wide trailer down the road, traipsing across the field as though they were in a parade, with Mrs. Beasley like a mule carrying the littlest one on her back. Going in a different direction were Mr. Ufford and his wife and their small yappy dog on a leash. Mrs. Ufford never left the house if she could help it, and she carried an umbrella, which she opened and closed as though testing it for when the sky fell. There was Mr. Wootton, the farmer across the field, who had eighty-six cows he milked in the early-morning darkness and again in the evenings. One of his boys was with him, running ahead and then waiting for his father to catch up, running ahead again. There were other people Bernie didn't know. So many. There didn't seem to be any organization, although there was a policeman shouting through a bullhorn, but Bernie couldn't hear what he was saying. He felt something slide around in his stomach. He didn't have the words for it, but some of the people out there had a look on their faces that frightened him. Not the ones who cared about his grandmother like Mr. Leroux or Mr. Wootton. But the ones who looked as though they were hoping for something exciting to happen, some calamity that would make the day worthwhile, even if it was something horrible happening to someone.

The sun broke through the clouds just after four-thirty and cast a golden light over the fields and the people searching, and that light seemed to say that everything would be all right. But then the sun went lower and the golden light disappeared, and a chill fell. Gretchen had fallen asleep upstairs, Eva was in the living room, Patty was in the kitchen making dinner, and Patty's mother had gone out in the car again to search.

As the light faded, a few of the volunteers drifted away. Only one police car was parked in the high grass beside the main road now. The TV van was still in the driveway.

Eva sat on the couch, clutching her bear. Bernie couldn't stand it anymore, and he went to find Patty, to plead with her. He stood by her quietly, hoping she'd see what a good boy he was. "My parents always let us go out and run around until dinnertime. We'll stay right by the house, I promise."

The voice that came out of Patty was Mrs. Huber's voice. "Didn't you hear what you were told? No is no. You can't go out. Who knows what will happen?"

"What? What will happen?" asked Bernie.

"Don't talk back."

"I wasn't. I just asked a question."

"And don't make things worse than they already are."

Bernie went back to the living room and looked out the window. It was still the same—just the one police car and the TV van and people wandering around aimlessly and the field darkening and the cool air deepening as though the whole world was falling down a well.

He turned on the TV, and a man's foot with a throbbing corn flashed on the screen. *Drop on Freezone, lift off that corn.* Mrs. Huber came back from searching and yelled at Fred because he'd gotten in her way.

Patty brought macaroni and cheese on a tray for Bernie and Eva, and things felt almost as though everything would be all right, but then they started watching the news. About ten minutes into the program, a reporter came on and said, "An elderly woman living off Burnt Harbor Road disappeared this morning and is still missing. Police have organized a search, and neighbors and volunteers are assisting. If you have any information or have seen a woman of this description"—they flashed the picture of Margreete with the seaweed—"please call the police."

"Are they talking about Grandma?" Eva asked.

"Shhh!"

On the TV screen, the reporter was walking down their very own road. And there was their own driveway laid bare, their house at the end of it in the dusk. A kind of unsteady-looking volunteer, who was searching for the lost woman, followed close behind the reporter.

They stared into the screen, and Eva was the first to recognize the familiar shuffling gait. "Grandma!" She jumped up and scattered her macaroni and cheese on the rug. She and Bernie shot out the front door and ran up the driveway, with Patty yelling behind them. A truck went by on the road, and the bright lights of the TV camera shone on the reporter, who was still talking. "That's Grandma!" Bernie screamed at the man. "The one you're looking for. She's right there behind you. Grandma!"

The reporter turned around and held his microphone up to Margreete. "What are you doing, ma'am?"

"Looking for the woman who got lost, what do you think I'm doing?"

"You're the one who's lost, Grandma," said Bernie. "They're looking for you."

"Me? I'm not lost."

Years later, Eva remembered the muffled sound of Bernie's bare feet running up the driveway, the scratchy feel of her grandmother's tweed coat, the way they walked back to the house holding her hands, her old-lady knee-high socks slipped down around her ankles and laddered with brambles, twigs in her hair like praying mantises. Her knees creaked up the porch steps. She didn't know where she'd been.

Patty's eyes were bright with relief. Mrs. Huber said, "I told you it would turn out fine." She'd said no such thing, but no one cared. Margreete took off her raspy coat, and underneath was a white-sleeved blouse and a brown wool skirt, and underneath that was her nightgown poking out. They sat her down on the couch and made sure she was all right and brought her tea with milk and sugar, and crackers with cream cheese and pineapple jam. Eva ran upstairs to get her grandmother's slippers and fell on the way up and scuffed her knees. What came out of her was the sound of residual hysteria, galloping like a horse out of a burning barn.

She sat next to her grandmother on the couch and stroked her arm like a cat.

"Stop that." Margreete pulled her arm away.

"We were worried, Grandma."

"Such a tizzy over nothing."

"We were watching the news on TV," said Bernie, "and Eva saw you behind the reporter, walking down the road."

"That man was a real blabbermouth."

"Haha, Grandma."

Fred stood with his black-and-white shoulder pushed up against her thigh. "Move," she said. "You're crowding me."

Fred shifted next to Eva, put his front feet in her lap, and pressed his nose against her chest. Eva saw things in Fred's face she'd never noticed before—the soft whiskers growing out of his cheeks, the hair on his chin a fine stubble. His ears drooped. His forehead was creased with worry lines. He might almost have passed for wise, but his eyes were shaded with bewilderment. He looked into Eva's face like a therapist, as though he knew something big had happened, his soulful eyes understanding all, understanding nothing.

18

"Our last day," Harry said, sitting next to Liddie on the edge of their hotel bed. "You know where I'd like to go? Don't laugh."

"Yeah?"

"Coney Island. It's warm today. Remember the first time we came to New York and we went to the boardwalk and bought a Nathan's hot dog and sat on the sand?"

"I do. . . . Just let me call the kids."

He grabbed her arm. "Honey? They're fine. Can't we just be here, this one day?"

"Okay." She kissed him quickly, and he returned for a longer one.

"I'm not ready to go back home," he said.

She smiled, grabbed her sweater, and slung her purse over one shoulder. "I am, and I'm not."

He held the door open, and they walked into a day with a bowl of piercing blue sky overhead.

On the subway, a couple sat across from them, he in a white T-shirt, she in a skimpy black sweater. Her face was wide and flat, and the boyfriend couldn't take his eyes off her. He grabbed her and pulled her toward him; she laughed and pushed him away. He chewed his fingernails for a moment, then looked at her ear as though he'd like to inhale her.

Liddie knew that look of hunger: Harry standing too close in the kitchen, wanting to talk when she needed quiet, pitting himself against the kids for attention. Sometimes she felt sorry for him, and she knew he knew it. But today it wasn't like that. She reached for his hand and pressed her hip against his as the train jostled forward.

In the tunnel, girders crisscrossed the black ceiling, the great iron skeletons of the city. They came into daylight like deep-sea divers coming up for air. Across from them sat a man with a big face and tiny ill-fitting glasses. A woman with dyed black hair, too much rouge, old eyes, a sharp nose. On a building: RUBINSTEIN AND KLEIN FINE FURNITURE. Then row after row of brick houses, a stone church with a crumbling tower, geraniums in a green window box, a factory belching black smoke, a patch of green at the intersection of two railroad tracks.

A couple got into the subway car with twin girls about Eva's age, their hair gathered into plastic barrettes stuck all over their heads like bright birds. The mother looked exhausted, and the father held a newborn infant against his chest. The hand that cupped the baby's head was careful and tender. He wiped the baby's mouth with a cloth, laid the cloth on his knee, and gazed into the small brown face. As they got off a couple of stops later, the father's love felt like a vapor trail wafting out the door behind them.

At the end of the line, Harry and Liddie walked down the platform, down the stairs, and out onto the wide street into autumn's slanted, wistful light. In the years since they'd last been to Coney Island, things had grown shabbier. The place had the forced jocularity of a guest making up for faded youth with a loud plaid suit. A muscle man all greased up and wearing just black bathing trunks stood beside a spangly woman with a placard saying, YOUR PICTURE WITH THE STRONGEST MAN IN THE WORLD, 75¢.

"No thanks," said Liddie.

"C'mon," said the woman. "This is his last weekend. Take a memento home to your kids."

"Just what they need." Liddie laughed.

They passed a circus sideshow featuring Wild Swamp Man. Shatzkin's Famous Knishes.

Out on the beach, a skinny, hairy man stood on the edge of the water in a bathing cap, poised to go in. The sun was bright, even warm, and an older man bulged in a folding chair, happy, everything sagging, his skin blasted from summer rays. His wife sat next to him on the sand, her head wrapped in a beach turban. A man who appeared to be their grown son sat next to her, shirtless, in shorts and long black socks.

"Flesh is king, even this time of year," said Harry.

"Flesh is king any time of year," Liddie said.

"Not for them." Harry's chin pointed to two little girls coming toward them, wearing lacy white communion dresses and small crowns with glittering rhinestones. The girls walked in front of their parents, solemn and pious.

"That's the strangest thing I've ever seen," said Liddie.

"You never wore a communion dress, did you?"

"Are you kidding?" She laughed.

Along the boardwalk was a round-shouldered trailer shaped like a huge mustard-slathered hot dog. NATHAN'S! STOP HERE! FROM A HOT DOG TO A NATIONAL HABIT.

"I think this is where we got a hot dog before," said Liddie.

"Yes. You had on a pair of white strappy sandals and one of the straps broke. You were in a chartreuse dress and a matching hat that looked so great I couldn't believe you wanted to be with me."

"Margreete got me that dress before I went away to the conservatory."

"What happened to it?"

"Must have given it away."

Harry bought two hot dogs, and they sat on the sand together, looking out at the water, eating, and listening to the rumble of the Shooting Star and the screams of passengers as the cars snorted up the steep track and hurtled down. Liddie dabbed mustard off Harry's bottom lip with a napkin. A woman in a pink swirly dress flounced past, her breasts so pointy they could have burst a balloon.

"Mr. Eyes Popping Out of Their Sockets." Liddie smiled at Harry. "Not really a breast kind of guy."

"Who?"

"Don't play dumb."

"How do her bosoms get like that?"

"It's called a bullet bra."

"Jesus. It stops bullets?"

Liddie laughed, and from behind them came the muffled cries of people on Rotor Ride, whirling around so fast, they were plastered against the sides of the huge drum.

She wanted to talk about the kids. About Bernie being picked on at school, about Eva's ear infections, about Gretchen being an odd baby. But she could see that Harry wanted to soak up the sun, to be as happy as that sagging man in the chair next to his turbaned wife, and she told herself to just shut up for once.

The next morning, they were at Penn Station early, waiting for the train north.

"I'm not going to listen to this!" a man near them roared at a woman. There were two suitcases between them like a barricade, one black, one beige. Harry and Liddie tried not to stare. The man swayed back and forth on his two wide feet, his face set hard, but he couldn't hold on to his precious rage, and he sat down next to the woman. She was talking to him softly, and he stared across the room at the far wall. The back of his head was bald, large, his neck thick. Behind one ear was the flesh-colored lump of a hearing aid.

Liddie pulled her suitcase closer and grabbed Harry's hand.

19

It was her children she'd been worried about. It never occurred to her that Margreete would disappear. Liddie hugged her so tight that her ears pounded.

"You're *squeezing* me."

She felt her mother's bones, more frail than she remembered, finally let go, and found herself crying. "Don't ever do that again," she said.

"What? What did I do?"

There was no point talking about it. Bernie told his mother that he could have found Grandma if Patty's mother hadn't been so dumb.

"You know, when you call people dumb, it makes you sound more arrogant than you already are," said Liddie.

"Even when they *are* dumb?"

"If that's the case, keep it to yourself."

That night, when Liddie was saying good night to the kids, Bernie said, "Mom? You said I was arrogant?" His voice was a little shaky. "But not about some stuff."

"What are you thinking about?"

"I'm the worst at basketball, even worse than the really little kids. I hit the wall instead of the hoop, and nobody wants me on their team."

"So what are we going to do about it?"

"I don't know. I could practice. But they close the gym when school's over. . . . Do you know how to shoot a basket?"

"I used to."

"How did you learn?"

"Did it over and over. I was mad at my gym teacher, and I wanted to show her I wasn't the klutz she thought I was."

"And did you show her?"

"Probably not. She didn't care."

That night, Liddie told Harry.

And for Bernie's birthday at the end of November, he poured a concrete footing and installed a basketball hoop on one side of the shed in the rear of the house. Bernie went there every day, shooting at the hoop in the dusk and into the darkness.

A couple of times, his father came out to throw the ball around with him, but Bernie didn't enjoy his father's cheerleading. Once, his mother came out, but usually she was teaching cello students by the time he came home from school. She tried to help, but her advice was to keep his eye on the ball, and even he knew that much.

His arms wobbled as he flung the ball at the hoop again and again. Every now and then it swished through the net, and he ran after it, thinking for a moment that this was how it was supposed to feel. Once, he made three baskets in a row. But more often than not, the ball bounced off the rim right back at him, or ricocheted off to one side, or hit the rim as though it planned to go in, rolled around lazily, and popped back out. Every now and then it hit him in the head, once hard enough to knock him down. Noah was good at basketball, and Bernie thought of asking him to come over to teach him, but he didn't want to disgrace himself. Sometimes he thought he was getting better. Other days, he knew he wasn't. Was it his hands that were the problem? Or more like his whole self?

He missed the basket and went chasing the ball out to the back field, where he could see almost nothing. His mother once told him that this time of day was called the *gloaming*, a word that had a strange sound, like the eyes of wild, watching things. He shuddered and felt for the first time in his life a sensation that would become more familiar as he grew older: a dread of things he couldn't see. The sky had grown darker now, and he searched with his feet over the rough ground and finally came upon the basketball, clutched it to his chest, and walked rapidly toward the lit house, feeling the tiny raised goosebumps on the surface of the ball.

He smelled the rubber close to his chest, the night ocean farther away, and saw the twinkling light of a boat anchored out in the dark waters. He wondered about the people on board, what they were doing, what they were thinking.

Once, he'd had a dream where every thousand years, just one ship appeared on the horizon. People waited for it, and they worshipped it as it passed out of sight for another thousand years. He liked to think about time stretching out like that, forever and forever, like a great lion with its paws out in front of it. It made him imagine that what was true now would not always be true, that maybe someday he would know how to play basketball and no one would laugh at him and call him a girl.

20

Eva glanced up when he came in the door and thought her brother's face looked strange. Cold air poured in behind him, and his hands were red. He was holding the basketball out in front of him, away from his body, the way you'd hold an animal you thought might pee on your shirt. "Did you make any baskets?" she asked.

"Two."

"Will you teach me how?"

"I don't know how yet."

She was sitting on the floor, cutting up a *Good Housekeeping* magazine with pinking shears, gluing pictures with mucilage onto purple construction paper. She'd just pasted down a picture of a woman in a yellow dress, whose skirt had flown up above her waist. Underneath was a white girdle. A horse stood behind her, with a jockey on its back. She wondered why the woman didn't seem embarrassed with her girdle showing like that. She cut out another woman, in a long white-and-purple dress, standing in front of a pond that looked as though it would have a slimy bottom. The woman was gazing at a little bird sitting on her hand, but you could tell the bird was fake, because it wasn't trying to fly away. As Eva turned the pages of the magazine, she saw a lot of women standing by their washing machines, holding up boxes of detergent and smiling with all their teeth. And other women bringing food to their families and smiling—*ta daaa!*—in the same way, as though life was the most fun ever when you were doing the boring things her mother hated, like washing clothes and cooking dinner. She didn't cut out those women, because they were as fake as the bird.

She cut out a picture of pinking shears, because it was so strange to be cutting pinking shears with pinking shears, and what if the one she was cutting out was also cutting out pinking shears, and on and on, until the pinking shears were so small you couldn't see them anymore. She pasted the pinking shears over the top of the head of the woman standing by the pond, so it looked like a tree branch. And then she stopped.

Her mother said supper was getting cold and she was tired of trying to get everyone there. Fred was underneath the table already, wagging his tail in readiness. Gretchen was in her high chair, smearing baby cereal through her hair, and Margreete was sitting beside her, trying to get her to open her mouth and eat something. Harry sat down at the head of the table, and Liddie brought out some lima beans in a Revere Ware saucepan. A casserole of rice and tuna had a large spoon sticking out of it. When the food was on her plate, Eva knew better than to say she didn't like lima beans or to add that she didn't like her food all mixed up together, like the rice and tuna fish. One by one, she dropped her lima beans under the table, where Fred ate them delicately.

Across the table, Bernie peered down at his plate and said, "There's a worm in my food."

"It's a piece of rice," said Liddie.

"It looks like rice but it's not. It's squishy and it has an eye."

"Your mother worked hard to put this meal on the table," said Harry. "The least you could do is respect . . . Eat your dinner, for godsakes."

Harry pushed things around on his plate for a while, then grew quiet as he squashed a small worm with the tine of his fork. "Darling."

Liddie examined her plate. At first it was hard to tell if she was going to laugh or cry. She lifted up her plate, turned the contents onto the floor, and went out the door into the night.

Fred cleaned up.

"Well, that's a pretty kettle of fish," said Margreete. "Over one little worm."

"It wasn't just one, Grandma," Eva said.

"Two, then."

Harry walked around the other end of the table and set the casserole on the floor for Fred. "Enjoy it, old boy. . . . Bernie, eat your lima beans. Eva's already finished hers. And if you kids find yourselves hungry tonight, just remember that half the world's children go to bed hungry every night."

"Always a lesson," Bernie said.

"What did you say?"

"Nothing."

Margreete was left sitting at the table. "All that fuss over one little worm." She fingered the tablecloth.

"Grandma," said Eva. "There were lots."

"I only saw one."

21

Margreete was headed there, she knew where, and she didn't need to be told. She lay on her bed on top of the quilt her grandmother had made for her years ago. The bed where she and Irving spent their Saturday afternoons making love, making children. *Oh, Irving. Where are you? I can see your finger, the third one, bent toward the little one after it was broken. Bent next to the little one like a sheltering tree. Liddie says we put you in the ground. That can't be right. That can't be right.*

Four children we made. One died before it got going. Blood in the toilet bowl. You cried. Don't worry, I said, we'll make another one.

The times she'd almost died. Falling through the ice on Crocker's Pond. The time under the car, when it began to roll. Wiring a muffler to the frame. Her neighbor's scream. "A stone! Put a stone under the wheel, you ninny!" The time of the great fever. Temperature rocketing up to 104. Alone with young children. Liddie and Peter helped her crawl across the floor to the bathroom and into the tub. "Cold water," she told them. "Cold as you can make it. Ice cubes." The shivers so violent a tooth cracked.

Peter was born on St. Valentine's Day. She loved Peter. He didn't come around much now.

Liddie. Her Lydia Marian Bright.

And the other one, the know-it-all, she almost forgot his name. . . . "You need to go into an old-age home," he said. She hung up the phone, and after she hung up, she told him what she thought of him. *Why don't you go into a home, you little bastard? I gave you birth and breath. Don't tell me what to do and where to go.*

He was right about one thing, though. It was time now. Time before it's too late, before she couldn't remember all the precious ones.

Lots of ways to do it. All you had to do was look at the television screen to see the ways. Car crashes, guns, explosions. But driving was out, and she didn't know anyone with a gun. She thought of the rat poison in the shed. She knew where it was, but no. Puking your guts out like that. Rope. She checked the beam in the attic. Sturdy enough. But she didn't know knots.

What would it feel like to die?

Nothing. It would feel like nothing. Like the black hole when you first drop off to sleep before the dreams come. Like a rock sitting in one place for fifty million years. Maybe a bird once perched on it. Maybe moss decided to grow on the north side. But the rock feels nothing. Not rain, not snow, not sunshine, not sadness, not happiness. It would feel like deep space, like Venus off there so far away, a tiny dot. Like the moment before the universe began. Not even the smallest movement of anything, not the smallest quiver. No memory, no wind, no clouds. Nothing.

The nothing didn't scare her. It was what came before the nothing. If you jump off the Golden Gate Bridge, the time it takes to fall. You know you'll hit the water, and all your bones will break and you'll go under where there's no light, and the pain will be terrible and your lungs will cry out and you don't know which way is up and your broken body will rise and finally it will be over. Or maybe not over. The water will pull you down and life will pull you up and you'll be dangling there between.

The time between was what scared her.

Or maybe you're one of the ones that survive the fall. And your body is so broken you don't recognize it, and your brain is more broken than your body. And you live forever in that darkness, only it's not the darkness of nothing. It's the darkness of something that suffers.

That scared her.

But she was old, and old dies better than young. If she jumped, she would die. It would not take long.

22

SUMMER 1958

The summer after Eva's year in kindergarten, Liddie's friend Nan came to stay with Margreete while the rest of the family set out for Ohio to visit Harry's brother and his wife, who was recovering from breast cancer.

"You're coming back?" said Margreete.

"Of course we're coming back." Liddie hugged her, and hugged her again. "Don't get lost, promise me. And take care of yourself."

"Why aren't I coming?"

"You wouldn't enjoy yourself."

"Why aren't I coming?"

"It just wouldn't work out, Mom."

It was a long, hot trip in the Plymouth station wagon, every member of the family sticky with sweat, Gretchen wallowing damply in her mother's lap. Bernie kept singing the same song over and over—*One-eyed one-horned flying purple people eater, sure looks strange to me. A one-eyed one-horned*—until Harry said, "Goddamn it, Bernie, shut up!"

Bernie looked out his window and Eva out hers at endless fields of corn and melons, at daisies and buttercups and black-eyed Susans, at cows standing in the shade of trees. Grain silos, dogs chained in yards, a farmer on a tractor under the skeleton of an umbrella, a falling-down bandstand, towering cumulus clouds. The only thing that relieved the sound of the tires on pavement was Bernie's excited voice, reading out the Burma-Shave advertisements, one signboard at a time.

> *Dinah doesn't*
> *Treat him right*
> *But if he'd*
> *Shave*
> *Dyna-mite!*
> *Burma-Shave!!*

"What does that mean?" asked Eva.

"Something about men and women," said Bernie.

The miles stretched out, and her father had a rule. If they asked for ice cream on a trip, they couldn't have any. But if they didn't ask, he never thought of it. So either way they didn't get ice cream.

Eva studied the back of her brother's big, round head as he looked out the opposite window—the curiosity and eagerness in his neck, the cowlick that made his hair stick up at the crown—and at that moment, she loved him with her conscious brain, maybe for the first time ever. But even then she knew it wasn't a love she could count on. At any moment, it could change. She remembered once when a storm was brewing and her mother rushed out to the clothesline to grab the clothes. "Where's Mom?" she asked Bernie.

"She's gone away and she's never coming back."

Eva had believed him and begun to howl, and Bernie was sent upstairs for the afternoon, where he messed up Eva's stuff and drew galloping horses on the walls of their closet.

There were the dozens of times he'd jumped out from behind a door and scared the pants off her. Or made fun of her when she tangled up her words. Or the night he promised her twenty dollars if she'd eat a green olive and she did, and he gave her the fake *That Ain't Hay* money.

But then the day after they arrived at their aunt and uncle's house, he called the tiny ants running around in the dirt under the high rope swing "those crazy little nervous people" and made sure she didn't step on them. What she learned on that trip is that you love and then you don't love. And then you love again. And the more you love someone, the more you hate them when you hate them.

23

FALL 1958

Bernie was standing alone at recess when Noah came up to him and asked if he wanted to come over sometime after school.

"Sure," said Bernie, trying to sound casual. He moved a little closer to Noah. "When?"

"I don't know. My mom said it would be okay today."

He wished it could be a different day, because he'd spilled tomato sauce on his shirt at lunch. "I have a stain on my shirt."

For some reason, Noah thought this was funny.

Bernie called his mom from the school office, and at the end of the day he and Noah climbed the steps onto Noah's bus. Charles Hicks sat alone behind the bus driver's seat, honking softly to himself.

"It's your birthday tomorrow, right?" Noah said to Charles.

"Yup," said Charles. "I'm going to be ten. . . . I'm supposed to be nine, but I started school late because I . . . *haw* . . . wasn't ready."

They sat down across the aisle from him.

"How do they know if you're ready or not?" asked Bernie.

"They just do."

A few more kids got on, and the bus driver mounted the steps and started up the bus. Bernie was sitting by the window and watched the school disappear behind them. The stain on his shirt was right where his shirt stopped and his pants started. He covered it with his hand. He liked sitting next to Noah, and it also made the words go out of his head. "I've never been to your house before," he said.

Noah looked at him. "I know."

The bus let them out, and they walked up a long driveway bordered with low evergreen trees. Noah's younger sister, Sarah, came running toward them and followed them around while Noah showed Bernie the garage, where his father had a workshop. "There's a mouse nest in the corner," said Noah. "Once there were mouse babies."

"I like mice," said Bernie, "except sometimes they get into the Rice Krispies box. Then they leave little black things behind."

"Poop," said Noah knowledgeably.

In the corner of the living room, Noah had a Lionel electric train that smelled of hot axle grease, almost like a real train. Noah showed him the transformer that made the train go. The engine was black and chuffed smoke and had a headlight. And behind it was a coal car, and a passenger car with lights inside it, and a car carrying logs, and a red caboose that said PENNSYLVANIA. The train went through a tunnel and then passed a tiny town with a grocery store, a couple of houses, and a church. The church was white with a steeple and cross on top.

Bernie asked if he could operate the train.

"In a minute." Noah showed him how to make it go slow and fast and how to back it up.

He slid the transformer toward Bernie. "Don't make it go too fast."

But Bernie pushed the dial the wrong way, and the whole train fell off the track on the first curve. He stood up to put it back on, lost his balance, and fell into the little town, crushing the church with his foot.

A flicker of horror crossed his friend's face and quickly disappeared. "It's okay," he said. "It doesn't matter."

"Yes, it does," said Bernie, picking up the white plastic splinters. Tears were leaking out around the corners of his eyes.

Mrs. Eagling came into the room. "I didn't mean to," he said.

"Mean to what?"

"I stepped on the church."

She glanced down at the floor. "I guess you smashed it up, all right."

"I have money in my piggy bank. I can buy another one. I'm going to buy a new one."

"You're clumsy, aren't you," said Sarah.

"That's not polite, darling," said Mrs. Eagling. Her mouth looked as though she wanted to laugh. She turned to Bernie. "When Noah's father comes home, he'll be glad to drive you home." To Bernie's ears, that meant, *The sooner we get you out of here, the better.* She left the room and went back to the kitchen.

"Want to watch television?" said Noah.

"No."

"What do you want to do?"

"Go outside?" There'd be nothing to wreck out there.

They sat on the porch steps, side by side, staring toward the driveway. The clouds were moving fast—dark and ominous below and fiery above with the oncoming sunset. The sun cast an odd gray-gold light that made dark things look extra dark and light things extra light.

"I don't think your mother and sister like me."

"My father does."

"I never met your father."

Noah smiled until he saw Bernie's face. "I'm just kidding."

The sky grew stranger, with alternating stripes of dark gray and bright coral. The ocean was just visible through the trees, with a lone fishing boat returning.

"Race you to the trees," said Noah. He got up and took off, then led the way toward a group of old apple trees and peered into a hole in the largest tree. "This was where the ducks had their babies. There were six eggs. And five small ducks. They came out of the hole and walked to the pond down there."

"Ducks can't climb trees."

"Wood ducks can. They have claws." Noah leaned over, picked up a feather, and gave it to Bernie.

Bernie touched it to his lips, brushed it across his cheek, and then tried to brush Noah's cheek, but his friend pulled away.

"Do you believe in heaven and hell?" asked Noah.

"No," said Bernie. "There's no such thing." He put the feather in his pocket and picked up a stick.

"What church do you go to?"

"I don't go to church," said Bernie.

"How come?"

"Because."

"You can come sometime with me, if you want."

"Maybe . . . I have a dog and my grandmother has a cat, and I have two sisters. My smallest sister is two. She doesn't talk yet. My mother says she's biding her time."

"What does that mean?"

"It means she doesn't feel like talking." The sky had purpled, and the clouds were galloping east, rolling over and over like tumbleweed. It was almost completely dark now, and they headed back toward the house.

Noah's father appeared in a shiny Chevy Bel Air and stepped out of the car with a briefcase. He looked tired, and his maroon necktie seemed to lie heavy on his chest. "Hi, sport," he said, rubbing Noah's head. "Who's this?"

"My friend from school."

"Does your friend from school have a name?"

Bernie told him.

"Furber? What does Furber mean?"

"My father said it's someone who polished metal in the olden days."

"So you're a polished, smooth-talking guy?"

Bernie laughed uncertainly. "I don't know, sir. I don't think so."

"I suppose you're going to want a ride home."

"Yes, sir."

"Let me put down these things and say hello inside."

Bernie sat in the backseat, with Noah in front next to his father. Mr. Eagling felt like someone you could easily admire, and also a bit scary. It wasn't just his deep voice; it was the way he carried himself. One hand held the steering wheel low down, and the other hand draped casually over the back of the seat where Noah was sitting, the way a father and son were meant to be.

When Bernie got home, he took the feather out of his pocket and put it in a little box where he kept his special things: The gum he was chewing when he won a race in Ohio on the Fourth of July while his family was visiting his aunt and uncle. A key he'd found on the ground near the swings at school. A tooth that Fred lost when he was chewing on a bone. But of all the things, the feather was the best. He took it out of the box again and felt its softness against his cheek. The tip of it was broad, with smooth black and white stripes. Under that, black and pale-yellow stripes made wavy lines, and below that was the fluffy, downy part.

Bernie sent for a Lionel train catalog and pored over it until he found a black-and-white church topped with a gold cross. A sign in front said, ST. NICHOLAS CHURCH, CHRISTMAS SERVICE 10.30 A.M., THE REV. P. TAYLOR. He filled out the order form, asked his mother to write a check, and gave her what money he had in return. He waited, and one day about three weeks later, a parcel arrived with his name on it. It was the first parcel he'd ever received.

Noah visited Bernie's house, and Bernie presented him with the box. "I thought you forgot," said Noah. He rummaged inside. "I like it even better than the old one."

"It was expensive," said Bernie. "My mom had to give me some of her money, too."

They crossed the brook and went into the woods where Margreete had showed Bernie a path. On the ground underneath a spruce tree, they found a dead robin, and Noah carried it back in his outstretched hands. "We can start a museum," said Bernie. "The rooms can be underground, with tunnels. Like the Lost City of Atlantic." They dug a hole, placed the robin in the hole on a nest of dried grass, and put old boards over the part they'd dug.

Mr. Eagling was the first visitor to the museum, and when they lifted off the boards to show him, the ants had already found the bird. "You better bury it," Mr. Eagling said. "Before it putrefies."

"What does that mean?" asked Bernie.

"Before it decomposes."

"It's part of our museum," said Noah. "We don't want to cover it up."

"Don't touch the bird," Noah's father said. "Just leave it alone. You don't want to be playing with dead things." He turned to Bernie. "Your father would say the same thing."

Bernie didn't think his father would. It seemed that Mr. Eagling felt a kind of horror when he stood over the hole and looked at the robin. "I'll bury him after you go," said Bernie. But he didn't. And the next time Noah came over, they uncovered the robin, and something had eaten the bird's eyes out of the sockets.

PART II

24

FALL 1962

Four years had passed. "It could all end with a bang," said Harry.

"What?" asked Eva.

"President Kennedy was just telling the nation—"

"Darling, the children don't need to hear this."

"—he was saying that Soviet nuclear weapons have been discovered in Cuba. He is imposing a naval blockade on the island. That means that U.S. ships are not going to allow any ships to enter Cuban waters. It's very dangerous."

"Where's Cuba?" asked Eva.

"Close to Florida."

Eva moved to her father's lap, where she seldom sat now that she was older. "What's going to happen?"

"I don't know."

"Are we going to get blown up?"

"It could happen," said Harry.

"No," said Liddie. "We're not getting blown up."

"How do you know?" asked Bernie.

"I just know."

But no one knew. At six years old, Gretchen was too young to understand. At ten, Eva was quiet and scared. At nearly thirteen, Bernie felt the inescapable fact: The world could blow sky-high with him in it, with his family in it, with Romeo and Fred, and the cows in the field, and everything and everyone living and breathing.

Everything was in danger, but everything was also beginning.

At the end of December, for the first time, Bernie and Noah were allowed to take a bus to Portland on their own, to see *Lawrence of Arabia*. They walked up the hill from the bus station and paid for their tickets. Noah liked sitting close to the screen; Bernie liked sitting far away. They sat halfway, munching popcorn and waiting on prickly cushioned seats for the film to begin. Then a curvy woman in a long white dress appeared on the big screen, holding a gleaming torch with its rays beaming out over COLUMBIA.

As the movie unfolded, Bernie's face went slack. Never in his life had he seen a more beautiful man than Peter O'Toole. Eyes of such intense blue, the lower lip fuller than the upper, movements like a tiger. He was surprised by a hard-on, which he hid under his bag of popcorn.

Sherif Ali asked, "Have you no fear, English?" And T. E. Lawrence answered, "My fear is my concern." He was a steely man who wouldn't think twice about murdering an enemy, who could withstand lethal temperatures in the desert, eyes caked shut from sandstorms, who knew no limits and never gave up.

Surfacing back onto the street after the film, they waited for the bus back to Bath. Noah turned to Bernie. "Have you no fear, English?"

"My fear is my concern," said Bernie, tossing his head.

"You look sappy."

"Not like Peter O'Toole?"

Noah laughed. "No, you don't look like Peter O'Toole."

"So you think *you* look like Peter O'Toole?"

"I don't sunburn like him."

"The manly Noah," he said, joking his way out of what was stirring in him again. "Rider of camels, killer of men."

Manly courage became a private joke between them: *My fear is my concern.* Lawrence of Arabia living in opposition to their fathers, who went off to work each morning in white shirts and choking neckties. What was manhood, anyway: the pale, unobtrusive lives of their fathers, or Lawrence of Arabia's heroics in the desert? Or something completely different?

Under Noah's mattress was a magazine that he pulled out and showed Bernie after school one day. "My mother would kill me."

They sat on the bed and Noah turned the pages. "Which one is your favorite? This one?" Noah pointed to a brunette, breasts flowing out of a zebra-striped bra.

"I like her outfit," said Bernie.

"But what about *her*?"

"I don't care much for her."

"Which one, then?"

Bernie looked at the women—glossy lips, tongues out lasciviously— and stabbed at a picture blindly, landing on a vapid blonde.

He hated himself.

"I don't think much of that one," said Noah.

"Yeah, kind of fake."

Noah closed the magazine and slid it under the mattress again. "Did I tell you I'm thinking of asking Melanie out?"

"You can't drive. It's sort of stupid to be driven around by your mom or your dad, don't you think? Besides . . ."

"She's white."

"Yeah, there's that, too."

25

Early that spring, the school principal opened the door of their eighth-grade classroom and whispered something to their history teacher, who looked at Noah and told him to collect his things and follow the principal. "You won't be coming back for a few days," she said. Bernie stood up, and the teacher said to sit down, it was none of his business.

Sleet slapped against the windows of the classroom, and Mrs. Buckenmeyer told them to close their books and get out a sheet of paper and a pencil for a pop quiz. "Write a paragraph about the causes of the fall of the Roman Empire." It was as though nothing had happened. Bernie left his paper blank except for three words: *What about Noah?*

Bernie thought that maybe Noah's father had lost his job and his parents had decided to move away. But later he learned that Mr. Eagling had not lost his job. He'd gone to work as usual that day, sat down at his desk after lunch, and died of a heart attack.

Bernie stood next to his father at Bath Memorial Baptist Church as the church elders wheeled an oversized coffin up the aisle. He watched Noah hold his little sister's hand and with the other hand hold his mother's elbow and then support her more firmly with his arm around her waist as they followed the coffin. At the front of the church, the organist pumped out "O Maker of the Mighty Deep":

In Thee we trust, whate'er befall.
Thy sea is great, our boats are small.

Like those boats, his friend looked very small, sitting in the front pew next to his mother and sister. The minister spoke about Mr. Eagling being called home, which made no sense. Dead wasn't home.

Afterward, in the basement of the church, there were tuna salad sandwiches cut into triangles, raw carrot sticks, potato chips, and Dixie cups of ice cream—chocolate on one side of the cup and vanilla on the other, with little wooden paddles to eat with. The food reminded him of a school picnic, but when he tried to eat a triangle of a tuna salad sandwich, he couldn't swallow it and had to go behind one of the pillars so he could wrap it up in his napkin and throw it away.

When they returned home from the funeral, his father tried to talk to him, but Bernie didn't want to talk. He went up to his room and thought about how Noah had stood by Mrs. Eagling and greeted people as though he was a grown-up. He didn't see him cry or falter or do anything that a kid would do.

Four years ago, when he was in fourth grade and first visited Noah's house, Bernie had noticed how tired Mr. Eagling looked when he came home from work and how he made an effort to be jolly. After that, every time he saw Bernie, Mr. Eagling would say, "How do you do, Mr. Furber?" and shake Bernie's hand. Mr. Eagling's hand was large and solid. He didn't seem like a person who'd drop dead.

After the funeral, Noah didn't come to school for a few days. When he did come, his face looked blank. Bernie watched the other kids stay out of his way. He didn't know what to say to him, either.

"Hi," he said.

"Hi," said Noah.

"Want to come over to my house sometime? Like this afternoon?"

"I told my mom I'd come home after school. I have to watch my sister while my mother does some stuff."

"Okay."

The bell rang.

"I'm sorry," Bernie said.

"Yeah."

"I liked your father."

"Me, too," said Noah, and Bernie watched him turn away.

Mrs. Eagling had not worked since Noah was born, but she had a master's degree in social work, and soon after Mr. Eagling died, she landed a job as director of a community organization in Wiscasset that ran a battered-women's shelter and a rape-counseling service. Noah went to work stocking shelves at Shop 'n Drop on the weekends.

Several weeks passed, and Noah told Bernie he wanted to start a dog-boarding business and earn better money. He was big on dogs, and dogs were big on him. Elders of his church helped him find lumber and fencing material for his project, and Bernie and Noah and a couple of church members built stalls in the Eaglings' two-car garage, with an outdoor run out the back door. Noah advertised "Noah's Bark" in the local newspaper, hung a sign by the road, and helped a local veterinarian on Saturdays to improve his skills in giving medications and dealing with aggressive dogs. One by one, the dogs came. By late spring, when Noah was fourteen years old, he'd signed up to take a dog-grooming course, which would qualify him to do toenail clipping and poodle and lion cuts.

"Like pink bows and stuff?" Bernie asked.

"They have to look a certain way at dog shows."

Noah was fiddling with a latch on a gate that wasn't working. Bernie liked looking at his friend when he was looking somewhere else. Noah was back in the world, sort of. He was sad, but he wasn't a drag to be around. If Bernie had lost his own father, he thought, he'd smash things, he'd yank off this latch that wasn't working, he'd holler and slam doors.

26

Bach was dead and not dead. At times, Eva felt she could reach her hand across the years between his life and hers and touch the sleeve of his coat. Except for her parents and grandmother and sister and brother, and Fred and Romeo, she loved no one more than this man she would never meet.

At the age of eleven, Eva began studying piano with a teacher her mother found for her in Brunswick. Miss Dyuzhakova had studied at the Franz Liszt Academy of Music in Budapest with Zoltán Gárdonyi and at the Curtis Institute of Music with Eleanor Sokoloff. She'd wanted to be a solo pianist but had needed to bury that dream because of the war, the death of her father and mother, and the need to look after a younger brother until he came of age.

Every Tuesday afternoon, Eva's mother dropped Eva off at Miss Dyuzhakova's house. Her teacher lived with an ill-tempered schnauzer named Louie, who bit Eva on the ankle at her first lesson.

"You must have done something to frighten him," Miss Dyuzhakova said. "Or maybe you don't smell right."

I smell fine, Eva wanted to say.

Miss Dyuzhakova could play anything and often rattled up and down the keyboard, shoving Eva out of the way to show her how it was done. Eva found her teacher's playing accurate and pinched and sad. Why would you be a musician if it didn't make you happy?

It never occurred to her to tell her mother that she didn't like Miss Dyuzhakova. It wasn't as though Miss Dyuzhakova did anything all that wrong. It wasn't wrong to be unhappy or to hate everyone but Louie. But it did seem wrong to wring the life out of everything she touched. Eva didn't mind so much about Mozart or Beethoven, but she minded about Bach. Miss Dyuzhakova assigned Bach the way she assigned Czerny, like an exercise, something to get your fingers moving faster.

Every year in May, Miss Dyuzhakova rented the community hall of the Methodist church in Bath and had all her students play a piece they'd memorized. This was Eva's first recital ever and, dressing in her bedroom, she felt a deep dread. She imagined her teacher standing steely-eyed behind the audience, watching every move her students made. Eva hated her yellow dress with the rickrack and her yellow socks and her clickety-clack black patent-leather shoes and the sparkly barrette her mother stuck in her hair and the way her hands felt cold, like the hands of a crocodile. She would be playing the first movement of a Haydn sonata, and the more she thought about it, the more she hated the piece.

Her mother yelled from downstairs that Eva had to come right away or they'd be late. She clattered down the stairs in her stiff shoes and climbed into the car and sat in the middle of the backseat, jammed in between her mother and Bernie, with Gretchen squeezed onto her mother's lap. Her father drove, and next to him, her grandmother sang:

> *Well, it's one for the money*
> *Two for the show*
> *Three to get ready*
> *Now, go, cat, go . . .*
> *One for the money, two for the show, one for the money,*
> *two for the show, one for the money, two for the show,*
> *one for the . . .*

"Mom, that's enough. You're making Eva nervous."

"No, I'm not."

"Yes, you are."

The frost heaves had chewed up the road, and Eva was thrown against Bernie and then against her mother and Gretchen. She thought of asking her father to turn around. She thought of saying she was going to be sick.

Miss Dyuzhakova stood at the door of the church, glowering. She didn't greet Eva. The room was a lonely-looking place, with a floor of gray linoleum and folding chairs, some with torn plastic seats. On a table near the back, someone had set out Ritz crackers, orange slabs of Velveeta, and radioactive-green punch, like something from one of those bomb test sites in Nevada her mother hated.

Miss Dyuzhakova arranged the pianists on the front-row seats in the same order as they'd be playing, from the least accomplished student to the most accomplished. Eva took her place in the middle of the row. Her hands were icy. She sat on them; she flattened them into her armpits. She found her name in the program and then peered down the end of the row to Jessica Petersen, who would be playing a movement of a Beethoven sonata as a grand finale, and she wondered what it would be like to be Jessica Petersen, the Most Favored One. Jessica's hair was pulled back from her face with a metal clip, her face impenetrable, and she wore a dress that looked as though it should be flouncing around the knees of a first-grader. The audience quieted, and the first student began. Then the next, and the next. Eva counted how many before she had to play. Five. Four. Her ears rang; her knees trembled. She had to clench her teeth so they wouldn't chatter. Three. Two. A boy named Ronald, with slicked-down hair, made a stiff bow and sat down. He played a Bach two-part invention as though he were a metronome. Then came Melinda Fox, who sat next to Eva. The people in the audience stared at Melinda Fox, who played a piece by Schumann as though she were the sky and the notes were little raindrops. It would be easy to hate her. Melinda finished and bowed to applause. Eva rose, stiff-legged.

It wasn't until she was in the car on the way home, silently weeping between Bernie and her mother, that she had time to think about what happened. She remembered walking to the keyboard and sitting down. The seat was too high, and she'd sat on her dress crookedly so it pulled at her neck on one side. Then her grandmother's voice rang out from the back of the room. "One for the money, two for the . . ." There was a *Shhhh!* and a snicker from somewhere.

She began the sonata, picturing page one of the music in her head, a page she'd practiced so many times that her fingers had grown spastic with familiarity. They slid over one another; it seemed they could play fast or not at all. The piano was a runaway trolley car. Faster and faster. She was aware of the bitter eyes of Miss Dyuzhakova on her. Faster still. She pictured page two and got halfway down the page before she ran right off the edge of her mind and capsized into silence. She began the piece over again, and her fingers raced over the keys. She got to the same place and stopped. For a third time, she began. She felt herself approaching the wall where memory darkened, and she crashed full speed into silence. Someone in the audience began clapping. It was her mother, she learned later, and then the rest of the audience joined in, and Eva stood up, bowed, walked to her seat, and sat down. If it hadn't been for her mother, she might have gone on forever—starting, getting to that unscalable wall, beginning over again, trapped in an endless loop.

The car lurched over a pothole. Bernie patted her leg and whispered, "It's okay, Shmoops. The first part sounded good. Three times, it sounded good." She slapped at him and felt a little better. On the other side, Gretchen's head nodded sleepily against her mother's neck.

"You're not going back to Miss Dyuzhakova," her mother said. "Maybe there was music in that woman once upon a time, but it's all dried up. I'm so sorry. I should have realized."

"It wasn't her; it was me," Eva said. "I'm the one that messed up."

"Who wouldn't in that atmosphere?"

"Melinda Fox didn't. Jessica Petersen didn't."

Her mother made a sound with her mouth, a fart-like noise.

In the front seat, her father said, "I'm proud of you, sweetheart." What did he know? He'd bob his head to any music in the world.

And her grandmother was snoring, her head bumping against the window.

Late that night, Eva heard her grandmother's footsteps heading toward her bedroom door. She could tell who it was by the way the footfalls hitched a little on one side, stopped awhile, started again softly, like a quilt thumping in a dryer. She'd taught herself not to be frightened, but tonight she felt afraid.

The doorknob turned.

"Irving, are you already in bed?" her grandmother asked. "Why didn't you tell me you were going to bed?"

"It's me, Grandma. This is my bed."

"You're such a joker."

"Grandma, it's Eva."

"Ha ha. Move over, sweetheart. Where are you?" Her fingertips grazed Eva's face, traveled to her hair . . . She moved away suddenly.

"You're not Irving."

"I know."

"Where is he?"

"He's dead, Grandma."

"No. That's not true."

"He'll be here in the morning," said Eva.

"He should be here by now."

"He got tied up at work."

"Well, that explains it." She settled back down. Her breath smelled stagnant, like cooked asparagus. Her hands clutched the top of the sheet. Eva reached up and stroked her grandmother's head and sang the song her mother had sung to her as a child:

> *Speed, bonnie boat, like a bird on the wing,*
> *Onward! the sailors cry.*

"I know that song," her grandma whispered. "Over the sea to Skye over the sea to Skye over the sea to Skye," she sang. "They dressed him like an Irish washerwoman to protect him from the British soldiers. Bonnie Prince Charlie was his name."

Her mother said that Eva was to call out if her grandmother wandered in the night, but she didn't want to, and the bed was almost big enough.

27

SUMMER 1963

School was out for the summer, and down in the dirt parking lot of Mr. Dream Cream, Bernie waited on his bicycle for Noah, eating a chocolate-and-vanilla soft serve with colored jimmies on top. Charles Hicks was also there, sitting off to one side on top of an old picnic table, with his feet on the bench, eating a cone. Charles couldn't stop his honking these days, even when he tried. The sound was like coughing up an eel, something deep and unhealthy stuck in his throat.

Bernie's ice cream cone, like Charles's, had begun to run down his arm. He'd forgotten to grab a napkin, but he couldn't now because Dennis Szwedko had just appeared with three of his scary, juvenile-delinquent friends, one of them already old enough to drive. Dennis had dropped a year behind Bernie in school and was about twice as big; he wore a white T-shirt and black leather jacket and smoked a cigarette, which he threw on the ground and stubbed out at the ice cream window with a pivot of his sneaker. Bernie heard him say he wanted a coffee shake, heavy on the coffee, which was about the coolest thing you could order. But he wasn't cool. He was alarming. His friends leaned on the car, smoking.

Out of the corner of his eye, Bernie saw Noah pedaling down the road on his bicycle, still far away. *Hurry the fuck up.*

Dennis paid for his shake, noticed Charles Hicks at the picnic table, and told him to do the snorting bull.

Charles choked out, "I don't want to," and took a bite of his ice cream cone. Dennis set his shake down, went behind Charles, lifted the back of his T-shirt up over his head, and pinned his arms. The ice cream cone fell onto the dirt, and Charles staggered around, trying to get himself free while Dennis and his friends laughed.

Bernie went over to Dennis. "Leave him alone, you jerk. Why don't you get your entertainment elsewhere."

"Else-where. Else-where." Dennis raised his voice an octave. "The fairy to the rescue." He kneed Bernie in the balls, threw him to the ground, and kicked him. Then picked up his shake and got back into the car with his friends. Bernie lay in a fetal position, eyes closed, afraid to move. The car door slammed, and the rattletrap clanked down the road.

Bicycle tires wheeled over dirt; a kickstand clicked down. "Whoa," he heard Noah say.

Bernie opened an eye and saw his friend.

"You okay?"

A sour taste in his mouth. He spat into the dirt.

"You want to lie there, or you want help up?"

"Up." Getting to his feet, he nearly went down again with the pain in his groin.

"Hurts bad, huh?"

He rubbed his mouth on his shirt and saw blood.

"Where?"

"My nuts."

"He messed up your face pretty bad, too."

Nearby, Charles was crying, chopping at the air, and Noah went to him. "You want another cone? I'll buy it for you."

Charles shook his head and tried to tuck his shirt into his pants. "I didn't want to . . . *haw* . . . do the bull for him. I'm not . . . not his little clown."

"You okay?" asked Bernie.

"Naw, I'm okay. You all right?"

"Yeah. More or less."

"Thanks for . . . you know . . . sticking up for me."

"Yeah, okay."

Charles turned and straggled down the road, and they watched as he stepped into a dirt lane and disappeared.

Bernie faced Noah. "And where the fuck were you?" He swallowed and spat again. "Didn't you see what was up?"

"I saw." He brushed the dirt off Bernie's back. "My father once told me that it wouldn't matter who starts a fight, it's me who's going to take the blame. . . . Strike one, I'm out."

There was nothing more to say. They turned around and walked their bikes in the direction of Bernie's house.

"Can you ride?"

"If I don't sit."

"Are you going to do anything to him?"

"Are you kidding? He'd end up blowing up my house. I shouldn't have said 'elsewhere.'"

"What are you talking about?"

"I said, 'Get your entertainment elsewhere.' It inflamed him."

Noah laughed. "You said 'elsewhere'? Elsewhere?"

"Sometimes I'm too dumb for my own good."

They rode slowly back up the road, Noah behind Bernie. When they came through the door of Bernie's house, they tried to sneak past his mother, but she saw them from the kitchen.

"Jesus! What happened to your face?"

"I went to get an ice cream cone and fell off my bike."

"Why don't I believe you?"

"I had a disagreement with a guy from school who was beating up this other kid."

"I stayed out of it," Noah said.

"You were smart," she said.

"Not really. Cowardly."

Bernie started to hobble upstairs, and his mother grabbed his shirt. "Where do you hurt?"

That was the last thing in the world he'd tell her, but he wondered if his balls were crushed. "I'll be okay by morning."

She tried to hug him, but he felt the tears coming and escaped.

"I'll run you a bath."

"It's okay."

"Please. Let me do that for you."

"Thanks, Mom. Me and Noah are going up to listen to some music."

"Sure?"

"See you in a while."

Bernie had moved his bedroom up to the third floor at the end of the school year. He climbed the stairs now, hanging on to Noah, with Fred stopping on every step behind them. In the bathroom, he looked in the mirror. "Fuck," he said. There was blood in his hair and dried on his neck. He took his shirt off and threw it in the laundry pile in the corner, dabbed water on his cheek, rinsed the blood off his neck.

In his room, one more flight up, he found another shirt and sat down gingerly on the bed. Fred tried to nuzzle him, and he pushed him away.

"I got hit in the nuts with a baseball last spring," said Noah, sitting on the bed next to Bernie, rubbing Fred's chest. "I iced it."

"That must have felt great."

"Want me to get you some ice?"

"No."

Noah turned on the radio. WJTO out of Bath. They sat side by side, leaning against the wall, their legs straight out in front of them, the radio on the wobbly table beside the bed. Noah laughed. "Ruby and the Romantics." He fiddled with the dial and came back to the same station.

> Our day will come
> And we'll have everything
> We'll share the joy . . .

"Mushy," Bernie said.

"Yeah," said Noah. "Great voices, though."

Something roared in Bernie's ears. Sitting next to his friend this close, their feet stretched out and almost touching, he hurt all over, but he wanted to kiss Noah. Hard. Never had he heard any man on TV or anywhere else admit to this.

He made himself say, "You like Bob Dylan?"

Noah snorted. "Naw. He's too smart for his own good—like you. B. B. King, 'You Upset Me Baby'. It's one of the best songs you'll hear in your life."

"I heard it," said Bernie.

"'You upsets me baby/Yes you upsets me baby . . .'" Noah sang, "'Like being hit by a falling tree/Woman, woman what you do to me.'"

"Yeah, it's a good song." Bernie moved away on the bed to give himself room to breathe, then got up and wobbled around.

"Hey, you know the March on Washington? I'm thinking of talking my parents into letting me go. You want to come?"

"Maybe. But my mom wouldn't let me do it." Noah studied his sneakers and whacked them together, looked at Bernie. "Are you being a good little white boy and trying to impress me?"

"No. Why would I be trying to impress you? I want to hear Martin Luther King speak."

"Don't try to impress me, okay?"

"I just said I wasn't."

"Anyway," said Noah, "King understands the South, but he doesn't get what it's like up here."

"What do you mean?"

"Same stuff, just not so obvious. You don't even have to think about it."

"And that's my fault?"

"It's not your fault, but you can ignore it."

After Noah left, Bernie's head hurt, his nuts hurt, his chest hurt, but mostly he just hurt. He hadn't spoken his truth, nothing like the truth. The only true thing he'd said was that he wanted to hear Martin Luther King speak.

28

At dinner Liddie tried not to over-mother Bernie. Harry noticed the gash on his cheek, and Bernie said he'd tangled with someone but gave no information beyond that, except for snorting when Eva asked, "Did you knock him out?"

Later, Liddie undressed and got into bed next to Harry. The night rang out with the barred owl's *Who cooks for you? Who cooks for you-aallllll?* She imagined the field mice crouched in the grass, listening, their black eyes wide, whiskers trembling. She pictured their tiny white feet shining in the moon's light and thought, *Hide your feet.* Their peril was so akin to human danger. Murderous things swooped down, ruthless in their indifference when it was already too late to save yourself. She imagined that something like this had struck Bernie, a coolly careless or cruel thing she'd never know about. Saturday night boiled up on the main road: Cars blasted down the peninsula. Beer cans flew into ditches.

Romeo was missing. She imagined his yellow eyes glowing in the dark, paws creeping through the night's stillness, a Dr. Jekyll lap cat turned into Mr. Hyde. She hadn't seen his large belly and battle-scarred black-and-white swagger for three days now. She said so to Harry.

"Nothing we can do," he said.

"How about if we go look for him?"

"You know? I never asked for a cat." They lay in bed side by side, not moving. "And I don't want to run around in the dark looking for him. I just want to be with you." Code for sex.

"Well, I'm going to look for the damn cat myself." But she didn't get up.

And then she said something she'd never intended to say: that his desire sometimes made her feel erased, as though she could be anyone. It wasn't her he wanted. It was . . . anybody. "I don't want veto power, but that's where I always seem to end up. On the other hand, I won't pretend I'm hot for you when I'm not. It's degrading for us both."

He didn't say anything for a while and then turned toward her. "Of course the last thing I want is you pretending. And I'm not going to pretend *not* to want you when I do—and by the way, it's you I want, not just anyone." There was an edge to his voice.

Is there something wrong with me?" she asked quietly.

"I don't know. Is there? Or is it me?"

She looked at the ceiling. A glow-in-the-dark star shone back like a rebuke; Harry had pasted it there after a trip to the planetarium in Boston with the kids. He'd pasted them on ceilings all over the house, like offerings. He was a more-than-decent father. He cared for Margreete. He'd moved here for her sake. How many men would have done that?

Tears trickled down and rolled into her ears. She turned to kiss him, and he pushed her away.

"I'm not that desperate," he said. "You know, Lid, I feel I have to prove myself over and over again to be worthy of sex with you. Like sex with you is the ultimate prize or something."

"You really feel that?"

"Much of the time, yes."

"The ultimate prize? You've got to be kidding. I'm the booby prize—I know four positions in bed. I've had one exciting sex dream in my life, ever. How pathetic is that?"

He turned toward her. "What was the dream?"

"Sucking Einstein's toes."

"Einstein?"

"Yes."

He laughed and reached for her hand in the dark. "I hope he enjoyed it. . . . And anyway, you're not so bad."

"You're not so bad, either," she murmured into his shoulder. "Turn over and I'll rub your back if you want me to."

She rubbed his wide back, and he made small moans of pleasure. She put her arms around his chest from behind and held him. Gradually, his breathing changed, and she felt his hand holding on to her wrist lose its grip.

She'd read articles in women's magazines about frigidity. But she knew what an orgasm felt like, and she didn't feel frigid. There was a man in the symphony, a violinist from somewhere in the Balkans, with a dark beard and undomesticated hair, like someone who slept in a cave in the mountains. He never spoke, but he had laugh lines around his eyes. Sometimes, watching him play, she wanted to jump into his smoldering bed with him.

With Harry she occasionally felt stirred, but the more he wanted her, the less she wanted him; and the less she wanted him, the more he wanted her. When they were in New York, it had been fine. Something about this house.

She stared at the starry ceiling and then got out of bed quietly, slipped on her sandals, and walked out the side door and into the field. The moon was half up the sky, and half full. Individual blades of grass shone in its light, and down the hill, its reflection shimmered in the water. "Romeo?" she called softly. She imagined him stuck in a steel trap or in the jaws of a fox or fisher cat. She walked as far as the abandoned foundation beyond the Woottons' barn, calling, and finally started home. The dew had fallen, and her feet grew wet in her sandals. She came back across the field, climbed the porch steps, and sat on the top one.

It wasn't this house. It was a kind of emptiness. Since moving, she'd taught cello, she'd played in the symphony, but there was a hole in the center of her life. She still missed the trio. When she practiced, it was for herself alone, or for the symphony—fine as far as it went, but not enough. She rubbed her bare arms in the night's chill. She thought of all that she'd asked of these arms until now, how gracious they'd been about it all. Cradling her babies. Embracing Harry in her wild youth. Hanging the washing on the line. Now these arms wanted music, to make their own damn music, the music they wanted to make.

Romeo was still missing in the morning, and Liddie went out with Gretchen and Margreete to put up notices along the road. Old Joe Weatherby, a retired boat captain, was out for his morning walk and raised his cap to them. "Have you seen my cat?" Margreete asked.

"What does it look like?"

Margreete said, "Black and white."

"Big neck," said Liddie. "Male. Lots of war scars, bent tail."

"Sorry, I haven't seen him. How you doin', Miss Margreete? Margreete blushed.

"Would you like to come over and see my garden? The raspberries are ripe."

She stood in the road. "How about now?"

"I've got to get back, Mom," said Liddie.

"It's okay, she's welcome to come with me," he said, "and I'll walk her home, safe and sound."

"I don't need walking," said Margreete. "I can walk myself."

"I can see that," he said.

"He's my boyfriend," Margreete said. "All talk and no action."

The captain laughed. "It hasn't always been like that."

Heading home with Gretchen, Liddie could imagine that Cap'n Joe really had been a boyfriend. Blue, blue eyes, the whitest hair, courtly manners, a gimpy walk as though he was still riding the waves. She could also imagine that in her day, her mother had known more than four positions in bed. Her mother called lovemaking "boom-boom." Growing up, Liddie had sometimes been jealous of her parents: how crazy they were for each other, and—later, when she was old enough to understand certain noises—how rollicking their sex life was.

That night, after the kids were in bed and the house was quiet, she crept into Harry's arms and asked him, shyly, if he'd like a bit of boom-boom. He looked at her, uncomprehending, then understood, got up to light a beeswax candle, and climbed back into bed, neither of them noticing how the burning wax was smudging a small circle in the wallpaper above it.

29

That summer, Bernie regularly babysat Gretchen while his mother taught cello students in her studio; he often read while Gretchen drew. He'd been reading *War and Peace*—partly to be able to say he'd read it at the age of thirteen but also because he adored it, especially Prince Andrei Nikolayevich Bolkonsky. Today, though, his head felt heavy and he needed to get out of the house. He was tired of sitting, fed up with hearing the sour notes of his mother's students, and worried about Prince Andrei, who had enlisted as an adjutant on General Kutuzov's staff when war broke out. He set the book facedown on a radiator and went to look for Gretchen, who was up in her room, drawing.

"How come you've always got the shades down in here?"

"The light is too light."

"We're going for a walk," he said. "I'm going to show you how to skip stones."

"I don't want to."

"I'm in charge this afternoon, and we're going for a walk. It'll be fun."

"I'm already having fun." Her Skinny Elfie in his little striped vest hung on the back of a chair by his upturned elf feet.

"Come on, Gretchen. I don't want to argue."

"Where's Eva?"

"Visiting a friend. Come on, put away your pencils." She finished the picture, ripped it off the pad, and crumpled it up.

"Why do you throw them all away?" Bernie asked.

"I don't know."

"Can I see it?" He smoothed it out, and Gretchen said that it was a mother standing by the shore; her girl, Melody, was down underneath the water of a deep lake speaking through a reed, but her mother couldn't understand her.

"Are you Melody?"

"I don't know."

"Can anyone understand Melody?"

"Skinny Elfie can." She crumpled up the drawing again and pushed her colored pencils into a pile and stood up. She was wearing red plaid shorts and a sleeveless white shirt with a blue smudge across the front.

Down in the kitchen, Fred heard the word *walk* and turned in wild circles, skidding across the linoleum floor. He rushed out the door ahead of them and flew into the field, his nose to the ground, ears flapping. Gretchen took Bernie's hand, high-stepping in the tall grass, her knees nearly up to her chin. She was small for her age, and it annoyed Bernie how slow she walked.

She sneezed. "Does the sun make you sneeze?"

"No," said Bernie.

"It does me. I bet you don't know what this flower is called. Yarrow. And this is a black-eyed Susan."

"How do you know?"

"I just do." She had a stick in her hand and whacked at the dried grass. "Do you like me?"

"Yes."

"Do you like me or Eva better?"

"I like you both the same."

"If you had to choose, who would you like better?"

"I wouldn't choose."

She seemed disappointed. Later, when Bernie recalled this moment, the field mad with bees and loud with the singing of summer, the pressure of Gretchen's hand in his, he thought he should have said, *You. I like you better.* Eva would never have known.

When they reached the water, it was low tide, just turning. Fred was already there, scrabbling over slippery rocks covered with rockweed, snapping at the waves. Bernie threw a piece of driftwood, and Fred was off into the water, paddling like crazy. He grabbed the wood in his jaws, turned, and made for shore.

Gretchen found an unbroken coconut onshore. "That's strange," said Bernie, throwing it into the water for Fred. It bobbed up, then went under, then back up. Fred's mouth opened like an alligator, trying to get a purchase on it. Finally he swam in with it, dropped it on a rock, and shook himself all over Bernie, quivering with excitement. *Again.*

Bernie watched Gretchen crouch down over a tide pool and stare into the water. The rock lining the small pool was granite—orange and green from minerals and the sea, with barnacles clinging here and there, tiny calcified mouths opening and closing. Shrimp-like creatures scooted around, and a couple of snails made their steady way across the bottom. Gretchen's wind-tangled hair blew across her eyes. Her neck was bent forward intently, and she reached for a snail and put it in the palm of her hand.

Bernie threw the coconut again and sat down on a dry rock a short distance from her and felt a happiness he hadn't felt in a long while: the sound of the water elbowing the shore rocks, a raft of eider ducks floating out beyond. The sandpipers with their fast cartoon legs running after bugs, swooping up together into the air like one organism, wings silver against the sun, and settling down again. He wondered why he didn't come down here more often. Looking at Gretchen, he thought what a funny little squirt she was. You never knew what she'd do or say. She was nowhere else but right here, staring into the pool, every sense in her awake, her feet damp with seaweed.

He threw the coconut again and again for Fred, who wallowed in and out of the water and over the rocks. The tide was coming in fast now. Fred paddled out, with equal measures of joy and desperation, and submerged his head, trying to get a grip. As Fred tired, Bernie began to worry and finally sat on the coconut. "Come here, boy. Just sit. Look, it's not here anymore. See, nothing in my hands," but Fred barked and dug away at the rocks around Bernie.

"Come on, sit down. Cool it, Fred." There was no stopping him. They'd have to go home.

He threw the coconut once more, and while Fred was bobbing for it, a wave surged onto shore and engulfed the tide pool where Gretchen crouched. She was knocked off her feet, floated for a moment, and then got up and started to run. Another wave came, and she pitched forward.

"Gretchen, wait! I've got you!"

She scrambled to her feet, panicked, and stumbled helter-skelter in the opposite direction from Bernie. As he ran toward her, she fell again. He saw her go sideways, and then came the sickening sound of her head against granite. A wave came in and nudged her as she lay there, eyes wide open.

At first he thought she was dead. He picked her up in his arms and brought her out of the ocean. Water streamed from her; blood flowed from the gash on her head. Bernie sat on a rock with her, stripped off his T-shirt, and wrapped it around the wound. Her eyelids fluttered, then her eyes closed. She opened them again, looked blankly at him, and closed them once more. He ran up over the rocky beach, stumbled up the long sloping meadow toward the house. Running, his lungs on fire.

"Mom!" he yelled, grabbing the screen-door handle, bursting into her studio. "Mom! Gretchen hit her head."

His mother took one look at Gretchen and put down her cello. "Call your parents," she said to her student, handing her the phone. "I have to leave." She lifted Gretchen into her arms. "Come here, darling. You're okay, you're okay now."

Her head, her head.

Bernie found his grandmother watching TV. "Grandma, we have to go to the hospital."

"There's nothing wrong with me."

He turned off the television. "Right now, Grandma."

"Wait, it's not finished."

"Gretchen hurt herself. You have to come."

"Who said?"

"Mom."

A car pulled into the driveway, and the cello student left.

"Who said?"

"Mom."

"Bernie, where are you?" his mother called.

He put out his hand, and his grandmother took it.

"I need my sweater."

"You don't, Grandma. It's hot out." He guided her toward the car, helped her in, and closed the door.

"I need my sweater."

His mother told him to get in the backseat and passed Gretchen in, placing her head in Bernie's lap. She'd forgotten the car keys and ran toward the house, stumbled up the steps, and then she was back, starting the car and roaring up Burnt Harbor Road.

"Where are we going?" asked Margreete.

"To the hospital."

"Where are we going?"

No one answered.

Bernie remembered when he was a little boy, his father driving him to the emergency room, up this same road, while he sat in the backseat holding his foot and the sun going down and dark falling. He laid his hand on Gretchen's skinny arm. "Are you warm enough?" he whispered. "Gretchen, are you warm enough? Gretchen, open your eyes." She opened them and looked at him and closed them again.

"Why is she lying down?" Margreete asked.

"Gretchen got hurt, Grandma," said Bernie.

"What?"

"She got hurt."

"What?"

He wanted to scream at her. *Stop asking the same stupid question over and over.*

30

It was just a silly sleepover with her friend Becky, but the next morning, Eva got the phone call from her mother about Gretchen. Becky Desjardin's mother drove her home in a lizard-green Chevy—Becky in the front seat and Eva in back. Mrs. Desjardin's sleeveless housedress looked like an apron, even though it was a dress; she was sweating in her armpits and on her upper lip. Eva thought that she never wanted to go back to Becky's house again, even though it wasn't Becky's fault that no one in her family had come to get her and no one had called until this morning to tell her about Gretchen.

When Mrs. Desjardin drove up Eva's driveway, she tooted the horn and waited while Eva got out. Romeo came to meet her, his tail held high.

"Romeo's back!" Eva yelled at no one.

She ran into the house. "Romeo's back!" she told her mother.

"He was trapped in the cellar."

"He could have died down there."

"I can't even think about it," her mother said.

"Why didn't you call me?"

"We were in a rush to get to the hospital."

"But after? You forgot about me, didn't you." Her mother didn't want to answer.

"I'm sorry, darling." She grabbed Eva's hand. "We didn't really forget you, but I was scared. Well, that's not true. We really did forget you."

Gretchen was lying on the couch with a white bandage wrapped around her head, her face pale. "I got stitches," she said to Eva. "They gave me novocaine. They made me lie down and I didn't want to. Grandma got upset, and they had to take her out and put her next door while a nurse stayed with her.

"A big wave came and knocked me down. The doctor said I probably had a concussion and I shouldn't go to sleep. Every time I closed my eyes, Mom and Dad jiggled me awake."

"Does it hurt?"

"Yes."

"Where the bandage is?"

"On the back of my head. Dad said that your brain is not attached to your skull. It just floats around in ceremonial spinal fluid."

"Cerebral."

"If your brain hits your skull and gets bruised, you have to stay quiet and not think about numbers and hard puzzles. I can think about other things, but it's impossible to turn your brain off all the way." They were quiet for a moment. "I'm not allowed to watch television, either."

"Do you want me to read you a book?"

"I want to have a nap."

"Want me to sit with you?"

"You don't have to." She closed her eyes.

The night before, Eva had been watching *Candid Camera*, sitting on the plaid couch with Becky and her brothers and laughing while Gretchen was at the hospital. She felt now as though she were watching herself laughing in front of the TV, like a girl who didn't care. She didn't know which made her feel worse—the girl who didn't care or the girl who everyone forgot about.

Gretchen's hair was tousled and there was still dried blood on the curly ends, the color of rust. Her hands were clenched into fists, as if trying to hang on to something.

Eva left her to sleep and waited to hear the whole story from Bernie, but the only thing he said was, "I don't want to talk about it."

"You don't want to talk about anything anymore."

"Maybe you'll understand when you're older. It's too hard to explain." He sounded like he was eighty years old.

"But I want to talk to you."

"Come on, Eva, don't bug me. I'm reading."

"Is *War and Peace* the longest book in the world?"

"Maybe."

"How many pages?"

"Over twelve hundred."

"I want to read it when you're finished."

"You're too young."

"I'm not."

"Fine, you're not." He went back to the book.

Prince Andrei was in the Battle of Austerlitz and had just been wounded and lay in the field, dying.

> There was nothing over him now except the sky—the lofty sky, not clear, but still immeasurably lofty, with gray clouds slowly creeping across it. "How quiet, calm, and solemn, not at all like when I was running," thought Prince Andrei, "not like when we were running, shouting, and fighting . . . How is it I haven't seen this lofty sky before? And how happy I am that I've finally come to know it. Yes! everything is empty, everything is a deception, except this infinite sky. There is nothing, nothing except that.

That was it, thought Bernie. The thing he couldn't explain to Eva. He'd felt something like this yesterday, before Gretchen fell on the rock, about the sky and the sea. It had to do with immensity. Sometimes when you're very quiet, everything grows huge, and you're part of it but such a small part that you dissolve. It was right in front of you, every day, even in the small things: Gretchen crouched over the tide pool, her hair blowing into her eyes, her red plaid shorts and spindly little legs. When for a moment he thought she was dead, everything stood still, like action frozen in a nightmare. And then running up the hill, the terror. That wasn't empty or stupid, that was real, maybe the most real thing he'd ever felt in his life. Gretchen could have died, and what had happened was his fault, no one's fault but his.

Him. Bernie.

Normally he thought he was pretty smart, but after yesterday, he saw it differently. When his teachers told him that he wasn't living up to his full potential, he always said to himself that it was because he was bored. Why wouldn't you daydream when Mr. Barraclough was standing in front of your math class, hiking up his pants every time he thought he'd said something clever—which was never? If he was honest with himself, though, he'd have to say that he didn't pay attention because he just didn't. Every day, there were little things that mattered if you could only see them. Eva just now. He knew it hurt her when he brushed her off, but she made him kind of crazy. Brown eyes that were so large and drilled into him so deep, it was like she was a coal miner. She saw too much, more than anyone in the family. He had no privacy around her.

She was scarily smart and probably would read *War and Peace*, zip through it in a week, and have all the patronymics and family names and diminutives worked out the first day. And then she'd want to talk to him about what he thought of Natasha and Pierre and whether he thought Tolstoy was a better writer than Shakespeare and why.

At the hospital, an odd thing had happened. He saw that nurse again who'd given him the tetanus shot when he stepped on the nail. He was surprised she recognized him. He thought he must look pretty different now, but she knew who he was right away and even asked about his foot. How strange that she still worked there and that she happened to be the one who was assigned to help Gretchen. She'd turned into their family's own emergency nurse.

When they got home and they got Gretchen settled, he told his father about seeing that nurse again, but his father didn't seem to remember her, which was also odd.

31

Gretchen crumpled up her pictures, one after the other, and the wastebaskets in the house filled with them. One evening before dinner, sitting next to Bernie on the couch, she labored over a drawing: a large boy, a little girl wearing red plaid shorts, and a dog with a coconut. The blue water of the ocean and blue sky overhead looked placid, but in the distance, like a fold in the universe, a large wave was gathering. Bernie watched the picture emerge and asked her to give it to him. "But don't show it to anyone," she said. She smoothed it on her knee and handed it to him.

"Why?"

"It's private. Just you and me."

He took it from her and folded it carefully and put it in his pocket. Since Gretchen's accident, he'd felt something toward her that he felt for no one else in the family—a kind of mission to pay attention. "I want to tell you a secret," he said. "I'm going to tell the rest of them tonight."

"What is it?"

He lowered his voice. "I'm going to go to Washington. Just by myself."

"Can I come, too?"

"When you're older you can come with me."

"I want to come now."

"It's dinnertime. You have to wash your hands. Look, they have ink all over them."

It was a night for spaghetti and meatballs and green beans. Half-way through the meal, Bernie pushed a meatball around his plate and looked at his mother. "I've decided I'm going to go to the March on Washington."

"Oh, you just thought you'd let us know?" said Harry.

"Who did you think was going with you?" asked Liddie.

"Well, Noah might come, but probably not. He's got the dogs to take care of. They're chartering buses that leave from Portland. Only eight dollars round-trip."

"Who's 'they'?" asked Harry.

"The NAACP."

"You're not even fourteen years old yet," said Liddie.

"That's right."

"Don't be a smarty-pants. You're too young to go all that way on a bus by yourself."

"But Martin Luther King is speaking and Roy Wilkins and John Lewis. There'll be thousands of people coming from all over."

"That's the problem," said Liddie. "God knows what will happen down there."

"You could come, too, Mom."

"I'll go," said Margreete. "I like parades."

"It's not a parade, Grandma. It's political."

"Well, muckle on, then."

"What does that mean?" asked Eva.

"How should I know?" said Margreete.

"I'm going," said Bernie. "I'm serious." His jauntiness had left him; his meatball was untouched. "You think it's dangerous because they're Negroes."

"It's nothing to do with that," said Liddie.

"Prove it," Bernie said.

"That's not something that can be proved."

"Your mother and I will talk about it," said Harry.

"I know what that means," said Bernie.

"Why don't you enlighten us?" That tone again.

"You'll go into your room after everyone's gone to bed," said

Bernie, "and you'll have one of your talks and it will result in a UPF, a United Parental Front. And the answer will be no. Dad, you used to have a social conscience. What happened to that? You think teaching school in a nothing place like this, pounding on the desk to make your points to dull-eyed junior high kids, is some kind of substitute for going out and doing something?"

"Young man, you listen to me," said Harry. "Why don't you try growing up before you pass judgment and piss all over your father?"

What Bernie saw was the hair growing out of his father's ears. It looked rakish, vulnerable, and it made him a bit ashamed of himself.

Liddie's eyes drilled into him. "I'll have you know, Bernie, that your father risked his life for his country before you were even born, before you were even so much as thought of."

"I'm talking about now, 1963."

"We know what year it is," said Harry.

"Why don't you come with me, then?"

"Maybe I will."

"I know what year it is," said Margreete. "It's 1943. The year of my birth."

"Mom, you were born in 1893."

"That's what I said."

32

While Bernie talked, Gretchen cut her own meatball into six pieces—one for each year she was old. She put years one, two, three in her mouth all together, chewed, and swallowed, then stabbed year four and chewed it thoughtfully. Around the edge of her plate were bumpy grooves, like rays of a blue sun. Her father called their dinners "blue plate specials." The dinner with the worms was a blue plate not-special.

She didn't know exactly what Bernie wanted—going somewhere on a bus by himself to a march. She could not march herself yet—her head needed another few weeks before it was back to normal. She looked at Eva, who was wearing her yellow shorts and her yellow top and no shoes. Eva had already finished her spaghetti and meatballs but not her green beans. They were sitting in a little green pile, and her sister was poking at them and spreading them out and piling them up again. Bernie was still talking about the march, how he wanted to go hear a king.

Gretchen recalled she had seen people marching at a high school football game with their flutes and clarinets and tubas. Majorettes twirling their batons and throwing them up in the air and trying to catch them, but lots of times they missed. Their hands were cold because they were dressed in skimpy outfits, her mother said. That's why. The head majorette had extra feathers on her head.

She slid off the chair and went under the table. Fred was there, waiting for things to drop, but nothing was dropping except a green bean every so often from Eva's plate. He was waiting for Bernie's meatball. He had his chin on his paws and his eyes were shifty because he didn't like it when people argued. He could feel things, even though people thought he was just a dog and had no feelings. She could see he was worried, because the skin on his forehead was wrinkled.

He'd chewed the last green bean but hadn't swallowed it. The spit-up bean was sitting in a damp lump near her mother's foot.

Her mother was wearing white sandals, and her big toe was lifting and falling on the bed of her sandal, as though it was impatient. Her father was wearing brown shoes and brown nylon socks. One sock had fallen down his ankle. Her grandmother had on pink slippers with feather pompoms, like a ballet dancer, only her legs were not like a ballet dancer's. Very close veins she had.

She wished she could bring her dead grandfather's stereopticon under the table, but it was fragile, and she was only allowed to use it at her father's desk. On special days she was allowed to take it out of the box and put the slides in the holder, one by one.

"Plowing with Oxen" was her favorite picture. A man in a field had a white bandage-y thing wrapped around his head, like when she came home from the hospital. The man was wearing bare feet and walking along in a muddy field, holding a plow that was attached to a pole that was tied to an ox. She could feel how tired the ox was, how his hoofy feet sank deep into the mud and how hard it was for him to move on to the next step. He just pushed ahead and sometimes bandage-man hit him with a stick, and the ox put his head down and felt bad.

Her parents were still arguing with Bernie. Her father said, "Young man, you listen to me," and her mother's heel was going up and down now. Bernie had picked up his meatball and slid it under the table for Fred. It rolled onto the floor, and Fred looked at it like it was too good to be true, then grabbed it before it could escape and chewed with his mouth open.

Sometimes Bernie called Gretchen "Little Twerp." She didn't

really know what *twerp* meant, but the way he said it meant that he kind of liked her.

Her grandmother pushed her chair back and left the table. She didn't say where she was going. Maybe she didn't like arguments, either. At night when everyone was asleep, she drifted around the house here and there. When she came into Gretchen's room, her hands were as soft as Fred's tongue, and they lapped at her face in the dark, trying to make sense of things.

There were question marks in her fingertips, wondering whose face this was. Whose forehead, whose hair, whose nose? Her hands traveled in the dark over the corners of Gretchen's mouth, making her smile even though it wasn't funny. Gretchen felt her grandmother's fingers asking her ears questions and making them sound like wind inside. Sometimes she climbed all the way into the bed and lay down and said, "Move over. What are you doing in my bed?" Gretchen learned to lie very still next to her, and she hardly dared breathe, because if she breathed, her grandmother might throw her out of her bed and say she didn't belong there. She got scared with her grandmother creaking around in the night like a ghost who lived in the walls. She might come tonight.

She followed her grandmother up the stairs. Usually her grandmother went to her room, but this time she climbed all the way to the third floor, where Bernie's room was now. Gretchen crept up the stairs behind her and watched her go into his room, where she stood in the middle of the floor for quite a long time. Then she opened the window and looked down. Before Gretchen knew it, she'd put one leg over the windowsill.

"Grandma!" Gretchen screamed.

"Go away. This is none of your business, go away."

Her grandmother climbed back in and slammed the window shut. Mad. She looked at Gretchen and growled. Almost like a wild animal.

Afterward, Gretchen thought she should tell her mother, but then she thought she shouldn't.

33

Bernie had a hand on the newel post at the foot of the stairs when Harry came around the corner. "I've decided the march is definitely out for me," his father said. "I'm sorry. I'd like to go. School starts September fourth, and I can't get down to Washington and back and get myself organized for the start of the year."

"You teach the same thing every year."

"I've moved to the high school, remember?"

"You could go if you wanted to," said Bernie.

"Young man, I've said this before and I'll say it again. Don't be so quick to pass judgment when you don't know what you're talking about."

"Well, you'd go if it was life and death—"

"If it *were*."

"If it were what?"

"The correct usage is *if it were*, not *if it was*."

"You're thinking about grammar when people are fighting for equality."

"Look, I'd like to be there. I'm sorry to disappoint you."

"No, you're not."

"I just told you I am. Damn it, Bernie, I won't be reviled in my own home or told that I don't care."

Bernie pivoted around the newel post and headed upstairs. When he thought about it, he didn't know if he had what it took to go all that way by himself. And he didn't know whether his motives were all that pure. If he didn't care for Noah like he did, he probably wouldn't even be thinking about going.

The next day, while his mother was teaching, Bernie called the march organizers in Portland and reserved a place on the overnight bus. It would leave Portland at 6 P.M. on August 27 and arrive in Washington at 6 A.M. on the morning of the 28th. The call he'd just made would turn up long distance on his parents' bill, but by the time the bill came, he'd be home and could pay them back.

He made a local call about the bus schedule from Bath to Portland and found that the bus would leave Bath on the afternoon of the 27th and arrive in Portland at 4:58 P.M., in time for the 6 P.M. bus. The bus going to the march was going to make one stop at a turnpike rest area in Connecticut. He'd call his parents that evening from a pay phone and tell them where he was so they wouldn't worry. And he'd mow all the lawns on his list the week before, so there wouldn't be any last-minute calls from his customers.

He'd hardly need to take anything, since he'd be coming back just one night later. He'd bring his Swiss Army knife, and he figured he'd need maybe twenty-five dollars for emergencies. He'd pack a couple of candy bars, a peanut butter and jelly sandwich, a canteen of water. And his baseball hat in case it rained.

After he finished mowing Mrs. Ufford's lawn, she came out the front door and said she wouldn't pay him, because you couldn't do a good job right after it rained. "You didn't cut the grass, you just pushed it down," she told him. He wanted to ask why she didn't stop him while he was mowing instead of letting him do the whole lawn and then telling him. But he pushed the lawnmower out of the driveway and up the road to his house. His sneakers were wet from mowing. It had started to rain again, and he took them off in the kitchen and set them by Fred's dog dish. When the sun came out, he took his shoes outdoors and left them there to dry.

Noah called that night. "What's up?"

"The usual," said Bernie. "Mowed lawns, got screwed by my neighbor, who said you can't mow when the grass is wet."

"She's right."

"No one ever told me that before."

"The rain plasters the grass down, dingbat, and you crush it with the lawnmower."

"It looked okay to me."

"That's because you crushed it and it was lying flat. But tomorrow it'll pop right up again."

"Huh."

"So, do want to hang out tomorrow?"

"I'm going to Washington."

"You're really doing it?"

"I told you I was."

"Do your parents know?"

"No."

"Have you no fear, English?"

Bernie laughed. "Yeah, a little."

"What if you get lost?"

"I have a reservation on a bus."

"What if once you're there, you can't find the bus to come back?"

"I don't know. I can always hitch back. I'm taking some money."

In the morning, he discovered that some animal had gone off with one of his shoes he'd left outside. He searched the field and found what was left of it in a gully along the side of the road. He picked it up and smelled it. The top half had been chewed and the shoelace was in tatters, but nothing had peed on it. Still, his shoe almost felt like a reason for not going after all.

Have you no fear, English? My fear is my concern. Peter O'Toole would never flinch at riding a bus to Washington.

He rooted around in his father's toolbox for duct tape, put the shoe on, and wrapped the tape over and under what was left of it. He tried it out, and the tape stuck to his sock. He unwound the tape and went upstairs to think. He tried on his leather shoes, which were too small and made him look like a dork. He had a pair of flip-flops, but they were on their last legs, and for such a long trip, he thought he'd be better off with the duct-tape shoe. Rather than sticking the duct tape to his sock, he stuck it to itself, reconstructing the top of the shoe and then winding another piece around and around to anchor it. He wouldn't be able to take his shoe off for two days.

He'd already packed his knapsack, and all that was left was making a big breakfast and setting out. He told his mother he was hanging out with Noah for the afternoon and overnight. At eleven o'clock, he went out to the road with his one white sneaker and one shiny silver sneaker and stuck out his thumb. It was a hot, muggy day, and the foot inside the duct-tape shoe sweated like crazy. Standing out there waiting for a ride, he wondered whether something bad could happen when a part of the body didn't breathe properly. He remembered a story about a dancer who'd sprayed her body with metallic paint and died because her skin couldn't breathe. That story could have been made up, like the story of the young medical student whose friends tied an amputated arm to the pull chain of her light, and after she reached up in the dark and grasped the clammy hand, her hair turned white overnight. On the other hand, maybe those stories were true.

He walked back down the driveway and into the house, up to his room, sat down on his bed, and unwrapped his shoe. He tossed it into the wastebasket, took off his other shoe, and dug his flip-flops out of the closet. They weren't sturdy, but he already felt a lot better as he headed out again.

"You're back?" his mother called out.

"Had to get something." He went into her studio, where she was practicing, and kissed her. She seemed surprised. He shouldn't have kissed her and raised her suspicions, but it just came over him, how hard she worked, how he really did love her, how beautifully she played, what a pain in the ass he could be.

When he got out to the street, a car stopped almost right away. He wasn't a magical thinker, but it did cross his mind that this piece of good luck showed that his footwear decision was right. The car was a Chrysler with crazy fins, like a spaceship, driven by a middle-aged woman.

"Where you headed?" she asked, and he told her he was going to Bath and then on to Portland by bus.

His mother could have told him if this lady's hair was dyed or not. He figured it was dyed, because everything about her was fixed up: red nails, perfume, green dress to match her car, platinum hair puffed up in a beehive. He'd watched his sister try to beehive her hair once, and it was the last time they'd had a good laugh together. Eva's hair stuck out in all directions as though she'd slept on a pillow filled with nightmares. This lady's hair was perfect. She had the window down in the heat, but her hair didn't move.

"How come you're going to Portland?" she asked.

"There's a movie I want to see."

"What movie is that?"

"Um, *The Longest Day*."

"That movie's already come and gone." She looked over at him.

"Well, my friend told me about some movie, but I guess I forgot the name of it."

"You're not a very good liar, are you?"

"No."

"What are you really doing?"

"Going to see a friend."

"A girl?"

"I'd rather not say."

"I bet it's a girl." She fiddled with the radio.

> *You look like an angel*
> *Walk like an angel*

"Do you like Elvis?" he asked, trying to make conversation.

"Sure. Do you?"

"Yeah."

"Are you a devil in disguise?" She looked at him, he thought maybe seductively, although he wasn't sure, but just the thought made him feel creepy.

"I don't know. I don't think so."

"Well, I bet you are. People who look like angels, they're often devils in disguise, and you look like an angel. I bet your parents don't even know where you're going."

"Maybe." He was sweating now.

"I don't care whether they know or not," she said. "You seem like a nice boy, and I'm going to Portland. I'll drop you wherever you want to go."

He wanted to get off in Bath, but he didn't know how to say no. "Thanks, that sure is kind of you."

The song on the radio changed. "Stevie Wonder," she said, pointing to the speaker. "Thirteen years old."

"Yeah, that kid is on fire."

"You can't be that much older than him," she said.

"Well, I am." He hated it when people thought he was younger than he was, and he stopped trying to make conversation.

When they were on the outskirts of Portland, she asked where he wanted to go.

"You can just let me out wherever it's convenient for you."

"You can tell me, I don't mind."

"I guess the Greyhound bus station."

"You're not a runaway, are you?"

"No, I'm just meeting my friend there. She's coming in from Boston."

The woman pulled into the bus station and got out of the car. She pulled a cigarette and lighter out of her purse. "I don't like smoking in my car," she said. Her hands were trembling as she lit up, and he saw that she was quite a bit older than he'd thought. He knew nothing about her, not even her name.

"Do you have children?" he asked.

"I have one boy; he's a man now."

"He lives in Portland?"

"He's in prison, up to Thomaston."

"Oh." It made him feel bad that this whole ride he didn't know she had sorrows of her own.

"He robbed a gas station. With a gun. He got in with a bad crowd when he was about your age."

"I'm really sorry."

"Let me tell you something. Don't you ever do anything to hurt your mama. I'm sure she loves you."

"She does." He could feel the tears wanting to come, and he looked down.

She leaned over and stubbed out her cigarette on the asphalt with her shoe. "All right, then."

"I sure do thank you for the ride. For everything. My name is Bernie."

"Doris." She stuck out her hand, which was cold even in the heat. She got back in her car and slammed the door, and he raised his hand to wave. Later in his life, he would hear people say things like, *Be kind to people, you don't know what sorrows they carry*, and he'd think of Doris.

"Bye, Doris," he said when she was gone, and into his head rushed a hot wind of loneliness. He felt like going home.

But James Baldwin was going to be there. Martin Luther King was going to speak. And Medgar Evers's wife and Daisy Bates and John Lewis and Roy Wilkins. Marian Anderson was going to be filling up the whole sky with her singing, and there'd be Bob Dylan and Joan Baez, and Odetta, Mahalia Jackson, and Peter, Paul and Mary. Two thousand buses would be coming from all over, and twenty-one chartered trains. He'd be one tiny part of the biggest march ever. He heard Doris's words: *Don't you ever do anything to hurt your mama*. His mother might be mad for a day or so, but later she'd be proud of him. And his father would, too, even though Bernie expected he'd be mad, too.

He saw a man half-walking, half-staggering down the sidewalk. Without any warning, the man leaned over and blew his nose onto the pavement. It was like a cartoon. A huge crane was taking down an old brick building. It opened its big steel mouth, took a bite out of the flooring, dragged it away from the building, and dropped it in a pile of rubble. A private living space was now open to the street, where anyone could see the wallpaper and the place where a family had sat down and eaten their dinner.

Next to a bus, a woman held up a sign saying WASHINGTON OR BUST, and a man checked off names on a clipboard. He asked Bernie if he had parental permission. Bernie said yes, paid him, and it was as simple as that. He climbed aboard and headed to the very back, by the bathroom. It smelled there, but the smell was overridden by his instinct to sit where the cool kids sit on buses, a place he didn't normally get to occupy. At six P.M., the bus was under way, every seat filled except for an empty one beside Bernie and another couple of empty ones farther forward. He noticed that he was the youngest person on board except for a girl about Eva's age, who was with her mother. Quite a few of the passengers had white hair; about ten passengers were Negroes.

The bus rolled onto the highway, and Bernie's chest expanded with pride. He thought of buses and trains and cars and planes coming from all directions toward the nation's capital. Some people had already been traveling for a day or two. Others, like everyone on this bus, would be traveling through the night. Hope would sweep across the land tonight. He felt freedom and joy, except for the small worry about the phone call to his parents. He looked out the window at trees and streams, at houses with their vegetable gardens and chickens, the occasional cow or horse. He thought of what lay ahead, the speeches and music, the thousands and thousands of people, and how he'd be able to tell Noah.

He thought of his father's rumpled hair and wished he was beside him on the bus and was also glad he wasn't. His family would be sitting down to dinner now. Maybe pork chops and potatoes and green peas. His grandmother would be muttering to herself; Eva would bring a book to the table, which she'd be told to close while they were eating. Fred would be under the table, stationed under Eva's chair, where the opportunities were greatest.

He took the peanut butter and jelly sandwich out of his knapsack and realized he should have packed more than one. He ate half and was still hungry, but that was part of the gravity of this trip, to sacrifice in his own small way. He nibbled part of a Three Musketeers bar, unscrewed the top of his canteen and swallowed some water, and put everything back in his knapsack.

A large man came swinging down the aisle toward the bathroom, and Bernie watched as he fitted himself through the door. He wondered how far it was to the rest stop in Connecticut. He might buy something more to eat there, but maybe he wouldn't. He'd need to find a pay phone to call his parents; he got more scared now thinking about it. Maybe it would be better to call them on the way back from Washington, when he could be reassuring. They thought he was at Noah's tonight, anyway.

The man came out of the bathroom, followed by a cloud of chemical sweetness. Bernie drowsed a bit, woke, looked out the window, rummaged in his backpack for nothing, drowsed some more as the sun fell low enough to cast a bronze light over the fields.

Several hours later, the bus pulled into the rest stop in Connecticut. The trip was feeling more serious now, with trees lost in darkness, Venus staring down cold and lonesome. The driver announced that the passengers would need to be back within fifteen minutes. Bernie was the last one off the bus, following everyone else inside. He hadn't spoken to anyone since they'd left Portland, and the fluorescent lights inside the rest area gave everything a feeling of queasy unreality. He went to the bathroom, and as he was coming out, the rubber divider between the toes on his left flip-flop separated from the worn sole. He stood on one leg, fed the divider through the hole, but it came right out again. He checked the vending machines, thinking they might sell Band-Aids. No. He went up to the woman sitting behind a cash register to ask whether she had a Band-Aid or, even better, Scotch tape. No. He looked in the men's room and found a machine that carried condoms. He bought one, opened the package, unrolled it partway, tied a knot in the end to keep it from sliding through, threaded the rolled top through the hole, unrolled it further, and tried to hitch it onto the toe part of his flip-flop. The men washing their hands at the sink stared at him and moved on. He got his Swiss Army knife out of the backpack, split the top, tied a knot with the two ends around the toe divider, and tried a few steps. The knot on the bottom pulled through the hole in the sole. He went back to the cash-register lady for change, bought a second condom, thinking that he could fashion something on the bus. Then he thought he'd better buy another, just in case, and he inserted the rest of his change into the machine. It jammed, and he whacked the dispenser violently. Some of his money fell out but not enough. Back to the cash-register woman, and back to the condom dispenser.

He rushed out into the parking lot, half barefoot, with the doctored rubber and flip-flop in his hand and the two unopened condoms in his pocket. Bernie remembered perfectly where the bus had been when he'd left it. He looked around, thinking it had moved, thinking anything but what was true.

34

He walked back inside the rest area and sat down. The place was deserted, and the woman at the cash register noticed him, got off her stool, and came over. "Where are your parents?" she asked.

"Home."

"Where's home?"

He told her.

"Do they know where you are?"

"I guess not."

"Is that a no?"

He nodded. "I was going to the March on Washington, and the bus left without me. My flip-flop broke and I was trying to mend it with something in the men's room and it wasn't going all that great and I guess I forgot about the time and the bus left."

"How come someone didn't notice you weren't on the bus?"

"I wasn't sitting with anyone, and they just didn't remember."

"It must have been scary to lose the bus."

He wanted her to stop talking before he started to cry.

"How are you going to get home?"

A man with a mustache was over at the cash register, trying to buy a packet of cigarettes, and the cash-register woman went and took his money, then walked back toward Bernie. She had the kind of stockings that roll up just under your knee, and one had slid down so her leg was two different colors. Her uniform was Pepto-Bismol pink, and her name tag said FLO.

"So what's your plan?" She smiled a little, revealing teeth that were all crowded together.

"I'm going to hitchhike."

"You don't mean now."

"No."

"Have you ever hitchhiked before?"

He shook his head. And then he remembered he had on the way to Portland.

"Why don't you let me take you to the bus station in the morning? Do you have any money?"

"Yes, I do."

"You'd be welcome to stay at my house when my shift is over. I'm leaving at eleven. Or if you'd rather, you can stay here all night, and I can pick you up in the morning and drive you to a bus."

"I don't want to stay here."

"Well, I don't want you coming home with me unless you call your parents and tell them where you are. I'll talk to them if you want."

"That's okay."

"Will they be mad?"

"Yes, I think they will."

"You know how to do long distance on a pay phone?"

"Yes."

". . . Come over here, and I'll give you some change."

Walking over to the phone, he wondered how to get out of calling. If he could get home by tomorrow afternoon, they'd just think he'd been at Noah's. But the woman was watching him.

His grandmother answered, the worst possible person. "Hi, Grandma. Is Dad or Mom there?"

"What's that funny beeping noise?"

"I'm in a phone booth."

"What are you doing there?"

"Grandma, I need to speak to Dad or Mom."

"What for?"

"Please, Grandma, I'm running out of time. The phone is going to need more money soon."

"It's hot here today. Where are you?"

"Grandma, I need to speak to Mom or Dad. Can you call them?"

She didn't answer, and after a time the phone went dead. He waited a few minutes before trying again, hoping someone else would pick up. He inserted more money, and his grandmother answered again.

"Hi, Grandma. Please call Mom." To his surprise, she did.

"When will you be home?" his mother asked. "Grandma said you were in a phone booth?"

"It's like this . . ."

"Where are you?"

"I'm in Connecticut, Mom."

"You're kidding, right?"

"I was heading down to the March on Washington—"

"You were *what*?"

"I got on the bus, but it stopped in a rest area in Connecticut and then it took off without me."

"It's ten o'clock at night and you're in a goddamn rest area in Connecticut? . . . Harry!"

"Mom. There's a woman here who works at the cash register, and she said she could let me sleep at her house and bring me to the bus in the morning. She's very nice."

"I cannot believe this."

He heard his parents conferring, and his father got on the phone. "I'm driving down there tonight. Where are you?"

"No, Dad, please. Really. I'm okay. I don't want you to do that. I'll let you talk to the woman here."

"What the hell were you thinking?"

"I wanted to go."

"And we said no."

"Dad—"

"And you did it anyway."

His mother got back on the phone. "Your father is not driving down tonight. That would make two fools in one family. Do you have any money?"

"Yes."

"Then go ahead and stay with the woman and get a bus home. You're a complete idiot." She hung up.

That surprised him more than anything in his life so far.

"I guess they weren't too happy," the woman at the cash register said from across the room.

"No. But they were glad I'm with you." That wasn't exactly what they'd said.

"I've got another forty-five minutes, and then we can get out of here. You want a hamburger or something?"

"I guess not." He still had half a sandwich. Come to think of it, maybe he'd eat that. After that and a trip to the drinking fountain and the men's room, where all this trouble started, he drowsed a little until she shook him gently by the arm.

"Come on, kiddo, time to go. You still want to come?"

"Yes."

"Where's your other flip-flop?"

"In my backpack." He hobbled out behind her.

Her car waited in the parking lot; he opened the passenger-side door and sat down, aware of various cans and crunched up bags and candy wrappers on the floor. He was so tired, his head kept nodding toward his feet. In a half-waking dream, he was being taken somewhere by the KGB and had to remember the route so he could escape, and then he snapped awake and thought how odd everything felt, that he needed . . . but he lost the thought and half-slept again.

He couldn't see the house in the dark, but what he did make out was a scraggle-tree street with uncertain grass, cars dropped at the curb like refuse. Flo opened the front door, then showed him to a room that was done up in pink and purple and told him to make himself comfortable. "This was my daughter's room," she said. "I've left it pretty much the way it was."

The way it was before what?

"The bathroom's next door. I'll see you in the morning."

"Listen," he said. "I want to thank you very much."

"Don't worry. You've very welcome." She shut the door behind him, and he heard her footsteps going down the hall.

He found seven Chatty Cathy dolls lined up on the bureau, their vacant blue eyes staring into the room. Most were blonde; two were brunettes. They were dressed in pastel pinafores and playsuits and party dresses. Bernie wanted to lay them down and close their eyes, but he was afraid to touch them. He could feel that the room was a shrine to someone no longer in the world. Time stood still, like a creature peering into the future with those same unblinking eyes.

He sat down on the bed and thought he heard one of the dolls say something. Back home, he'd once tried pulling the Magic Ring on Gretchen's Chatty Cathy and found it creepy. "Let's play school." "Please change my dress." Gretchen found it creepy, too. Margreete was the only one in the family who wanted to talk to it. He lay down, so exhausted that sleep felled him like a blow to the head; soon his dreams came, stuffed with mayhem.

He woke the next morning to the smell of bacon and toast and coffee. Flo was in her bathrobe and asked him to sit down for breakfast. She said a bus to Boston would be leaving in less than an hour and if he wanted a shower after he ate, he'd find a towel in the bathroom. He noticed her unkempt hair, her pale lipstick-less mouth, her eyes smudged with eyeliner she'd been too tired to remove the night before, her face a kindness he didn't know what to do with. "What size are your feet?" she asked.

"Ten," he told her, munching on a piece of bacon.

"My former husband left behind a pair of shoes. They'll be a bit large, but they'll get you home. I have no use for them. He got a job in Denver after we lost our daughter, and that was that."

He held his breath and waited. He couldn't ask, but his chest felt full of the empty room he'd breathed in all night.

"She fell from a roller coaster."

"Oh."

"I saw it happen. I wasn't with her. My husband was. I was down below."

"I don't like roller coasters," said Bernie. "I throw up." And then he thought that was a really wrong thing to say and added, "I'm very sorry for your loss." But that sounded like something on a Hallmark card.

"It was a long while ago," she said.

"That doesn't make it any better," he said, and went quiet.

She excused herself and came back with a pair of brown-and-white wing-tip shoes.

"Oh, no, I couldn't," said Bernie. It sounded as though he was saying she was too kind and he couldn't possibly take them, but he really meant that he couldn't be seen in shoes like that.

"It's all right," she said. "Really." She thrust them into his lap.

"Thank you so much." He put them on.

She drove him to the bus station and made sure he had enough money. He thanked her, and just before he closed the door of the car said, "I'm really sorry about your daughter."

She reached for his hand. "You're a good boy," she said. "Good luck."

Noah laughed, out by the dog kennels. "Holy Moly, what a knucklehead." He was holding a hose, filling up the water dishes of his boarding dogs.

"It could have happened to anyone," said Bernie.

"No, it couldn't. It could only happen to you. What did your parents say?"

"My mother isn't talking to me. She slapped me—my father couldn't believe she did that. And she told me if I ever pull something like that again, she won't let me back in the house."

"She was scared," said Noah.

"She was furious."

"Did she ever hit you before?"

"No. But in a funny way I'm glad she did. She might get over it sooner."

"Maybe."

"What do you mean?"

"I don't know."

"My father was kind of too reasonable. He said he was disappointed in me. He said when I was a parent, I'd understand what it's like to be afraid for your kid."

Noah passed Bernie a can of dog food and asked him to fill a couple of dishes. "Would you ever want to be a parent?" asked Noah.

"No."

"I watched some of the march on TV," said Noah. "It's unreal how many people were out there."

"I can't believe I missed the whole thing."

A cocker spaniel came up to the fence, and Bernie rubbed her under her chin. "Are we done here?"

"Yeah." They started back to the house.

"Is your mom at work?"

"She's up at a conference in Augusta. Mrs. Lorinda Eagling, Executive Director of Safe Harbor, has been asked to speak about the roots of domestic violence."

"Does she like her job?"

"I think so. When I leave home for good, she's at least not going to be stuck here doing nothing. Which is what she'd be doing if my father were still here. I'm not saying it's good he died."

"What do you mean for good? Where are you going?"

"I'm not sure." He wiped his forehead with the sleeve of his shirt. "I'm thinking about the Air Force."

"You're joking."

"No. I've looked into it. They'll pay for college plus a living allowance. All four years free and clear."

"Why don't you just get a scholarship?"

"I wouldn't get a full one, and my mom is just getting by. Plus, my father was in the Air Force and it worked out for him."

"Is this some kind of tribute to him?"

"No."

Bernie followed Noah into the house, and the screen door slammed behind him harder than he intended.

"They'll own you for four years. It's a horrible idea."

"I heard you. Just cool it, okay?" Noah got some crackers down from the cupboard and a jar of peanut butter and took them into the living room and set them on the coffee table. "I saved this for you," he said, handing Bernie a copy of the *Portland Press Herald*. "You know how many people were at the march? More than a quarter million."

Bernie opened the newspaper to the page printed with King's speech, sat down on the couch, and read part of it out loud: "'Now is the time to rise from the dark and desolate valley of segregation to the sunlit path of racial justice. . . . The marvelous new militancy, which has engulfed the Negro community, must not lead us to a distrust of all white people . . .'" He could hear King's voice soaring and falling. He looked up from the newspaper and saw Noah standing on the other side of the coffee table, watching him.

"Do you distrust me?" asked Bernie.

"Don't be an idiot. But that dream he's talking about? Not going to happen. Not while I'm alive."

"You can have any kind of life you want."

"Just like you made it to Washington."

"Get out, I would have made it."

"But you didn't."

35

FALL 1963

Eva got off the school bus and found Fred waiting for her, the way he did every afternoon. She emptied the mailbox—a letter from Uncle Peter for her mother, a bill from the electric company, some other stuff, and the newspaper. Fred pranced up the driveway ahead of her and led the way into the kitchen, where he ate a few leftover pieces of kibble, slurped up some water, and lay down under the kitchen table. She poured herself a glass of milk, and her fingers left imprints in the glass's condensation as she drew lines down the side with her nose. She had a headache and laid her cheek against the yellow tabletop.

She snapped the rubber band off the *Portland Press Herald*, unrolled it, and spread it out. September 16, 1963. The headline read, BOMB BLAST KILLS FOUR CHILDREN. At first she thought the bomb had gone off in Maine. She hardly knew where Birmingham was.

Four schoolgirls died. Addie Mae Collins, Cynthia Wesley, and Carole Robertson, all fourteen years old, and eleven-year-old Denise McNair. The girls were buried beneath the rubble in the basement restroom, where they'd been putting on choir robes and tying on their sashes for the service. The Reverend John Cross said their bodies were "stacked on top of each other, clung together." He had been leading a women's Bible study group, "A Love That Forgives."

Eva pictured the girls in the basement restroom of the church, laughing the way she'd been laughing with her friends in the restroom at school this afternoon. She stared at their pictures. Denise

McNair, the girl who was eleven years old like her, had a pretty hat on. Everything about her was pretty and bright.

In the newspaper, the faces of the girls were all jammed up next to each other, which made Eva think again about what the pastor had said: *stacked on top of each other.* Their families were wrecked, the way her family would have been wrecked if Gretchen had died. The paper said it was probably the work of the Ku Klux Klan. She'd heard of them and seen pictures of the white robes, the eyeholes filled with emptiness, like ghosts.

In the paper, she read President Kennedy's words: *I know I speak on behalf of all Americans in expressing a deep sense of outrage and grief over the killing of the children yesterday in Birmingham, Alabama.* But it wasn't true what he said. He didn't speak on behalf of all Americans. There were Americans who wanted to blow up churches and kill children like these four girls, who didn't care what the President said.

Later, it turned out there was at least one person who wanted to kill the President himself, and did. News of his assassination came over the loudspeaker while Eva was in her sixth-grade gym class. Her gym teacher, Miss McCann, had just told the girls that they'd have to run around the football field five times as punishment for giggling. Miss McCann was a sadist. A brisk wind blew off the ocean, and their bare legs would be apple red with cold. Eva was standing under a basketball hoop, wearing her gym uniform, a short, ugly one-piece bloomer with snaps up the front and short sleeves that stuck out stiffly.

The President has been shot. The loudspeaker crackled, and the girls huddled in their clownish gym suits in horror. Katie Farnsworth grabbed Eva's hand and pulled her over against the wall, squeezing her hand so hard that the cheap ring Eva was wearing dug into her palm. The principal was sending for the school buses to take them home early.

Into the silence, Mariah Littlefield said, "My parents didn't think a Catholic should be President anyway." Miss McCann looked at her with her hard, small eyes and told her to "shut the hell up, you little fool," and Eva saw with a shock that their gym teacher was a human being after all.

Bernie was in an earth science class taught by Mr. Dimsby, who weighed 430 pounds and was going into the Parkview Adventist Medical Center the following day to lose weight. Bernie and his lab partner were measuring the effect of temperature on the volume of a gas when the principal's voice came over the loudspeaker.

Harry was teaching a world-history class and had just told his students about the atrocities of the Japanese during World War II. "You won't find this in your history book, but Americans also tortured enemy soldiers. Our country was not as blameless as these pages imply." He held up their textbook, *History of the World*. "You'll find that Americans are inevitably portrayed as the good guys, but this is not always the truth."

Rosemary raised her hand.

"Yes?"

"My uncle died in World War II."

"I'm sorry to hear that."

"And I don't think it's right for you to say that he wasn't a hero."

"Did I say that?"

"You said American soldiers tortured people."

"I didn't say your uncle did. One of the main reasons for you to become educated is so you learn to ask questions, to recognize propaganda when it occurs. It can come in many forms, through radio and television, through newspapers, even through your own history textbo—" The principal's voice interrupted him, and he put the book down on the desk. After the loudspeaker went silent, Harry looked at his class. "You will never, as long as you live, forget this moment." He sat down, turned his face to the wall, and cried. And finally turned back around, wiped his eyes, and told his students they were dismissed. "I'm sorry. What the hell is the point of being here? Go home and be with your families. Don't just look at me. You're dismissed." They shuffled out of their chairs in confusion and went into the hall.

Liddie was practicing Stravinsky for the next symphony orchestra concert in Portland and didn't hear the news.

Gretchen was in her second-grade classroom, and no one told her anything. Margreete was at elder care for part of the day, and no one told her anything, either.

That night the family sat in front of the TV as witnesses described the mayhem. Shots ringing out. President Kennedy being rushed to Parkland Hospital. Their youthful President gone.

Liddie thought of JFK's children running around the halls of the White House, bringing laughter to its sedate walls. All that life. They watched Jackie Kennedy in a small room aboard *Air Force One* in her pink bloodstained suit, standing next to Lyndon B. Johnson, with his long, sad face as he took the oath of office.

"What happened?" asked Margreete.

"The President was shot," said Harry.

"What happened?"

"Harry just told you, Mom. The President was shot."

"What did you say?"

"Don't keep asking," said Bernie. "He's dead."

"And now the whole country is broken," said Gretchen.

That Sunday, on national television, Jack Ruby shot the man who shot the President. Lee Harvey Oswald's mouth opened wide, like he was saying *Oh!* Gretchen grabbed her mother's hand. Jack Ruby wore a black suit and had a fat neck. "I don't want to watch," Gretchen said. But they showed it over and over, Oswald's mouth open like someone had punched him in the stomach.

"Why did he get bumped off so quickly?" asked Harry. "Was someone afraid he'd talk?"

"Why even speculate?" said Liddie. "Kennedy died. It's a national tragedy. And then to see his murderer murdered on live TV. What kind of country is this?"

"A violent one," said Harry.

"Sometimes I don't even want to live here anymore," said Bernie. "Who's going to get killed next? And what about Superman's never-ending battle for truth, justice, and the American way? Oh, I forgot. This *is* the American way. Guns, guns, and more guns."

"What are you talking about?" asked Eva.

"This country. I'm talking about our country."

Together they watched footage of the two white horses pulling the carriage carrying the casket. Liddie wept at the sight of the black riderless horse, the eerie beat of the drums.

Only much later would they see the complete footage of President Kennedy sitting in the backseat next to Jackie Kennedy in her pink Chanel suit and pillbox hat, with John Connally and his wife, Nellie, in front, traveling down the Dallas street in that great wide convertible and everyone smiling and waving as though tomorrow and tomorrow would always be this happy and free. And the President suddenly slumping to one side and Jackie trying to hold his head upright, the second bullet striking, and her husband broken beyond repair.

36

On the night of the school's parent–teacher conferences, Harry met the mother of Rosemary Bialas, who wore so many silver bangles on her arm, they tinkled as she talked. Rosemary's mother told him that Rosemary was a good girl but that she was a little too interested in boys. That was an understatement. Rosemary was a nitwit who probably hadn't opened a book all year. The family lived in a house farther up the peninsula that had a two-car garage out front, with HIM on the left and SHE on the right. When he drove by, Harry always smiled and then often felt bad about being so smug.

Rosemary's mother did not let on during the conference that her daughter had complained about him or that Rosemary's outraged father had told Frank Duffy, the principal, that Harry was a traitor and ought to be fired.

"There are a few things we need to discuss," Frank said later that week when he called Harry into his office. Harry was now sitting in a straight-backed chair, like a naughty boy, facing him.

"First of all," Frank said, "we don't swear in our classrooms. I understand that you swore after you heard the news that President Kennedy had been killed."

"I don't actually remember what I said."

"Our job is to act as role models at all times, no matter what the provocation."

"It seems to me that 'provocation' is a pretty mild word to use about the assassination of the President of the United States of America."

"The point is—"

"—we don't swear in our classrooms."

"Yes, you get my point." He squeezed his hands together. "Second, you dismissed your class the day of the incident. *I* dismiss school, or my assistant principal dismisses school. Teachers do not dismiss school. Your students were found out in the corridor, milling about, not knowing where to go or what to do."

"I understand it would have been better not to dismiss them. I was devastated."

"The point is—"

"—teachers do not dismiss school," said Harry, "and our job is to act as appropriate role models at all times."

"Exactly." Frank paused to get his bearings. "Third, I understand from one of our parents that you referred to American soldiers serving in World War II as dishonorable."

"Was this one of Rosemary Bialas's parents?"

"Yes. Well, I'm not really at liberty to say. It might have been."

"I didn't refer to American soldiers as dishonorable. I said that atrocities had been committed on both sides, that our country was not blameless."

"Was that in the history book?"

"That was my whole point—that good citizens must ask questions, not swallow everything they read or are told. This is the foundation of a strong democracy. Not all American soldiers behaved honorably in the war, even though the history book implies that every U.S. soldier was a hero."

"Rosemary's uncle, Doug Bialas, died in the war."

"And I told Rosemary that I was sorry."

"You implied that he was a torturer."

"For Pete's sake, I did no such thing."

"That's what she understood."

"She most definitely misunderstood. I even clarified the point for her that I was not talking about her uncle."

"Well, it's inappropriate for you to make statements of that sort, statements that are not supported by the history books we provide."

"Who's 'we'?"

"Myself. The school board."

"I see."

"And one other thing."

"Yes?"

"I understand from Mr. Bialas—I mean, from the parent in question—that you didn't serve in the war."

"I don't see how this is any business of Mr. Bialas. I did serve. I served in a different capacity."

"In intelligence?"

"No."

"Would you say, Harry, that you're loyal to this country?"

"I beg your pardon?"

"Are you a loyal American?"

"Is your name Joseph McCarthy?"

"I don't appreciate that."

"And I don't appreciate the question. In fact, I'm deeply offended by it. I was not required to sign a loyalty oath when I was hired, and if I had been, I wouldn't have taken the job. Not because I'm disloyal but because requirements like that, and a question like the one you just asked, smack of totalitarianism. So, Frank, go ahead and fire me if you can't support me. And if you do fire me for what I've taught in my classroom, the first thing I will do is call the American Civil Liberties Union."

"Is that a threat?"

"It's just what I'd do. I'm not threatening you. You can do anything you want. You're the principal. Are we finished?"

"Yes, we're finished."

"Am *I* finished? Do I still have a job?"

"I have to run this by my superintendent."

"So I might be finished and I might not be."

"That's the long and the short of it."

"And, furthermore, I might *want* to be finished and I might not want to be. Have a good weekend." Harry stood up, went back to his classroom, gathered his papers into his briefcase, stuffed *History of the World* into a drawer of his desk, and walked out to the parking lot. He looked for his car and then remembered he was driving a loaner while the station wagon had some body work done. The loaner was a large-finned canary-colored Plymouth Fury that looked as though Harry might be planning an exit by air. On the driver's side fender, about knee high, *Fury* was written in chrome.

He drove to the hardware store and parked out front. He was supposed to pick up something, but for the life of him he couldn't remember what.

"Damn it," he said out loud. He sat there for a minute. It was a dustpan he was supposed to pick up for Liddie. Well, fuck the dustpan. *Go buy your own fucking dustpan.* He was tired of being a good boy. Tired of teaching students who didn't give a damn, tired of saying yes to Frank when he meant no, tired of keeping the lid on in his own house. The roof would blow off if he ever gave vent to what he was really feeling. Did he even know what he was feeling? Fury.

He stared through the windshield, where the sun glinted. A small spider trailed through the light, casting a tiny shadow on the dashboard. He stopped and watched. To that spider, the shining light and the cool glass under its feet were the whole world. That spider wasn't thinking about how the car had just transported it from somewhere else. It didn't know "car" or "somewhere else." As humans, Harry thought we weren't all that different—we have no idea how much we don't know.

He'd always wanted to visit the Lascaux Caves, to set his feet where humans had walked twenty thousand years ago, to take in with his own eyes the beauty of those ancient paintings, the subtlety and vigor of the animals depicted: the great black bull, the running horses. He longed to understand what it had been like for the men and women who had made those figures. Perhaps they were not so very different from us, not in the most essential ways. Photographs of their ancient handprints moved him so deeply, gave him a pleasure so deep, he had no words. As though they were reaching, beckoning from that ancient world, trying to tell us where humans had gone wrong, showing us a way forward.

Here he was, a man of the twentieth century, sitting on the warm plastic seat of a Fury, looking out the windshield at the front door of the hardware store, the blue and red wheelbarrows sitting out front, the rakes stacked up alongside snow shovels for the coming onslaught, and in his rearview mirror the last of the russet oak leaves hanging on. To have had his knuckles rapped by a principal with not one bit of imagination, vision, or insight. To have had to prostrate himself to keep his damn job. If he didn't have a wife and kids and a mother-in-law and a dog and cat and an aging house, he'd have quit on the spot.

He reached into his pocket and brought out his wallet, not knowing what he was doing until he was doing it. Under his driver's license, buried deep, was the slip of paper bearing Molly's phone number.

He'd never believed in a universe that neatly arranged things for people, that created certain inevitabilities, but it was hard to believe that the coincidence of Molly looking after both his children in the emergency room was merely another example of random billiard balls flying into each other.

"I'd like to see you again," he said into the windshield, into the sun and the spider and the sky.

He tucked Molly's phone number back into his wallet, got out of the car, coaxed the spider onto his palm, and found a shrub where it could make a modest living. He backed away from the hardware store and started home. He wouldn't tell Liddie what had happened at school. There was no point worrying her until there was something to worry about. She'd be teaching, and the babysitter would be there making dinner, he hoped.

Arriving home, he found Gretchen and Eva weeping and Bernie up in his room, doing homework with Noah. Romeo was dead. The old cat had made it up the steps onto the back stoop, perhaps heading in for his supper, and breathed his last breath on the doormat. Margreete was sitting beside Romeo, wailing, patting him frantically from head to tail, head to tail.

Harry sat down on the steps next to her. "I'm sorry."

"You poisoned him, didn't you."

"Nobody poisoned him. He was an old cat. He didn't suffer, he just lay down as though he was going to sleep."

She stroked Romeo again fiercely. "What do *you* know?"

"I don't know anything."

"Were you the one?"

"The one what?"

"Poisoned him."

"No one poisoned him, Margreete. His time had come."

Harry stared at the old cat. He was lying on his side, his feet splayed out in an odd relationship to one another and his mouth slightly open, as though he'd labored for breath at the end. His eyes were half open, with nothing there. Less than nothing, like a subtraction. His black-and-white fur, his bullish neck, his wide tail, his large tummy—it was shocking to see every vital force gone. His whiskers were bent into the doormat on one side, and Harry wanted to adjust his head, but he couldn't bring himself to touch it.

"He was a fine cat," he said. "He ruled the roost. He loved you, Margreete. You gave him a good life."

Margreete's tears broke his heart.

"Do you have an idea," he asked, "where you'd want to bury him?"

"A bonfire," she said.

"You want to burn him?"

"The Romans did that."

"The Romans buried their dead." He didn't actually know what the Romans did, but he would not incinerate Romeo. And he wanted to get him into the ground before Gretchen got involved and became even more morbid than she already was. "How about if you get one of your shirts or sweaters to wrap him in and I'll start digging a hole." Margreete rose to her feet and disappeared.

He scouted around for a good burial spot and decided on a patch of ground not too far from where he'd planted the peonies from Michigan. He'd seen Romeo sitting there, blinking into the setting sun, and it seemed like as good place as any from which to view eternity. The ground had still not frozen solid, and he plunged the point of the spade close to his two favorite peonies: Pride of Essex and Departing Sun. He'd enriched the soil there with compost, which made it easier to work; he enlarged the perimeter of the hole and started downward. From inside the house, he heard the sound of one of Liddie's more promising students. There was a chill in the air, which seemed to rise from the ground, and he leaned on the shovel to rest for a moment and listen. He didn't know who the composer was, but the music was lush enough to be Brahms, perfectly suited to an autumn evening with its steadily growing accumulation of fallen leaves, the yearning in the air, and a befuddled, middle-aged man digging a grave for a dead cat.

He finished deepening the hole, Liddie's lesson ended, the student came out—fortunately through the front door and not over Romeo. Out came Fred, too, who discovered his former enemy lifeless on the doormat. He nudged Romeo's head with his nose, his tail wagging. *I know you're just playing; get up now.* He nudged again with his nose and suddenly leapt backward.

It seemed that Margreete had lost the thread of the narrative, and Harry went to find her. She was at the kitchen sink, washing an old blue sweater.

"Did you forget about Romeo?" he asked. "I'm going to bury him now. Do you want to come?"

"No, I guess not. I don't know," she said, lifting the dripping sweater out of the water. "Maybe I should come with you." She didn't follow him, though, and Harry picked one of his flannel shirts off a hook in the kitchen and went outside.

It was nearly dark now, and a heavy dew, saturated with the sea, was settling over grass and leaf. Fred, with his head dampening, sat at the bottom of the back steps, keeping watch.

"He died," Harry said out loud, and Fred's tail wagged, just the tip of it.

He thought for a moment. He'd wrap his shirt around Romeo and not actually have to touch him, but he didn't know what would happen when he picked up the shirt in his arms—whether Romeo had been dead long enough that he'd be stiff or still limp. Either way, he didn't want to do it. Would his head flop to one side and his mouth open further? He was afraid of unexpected movements from the cat, who wasn't a cat anymore. He wanted to yell for someone— his father—who would have just gotten it done, like the man he was.

With his shirt stretched out before him like a cloak, he knelt down beside Romeo. His heart beat into his forehead. "Sorry, old boy," he whispered, and laid the shirt over the top and tucked it carefully around the sides and felt the body give a little. He got all the way down on his haunches and picked Romeo up with his forearms, making a kind of trough with his arms. It wasn't easy to walk that way, bent over, and he staggered along toward the hole, surprised at how heavy Romeo still was with all the sap gone out of him.

Fred walked along beside him, a lone pallbearer. They reached the hole, and now there was the problem of how to get the dead cat in. He set him down, wishing he'd made the hole longer. It seemed as though Romeo/not Romeo was quite stiff, but Harry didn't trust him not to buckle if he picked him up just with his two hands. He went into the shed and flattened out a cardboard box and lifted Romeo onto that and slid him gently into the grave, tucking the shirt around him. And then went back to the shed and brought out another piece of cardboard and laid it over him. Fred trailed him, back and forth, sniffing cardboard, sniffing him, poking his nose into the hole.

Let the sea roar, and the fullness thereof. The words jumped into his head. He thought they must be part of a psalm he'd learned in his youth, nickering at him from the past. He scooped up a spadeful of dirt and tipped it onto the cardboard. He shoveled in more dirt, hating to think what would happen next: the worms exploring, the tunneling roots, the soft fur sloughed from Romeo's bones. The first star came out, and again he thought of Brahms, who loved Clara Schumann and finally had a chance to marry her after Robert Schumann died. In the end, though, they never married. It seemed Brahms had preferred longing to marriage. *The state of longing is not something often celebrated,* he thought, *but look at the music it created.*

Harry kept shoveling until the hole was filled. He tamped it down with the spade and carried several granite foundation stones from a pile he'd been saving and laid them over the grave. A sliver of moon rose over the ocean, and Harry stood with Fred and looked at the sky. He felt oddly at peace, unencumbered. He knelt in the dirt—something he'd never before done for animal or human—said goodbye to Romeo, and headed toward the lighted house.

37

Liddie looked out the kitchen window as Harry was shoveling dirt into the hole and felt a wave of affection for him. Her last student had left, and she wanted to join him out there, but if she went, Gretchen might get involved, and she was already too focused on death as it was. In the twilight, Liddie could just make out his outline with the spade. Harry was squeamish about dead things, and he would have had to force himself to pick up Romeo. He hadn't ever wanted a cat, and he hadn't wanted to live here. She worried that he didn't complain enough. Sometimes she wished he'd swear more, maybe even throw a cup of coffee across the room. She felt things simmering in him. People got cancer like that. And heart attacks. Or both.

She remembered when they'd first known each other. An evening in Boston. A sudden rainstorm. She was wearing a light summer dress; Harry was wearing his basketball sneakers. Black high-tops. One of his shoes was coming apart at the sole, and with every step it made a flapping sound. And then Harry's other shoe started flapping. When the deluge came, they made a run for a movie theater, and Harry flapped furiously, and Liddie laughed so hard, she wet herself and had to wash her legs in a puddle and step out of her underwear and throw it into a bin on the street. They held hands and ran like crazy, laughing, splashing through the streets. Water dropped from the end of Harry's nose, from his eyelashes. He picked her up and twirled her around under a streetlight and the rain whirled off her hair into her eyes. They never made it to the theater, and by the time they turned the key in the door to her apartment, she was so wet, her dress clung to her like the skin of a seal. She wasn't wearing a bra, and her nipples pointed through the thin cotton. Her roommates weren't home, and she slammed the door shut with her foot at the same time that she peeled off her dress and flung her sandals from her. And then she helped Harry rid himself of his floppy shoes and his wet socks, which she wrung out into a houseplant, and, hardly breathing, she unbuttoned his shirt and unzipped his pants and pulled them from his legs. She was shaking with lust, her teeth chattering, and her knees trembled all the way to her chest and into her throat. She was a virgin when the rain began, and when it stopped, she wasn't. There was wind that night, a howling summer wind, and the lights went out. Up and down the street, every house was dark, and things went quiet with the darkness. She took it as a sign of something, an electricity between them so potent that they blew fuses all over the neighborhood.

Virginity had never mattered all that much to her; what mattered was the search for a soulmate, an idea that felt almost as silly now as the protection of one's virginity. As though there could be just one person in the world meant for you. You bumped into someone at a certain urgent point in your life. It could be any number of people, as long as you smelled right to each other, as long as you could believe the story of the two of you. She'd always thought she would marry another musician, but somehow her story never combined with anyone but Harry's.

She looked out the window again, and he was putting the spade in the shed. He came in and washed his hands. She kissed him. They ate dinner, washed up, said good night to the kids. Upstairs in their bedroom, Liddie undressed Harry, not ravenously but slowly, kissing here, there. She could see how much it surprised him, and it made her sad that he was that surprised.

Later, Margreete wandered into their bedroom and climbed in on Liddie's side. Her mother startled her out of an almost-sleep, but she found an odd pleasure to have Margreete speaking to her with her fingertips in the dark, her hands moving between her mouth and ears, as though trying to connect the dots. And then her mother began to whimper that she wanted to go to bed, and Liddie stood up and shuffled her back to her room and helped her lie down and tucked her in and kissed her on the forehead. Her mother said, "Don't go," and she folded back her covers and patted them. Liddie climbed in and smelled her mother's old-woman smell of boiled eggs and dried raspberry canes, an overcooked outdoorsy smell.

"Where did he go?" asked Margreete.

"Who?"

"The furry person."

"Romeo? He died, Mom. Harry buried him out in the yard. He died of old age."

"Old age."

"Yes."

"Old age."

"Yes."

A few minutes later, her mother got out of bed. Liddie followed her over the creaking floorboards of the hallway and downstairs. "Open the door," Margreete said.

Liddie found her key in her purse, unlocked it, and kept following her mother out into the yard under the apple tree, where Margreete scratched with her hands at the fallen leaves under the tree.

"Mom."

"Go away. I'm looking."

"Mom. Please don't do that."

"He's under here."

"No, he's not there. Tomorrow I'll show you where Harry buried him. . . . You remember you mustn't go out of the house at night unless I'm with you? It's not safe for you to wander around in the dark. Do you remember the time you were on TV?"

"I was on TV?"

"It wasn't a celebrity appearance. You were lost, remember?"

"I do seem to recall something of the sort."

"You don't remember, do you? I don't want you getting lost at night."

"I'm not lost. I'm looking."

Liddie put her arms around her. "Romeo died, Mom. Harry buried him in a good spot."

"No."

"Come on, Mom, let's go in. It's late. I'm tired."

"I want to walk down there." She pointed across the meadow toward the water. "Just this once."

Liddie was cold. But in a month the field would be deep with snow. "All right. I'll get our coats. Stay right here." She came back and helped her mother into Irving's old lumberjack coat. "Can you see all right? It's only half the moon."

The grass in the field had withered with a frost, and it shone silver under the dried stalks of daisies and lupine. Liddie lifted her nose to the clean, gritty smell of ocean and heard the waves breaking down on the shore. The ground was uneven under their feet, and the grass crunched slightly. They were quiet as they walked down the long hill. She felt the strength still in her mother's arm, an arm that had stacked and split firewood, forked up potatoes, changed the chains on the tires of cars in winter.

Margreete had been an imperfect mother, but who isn't? Liddie remembered her yelling about small mishaps, how she'd pushed her into scratchy woolen leggings in the winter, secondhand leggings with rusted clasps. And how at school Liddie couldn't get the straps down fast enough and had to walk home with pee dribbling down her leg into her socks, and the leggings growing colder and colder and her brother Willard refusing to walk beside her because she smelled. Her mother's hands were chapped and rough as she pulled off her daughter's boots and socks and stripped off every stitch of clothing and said under her breath, "Seven years old and still wetting her pants like a two-year-old."

Beyond on the horizon, a ship was moored far out, with its small, beckoning lights. Over it was the wild, ancient light of the largest planet.

"Can you see Jupiter, Mom?"

"That's not Jupiter."

"What is it?"

"Lola's. We can take the boat out. Get our hair done."

"Maybe tomorrow," said Liddie.

Her mother had been one tough cookie. One New Year's Day, she told the family that they were going for a winter picnic. She poured split-pea soup into a big Thermos and made mayonnaise and sardine sandwiches, and Margreete and Irving and the three kids went traipsing out into the woods on a blisteringly cold day and sat miserably on a log, their hands chapped inside their mittens. "Can we go home now?" Liddie had asked, and her mother had said just because she was a girl didn't mean she had to act like one.

And now here were the two of them feeling their way with their feet in the dark of night, the wind coming up, girls who weren't acting like girls. Her mother was walking fast in the dark, as though she had a destination in mind. She wheezed a little in the cold and stumbled along.

Her mother had never been reliably affectionate. Liddie often suspected her of loving Irving more than her children. On Saturday afternoons, the kids were banished, and jumbly noises and odd cries came from behind their parents' closed door.

But her mother had been smart enough to realize that Liddie could be crowded out by two brothers, and she told Irving that her daughter would play an instrument, come hell or high water. "She's not going to turn out like me."

"And what's that like?" Irving had asked.

"Talented, without a talent."

Liddie put her arm around her mother and felt her shudder against her. "Are you warm enough?"

"Yes." Margreete was crying.

"What, Mom?"

"The moon is disappearing."

"It's going to get bigger again, you'll see."

"No."

"Later this month—"

"No, it won't."

"You know what I think? I think there will always be this grass and this moon and this ocean. And somewhere you and me."

Her mother stopped walking. "No, not somewhere you and me," she said. "Not me." They were at the bottom of the field now. Her mother's hand felt large and bony in hers.

"Let go," her mother said.

"The rocks are slippery. This is where Gretchen fell." They made their way over the wet granite, across a narrow strip of sand, and sat down on an old, battered aluminum rowboat that had been there forever. The metal was cold on her bottom. She wondered why no one had ever hauled it off. There were ancient oars in the sand beside it, and her mother picked up the end of one. "A paddle," she said.

"An oar."

"Or what?"

"An oar for the boat."

She wanted to ask her mother whether she remembered that cold New Year's Day when they'd sat on the log eating sardine sandwiches, but it seemed mean to keep asking if she remembered things. Tusks of moonlight played in the waves, causing them to shimmer silver like fish scales and turn somersaults. Clouds were moving in. A great sheet glided over the face of the moon, and the water went dark.

Liddie took her wool hat off and put it on her mother's head. "What are you thinking about?"

"I don't know."

"Funny. I was just thinking about the Latin you made me take in high school."

"Did I?"

"You thought I was going to be a doctor and I'd need Latin."

"You were the clever one."

"You thought I was going to do all sorts of great things. Mrs. Gilooly was the teacher. She wore a fake yellow rose on her brown dress every day. She thought there was no need for us to be stupid, that we could read the *Aeneid* if we tried. She was proud of us."

"Me, too."

Her mother had never said anything like this to her before, and Liddie sat very still, not wanting to break the spell. She felt the tears beginning to come, not for the small moon but for the day her mother would be gone. "You've been a good mom to me. It's not easy being a mom. I used to get mad at you a lot."

"What for?"

"I don't remember. It doesn't matter anymore, even though it used to matter so much, the things that made me mad."

"What were you mad about?"

"Things you wouldn't let me do."

"Are you mad now?"

"No. Did you think I was?"

"Did I think what?"

"Never mind. Don't you love the sound the waves make when they lap at the rocks?"

"Everybody is asleep now," said Margreete.

Her mother's hand was cold in hers. "Shall we go back?"

"Not yet. This is my harbor, you know."

"I know. It's a lovely one." The light of a buoy blinked on and off, and a breeze came off the water, almost as warm as September. Liddie wrapped her arms around her mother and felt her shivering, the absence of flesh over bones. Margreete had begun to stash food away, not eat. Tonight she'd dropped a whole hamburger under the table for Fred.

"You're getting cold, Mom. We're going back now." She pulled her mother up, and they started up the hill, their footsteps crunching on the cold grass. "I'm going to miss you."

"Me, too."

"Do you think anything is left of us after we go?"

"No," said Margreete.

"Nothing?"

"You won't find me in the usual places."

"Where will you be?"

"Lola's." She stopped a moment to catch her breath. "The haircuts aren't so great, but they give a good perm."

They climbed a little farther and rested. "When I was learning Latin," Liddie said, "I read a story about Aeneas."

"I know him!" said Margreete. "I met him way back when."

"You remember his father died and Aeneas missed him so much, he went down to the underworld? When he found him, he tried to reach his arms around him, but his father was hollow, like the bones of a bird."

Margreete chuckled. "Hollow like my head."

"Oh, Mom."

"Hollow like my head."

She felt her mother shivering harder against her now and said, "Let's get you home to bed." They reached the house, hung up their coats, and climbed the stairs to the second floor. Liddie helped her under the covers and tucked the quilts around her, the way her mother had tucked her in as a girl, then waited until she heard her breath deepen into sleep.

38

WINTER 1964

Ratul Charan Mukherji and Paritos Sengupta came to Maine with twenty-five other men, arriving in snow and leaving in snow three months later. They'd left Calcutta to study shipbuilding at the Bath Iron Works, courtesy of the Indian government. Liddie signed up her family to host them for an occasional meal, thinking it would be good for the kids, good for everyone.

Eva had practiced their names, and she watched out the window as the two men got out of her father's car, one wearing sunglasses and the other scarecrow-like in a coat that hung off his long frame. Snow fell in big, sloppy flakes. They walked toward the porch steps, and Eva ducked down under the window.

Ratul Charan Mukherji moved with an easy grace as he took off his sunglasses and entered the house. His face was square, his skin very smooth. Paritos Sengupta was a stumbly fellow with a gap between his front teeth, his wavy hair combed straight back from his forehead.

They sat down in the living room, and her mother introduced the family. "Who are you?" asked Margreete.

"I'll just repeat it one more time, Mom," Liddie said. "This is Ratul Charan Mukherji and Paritos Sengupta."

"We are Indian trainees," Mukherji said.

"What about your feathers?"

"Our feathers, madam?"

"I'm sorry," said Liddie. "My mother is senile."

"Ah," said Sengupta. "How old is she?"

Margreete looked at him. "I am older than you were when you were born."

"In our country," Mukherji said, "the old ones are the wise ones."

"They don't think that sort of thing around here," said Margreete.

"I am still young and unwise," said Mukherji. "Only thirty-seven this month."

"My. You don't look that old." She paused for a moment. "How old are you?"

"Thirty-seven," said Mukherji.

"My. You don't look that old."

Gray hairs intermingled with his black, glossy hair; Eva thought he did look that old. Her mother invited them into the dining room and brought out cooked carrots, then went back for the macaroni and cheese. "This probably isn't what you're used to eating." Her face was pink with exertion.

"We are used to spices," said Mukherji.

"I'm afraid this couldn't be much blander. I wasn't sure what you'd want."

"Never mind," Sengupta said. "I have had stomach problems all my life, and now no spices, no problems."

"You will stop eating spices when you go home, then?" asked Harry.

"No, I will start again. It's impossible. Everyone eats spices."

Gretchen slipped down under the table and crawled to each man and inspected his footwear before she resurfaced and asked, "Do you like sled riding?"

"What is that?"

"You know," said Eva. "You get on a sled and slide down the hill in the snow."

"We have never done it," said Mukherji. "We have no snow back home."

"We'll take you after lunch," said Harry, "if you'd like."

"I like your teeth," said Margreete, looking at Mukherji.

"Thank you, mum."

"They're very white. Do you have a grandmother?"

"My grandmother is no longer alive."

"That's where I'm headed," she said.

"That's where we're all going," said Harry.

"Not me," said Bernie. "I'm going to live forever."

"Would you like that?" Mukherji asked.

"Wouldn't everybody?"

"No," said Sengupta, who'd been quiet over his dinner. "After some years, you find that you have seen enough."

"And things begin to repeat themselves," said Liddie.

"Exactly, madam."

"You can call me Liddie."

"Perhaps next time," said Sengupta. "And next time you can call us Paritos and Ratul. Or this time, too."

"How do you say something in your language?" asked Eva.

"Nomoskar," said Mukherji. "Hello."

"Nomoskar," said Eva.

"Amar naam Eva," he said. "My name is Eva."

"Amar naam Eva."

Bernie interrupted. *"Amar naam Bernie."*

"My turn!" cried Eva.

"Amar naam Bernie. Amar naam Bernie."

"Stop it, Bernie!" She felt such sudden hatred for him, she could hardly breathe.

They had vanilla pudding and frozen strawberries for dessert, and then they were finished. Eva had never heard anyone burp like Mukherji. She held her paper napkin over her mouth so hard it ripped, and then she made the mistake of looking at Bernie, whose laughter exploded beneath his hand.

"You're a big burper, aren't you?" said Margreete.

"For us, it is a sign of politeness. We have enjoyed our food."

"For us," said Margreete, "it is a sign of not-politeness."

Mukherji laughed, and Eva laughed so hard, milk came out her nose, and she couldn't stop until they got their winter coats and hats on and polished the runners on the sleds and put them in the trunk of the car.

They took both cars, and Eva insisted on sitting next to Mukherji.

When they arrived at the hill, Sengupta said, "You go first. I want to watch."

"You and me together, Bernie," said Eva.

"And me," said Gretchen.

The three of them piled onto a sled and screamed down the hill, and Sengupta's eyes watered and grew bright with cold and happiness.

Liddie went down with Margreete, who was wearing a pompom hat like a little girl, and they picked up so much speed, they cleared the bank at the bottom of the hill, tumbled over the top, and disappeared.

Eva gave a sled to the two men. Sengupta was frightened, and Harry and Mukherji streaked down, spilling over and laughing at the bottom. Then Sengupta and Bernie, and Liddie and Gretchen, and Eva and Mukherji, and Harry and Margreete, around and around, until the sun dropped low in the sky and the wind rose and Mukherji and Sengupta went back to the dormitory.

That night in bed, Eva whispered, *"Amar naam Eva. Amar naam Eva."* When you say words over and over again, they stop sounding like what they are. *Couch . . . couchcouchcouch. Amar naam Eva. Amar naam Eva.* Her name began to disappear. And then she disappeared, except for her eyes, looking toward the dim light at the window. She thought of her mother's face when she looked at Ratul Charan Mukherji, a brightness, as though she'd been waiting for him to come to dinner all these years. If there was a country where people looked like Ratul Charan Mukherji, she would like to go there. But the only words she would know were *Amar naam Eva*, and she would have to say them over and over like an idiot. There was the other word that she'd forgotten. *Osh . . .* something. Like soft music.

Sometimes she was tired of her family. What would it be like to sit quietly with Ratul Charan Mukherji and have no one else—like

Bernie—interrupting or saying stupid things? But then maybe she'd feel shy and not have anything to say. You wouldn't know unless you were in that situation.

She closed her eyes, and her breathing grew steady and deep until the night swallowed her.

39

Harry woke to the eerie sound of winter thunder rolling across the fields. When he went to the window, snow blanketed the road, and lightning sparked the dull sky and found its mirror on the icy ground. Up the road, a dog barked. Liddie was already up. Harry turned on the radio and heard school-closing announcements all through southern Maine and up the midcoast. Eighteen inches were predicted. Liddie would be home all day, cello lessons canceled this afternoon.

The thought of being trapped within these four walls made his head feel ashy. What came to him was an army of boots tramping in smaller and smaller circles. The pale sun would set just after four. He had to get out. He could say he had to prepare a test for his sophomores and had left the materials at school. He could say he had to buy a new snow shovel. He could say he was fed up with this life and had nothing to look forward to. He could get hold of himself and take the kids sledding. Or make breakfast. Or go downstairs and kiss his wife.

He went down and kissed Liddie, who'd made an early pot of coffee and was already mixing pancake batter. He poured two cups of coffee and passed her one.

"You're up early," he said.

"Banana or plain?" she asked.

"Banana."

She poured three pancakes into the pan and placed some banana slices on top, cooked one side, flipped them over, and put them on a plate for Harry.

"You're not having any?"

"I already did."

She looked the way he felt—restless, about to jump out of her skin. "What do you have on today?" he asked.

"Yesterday one of the members of a local piano trio asked me to play a concert with them, pinch-hit for their cellist, who's on maternity leave. I didn't give them an answer yet. When would I put something like that together? This morning I was going to take a look at the music and let them know tomorrow, but the kids are home . . ."

"When's the concert?"

"In a little over a month. A Kodály Duo for Violin and Cello, the Brahms Piano Trio in C Minor, some other smaller things. I don't know the Kodály, but I played the Brahms in Michigan."

"Of course you should do it. I'll take the kids sledding when they're up. More coffee?"

"No, thanks." She disappeared, came back for a sweater, kissed him on one ear, and disappeared again.

He turned on the oven and began stockpiling pancakes for the kids for when they woke up. Margreete came down and sat by the woodstove, looking out the window at the falling snow. Harry asked her if she wanted a pancake and a cuppa.

"Cuppa what?"

"Coffee. Can I pour you some?"

"What's in the cup?"

"Coffee."

"That's all?"

"That's all. What were you hoping for?"

"Coffee."

"You're in luck. This is coffee." He added milk and two sugars, handed it to her along with a couple of pancakes, and sat down at the yellow table while she wandered out with her cup.

Music—he didn't know what—wafted out of Liddie's studio,

each note seeming to journey along a tightrope strung between past and future. He could never begin to describe this to Liddie. He'd never tried. And he'd never told her what solace and joy her playing gave him. He felt unequal to speaking about it, as though he were trying to assemble something delicate and complicated with his elbows and knees. Last night after dinner, she'd played the adagio movement of a Bach cello and piano sonata, and such sweetness flowed from her bow that he thought his head would explode. He was sitting with a book, not reading, just listening. She balanced on a note, lingered over another, each note spilling into the next, stretching out to meet and receive the other.

He made more pancakes, turned off the stove, shoveled the porch and enough of the driveway to get out, and after breakfast took Noah and Bernie and the girls sledding on Brydon's Hill, then brought the kids home at around lunchtime. When the snow tapered off, he said he had to go into school and figure out an exam. He knew where he was going. He'd known all along, and it wasn't to school.

The snowbanks beside the road had risen so high today that in places he could no longer see into the adjoining fields. He pictured Gretchen on Brydon's Hill with her sideways ponytail making her woolen hat stick out lumpily, waiting at the top of the hill for a sled. Her cheeks fiery red in the cold, so excited, jumping wildly up and down, sledding down and screaming all the way. And then he thought about the damage he might do, how he was willing to risk it.

One summer in high school, he'd worked on a demolition crew, his job to tear out the innards of old apartment buildings. They ripped out old toilets and sinks, busted through doors. His favorite were the walls, sledgehammering a hole through old plaster, enlarging the hole, finally bringing the whole thing down. That's what this felt like, driving up the peninsula, parking in front of the hardware store where he and Molly had run into each other that time, opening the door to the phone booth and digging Molly's number out of his wallet.

He put the dime into the pay phone and listened.

The phone rang eight times and stopped. The dime rattled down inside the phone and appeared. He reinserted it and dialed again. It occurred to him that this wasn't the best day to call. Her kids would be home, maybe her husband, too. Maybe she'd have an extra shift because of the snow. The phone rang and rang. It was a relief, really. How easily things could be broken.

Two days later, she picked up on the third ring. "I kept your number," he said.

"I found yours in the phone book," she said. "But I never tried to call."

"And I didn't try to call you, either."

"Why was that?"

"Too scary."

"And now?"

"I'd like to see you."

They met at the dam again. He was there first, turned off the car, and hung on to the steering wheel of his Plymouth as though he were still going somewhere. More of the asylum structure had caved in. There wasn't a window unbroken now. Molly pulled in front of him, stopped, and looked over her shoulder. He climbed out of his car and into the passenger seat of her Rambler station wagon. He put a hand at the back of her neck and gently pulled her close.

Her hair was shorter, giving her a harried, businesslike look. She wore glasses now, stylish ones. Beside her, he felt the simplicity and longing of his animal self.

"I like this place," she said, looking toward the old asylum.

"What about it?"

"How wild and wrecked it is."

"It depresses me." He picked up her hand. "But you don't."

"I hardly even know you," she said, smiling. "But when Bernie walked into the hospital with Gretchen and your mother-in-law and your wife—who's lovely, by the way—it crossed my mind that it was fate."

"I don't believe in that crap."

"Ha. Okay."

"Do I sound opinionated?"

"Arrogant." She laughed.

"Bernie's teachers are always accusing him of that. I guess the apple doesn't fall far from the tree."

"How is he?"

"Doing well."

"And Gretchen?"

"Also."

"Your mother-in-law is quite a handful."

"I understand she got pretty upset there."

"She was scared."

"Sometimes I get scared for her."

"Harry, do you ever feel that you can't keep all the balls in the air one day longer?"

"There isn't a day that goes by when I don't feel that." He touched her hair. "I like it this way. It looks sporty."

She put her hand up and covered his. She took a breath as though she was going to say something, but nothing came out.

"What?"

"Here's the thing. I love my kids. I used to love my husband. Maybe I still do. It's funny—when he's out of town, I love him, but when he comes back, I don't like him. I don't like how self-satisfied he is; I don't like the way I am when he's in the room."

"What do you mean, you love him when he's away?"

"I think of him fondly, I have good memories, I wish him well. But then he comes back. Shouldn't there be joy? And shouldn't you feel that someone's watching your back, that there's a generous presence in your life, someone who's going to forgive your weaknesses and believe in your future? I don't think he believes in me that way, if he ever did. I'm a workhorse. Like those horses who used to work underground in the coal mines in darkness until they went blind."

"That's horrible."

"I'm being overly dramatic. That's one of my faults."

"Did he tell you that, or did you tell yourself?"

"He did."

He couldn't have referred to his wife as "she" that way. Liddie didn't really watch his back, she probably had little faith in his future, but he didn't feel cold toward her. He didn't blame Molly for that cold "he." It just made him sad. And scared, if he was honest with himself.

A rusting refrigerator teetered on the edge of the dam, and he shivered involuntarily.

"What?" she asked.

"Just looking at that water turning to ice."

"I'm scaring you, aren't I?"

"I guess you are. How did you know that?" He put his hands on either side of her face and brought her close. "Do you want to get in the backseat with me? Like a teenager? Or do you want to talk?"

"Yes."

"Which?"

"Backseat."

They got out each side, closed the doors, opened the back doors. "Like a clown car," he said. She laughed and slammed the door on her side. She opened it again and got back out.

"Going to start up the heater." She moved quickly, like an athlete, slid into the front seat, turned the heater on full blast, stood a moment outside the car, her feet crunching down the snow and dried leaves, and shrugged out of her coat. She jumped in beside him, threw her coat into the front seat, and unzipped his coat.

"Do you have to be home any particular time?" he asked.

"Soon. Too soon." Her hands traveled over his shoulders, down the small of his back. She nipped through his shirt at the tops of his arms and unbuttoned his shirt and gently nibbled his chest, pulling at his hair like a little goat.

He felt sick with desire and just as sick with something that made him want to run.

She sat up quickly, as though she sensed the war in him. "I really wanted to see you again, but I'm frightened." She took her hand away from his. "I think I'd better go, I'm sorry."

"Wait. When can I see you? Is it all right to call your house?"

"Hang up if he answers."

"Of course."

"Is it all right to call yours?"

He looked at her. "No. I'm sorry."

"I understand." She grabbed her coat from the front seat. "But that makes me the one who waits, and it makes you the one with my number in your wallet."

"That's not right," he said.

"No, it's not." She buttoned up her coat and the top button of his shirt.

"What?" he asked.

"No, I said, it's not. You could get a post office box," she said.

"Maybe we should pick a regular day every couple of weeks?"

She looked at him strangely, almost with hostility. "No," she said. "Nothing marital like that." They didn't have time to resolve anything. He felt breakable and confused as he buttoned his shirt. They climbed out of the backseat. She kissed him on the lips, returned to her car, and drove away. He stayed and looked at the water beginning to freeze over the trash on the top of the dam. What had just happened?

Liddie had once told him that she'd loved men as a child. She loved their smell and their cigars and their confidence in themselves, their whiskers and the way they put their hands into their pockets, the way they shouldered their burdens so silently. "Perhaps," she'd said to him, "I loved them too early and too eagerly." He wondered now, sitting in the car and looking at the wreckage of the asylum, what kind of a man he was. He felt the shambles of the last half hour, an embarrassed tactile echo that made the chest hairs Molly had pulled with her lips shiver like grass.

40

While Harry had been sitting at the dam, Margreete was busy throwing birch logs into the woodstove at home. She vacuumed up the live coals that spilled onto the floor and set the Electrolux on fire. Liddie was teaching a serious young girl at the time, who ended up having to watch out the window as her cello teacher heaved the vacuum cleaner out the door like a shot-putter and buried it in the snow.

Coming back into the house, Liddie found Margreete standing at the door, holding the black metal shovel from the ash bucket. "I told you, Mom, stay away from the woodstove. You'll burn down the whole house."

"I never," Margreete stammered. "I never. Who burned down the house?"

"You didn't. But stay away from the woodstove. I repeat, do not go near the woodstove. . . . Where are you going?"

"To look for the chain saw."

"Chain saw?"

"Go right through the middle of the vacuum, slick as a whistle."

"Mom." There was nothing more to say. She went back to her studio and finished the lesson.

She couldn't be trusted now. Not for one minute. The mother of one of her students had told her about a competent older woman named Mona O'Hearn, who lived farther down the point. Mona had been tending to a woman who'd recently died, and she was looking for work.

Mrs. O'Hearn turned up two days later to meet Margreete and get herself oriented to the house. For now she would only come while Liddie was teaching, but if things worked out, she could spare additional hours, she said. She had a large bosom and thick cotton flesh-colored stockings.

Margreete said, "What's she doing here?"

"She'll help look after things while I'm teaching."

"What's she doing here?"

"I just told you, Mom."

"You've got big biceps," said Margreete. "Do you wrestle cattle?"

"What's she saying?" asked Mrs. O'Hearn.

"You can ask her," said Liddie. "My mother understands."

"I said you have big biceps," said Margreete.

Liddie's first student arrived, and as she turned toward her studio, she heard Mrs. O'Hearn ask, "Did you make a stool today?"

"I don't do carpentry," Margreete said. "I leave that to the boys."

Liddie paused at the door before greeting her student. "A stool!" cried Mrs. O'Hearn. "A stool!"

"I don't know what you're getting so excited about," Margreete said. "I just told you."

Toward the end of the week, signs began to appear around the house: *This is your bed. Do not get into it in the daytime.*

Shoes belong on your feet, not in the washing machine.

Mrs. O'Hearn's final day was a Friday when Eva overheard Margreete whining about not being able to have a piece of toast, and Mrs. O'Hearn saying, "Stop your fussing or your next stop will be the old-age home."

Eva came into the room and stood in front of her. "My grandmother is not going anywhere. Look how upset you've made her. . . . Look, Grandma. I'll play something for you."

After that, Liddie arranged for Margreete to go to elder day care every afternoon while she taught. "You're going to see Janice and Edna," Liddie told her mother in the car. "You've been here a few times before, remember?"

Margreete whimpered. "I don't know them."

"Yes, you do. They're your friends."

"I don't know them."

She clung to Liddie at the door while one of the caretakers tried to interest her in an arts-and-crafts activity. "I don't know these people," she said. "I don't know these people."

A woman rocked in a chair, chanting, "All-American boy. Pop, pop, bang, bang!"

Margreete had on her favorite red hat with the navy-blue feather. The feather trembled, and Liddie had to leave her like that. She had to peel her fingers from her arm and drive away. It felt like one of the worst things she'd ever done.

Heading home from the center, she saw the fog thickening over the islands in her mother's brain, traveling in backward chronology, swallowing first the days and months and years closest to now, then engulfing the 1950s, the '40s, the '30s, lingering on the threshold of her early marriage, her adolescence and childhood. Soon those would be gobbled up, too, and sent whirlpooling into the darkness. Margreete was beginning to live in a country of her own, where time had no meaning. Liddie used to believe that time went in a straight line, arrow-like. Now it seemed more like water.

She tried to imagine her own life without memory: like a flat sky, like food without taste. So many thousands of memories lived in her, small and large, distant and close, potent and insignificant. A rooster crowing on a farm in Mexico. She'd forgotten the farmer and the farmer's wife but could still hear that smart-ass sound. Her friend Judy's barrettes in fourth grade, shaped like frogs. The way her first landlady's front teeth were two different colors. The smell of her father's chest when she climbed into his lap. A wedding she attended with her brother Peter when they were young. Why did it matter now that Liddie had worn a homemade pale-lilac organza dress with a sash of the same color? Why did it matter that her white shoes were slippery? But that day did matter, somehow. The fabric of her life all these years later was richer for remembering the way Peter's hair was slicked down, how he wore a white shirt and a clip-on bow tie, which had become unattached on one side, like a squirrel hanging upside down.

She and Peter had sat on the floor, eating wedding cake. Then all the girls stood in a clump, waiting to catch the bride's bouquet. They put Liddie in front because she was the youngest. The bride stood with her back to them, and when she threw the bouquet, it hit Liddie on the head and knocked her down. She wanted to cry, but so many people were laughing, she laughed, too. The only person who asked if she was okay was Peter.

What would it be like not to remember that? She wouldn't know, because she wouldn't remember. But it would matter. The memories she carried were unlike anyone else's who had ever lived or would ever live again: the weight of them, their color and sound and texture, their abundance and power.

When she returned home, her first cello student was waiting for her in the driveway. He got out of his mother's car, wrestling with his cello case, and Liddie led him up the driveway. Sammy was as unpromising a student as she'd ever taught, except that his excuses were so baroque, she almost looked forward each week to hearing what he'd come up with.

Sammy tightened his bow. "I couldn't practice this week because my sister kept turning the record player up, and I couldn't hear my notes."

"Did you think about going into another room or asking your sister to turn the record player down?"

"No," he said. "And then I got a splinter in my foot."

"But I don't think you play with your feet."

"I couldn't think about anything else."

"Ah," she said. "Well, why don't you try today anyway." She'd thought about talking to his mother and saying these lessons were a waste of good money, but she liked the kid. Near the end of the lesson, though, she said, "Do you want to keep on with these lessons, Sammy? It seems as though you don't really want to play the cello. I like you, and I want to know. Is this torture for you?"

His cowlick had ridden up with today's efforts and sat awkwardly at the crown of his head. "I guess," he said. He bounced the bow against the strings.

"You know, that's not so good for the cello. . . . Do you think you'd rather not keep going?"

"I want to play the trumpet, but my mother says it's too loud."

"Why don't I talk to your mother?"

That was Sammy's last lesson. She'd miss him but not so much. And she hoped he'd be allowed to play the trumpet. He was a trumpet kind of kid.

Liddie had said yes to the Kodály and Brahms concert. This would be the only concert she'd play with the trio before the regular cellist returned. She felt utterly grateful to be playing like this again: a kind of rapture she'd almost but not quite forgotten. It was the intimacy of the small group and also the music itself—the way Kodály's violin and cello spoke so tenderly to each other, the sweetness of Brahms, the longing pouring through his melodic lines.

41

Fifteen miles distant from Burnt Harbor, Harry walked next to Molly along the Kennebec River, where ice crystals tinkled on the bank like glass bells. Only the middle of the river flowed free, rushing pell-mell past the icy edges. They were seeing each other every two or three weeks now, meeting before her shift at the hospital began and after his school day ended. They mostly stayed away from public places, meeting at the dam sometimes, on the shore of Nequasset Lake, along the river where they walked today. Often they took to the backseat of his car or hers, the heater pumping out warmth. They talked, they laughed, she occasionally cried, their bodies reached for each other. They'd talked about spending the night somewhere.

Now he put his arm around her, but she slipped out. He didn't ask why. He told her about the Indian shipbuilders: how Paritos could bounce a ball on the end of a bat for minutes at a time, how Ratul was teaching Bengali to Eva. She didn't appear to be listening. Her face was wistful, her eyes sheltered from him. After walking a few miles, they passed under the Union Trust Company bank clock, another of their regular meeting spots, and went up the street to the café. The Formica table, once red, was polished down to beige by the arms and elbows that had leaned there.

He poured cream in his coffee and said, "You're quiet today." He reached for her hand.

"Harry, I can't see you anymore. Please don't try to talk me out of it. I've thought about it night and day, and I'm not changing my mind."

"Wait, please don't."

She put her fingers over his lips. "It's too hard. My body is in a constant state of grief. If I let it take me where it wants to go, my marriage will be over."

He made a sound in his throat that wasn't a word. "But we're not all that much more than good friends."

"We are, and you know it. You're a man, I'm a woman. We have bodies. It's simple. My body wants yours." They fell silent. She stirred her coffee round and round with the spoon, clinking the side of the cup. He wanted to ask her to stop—he couldn't bear the sound.

"But it's not just that," he said. "If that's all it was, we would have found a motel by now. You matter to me. Your friendship matters."

"I know that."

"I want to see you. I want to know how you are."

"You could throw one of your kids down the stairs every so often," she said, "and I could see you then."

"Not funny." He rubbed the back of her hand with his thumb. "It's all chapped."

"Winter," she said, taking her hand away, gulping her cold coffee. "We could try making it this day every year. At least, know . . ." She didn't finish.

"If that's what you can manage, that's what we'll do."

"I shouldn't say this to you, especially not now, but I read somewhere that you know you're in love when someone smells right. There's a smell coming from his skin. It's like . . . you know when you open a door that's been shut for a long time? Like he's been in the basement."

For a moment, Harry thought about his father smelling like a cornflakes box.

"I'm sorry," she said. "He's not a bad man." Her hands trembled.

"You're scared."

"Yes."

His eyes were hot, welling up. He touched her chin but didn't kiss her. "I'm not going to try to talk you out of this, because you asked me not to. I should go, yes?"

She nodded.

"Here's looking at you, kid. Next year, four o'clock. I'll be right here." He raised his cup to her, left some money on the table for their coffees, and stood up. He didn't want to cry, and he didn't, not until he got into his car. He drove a short distance, pulled off the road, and waited awhile until his vision cleared. She was right to end it. Their bodies wanted what they wanted. His heart did, too. She was right, damn it, she was right.

The year before, he'd watched the ice break up on the Allagash River. It was thick, riven with cracks, moving fast downstream, tumbling over itself. Open water appeared and more ice came downriver, groaning with the upheaval of spring. Great gray chunks littered the shore, and in the cross section of the ice, you could see striations—the history of how the river had frozen, bit by bit. He'd always remember how that river broke.

He blew his nose, waited a bit longer, and drove toward home, thinking of Molly's courage. In some part of his reptilian brain, he'd known, too. But he'd convinced himself that this was possible, that everything was possible.

42

The Calcutta shipbuilders were scheduled to return to India, leaving early on a Sunday morning from Portland. Liddie had promised them that the whole family would drive to the Greyhound station to see them off. Snow was predicted overnight, but it wasn't a worry. It was March, and winter was almost over.

She set the alarm for six, but her sleep was turbulent, and she snapped awake just before five. She got out of bed, looked out, and saw that the wind had roared down the peninsula and hurled snow halfway up the windowpane. Downstairs, she pushed open the kitchen door against a mound of snow. When she flicked on a flashlight and shone it toward the outside thermometer, it read nine degrees. She ran back upstairs, woke Harry and Bernie and Eva, and told them to hurry, to dress warmly, grab a shovel.

It felt like January again. Snow swirled around them as they shoveled a path for the car. Liddie glanced at Bernie and Harry, working close to each other. Bernie was just about the same height as his father now, wearing one of his old hats. His head had grown, and the hat rode up over his ears. And there was Eva, bulldozing straight ahead with her shovel. She felt proud of the four of them in the near darkness, with the snow gusting up from the ground, blowing sideways, coming down from the sky. They shoveled for three-quarters of an hour but were only a third of the way out the driveway.

"Why didn't we leave the car out by the road?" said Bernie.

"The forecast said light snow."

"No way we'll make it in time," he said.

"Not with that attitude," said Harry. "Why don't you just keep your mouth shut."

Bernie threw his shovel into a snow drift and went to sit in the car. The three of them shoveled in silence before Harry walked over to the car and yanked the door open. "Think about someone besides yourself for a change. Look at your sister."

"I'm not feeling well. I have a sore throat."

Harry thrust the shovel at Bernie, and Bernie got out of the car, bumped Eva with his hip. "Goody-goody." He turned and plowed thigh-deep through the snow to the end of the driveway and started shoveling toward them. An hour later, they were still at it, but they needed to leave now, right now. Liddie ran inside, stuffed Margreete and Gretchen into their coats over their nightgowns, and hustled them out the door.

Margreete yelled that the wind was blowing her over, and Liddie held her hand and pulled her along toward the car. All at once, Gretchen stopped. "Mommy! There's an animal."

"Not now."

"Mommy, you have to look!"

A little brown bat, motionless, was lying in an indentation in the snow. It would die. Harry honked the horn, and Liddie dragged Margreete and the weeping Gretchen toward the car. "Get in," she said. "Hurry." Margreete scrambled into the front seat, Gretchen into the back, screaming, "No, Mommy! No, Mommy!" Liddie closed the back door and got her mother settled in front. She told Harry he should go on without her. There was a bat in the snow.

He argued, told her he'd stay behind instead.

"Go!"

Harry gripped the steering wheel. His green hat was askew, and his eyes looked wild. She watched as the car fishtailed up the driveway. It paused at one drift, floundered like something drowning. It sank and lurched, now propelled forward, then sideways. It labored a few feet, straightened out, went sideways again, and lurched to a stop. Harry backed up and made another run for it, tunneling through the path he'd made. With a backward flurry of flying snow, the car almost made it through and stopped. Harry backed again and launched the car toward the last drift. It made it most of the way through, teetered on the edge of the plowed road like a climber hanging on to a cliff. The wheels spun like crazy, and, at last, the rear tires grabbed hold and the car plunged onto the pavement. Liddie saw the backs of her children's heads through the rear window, her husband hunched over the wheel.

They disappeared, and her eyes welled up, thinking of Ratul's impeccable British accent, his virtuoso burping, his square, smooth face. Paritos, with his wide-open smile, his coat hanging from his skinny frame. She'd never see him again.

Fred met her at the door, tail wagging, and as though he understood, he brought her a squeaky toy, drank noisily from his water dish, and pushed his snout under her elbow. She found a small square box, lined it with a towel, picked up the leather gloves by the woodstove, and went back out, closing the door on Fred. In the driving snow, she bent over the bat and looked at its face, part snub-nosed weasel, part tiny bear with huge ears. The snow was blanketing it by the minute; its knees and elbows were all bone and sinew. The wind shrieked around the small body, and the bat hardly moved when she placed it in the box. It was either frozen or hibernating or dying.

She took a heating pad from her mother's room, plugged it in, and put it under the box. "Hey, little guy," she said. It didn't move. Fred nosed at the box, and she put it up on the mantelpiece and pulled out Romeo's old cat carrier, slid the box inside, and closed the door. She built a fire, got Fred his breakfast, filled a bowl with warm water, and sat and thawed out her hands, rubbing the prickly needles from them as they came back to life.

Fred looked at her, doggy kindness pouring out of him. His ears hung over the sides of his head, lifted slightly. He pawed at her lap and whined. She patted his head and told him about what Tibetan Buddhists say, that you get reborn as a human if you lead a meritorious life and as an animal if you messed up your previous life. "That's not true, though. Who wouldn't want to have your life?"

She checked the bat, moving a bit now in the warmth, its pulse visible in the near-transparent skin of its neck. She tried giving it some water with an eyedropper, but it wasn't ready to take it and the drops fell onto its fur. She could picture, as though from a distance, the car on the road, making its way to Portland through the storm, all her precious ones on board.

But all was not well inside the car. "Let me out," said Margreete.

"Take your hand off the door, Margreete. Bernie, lock the door."

"Kidnapper!" she shrieked. She rattled the door handle and tried to open the window.

"Stop it right now!" yelled Harry.

"Don't talk to me. My mother wants me back."

"Your mother's dead," said Bernie.

"No, she's not."

"She's dead, Grandma."

"Leave her alone," said Harry. "Let her think what she wants to think."

Bernie stared at the back of his father's head, at the hair dusted with gray turning backward on itself as it disappeared under his green hat. "You've been at me all day," he said. "Why don't you cut me some slack?"

"Because you haven't pulled your weight from the moment you got out of bed."

"I told you, I wasn't feeling well. My throat's sore."

"Bullshit."

The car got quiet, and Bernie lifted his hand. Later, Eva remembered it like the paw of a bear, the suddenness. He swiped at his father's head, and the green hat fell into the hole between the seats. Eva thought they would all die when her father turned around, still driving, and went to belt his son. He couldn't reach him, and the car bounced off a snowbank and back onto the road.

He turned back around. "Don't you—ever—do that again. You hear?"

"Don't tell me I'm talking bullshit when I'm not."

"Shut up, Bernie. Just shut up."

They drove on in silence while the wipers passed across the surface of the windshield, snarling against snow. The sun struggled from behind a cloud, and Eva saw the shadow of their car moving along a snowbank like a black-and-white photograph. Not too many years later, she understood that much worse things happen in families. Knives. Boots. Fists. Guns. But now she could not imagine anything worse.

They passed through Bath, faster and faster, on to Portland, arriving at the Greyhound station just as the bus was pulling out. Harry stopped the car inches away from the front bumper of the bus, and the air brakes groaned and the sleek Greyhound on the side of the bus stopped running, and the bus driver scowled through the big windshield wipers. Harry jumped out of the car and pounded on the accordion door. It opened, and Ratul and Paritos ran down the aisle and down the steps, and Eva ran into Ratul's open arms.

"But where is Liddie?" asked Ratul, who'd learned to call her by her first name. He was crying—they were all crying.

"She had to stay to save a bat, a little animal," said Harry. "It was freezing in the snow. She's very sorry not to be here."

"It is good karma, saving this animal," said Paritos.

"Tell her," said Ratul, "that I will hold her in my heart always. I will hold you all in my heart always. Don't cry, dear Eva. One day, perhaps we will meet again. Goodbye, Master Bernard. Goodbye, young Gretchen. Goodbye, Harry. And Mother Margreete." He made a deep bow to her. The two of them mounted the bus steps, the driver closed the door, and Harry moved the car out of the way.

The bat did not make it.

43

1965

On the twelfth of March, Eva turned thirteen. She heard her mother's footsteps slapping the floor softly in her too-big slippers.

"Happy Birthday, darling."

"Do I have to go to school?" she asked, her eyes shut, her voice muffled in the covers.

There was silence for a moment. "No."

"You mean that?" She opened her eyes and looked at her mother, who was still wearing her nightgown, slipped down on one shoulder.

"You can do whatever you want today," she said, sitting on the edge of the bed, her breath smelling like sleep. "You know what I wanted to get you for your birthday? But it wasn't possible."

"What?"

"A new piano."

"Oh." Eva sat up in bed.

"Someday we'll be able to. . . . But I got you this." She handed her a present wrapped in brown paper and tied with red and blue yarn twisted together. "I ordered it from the Frank Music Company. It's a place on West Fifty-fourth Street between Broadway and Eighth Avenue in New York. You go up the elevator to the tenth floor, and you come into a room . . ." She waited for Eva to unwrap what was in her lap. "The store is jam-packed full of music. Frank Marx knows where every single piece of music is. You can get anything there. Anything at all. A lot of famous musicians shop there. I couldn't decide between the Kalmus and the Peters edition, and I finally decided on the Peters. I thought you needed both volumes, even though it'll be a while before you're playing much of *The Well-Tempered Clavier*. Still, it won't be so long."

Eva hugged her. "Oh, Mommy."

Her mother hugged her back and stood. "I love you more than the wind and the sky." She left, and Eva heard her heading to the foot of the stairs leading to the third floor, calling to Bernie. Then to Gretchen's room, where a small, grumpy voice said, "I don't *want* to."

As her father came in, his body passed through the spring light coming from the window. He hadn't shaved yet, and his chin scratched when he leaned down to kiss her. "Thirteen," he said, patting her awkwardly. "My sweet daughter is all grown up." He wiped his eyes with the heel of his hand and pulled a small parcel with a pink bow out of the pocket of his pants. He must have had it wrapped at a store—his wrapping never looked this tidy. She opened it and found a tiny heart-shaped locket. "You can put whatever picture you want in it," he said. "It has two sides." He smiled. "But one of them better be me. Just kidding."

"Put it on me?" she asked.

He bent and fiddled with the clasp and kissed her forehead. "Have a good day, kiddo. Your mom says you get to stay home. Lucky you. Happy Birthday. I love you." She heard him go into the bathroom and imagined him running his shaving brush around and around in the shaving soap, getting a lather up and scrubbing the brush over the bottom half of his face.

She thought she'd remember this day—her mother and father coming into her room, the light from the window, the wrapping paper lying on the bed, the precious Bach volumes, her father's eyes welled up, the necklace. A bit old-fashioned, it was. She pulled the heart gently back and forth on the chain and felt and heard the tiny ratcheting sound of it. She liked the idea of the two sides empty, waiting for something.

She'd miss a math test at school. And, best of all, she wouldn't have to deal with Sharon Peavey. That girl had mean down to a science and never quit. And now there were other girls in the Peavey orbit, who thought snide was a riot. Eva had a good friend, Arlo, and another friend, Ruby, and without them, she couldn't even imagine her life. Maybe when she got to high school, things would be different; maybe Sharon Peavey would go to a different school, move to Walla Walla, choke on a chicken bone.

Her father's car started up. She heard Bernie's feet clomping down the stairs, pictured him half-slurping, half-gobbling his Wheaties, then there was the slamming of the kitchen door on his way out to the road to wait for the bus. There was her mother tussling with Gretchen, who wanted to wear her sandals when there was still snow on the ground. Lying here when everyone was stirring made her feel as though she was sick, but she wasn't. She was thirteen.

The first thing she remembered in her whole life was Bernie's face outside the bars of her crib and the sound of gnawing. When she was older and Gretchen was in that same crib, her mother showed her Bernie's tooth marks, and she realized that she hadn't made it up: Bernie had been a Beaver Boy, trying to spring her free with the only tools he had. He'd lost interest in her now. She wondered whether it was her fault, or his fault, or nobody's fault.

A seagull flew high in the sky. She held her hand up to the light. Like a bird's wing. Mrs. Chapin had been her piano teacher now for the last couple of years. "Very good, Eva. My, you're a talented young lady . . ." was often all she could think to say after Eva had played something for her. Her mother thought she'd outgrown Mrs. Chapin and had arranged for her to meet a man on the piano faculty at Bowdoin College. Mr. Darius Zukauskas. The meeting was tomorrow, and she was scared.

The whole day of her birthday, she practiced the first movement of a Mozart sonata and the Allemande from a Bach French suite that she'd picked out to play for him. And between the practicing, she leafed through her new piano books. There was a universe inside the covers—two sets of preludes and fugues in all twenty-four major and minor keys. Seven flats, seven sharps, how could anyone ever play that?

She wrung her hands as her mother drove her to meet Mr. Zukauskas the next day.

They knocked on the door of his studio. Two grand pianos, end to end, sat in a room. One gleaming black like a racehorse, the other more like a regular horse. Mr. Zukauskas was tall and lean, with a long, pensive face, his dark hair combed back from a high forehead. His hands were large and his eyes dark and penetrating. He asked Eva's mother where she was playing these days.

"Just the Portland Symphony," she said, "except for one concert last winter with a piano trio—I was filling in for their cellist. In Michigan, I was a permanent member of a trio. I'd like to play chamber music regularly, but it hasn't happened here, not yet."

"You miss it."

"I do."

He turned to Eva. "So," he said, looking into her face, "this is the girl you spoke of. How old are you?"

"Thirteen. My birthday was yesterday."

"Thirteen . . . And you play the piano well?"

She didn't know what to say. She wanted to say, *Yes, yes, this is my life.*

"Who is your favorite composer?"

That was easy. "Bach."

"And after Bach?"

She thought for a moment. "Stravinsky." She didn't know why she'd said this. It could have been anyone: Brahms, Mendelssohn, Beethoven, Dvořák.

"You will play for me." It was neither a question nor a command.

She was so frightened, her ears thundered. "Which piano?"

"You choose."

Her mother said that she'd step out for a bit, give them some time, just the two of them.

Eva walked to the older of the two pianos.

"There's nothing to be afraid of," Darius Zukauskas said.

The only people in her life who'd ever said that were people who gave her everything to be frightened of. Doctors with injections. Her father urging her to jump off a ten-foot bridge into water below.

She sat down, looked at the keys, and began. She could feel him listening, his intensity winging around the room like a smart black raven. She loved this Bach Allemande. Usually, she was calm and happy when she played it. But now her forehead felt large and stupid. To her ears, her playing sounded wooden, all wrong, while this was one of the sweetest of pieces, meant to be like water, the notes singing themselves. When she ended, her eyes were hot with frustration.

"Yes," he said. "Why are you so frightened?"

She began to cry. "I want you to be my teacher. I want it so much, I can't play."

"So." He looked at her. "You can play. You just showed me. But you can play better. I understand. Don't worry. I will teach you."

Every Tuesday afternoon when she knocked and entered his studio, she felt the galvanic force of him. He had long, thick eyelashes, dark, as though fed by tears. His eyes stilled her. When he spoke, he used only the words he needed, nothing extra. He had no sense of humor, but she didn't care. She wanted to babble around him, but that was unthinkable.

Bernie said, "You're in love. Eva's in love, Eva's in lo-ove."

"Shut up!" she said, pounding his chest with her fists until he grabbed her wrists.

She played Beethoven and Chopin, Schubert and Bach, Ravel and Scarlatti and Debussy. Mr. Zukauskas never praised her. He only told her what needed improving. One afternoon, her mother drove her to her lesson, and they were all the way there before she realized she'd forgotten her music. It was too late to go back.

"I'm not going in," she told her mother.

"You're going."

"My little lost sheep," Mr. Z. said. "How did you forget? Maybe you wanted to forget?"

"No. No, I didn't mean to."

He went to a closet and pulled out several scores for two pianos. "We'll sight-read today, you on one part, me on the other." He made her sit at the racehorse piano. Schubert first, then Arensky and Moszkowski. She lost her place, she bumbled through, but every so often she found herself playing real music instead of just notes. They finished one piece, and she looked over the top of the piano and smiled. That day, her teacher hugged her goodbye, the way a grandfather might hug a child.

She heard him play in public only once: a concert of Mussorgsky's *Pictures at an Exhibition*. He played without music, without missing a note, moving from the tonal paintings of laboring oxen, to squabbling children, to young chickens, to the final bells of the Great Gate of Kiev with its avalanche of chords. The music was impossibly difficult; sitting on the piano bench, he looked like a man driving a team of wild horses.

"You like your teacher?" her mother asked afterward.

"I love my teacher."

"I can see why."

Some nights she dreamed of him. There was always water. The ocean. Near drownings. Swimming under the cool surface of a lighted pool. Water so blue. She had never seen such blue.

44

FALL 1965

That fall, Harry yoked himself to his classroom, put his shoulder to the wheel, and it all began again. Every school year seemed less tenable—his temper shorter, moments of satisfaction fewer. His colleagues in the history department appeared serene enough: trooping along, cracking tasteless jokes in the teachers' room, cutting corners where they could, going home to their families, and doing it all over again the next day. But for Harry, each day seemed like the day that might end it all.

It finally happened at the end of a week filled with inattentive, mouthy kids. Outside his classroom window, the leaves had fallen, all except the large bronze-colored oaks. The naked trees looked bleak in a sky threatening rain, or snow, or something in between. His class had been studying the Korean War, if you could call it studying. Out of the corner of his eye, he saw Darlene pass a note to her new boyfriend.

"You thought I didn't see that," said Harry. "Give it to me."

Randy crumpled up the small scrap of paper and put it in his mouth.

Later, Harry knew he should have just left it at that, finished out the last period, and gone home. But he found himself filled with rage. The kid knew nothing about the Korean War, and he would almost certainly blunder into soldiering in Vietnam, flags flying. "You won't think you're so smart," said Harry, "when you're drafted in a year or two to fight. For a war as reckless and morally reprehensible and bankrupt as anything our country has ever engaged in. Tell me something: Why did Norman Morrison set himself on fire last Tuesday outside the Pentagon?"

Randy was still chewing on Darlene's words and didn't answer.

"That's right, swallow it."

Randy's Adam's apple slid violently up and down, and the love note was gone.

"Jesus!" said Darlene under her breath.

"I'll tell you why. Norman Morrison took his one-year-old baby with him to the Pentagon to remind himself, in his last moments, of all the South Vietnamese children being slaughtered by American bombs carrying napalm. At the last moment, he gave his baby to someone, doused himself with kerosene, and lit the match. He was sitting under Robert McNamara's window at the Pentagon. You know who McNamara is, right? He's the secretary of defense, one of the people responsible for the deaths of thousands of men, women, and children in a country that should be allowed to decide its own fate."

Harry couldn't stop himself, even with a voice inside him yelling at him to stop.

"Have you ever seen what napalm does to children? Their skin is on fire. It hangs off them in strips. Water boils at two hundred twelve degrees Fahrenheit. Napalm burns at two thousand degrees Fahrenheit. That's why Norman Morrison set himself on fire.

"It's time—and I'm not just talking to Randy, I'm talking to you all—it's time that you took the study of history seriously. You've heard the phrase *history repeats itself*, right? Well, it's true. If we're not wide awake, history repeats itself in the most terrible ways. It's happened throughout the history of the world. Senseless wars, murders, assassinations, more and more sophisticated weaponry in the hands of ignorant people, the deaths of countless innocent civilians, the arrogance of politicians wielding the tool of fear, the rise of police states, bully governments that believe it's their role to police the world, governments like ours, lying, overstepping the bounds, running amok in cultures we don't take the time to understand, sending soldiers to Vietnam for no reason. Half of you boys will end up in Vietnam, and how many of you will return? Those of you who do return will return bruised and broken in your souls."

Harry stopped for a breath and looked around at his students. They were silent, many with their heads down, looking at their desks.

"Open your books to page two seventy-two," he said quietly. "Harriet Boudreaux, what was the turning point of the Korean War? Can you find it on this page?" Harriet never let him down, but this time she just looked at him with alarm. "Can someone help her?

"No? Well," he said, his voice softening, "the problem with studying history through wars, one after the other, is that we get the feeling that war is what matters, that if we're not having a war, our contributions to history are unremarkable. War gives us the sense that we're involved in something grand and meaningful. Nothing could be further from the truth. If we had a generation of peace, imagine what could be done to improve the—"

The bell rang. His students picked up their books and bags, bumping into one another in their rush to get out.

By the time Harry had gathered everything he needed for the weekend, it was four o'clock and the sun was low in the sky. Next to January, November was the worst month of the year. It felt like a shroud closing around him, every day darker, colder. He missed Molly.

An odd mist was settling over the road and fields as he drove home. He thought of the story of the 5th Battalion Norfolk Regiment, which was said to have disappeared into a cloud of mist as they marched toward a wood in Gallipoli during World War I—sixteen officers and two hundred fifty men. None of them were ever seen again. They just vanished into that strange cloud. There were speculations about what had happened—that eerie mist spiriting them away—but the truth was that they were mowed down by enemy fire.

Another story from another war. What he'd said in his classroom was true, every word of it, but he was not proud of himself.

Especially threatening Randy with the draft. That boy came from a poor family. He was a sitting duck, and after high school he'd be one of the first to be taken.

He drove down the peninsula and along the slendering waist of the road toward home. The mist still hung over the meadows, and he saw Mr. Wootton's black-and-white cows bunched together a little way from the road. Gretchen loved pulling up stalks of grass and holding a handful out for them, her arm trembling as a long gray tongue wrapped around her offering and took it. Once, when he'd been driving home, he'd seen Mr. Wootton walk up to one of his cows and embrace her. They stood there for a while, cow and man. His neighbor rubbed her chest, and the cow's big, blunt nose nuzzled up against his neck and then pointed to the sky.

Liddie didn't teach on Friday afternoons, and Gretchen and Eva would be home with Margreete. Bernie was driving now and would probably be helping out at Noah's Bark. Harry had promised to make sloppy joes tonight, one of his Friday-night blue plate specials.

He went into the kitchen and set a skillet on the stove. Liddie came in a few minutes later and asked him about his day.

"A student made me angry last period—well, if the truth be told, the whole week made me angry—and I became everything I detest in a teacher. I humiliated a student. I badgered the entire class with a rant about the war. You'll be thinking, so what else is new? I couldn't even make it to Thanksgiving this year before I lost my head."

"It can't have been that bad."

"It *was* that bad. I feel like getting drunk."

"Want a beer?" She went to the refrigerator.

"I want a dozen beers. Whatever made me think I had the patience to teach? I'm telling you the truth: I hate every day I go into that school."

"Then you shouldn't be forcing yourself to do it."

"I have to work."

"You could find something else."

"They're not bad kids. They're just ignorant." He took a swig of beer, set the bottle on the counter, and grabbed an onion from the refrigerator. He handed her a knife and cutting board and started the tomato sauce.

"What are you going to do?" she asked.

"What kind of question is that?" he asked. "I'm going to get through the year."

She turned away. "You don't need to snap at me."

"I'm not snapping."

As they were sitting down to eat, Gretchen said, "How come our family doesn't say 'thanks be to God' before we start?"

"Where did *that* come from?" said Harry. "Do you want to say 'thanks be to God'? Go ahead, I don't mind."

"It's what the father is supposed to say, not the kid."

"Who said? You go ahead."

"I don't want to."

"I'll say it," said Margreete. "Thank you for nothing."

Liddie laughed.

"Who is God, anyway?" asked Gretchen.

"Dad doesn't believe in God," said Eva. "Some people think God is an old man in the sky with white hair and a white beard who's kind and gentle and sits in front of fancy gates and lets people into heaven after they die if they've been good. And heaven is where people are nice to each other all the time. And no one is hungry or scared or sad or anything. They're just happy forever. And the angels play music on harps and sing and float around."

"Do you believe that?"

"No," said Eva. "How could people stay up in the clouds like that? They'd fall out of the sky."

"Why do people believe it?"

"Because," said Liddie, "it helps them."

"Would it help me?"

"You have to decide that for yourself."

"How old do I have to be?"

"You can decide right now if you want to."

"I think I'll believe it for a while and see."

"Fine," said Harry. "We'll have a little Holy Roller in our family. . . . Seconds, anyone?"

Bernie passed his plate, and Gretchen said, "Sing the state-capital song, Grandma."

"Let's not start that," said Liddie.

But she already had. "Rhode Island has two capitals, Providence and New-port, Rhode Island has two capitals, Providence and New-port. New Hampshire, Concord, on the Merrimack Ri-ver, New Hampshire, Concord, on the Merrimack Ri-ver. Massachusetts, Boston, on the Boston Ba-ay, Massachusetts, Boston, on the Boston Ba-ay."

"Mom? That's enough now."

Margreete tipped her plate onto the floor for Fred.

Tuesday morning, the ax fell. "Have a seat," his principal said.

"I know what this is about," Harry said to the jowly, self-satisfied face sitting across from him, trying not to focus on Frank's ugly brown-and-yellow-striped tie.

"Then why don't you tell me?"

"Friday, last period, Randy Shaw and I got into a contest of wills. He made me angry, and I told him he wouldn't think he was so smart when he was drafted into Vietnam and found himself fighting another one of those useless, morally reprehensible wars, fought by a country that had no business being there. Many soldiers wouldn't come home, and those that did would have their spirits wounded beyond repair."

"Go on."

"That's about it."

"You forgot about making him swallow a wad of paper. His mother told me yesterday that you made him swallow it."

"That's not true. I didn't make him do that. He did it of his own accord. It was a love note he didn't want me to see."

"And you left out the part about Vietnamese children with their skin hanging off them in strips. Cynthia Demitre's father called and said she'd been so upset, she couldn't eat dinner."

"That's right, I did say that. I wanted to drive home the fact that the Vietnam War is not a venture we can be one hundred percent proud of."

"You know, Harry—I don't need to remind you that we've had this conversation before—it's not your business to comment on politics in your classroom. Vietnam is a matter for families to discuss in the privacy of their own homes. Your classroom is not a soapbox for your radical views."

"Hold on a moment, Frank. With all due respect, it's 'radical' to disagree with this war? Vietnam is a matter of life and death for some of these kids. Many of them are going to end up there, some will be blown to smithereens, others will come back scarred for life. You know that as well as I do. And I'm supposed to act like a robot, without any views of my own or a sense of responsibility for my students' lives?"

"There's a pattern that's very familiar here."

"What's that?"

"You bring your inappropriate political views into the classroom."

The word *inappropriate* was on the top-ten list of words Harry despised.

"What I'm saying is this. If the material is not in the history book, it does not belong in your classroom. End of story."

"That book is hopelessly outdated."

"It doesn't matter. You've insulted our servicemen; you've offended the patriots in our community. You've described and shown images that are disturbing to your students. Mr. Demitre said that earlier this year you showed the class a picture of the public lynching of a black man."

"That lynching took place in Marion, Indiana, in 1930. I wanted them to know that racism didn't end with the Civil War."

"That, Harry, is exactly my point. Was that photograph in the history textbook? No, it was not. That photograph would never have been chosen for students in the tenth grade. That material is inappropriate for this age bracket."

"You've been gunning for me since I started working in this district."

"Let me finish, Harry. You need to understand you're on very thin ice. Now, I know that you're a very caring and hardworking teacher. I know you have an excellent grasp of your material. And I personally like you, even though I do not share many of your views."

What a load of crap.

"However, we need to get this straightened out if you're to continue on with our team here. I've made the decision that the renewal of your contract this coming year is contingent on you proving that you have a better grasp of what you can and cannot say in your classroom, what you can and cannot do. Have I made myself clear?"

"Basically, if there are any more complaints, I'm out."

"In a word, yes."

"I suggest you install a monitor to sit in my classroom to see whether I continue to make incendiary remarks."

"That sort of sarcasm is not appropriate, either."

"All right, Frank, I'll let you know my decision by the end of the week."

Frank looked at him. "What decision?"

"Whether I can continue to teach under those circumstances."

"I'd like to think that you can make those adjustments. It's not every day that a teacher of your caliber comes along."

Harry disliked this man so intensely, it hurt. He stood, wished Frank a good day, and walked down the hall to his classroom. On his way home, Zorba the Greek came to him, answering a question about whether he was married. *Am I not a man? And is not a man stupid? I'm a man . . . so I married. Wife, children, house . . . everything . . . the full catastrophe.* Zorba pronounced *full* like *fool.*

Was he, Harry, a fool? No more than any other man. Was he a coward? Less than some men. Was his life a catastrophe? Maybe.

But he wouldn't regret his family. The house, yes, with its clogged gutters and tipping-over porch.

One thing was clear enough: He wasn't going to make it through the school year, not even to Christmas. He couldn't change his stripes any better than Frank's ugly necktie could.

45

SPRING 1966

Gretchen watched her mother take two socks off a big pile of clean laundry in her bedroom, put them together toe to toe, roll them up, and turn one cuff down to make a ball. "I'm almost ten years old," she said.

"I know," said her mother. "I was there when you were born."

"Soon I'll be a double-digit girl."

"How about that?" It was the voice her mother used when she wasn't really here. It was friendly and pleasant and didn't mean anything.

Gretchen lifted one of her shirts off the pile and wrapped it around her neck.

"Just leave it," said her mother.

"Do you know the saddest sound in the world?" Gretchen asked.

"No. What?"

"Mr. Wootton's mama cow looking for her baby." Across the field, Mr. Wootton had put the mother cow in one field with the other cows and the baby in the barn.

"It's time for bed," said her mother. "Don't dillydally now. And don't forget to brush your teeth."

Gretchen went to her room and took off her socks and shoes. Her father told her the cow and calf were separated because that's what had to happen. Mr. Wootton's cows produced milk for him to sell. But if he let the baby drink all the milk, then he wouldn't have any milk to sell from that cow. Gretchen told him that she wasn't going to drink any more milk if she was taking it from babies. But her father said, no, when the baby cow was ready, then the farmer took the mother away and kept the milk.

But that wasn't right. This baby wasn't ready, and the mother was crying in the field. She took off her pants and underpants and shirt, lifted her nightgown off the hook, put it on, and went into the bathroom to brush her teeth. She sat on the toilet and listened to the cow, and she brushed her teeth but not really, just chewed on the bristles the way she wasn't supposed to.

When she got into bed, the cow was still crying. She was crying, too, and her mother came to say good night and said, "The mama will forget about her baby in a few days, and then it will be all right. Cows aren't like people."

"How do you know?"

"I just do. Now, go to sleep."

"I can't."

"Please, Gretchen, I have other things on my mind."

"What?"

"Your father is going for a job interview tomorrow, and I need to iron his shirt."

"The cow is more important."

"That's enough."

"Do you think he'll get the job?"

"I don't know."

"What if he doesn't?"

"He'll have to keep looking."

"And we won't have enough money?"

"That's right. Go to sleep now, honey." She kissed her on the cheek, smoothed her hair, and turned out the light. The cow kept bellowing. Gretchen got out of bed and got the flashlight from the bureau and turned it on under the covers so she could read the book about Lassie to make her feel better, but the book was as sad as the cow. She kept reading after her parents went to bed. The cow went quiet, and then she started again. Gretchen thought of the baby in the barn, all by itself in the dark. She thought of all the creatures in the darkness, the baby rabbits in their tunnels snuggled together, the footprints of mice she'd seen in the snow and the track between the footprints where the tail had dragged. Every small creature in the world needed its parents.

Jeremy, her friend at school, would know what to say. He'd been her friend since second grade, when she'd had to find a partner for a science project. She and Jeremy chose each other, and they did a project on the luna moth because Gretchen had found one clinging to the shed door one morning with its pale-green wings and its pretend eyes and streaming tail. It was the most beautiful thing she'd ever seen. Jeremy had a picture of a night-blooming cereus, which they put in their project next to the moth. Their teacher, Mr. Daniels, said the flower didn't have anything to do with the luna moth, but they said, yes, it did, because they were both beautiful. "Beautiful and fleeting," said Jeremy, and Mr. Daniels left them alone. Jeremy had the right words for everything.

She could hear her grandmother coming, because when she walked, she put her hand on the wallpaper to feel her way in the dark, and her hand made a kind of dry sound. Just before Gretchen's room, the wallpaper was loose and the sound was different, and then Gretchen knew she'd be stepping through the doorway.

Gretchen shone the flashlight on her grandmother's face next to her in bed, and she went blinky; her face was so close, Gretchen could see the white whiskers growing on her chin. She told her about the mother and baby cow and asked whether she could help her open Mr. Wootton's barn door and let the baby out. "No, not now," her grandmother said.

But then she got out of bed and took the flashlight. Gretchen called to her, but she kept going. She went down the stairs and Fred's toenails click-clicked after her. In the kitchen, Margreete stood at the door, rattling the knob. "Open the goddamn door."

Gretchen found the keys in her mother's purse, opened the door, and followed her grandmother out, with Fred close behind.

Margreete sat on the porch steps. "Get away, dog," she said. "You're bothering me." The moon was bright, almost like day. The face in it was her mother's.

When her mother died, Margreete had found her sitting in her favorite wingback chair, leaning with her head against one of the wings and her mouth open as though death had surprised her before she'd had time to wipe her glasses and gather herself. Her coffee was spilled on the floor, and the cup had rolled under the table. It was July, and the raspberries were bright on the bushes, and her mother's newly washed clothes were on the clothesline, moving in the wind as though they were alive.

"Grandma, did you forget about the cow?"

"No. Yes."

"I'm too little to go by myself. And you're too old to go by yourself. Stand up, Grandma."

"All right, all right, don't hurry me. I'm coming, I'm coming."

46

Bernie stood at the base of the apple tree and told Gretchen if she came down he'd take her to Bath for a special treat as soon as their mother came back with the car.

"I don't want to go to Bath."

"Gretchen, sometimes you just have to accept the world the way it is. She's not our cow. And Mr. Wootton can't have you reorganizing his cows. Come on, Gretchen. Come on down. Your hands are getting all cold and red and chapped."

She began to cry. "I'm not coming down."

"You know, there are things I feel like protesting, too."

"Like what?"

"Lots of things. But you have to choose your battles. Come on down."

"No."

"Mom will be back soon with Grandma. She'll be mad if she finds you up here. She'll be mad at me, too."

"I don't care."

Bernie looked up into the branches again. The tight buds were swelling. Before long, the red-winged blackbirds would be singing. Today, though, the cold stung. Gretchen was wearing her rubber boots and winter coat, and her nose was running. In the wind, her brown hair lifted out from under her hat and swept across her face. She reached for a higher branch.

"Stop it, Gretchen. You'll get hurt. It's going to get dark soon.

Come on down now. Idealism can go too far. Do you know what idealism is?"

"Yes . . . What?"

"Dad is an idealist—at least, he used to be. Now he's just unemployed."

"Do you like Dad?"

"I guess." That wasn't really the truth, but he couldn't say what was in his head. Last week, the day after St. Patrick's Day, he and Noah had driven to Bath to get supplies for Noah's Bark. They stopped off in a coffee shop on the way home and and saw his father locked in conversation with the nurse his dad had said he didn't remember. His father was so engrossed, he didn't see them. Not only was he an idealist, he was a liar. Now Bernie couldn't even look at him. It was tempting to blow the whistle on him, but his mother had enough stress in her life, holding everything together while his father looked half-heartedly for work, or gathered seaweed to sell and came home smelling like a seal, or wrote articles to radical magazines and leftist rags like *Ramparts*. The other night, Bernie had met him on the stairs, and his father shoved a sheaf of papers toward him and said, "You might want to have a look at this. I've just finished a two-part series on the classist roots of the Vietnam War." Bernie said he was busy and left his father standing with the pages in his hand. It was awkward, very awkward, and, he had to admit, sad.

He looked up into the tree again at Gretchen. "You're cold, aren't you."

"Yes."

"Want me to get your mittens for you? And some hot cocoa?"

Bernie disappeared into the house and heated up milk on the stove and stirred in cocoa and poured it into a cup for her. Fred was lying by the woodstove, and the end of his tail wagged when he saw Bernie. Eva's piano music was coming from the other room. Bernie warmed Gretchen's red mittens in the oven for a couple of minutes and went outside with them and the mug of cocoa. The sky was going dark.

"You have to come down farther. I can't reach that high."

"You're going to grab me."

He hadn't thought of that. He set the cocoa down on the ground. "Come on, Gretchen. I warmed your mittens in the oven. They're nice and toasty for you."

She turned around, facing the trunk of the tree, and slithered down to a lower branch.

"I can't reach up that high."

"Yes, you can."

"No, I can't."

"You're going to get me."

"I won't."

She came down farther, reached for her mittens, and he grabbed her hand and yanked her out of the tree, raking her leg against the bark on the way down. She turned into a wild animal, biting and hitting and scratching. "You lied! You lied!" He held her tight and carried her into the house and straddled her on the floor and held her hands over her head. He didn't know what else to do, except maybe lock her in the bathroom.

"Gretchen, calm down, you were freezing up there."

"You're not my brother!" She kicked and screamed and threw her head from side to side.

The piano stopped and Eva came into the kitchen. "What are you doing?"

"She was in the tree and wouldn't come down."

"Let her go."

"She'll go up the tree again."

"What happened to her leg?"

"She scraped it on the bark."

Gretchen sobbed, "He promised, he promised!" And then all at once, she gave up and grew still. Eva got a basin of water, and they washed her leg and dried it.

Soon after, Bernie heard a car come into the driveway, then his grandmother's and mother's voices. His mother was angry when she learned what had happened. "She could have fallen out of the tree and gotten another concussion." She turned to Margreete. "And,

Mom, you encouraged her last night. You opened the barn door and let the calf out."

"When did I do that?"

"Last night. And some of the cows got out, too."

"Well, I never . . ."

Bernie looked at his grandmother pulling at the sleeve of her sweater, her mind as smooth as a boiled egg. "Sit down on the stool, Grandma," he said. She stretched a foot out in front of her, and he helped her take off her shoes and socks. Like old turtles, her feet were, cracked and ancient.

His mother came out of the mudroom and told Bernie that she had to be able to depend upon him.

"I was doing my homework. How was I supposed to know she'd go up a tree and decide to stay up there? I didn't know she'd do that. I had to pull her down. It could have happened with you here, too. It just happened to be me. And what about Dad? I've got homework, but he's not even working, and he stays away all day pretending to be looking for a job and writing those articles no one reads." He'd said too much already, and he saw by his mother's face that he'd hit the mark and needed to shut up.

His mother put her hand over her throat and left without saying a word. "Gretchen?" she called. "I need to speak with you." There was no answer.

47

The car puttered down the peninsula, and for the first time, Harry noted the signs of spring that he'd been too depressed to see until now. Nearly five months he'd been looking for a job. For his most recent try at bringing in some money, he'd teamed up with a guy named Clarence Dexter, who, he discovered, excelled at guaranteed-to-fail entrepreneurial schemes. Harry had already been out three times with Clarence, collecting kelp at the turn of the tide, stuffing the long, slimy ribbons into canvas bags—four hundred to five hundred pounds a tide—hauling them back to Clarence's place in a rattletrap pickup, and hanging each ribbon with clothespins on special wooden frames Clarence had built and Harry had paid for. Harry had also paid for two pairs of chest-high rubber boots, a set for each of them. The idea was to dry the kelp, package it up, and send it to a health-food outlet in Massachusetts, which would pay them ten dollars a pound for it. Four hundred pounds wet equaled forty pounds dry. The fly in the ointment was quality: The distributor would not buy spotted seaweed. Rain blemished the product, or else the fog rotted it before it could dry. They'd been out three times, and their failures were three for three.

But today! Today was the day he was offered a job to organize Bowdoin's historical archives and to research the college's early years, from 1794 through the beginning of the First World War. It was a full-time job with decent pay and benefits. If all went well, he was likely to be offered a permanent position as college historian, a position that hadn't been created yet but was in the works. He liked his new supervisor at the college, a Miss Braxton. No nonsense, no dazzle, but a spunky sense of humor. When he'd asked her how long she'd been there, she told him since sometime before the Boer War. Not the funniest thing he'd ever heard, but still. He imagined they'd get along fine, and unlike the principal he'd left behind, she didn't wear ugly neckties.

He now saw the classroom as an environment that had encouraged the toxic, hectoring side of him. What a relief to put that behind him and to hold his head up again. Liddie still spoke to him, but her anger had been building over the months, in direct relation to their bank account bottoming out. His job-hunting necktie had been feeling like a noose around his neck for weeks. He loosened it and flopped it down on the seat beside him. Only yesterday, he had been Nowhere Man, like in the song. Harry had noticed that his son had been avoiding him. Not that he could blame him.

He turned on the radio, and there were the Beach Boys, singing *Bar bar bar bar Barbar Ann*. He liked this stupid song, and he knew it would be in his head now for the rest of the day.

He parked the car next to the house, still humming, and walked in. "Honey, I'm home!" like some dimwit on a sitcom. The whole house seemed to be saying, *So what*, except Fred, who grabbed his empty dog dish in his mouth and brought it to him.

Harry got the bag of kibble and filled the bowl and went to the bottom of the stairs.

"Hello? Anybody home?"

"We've got a problem," said Liddie.

At the top of the stairs, he found Liddie sitting on the floor outside Gretchen's bedroom door. "It's that cow," she told him. "Gretchen's not eating, and she's not coming out until the mama and baby are reunited. Mr. Wootton separated them again, and the mama is crying."

"And you said?"

"I told her to come out and have some dinner and we'd talk about it. That went nowhere."

"Gretchen!" he said. "Unlock the door. Do I have to break the door down?"

"Well, that's effective," said Liddie.

"And you're not being all that helpful, either."

"It's *your* DNA that we're dealing with here."

"How do you figure that?"

"Who's the protestor in this family? How do you think she learned this?"

"C'mon, honey. What about the TV? People are protesting all over the goddamn country. I just walked into the house. All I wanted to do was bring you some good news."

"What kind of good news?"

"Forget it."

"Tell me now."

"I don't feel like it," he said.

"The job?"

He turned and went into the bedroom, threw down the tie, took off his suit jacket and good pants, put on a flannel shirt and his favorite old khakis, and went downstairs.

Margreete was in the kitchen, eating Ritz crackers out of a box. "Hungry?" he asked.

"Not as hungry as I was before the next cracker."

"What do you want for dinner?"

"Lobster thermidor."

"Coming right up." He looked in the freezer and found a package of fish sticks and frozen peas.

"Where have you been?" asked Margreete. "I've been expecting you all day."

"Who am I?"

"Irving, you silly boy. Such a joker."

"Margreete, if I told you I wasn't Irving, would you believe me?"

"I know you're Irving, because you're wearing that shirt." She picked another cracker out of the box and munched it thoughtfully.

"You were the one who let that cow out of the field, weren't you."

"Not on your life. I don't know any cows."

"Well, who did, then?"

She ate another cracker.

He tipped the freezer-burned fish sticks out onto an aluminum cookie sheet and popped them into the oven. He searched the pantry for potatoes, found five edible ones, and peeled them and put them in a pot. Same with the peas. While he was waiting for the potato water to boil, he picked up the phone and called his neighbor.

Wootton's wife, Millie, said he was in the barn, milking the cows. Probably a good thing. Mistake to get in touch by phone. Better to see him face-to-face.

Harry optimistically set the table for six. Bernie came into the kitchen, saw him there, and left. Harry stood over the bubbling potatoes and considered what to say to his neighbor. If he, Harry, had a bunch of cows, and a little girl next door was upset about the way he was looking after them, what would it take for him to feel sympathetic? Money? Services rendered? Was it possible Gretchen would wake in the morning, eat breakfast, go to school, forget all about it?

No.

Liddie came into the kitchen. "Mom, that's enough crackers. You'll ruin your appetite."

"My appetite is already ruined. Bozo here is cooking up a storm."

"What's for dinner?" Liddie asked.

Harry opened the oven door.

"Oh . . . That looks appetizing."

"It's all there was."

"So, what's the good news?"

"I've accepted a job. The historical-archives position at the college."

"That's wonderful, darling." She put her arms around him.

"A respectable offer, too. It starts two weeks from Monday. And there might be a permanent position coming down the pike."

"Thank God. That's wonderful," she said again. "This hasn't been the happiest five months."

"For me, either."

"I'm *talking* about you, silly."

"I thought you were talking about you."

"Occasionally, I do think about someone other than myself. Times even when I think about you. I'm happy for you, darling."

"After dinner, I'm going over to talk to Wootton."

"Why don't you let me go instead? He might not get his back up with a woman."

"Can you just trust me on this one?"

Five people sat down to dinner. Eva suggested that they ask Gretchen to talk to Mr. Wootton herself.

"Or take Grandma," said Bernie. "Or we'll all go. Overwhelm him with our collective logic. Jesus, Dad, you're going to make a fool of yourself. What's he going to say? They're his cows."

Harry got up from the table without another word and left the house, with Fred trotting after him. "Go home, Fred."

He headed across the field, opened a gate, went through, closed it behind him, went through another gate, and ended up outside Wootton's barn. The lights were on. Inside, Wootton was moving around slowly among his animals in that comforting way of his, the portable milking machine hissing and clanking. With their heads in the stanchions, the cows were like ships anchored in a harbor, their bellies round as hulls. It was their eyes that Harry loved, the straight, blunt eyelashes and deep, mysterious animal gaze. He looked at the cow nearest him: her eyes placid, her mouth straight across, a kind of dignity in her expression.

Wootton looked up. "Twenty to go," he said, cleaning a cow's udder before clamping on the milking machine. "Have a seat." He gestured toward a stump by the door.

Harry sat. The barn was filled with the steamy expulsions of large nostrils. He could imagine sleeping here with these broad-beamed, forgiving creatures on nights when he was discouraged by the sins of his own blundering, misbehaving kind. Better an oaf of a cow than a lout of a human.

About three or four milking machines were going at once, their collective choo choo a reassuring, rooted, industrial sound. Harry remembered from his childhood the sound of milking before machines: the hollow, ragged sound when the first squirts of milk struck the bottom of the metal bucket, the swish as it filled, the bucket scraping against the concrete floor as it moved from cow to cow. He closed his eyes, dozed, and was surprised suddenly to see Wootton standing over him.

"What can I do for you?"

Harry fumbled to his feet. "Sorry, long day."

"You want to come into the house?"

"This is fine."

Harry didn't know what to do with his hands. "First, let me just say that I'm sorry that my mother-in-law and my youngest daughter caused trouble for you. My mother-in-law is senile, and sometimes she wanders at night."

"You'd best keep the doors locked," Wootton said.

Harry could have told him they already did that, but he let it go. "Yes . . . Here's the thing. My youngest daughter got it into her head . . ."

His neighbor hiked up his blue jeans.

"I'm taking you away from your evening."

"I'm listening."

"Have you met my daughter Gretchen?"

"Probably seen her from a distance."

"She's an unusual child. What happened is, she heard your mama cow crying for her baby after you separated them, and she went to pieces."

"What I did is common practice. Has to be done."

"I'm not questioning the practice, although I have to admit it's hard to hear."

"Yep."

"You obviously have a herd of fine-looking cows here, and you've worked out what—"

"So your daughter is upset. Is that what you came to say?"

"She's more than upset. She went up a tree this afternoon and wouldn't come down, and now she's locked herself in her room, and she refuses to eat until the cow and the baby are reunited."

Mr. Wootton looked at him. "Sounds as though you got a heifer on your hands who needs straightening out."

"I beg your pardon?"

"That little girl of yours is ruling the roost."

"Ordinarily, I wouldn't have bothered you. She's only nine years old, but once she's going down a track, she's like a freight train."

"Mr. Furber, I've put up with shenanigans from your mother-in-law over the years. This isn't the first time she's left one of my fences wide open."

"I'm sorry to hear that."

"And now your daughter is in the act, running around all hours of night, and you're expecting me to change what I do with my own cows so she'll go back to eating her cornflakes."

"When you put it like that . . . But I'm wondering if you might accept monetary compensation . . ."

"For my trouble? No, I took care of it."

"I mean is there anything that would make it worth your while to keep that cow and calf together for a while?"

"And what happens next time I have to separate a cow and calf?"

"I would hope she'd be over it by then."

Wootton took off his cap, ran his hands through his hair, positioned his cap back on his head. "You give me twenty dollars and we'll call it square. And you can tell her when she's older, I expect her to give me some afternoons mucking out the barn."

"I'll have her bring over the cash tomorrow."

"And let me give you a piece of advice. You want to straighten her out before she hits the crazy years. My girl, she ran wild, got herself pregnant, ran off with a guy, nearly broke her mother's heart, lost the baby to pneumonia."

"Is she still with that guy?"

"He was a no-good asshole. No, she's working over to Raymond's Auto Body. Met another feller and got married, had a baby, sweetest little gal, apple of her granddaddy's eye."

"Well, you never know with kids. I'm glad it worked out for yours. And I sure do thank you. I wasn't looking forward to going home with that cow still crying and nothing to be done, I can tell you that. I would have been back, asking to sleep in your barn."

"Wouldn't be the first time a man slept in this barn."

48

Harry let Bernie know about the Masters Tournament on television, and, to his surprise, Bernie sat down to watch it with him: men sending balls through the sunny air, carefully calculating the slope of the turf and the trajectory, so meditative and agreeable.

An Ajax commercial began. *Ajax men of science, they've harnessed bromine bleach . . .* Bernie sat next to Harry on the couch. Jack Nicklaus was ahead. Bernie was cutting his toenails, and the shards were flying.

"You couldn't do that somewhere else?"

"I'm almost done."

There was a commercial break, and on came a song advertising G.I. Joe.

G.I. Joe, G.I. Joe, fighting man from head to toe, on the land, on the sea, in the air! And then a blond kid with an unpleasant face yelled, "G.I. Joe attacks! Boom! Boom!"

"Little Nazi," said Bernie.

Dozens of G.I. Joes gathered on the screen, and the commercial said never had anyone had so much fun playing soldier. Harry snorted.

"Dad, there's something I've been wondering."

"Yeah, what's that?"

"Did you ever cheat on Mom?"

Harry looked at his son and felt himself standing on the edge of a cliff. "What makes you ask that?"

"Just wondered."

"If you mean did I ever sleep with another woman, no, I didn't." His heart beat faster.

"Did you ever want to?"

"I don't know of many people who don't want to at some point in their marriage."

"Do you remember when I stepped on the nail and you took me to the hospital and there was a nurse there who got me ice cream?"

"Yes, I remember that night very clearly."

"And?"

"And what?"

"What about that nurse?"

"She was a lovely person. I'm glad she was the one who was there to fix you up."

His son was no fool. They weren't talking about that nurse fixing up Bernie, and they both knew it. For one small moment, with Bernie looking straight at him, Harry thought his son would think less of him if he told the truth. A moment later, too late, he knew the opposite was true.

"Right, Dad," said Bernie. They stared at Jack Nicklaus reading the green, lining up his next shot. Nicklaus's concentration was absolute, as though the outcome would shape the world.

Bernie began to squirm, got up, and mumbled that he was going out. Harry resisted the impulse to hug him, to speak what he'd failed to speak. His son didn't like hugs, at least not at this stage. Harry heard the car start in the driveway and stared at the television screen: the fairway and sky and crowds standing around looking to see where a small white ball would go.

Which was worse: telling a lie, or telling the truth with the intent to deceive? Almost certainly the latter, with its willful manipulation and convoluted layers of deceit.

Many times he'd imagined saying something to Liddie about Molly, but he was pretty sure it would go badly. The more time went by, the less certain that seemed, but also the more impossible it was to admit he'd kept this from her since that first meeting back at the dam in 1957, nine years ago. Now, a once-a-year assignation hardly seemed worth mentioning. Molly mattered, but a conversation in a coffee shop was not marriage-threatening.

He'd never met Molly in his town or hers. When he thought about them sitting in her station wagon next to the dam, what he felt was how naïve he'd been and how his motives had not been altogether despicable. He'd craved comfort and connection, although what was despicable was not caring that he could have brought the walls of his home crashing down.

Harry still remembered one particular day after World War II, when he'd gone to Europe to help with relief work. It had rained in the afternoon and the sky had cleared just before sunset. Light gilded the sides of buildings, many of them bombed out. Streets glistened, and the pigeons waddled among the ruins. He was walking back to the hostel where he and the other relief workers stayed, and something made him turn and cross over the stone threshold of a church. So many feet had crossed that threshold over the centuries that the stone was cupped.

It was like this with him and Molly: So many millions had walked a similar path that if it had been stone, it, too, would have been cupped. His loneliness, the way she lit him with a kind of hope—these were elements of emotional cliché, but he didn't like to think of it that way. He thought of her with fondness, he recalled the way they had lived their lives, storing up things to tell each other, bringing morsels to one another. Back then, the world had been more noticeable because of her.

Was it wrong? No. Was it wrong? Yes.

When Harry heard Bernie come home that night, Liddie was asleep. He got out of bed quietly, put on his shirt and trousers in the hall, and went downstairs in his bare feet. He found Bernie in the kitchen, standing in front of the open door of the refrigerator, not doing anything, just standing there. He'd been drinking, his rosy ears the giveaway.

"That nurse you were asking about?" Harry said. "Her name is

Molly. I'm sorry I didn't tell you straight. We never slept together, but that doesn't mean nothing happened."

"I know. I was with Noah one afternoon in Bath, and we saw you with her. You didn't see us."

"No. No, I didn't."

"You were sitting in a booth, wrapped up in each other."

"Did you never think of saying anything?"

"I said something. This afternoon."

They were quiet.

"I mean before."

"I didn't want to talk to you. I was angry with you for cheating on Mom. Do you remember when you were looking for your green hat? I threw it away. I watched you look high and low for it."

"I liked that hat."

"I know you did." He shut the refrigerator door.

"I'm sorry I hurt you," Harry said.

"Does Mom know?"

"I don't know. It hardly matters anymore. The temptation is past now. There was a time . . ." His voice dropped away.

"What?"

"It's past. A few years ago, Molly and I agreed to see each other just once a year, the day after St. Patrick's Day always in the same place, where you saw us."

"You should tell Mom."

"I used to think she'd leave me if she knew. Now I kind of doubt it."

"Telling the truth is better than living a lie."

"Is that what you think I've been doing?"

"Sort of. But not the kind of lie I thought you were living."

"I'll give it some thought," said Harry. He stuffed one hand in his pocket and jingled the coins. Nickels and pennies by the feel of them. "Your mother and I had some lonely years together. I'm not saying that to justify myself."

"I know."

"I thank you for speaking up."

Bernie shrugged.

"It can't have been easy for you to say what you did."

"Do Eva and Gretchen know?"

"No. Anyway . . . thank you." He didn't know what else to say.

Bernie turned on the faucet, filled a glass with water, and left the room. Harry imagined him stretched out in his bed on the third floor in the semi-darkness, thinking God knows what about his father.

As Harry passed out of the kitchen into the hallway, he caught sight of himself in the mirror, a slightly slumped, uncertain figure. The last time he'd seen Molly, a few weeks back, she was still working as a nurse, still married. Her kids were teenagers now. The brightness was still in her but dimmed. She said she planned to leave her marriage once her kids were out of the house. That didn't seem right to him, to know and not act, and he told her so. In a way, it was the same conversation he'd just had with Bernie. Don't live a lie.

He crossed into the living room, sank into the red chair, and heard his father's crusty, defeated voice: *Women. You can't live with 'em and you can't live without 'em.*

He himself had been an idiot about the opposite sex from the get-go and still thought of himself as a semi-idiot. Leslie—the first woman-of-his-dreams—popped into his head. One of Harry's buddies in college tried to warn him that she was a taker, a cold-hearted girl. She did say mean things about people they knew in common, but if he was honest with himself, her meanness was one of the intoxicants. Not to mention the way she touched him conspiratorially on his arm and tossed her hair. He ran track in those days, and he remembered his raw, animal desire as he jumped the hurdles, blowing out his blood vessels to impress the only spectator who mattered.

Never had he seen this kind of desire in his son. Bernie's need to hide it seemed a rebuke of his father. But maybe it wasn't there at all. There were men who lived in their heads, their brains a kind of sex organ. He'd thought about asking Bernie if he had a girlfriend, but something stopped him.

Leslie, of course, dumped him. But before that, he'd taken her out to dinner, worked extra hours sweeping out the dorms to afford a pair of earrings that she never wore. He gave and gave, and even when she told him it was finished—*Don't call, don't write, I'm going to Paris*—he hastened to the airport and ran down to her gate with some cheese-and-tomato sandwiches for her journey. Oh, even now it pained him to think of dashing after her with those sandwiches. She would have tossed them into the nearest bin. After she left, he found out she'd been sleeping with at least two other men: a professor, and the friend who'd warned him about her.

He thought of himself as a natural pursuer, a maker of cheese-and-tomato sandwiches. It had proved impossible to overcome. He was the one who wanted; Liddie was, more often than not, the one who didn't want. If he'd been born a dog, he'd be rolling on the floor with his feet in the air, exposing his tummy.

Was it his paternal duty to ask Bernie the questions that would embarrass them both? His only son would be gone soon, pulling up anchor. It crossed his mind that Noah was Bernie's romantic interest, but no. There was no history of that kind of thing in the family. Well, except for Liddie's brother, Peter. Harry didn't know much about these proclivities—in fact he'd only known one other such man, back during the starvation experiment. Howard was his name. Everyone ostracized him, as though they could catch what he had. Without the support of the rest of the group, Howard was one of the first men to break when starvation set in. Harry was ashamed he'd never tried to befriend him. Maybe he'd feared the possibility of contagion as much as anyone else.

Things were changing. The thundering herds would trample past, and all of a sudden he'd be left in the dust, sitting on the soil of a planet he no longer belonged to. Already, look at how you took your life in your hands if you held a door for a woman. One day his daughters would look at him as though he were a dinosaur. He'd see it in their eyes, the way he already saw it in Bernie's.

49

They turned on the *CBS Evening News*, Liddie on the couch with her mother and the girls, Harry in his chair with Fred at his feet, Bernie in a separate chair. Night after night, they watched the war. On and on it went.

A Vietcong soldier wearing a black blindfold, pushed along by a bayonet. Two children hunched in a drainage ditch for protection, clinging to their mother. A man in a conical rattan hat, holding the limp body of a child, thin legs dangling down over his arm. A Marine on his knees, his ear to the chest of a fallen buddy. Bombs falling and falling out of the sky.

They listened to the fatherly voice of Walter Cronkite making the unimaginable imaginable. A village had been leveled, one hundred fifty houses burned down; from across the world, they could hear the choked and huddled sound of women and children. The men were nowhere, disappeared into tunnels, hidden under the cover of rice paddies and jungle leaves and vines.

"Why did they do that?" asked Margreete.

"I don't know, Mom."

"Why did they do that?"

"I don't know."

"Why are they doing that?"

"Mom. It's a war. It doesn't make any sense. If we didn't have a war, we wouldn't know what to do with ourselves. What would we do with our billions of dollars? How would we make ourselves feel important? How would the world know how strong and righteous we are?" She stood up and turned off the TV. "We're not going to watch this. It's too terrible."

"We have to," said Bernie, turning it back on.

"Who said?"

"We have to, so we know."

"And you don't mind that one of your sisters is crying and your grandmother is upset?"

She went into her studio and sat and looked at the picture she'd stuck on the wall, of a mother orangutan holding her baby. The baby was newborn—bald, with an irresistible, imploring face. The mother's body was large and calm; her arms enfolded the baby, and her face held pure love. When Bernie was a boy, Liddie had loved his singing. He opened his mouth wide, and sweetness poured out. That boy was still in him. He'd be seventeen years old in November. Within thirty days of his eighteenth birthday, he would need to register for the draft. That was bad enough. But to imagine him in Vietnam, or to imagine Noah . . .

Politicians were always saying they'd fight for you, that they'd never stop fighting for you. But she didn't want them fighting for her; there was too much fighting already. War had become the most solemn and momentous thing people could imagine. What if the most momentous thing was a baby orangutan in its mother's arms?

Bernie would not be sent to Vietnam because he'd go to college, but this afternoon Noah had been at their house and she'd ended up in the kitchen with him alone while Bernie went upstairs to the bathroom. Noah told her he was thinking about signing up next year. She was rooting around in the refrigerator, wondering what to thaw for dinner, and his words stopped her dead in her tracks. She came over to where he was leaning against the cupboards, held both his shoulders, and said, "Please tell me what you just said was idle chatter."

"It wasn't," he said.

She looked into his face. "You must know after all these years that I think of you almost like a son. You're young, and you think you'll live forever. But you could die."

He met her eyes. "I know that."

"If something happened to you, your mother would never get over it." She paused. "Neither would I."

"But nothing's going to happen to me. I'm thinking of the Air Force, which isn't like the Army."

"You mean you don't have to see the people you kill."

He winced. "My father was in the Air Force."

"But it wasn't Vietnam."

"Maybe they wouldn't send me there."

"They're sending everyone they can get their hands on. And they're lying to people, trying to pretend this is an honorable war. It's not. Is money the issue? If so, Harry and I will do whatever we can to help you pay for college. We have two incomes now."

"I wouldn't feel right taking your money."

"What better use could there possibly be for it?"

Bernie returned, and Noah excused himself as soon as he could. "Thanks, Mrs. Furber."

She waited a day and called Noah's mother, and they sat in Lorinda's kitchen on a school-day morning when Lorinda had planned to work at home. Noah's mother said, "That boy thinks this is what his father would want. He was hardly old enough to know his father. Honest to God, I'd rather see my son locked up than sent over there."

"I talked to Noah over at our house. I told him Harry and I could help with college expenses if that would keep him out of the Air Force. I wanted you to know if it makes a difference."

"I couldn't allow him to take your money. Thank you. Nothing's going to change his mind anyway."

"There are draft counselors he could talk to."

"He wouldn't talk to them."

"Can't you refuse to sign a paper or something?"

"Once he's eighteen, it's out of my hands." She poured more coffee. "Maybe it's the only way he can get away. Live his own life. He might think that fighting for your country is a good-enough reason."

Liddie stared at her hands. And then glanced at the hands across the table from her. Lorinda's were delicate and shapely, the nails polished a light pink like the inside of a seashell, her fingers folded together. "What do you mean 'get away'?"

"He thinks it's his job to take care of me. He needs his own life."

"He's a sweet young man. You've been a great mother to him."

Lorinda made a noncommittal noise and stopped a moment. "I need to ask you . . . Is your son a homosexual?"

Liddie looked at her, stunned. "He never said that he is. Why? And what if he was?"

"If he was, I would not countenance it. No, I would not countenance it. Nor would my pastor. Nor would my husband if he were alive. My Noah has enough to deal with, without that on top of it. He is a God-fearing young man."

"I can see that. He's as good a young man as there is, and I wouldn't want any harm to come to him, not from any direction. But no harm will ever come to him from my son." Inside, she was shaking with anger. All this time, she'd thought she wanted to know Noah's mother better. She told her that she had work to do and left soon after.

That night, she dreamed of a vast airplane hangar, the size of two football fields. Inside, the building was shaped like an airplane wing, tapering down to a flat wrinkle of metal so narrow that when she walked out to the very edges, there wasn't space to breathe. The inside was white, scary white, and when she woke up, she could imagine Noah sitting in the cockpit of a fighter jet, its belly pregnant with bombs.

50

FALL 1966

Love is a sacrament that should be taken kneeling, Bernie wrote in a notebook, and then he wrote it again. And again, until the page was full. He didn't know exactly what Oscar Wilde meant, but once words were freed from the prison of their inventors, they could mean anything you wanted them to.

Noah called. "My mom and sister went to Boston. My aunt's in the hospital. Want to come over, spend the night?"

"Sure," said Bernie. It was homecoming weekend, and the last thing he wanted to do was go to the game and watch Lily Alessandrini flounce around and get crowned homecoming queen.

Noah suggested they do a ten-mile run—they were in training for a statewide cross-country meet—and Bernie bicycled over after raiding his parents' liquor cabinet. He'd come up with a bottle of tonic and a half bottle of gin for later.

"Hey," said Bernie, poking his head in Noah's kitchen door.

"Hey," he heard from inside.

The leaves were past their height, with just the oaks still clinging to the branches, bronze against dark-green spruces as they ran down the peninsula toward Barrow's Point. The two of them were nearly the same height, but Noah's stride, unlike Bernie's, looked close to effortless. He wore old running shorts and a navy-blue nylon shirt several times too large that flapped when he ran.

"How's your aunt?"

"Looks like she's not going to get better. It's kidney cancer."

"Is your mom close to her?"

"Yeah."

Noah speeded up. He was nearly a quarter mile ahead by the time they came to the point of land that looked out in the direction of Portugal. Bernie stopped and stood, breathing hard as the wind blew from the northeast and chopped up the navy-blue water. Far out was a schooner with its sails up.

"Leaf peepers," said Bernie, still panting. "Look at them pretending to be all nineteenth century."

Noah laughed. "Don't tell me you wouldn't want to be on that boat."

"Course I would. Wouldn't you?"

"Water's not my medium, man. You know that."

"I thought it was just swimming you hated."

"Yeah, and what happens when the boat goes down? You have to swim."

"A sadist tried to teach me swimming when we still lived in Michigan," said Bernie. "My mother wanted me to learn before I could drown somewhere, so she sent me to the YMCA. I was so scared, my teeth chattered."

"Aww, I can just see your skinny little concave chest. Holding yourself with your arms."

"Exactly. And this guy just threw us in, one by one, and watched us sputter. When we went under, he rescued us if he felt like it. It took him a while to rescue me, and he almost had to give me artificial respiration."

"You're exaggerating."

"No, really."

"So how come you like to swim?"

"I don't know. I got over it."

"I didn't. My grandfather had similar ideas." Noah took off running again, and soon was far ahead. He was already feeding the dogs by the time Bernie got back.

He looked at Bernie accusingly.

"What? I'm faster than I was."

"I bet you still weigh ten pounds more than me."

"It's all muscle."

"Right."

A Jack Russell terrier leapt in the air like a helicopter. "Who's this little guy?" asked Bernie, holding out his hand.

"Sparky. Belongs to the head of the volunteer fire department. He and his wife went to Bermuda. And over here, this girl is on antibiotics. She's got an infected paw."

"Her bandage is dirty," said Bernie.

"And you're going to hold her while I change it."

"What's her name?"

"Dolly."

"Come on, Dolly, we're going to have a cuddle." Bernie sat down on a wooden crate and rubbed her behind the ears. "Her lips are all droopy."

"That's what English bulldogs look like. They're cute when they're puppies. Pick her up and hold her with her tummy out. Stick out your foot, Dolly."

"She's drooling on me."

Noah took off the old bandage and threw it in a bucket, then wrapped her foot with new gauze, securing it with adhesive tape. "Hold her a minute more. I've got her pill." He pried open her mouth and shoved it in back and held her mouth shut. She swallowed.

"You'd be a great vet."

"Don't."

"What?"

"I'm tired of you telling me I could do this, I could do that. Your mom already talked to me. She's against the Air Force, and so is my mom, but I've thought it through. I might go into politics someday, and it's good if you've served. Besides, if I sign up, I won't get drafted."

"You don't want to go into politics. And they can't draft you in college."

"How many times do I frigging need to tell you? My mom

doesn't have any money. After four years, they'll pay for college. No debt. I can do whatever I want."

"Four years is forever. They'll fuck you up. And you really want to be part of that—those lies and patriotic crap? You're way too smart for that."

"Did it ever occur to you that I might know what I'm doing? Did you ever consider that the wind at your back is blowing the other way for me? Think about it."

"I am. Damn. Get off, Dolly." Bernie pushed the dog away.

"You're not. You've got all the answers."

"It's called trying to be your friend."

"Friends respect each other."

"I respect you, damn it."

"No." Noah looked straight at him. "You really don't."

Bernie turned and pushed out of the gate and jumped onto his bike. He pedaled down the road, his left eye crying in the wind, his right eye dry. He rode for a couple of miles against a headwind before he began to hear Noah's words. He slowed down, stopped, and straddled his bike, then got off and sat on a stone wall looking out over a field. A crow landed on a fence post a couple of feet away, and Bernie's eyes met two beady, black, wild eyes.

He wanted to believe the world was open to him and Noah in the same way. But, no, it was not. It might have been true back at the beginning of the world, before people messed it up, before whips were used on humans, before white crowds stood grinning at a black man hanging from a tree, but that stuff happened, and it didn't just erase itself. You couldn't see history, you couldn't taste it or smell it, but it was lodged like a snake under a house. It was still happening, the same old snake coming up into the house, through different holes. It wasn't over, not for his friend and not for him. He wasn't mad at Noah, just at himself. It was stupid and insulting to pretend the two of them had the same future in front of them when they didn't have the same past behind them. What would it be like if he had a different history inside him, if his great-great-great-grandfather had been tied to a post and whipped senseless? Or if that man's wife had been raped again and again, lost five out of six of her children to slavery, and wept at night until she was in her grave? It would change the way he felt about the world, make him wonder if he could trust anything.

It was nearly dark, and he got back on his bike and started for home, then changed his mind and headed back to Noah's. The fields had turned a deep gray, the birds flying into the shadows to roost. By the time he returned, Noah was taking a shower. Bernie waited, and then he went into the bathroom and sat on the closed toilet seat. "I'm here," he said.

The water ran awhile longer and stopped. Noah stepped out and grabbed a towel.

"Look, I'm sorry," said Bernie. His head was full to bursting, and the words spilled onto the linoleum floor, spangled the walls, flew toward the steamy window. "I wouldn't be going on about what you should do if I didn't care. You're a better person than I am, and it would be too horrible if you died." He stopped to gather himself. "I don't mean I just care about you, I mean I love you, man. And you're right, I don't know what's best. So I'm going to shut up about it."

The water condensing on the mirror ran down slowly, one drop crawling into another. There was silence for a moment. Noah dried off one leg, then the other, wrapped the towel around himself, leaned on the sink. "Yeah, okay. No sweat."

Later, Bernie made gin and tonics and they sat on the couch and watched TV. He got up to go to the bathroom, and when he came back, he sat down closer than he meant to. Noah moved over. "What are you doing?"

"I'm just drunk."

"You're not, like, coming on to me, are you?"

Bernie's head clouded. "You're joking, right?"

"No," said Noah. "I'm not, and I'm also not that kind of guy."

"I know that. . . . What? You thought *I* was?"

"Not really." Which could mean maybe yes.

"Well, I'm not," said Bernie. "You thought I was?"

"For a minute, yeah."

"Well, I just told you. I'm not, for fuck sake."

"You don't have to get all pissed off. I get it." He paused. "My mom asked me the other day if you were a homo. I told her you weren't."

"What if I was?"

"You couldn't come here anymore."

Bernie sank back into the couch. He was pretty sure his friend still wasn't convinced. They slept in Noah's room that night, Noah in his bed, Bernie on the floor in a sleeping bag. Into the darkness, Noah said, "I'm glad you're not, you know, one of them. . . ."

"Why?"

"I don't know. I'd be . . ."

"Like, on guard?"

"Yeah. It's not like there's that much wrong with it, I guess. It's just kind of—I don't know. Perverted."

"Dennis thinks I'm one," said Bernie.

"Dennis calls me *princess,* too. Probably 'cause I don't go out with anyone."

"He's an animal."

"I never told you. Once I called Wendy Tuttle and asked her to go to the movies. She said yes, and then she called me back and said no."

"You think she asked her parents?"

"Probably. I didn't like her that much anyway."

"Still."

"Yeah."

They were quiet again until Bernie said, "Do you remember the museum we made a long time ago? With the dead robin?"

"Yeah. And remember you said it was going to have tunnels and underground rooms like the Lost City of Atlantic?"

"Did I?" Bernie laughed. "I was such a little dipshit know-it-all."

"And you're not now?"

Bernie lay awake, not moving, making his breath deep and even. He stared into the dark at a small patch of moonlight shining through the window and reflecting off the limbs of a tree onto the ceiling. It was like being underwater, the way when you open your eyes you can sometimes see rays of sun playing under the surface.

He'd known from the moment his mother explained to him what *weird* meant that it fit, what they called him in school. But being weird was different from being queer. You might get beat up for being weird, but you might get killed for being queer. He wondered if freezing his balls with ice cubes would make him normal. He was still a little drunk. Maybe he should ask Stacy out and see how it felt to kiss someone. But the thought grossed him out.

He heard Noah's breathing change, like a diver into the deep. He could barely see the outline of his body under the blankets, curled into a cocoon of himself. He wished he hadn't said what he had about loving him. It just burst out of him.

The moon disappeared behind a cloud, and he remembered a line from a poem he'd learned in first grade: *Blink went the moon and black went the sky.* Once upon a time, he thought that was the cleverest thing he'd ever heard. He'd imagined the moon's big eye blinking and everything around him going black. Like now.

51

At fourteen, Eva still hadn't gotten her period. It made her wonder if there was something wrong with her—like maybe she was screwed up not just in her mind but in her body. She didn't talk about it, not with her mother or anyone else.

Starting that fall, she became the accompanist for the school chorus, a ragtag group of sopranos and altos and a smattering of pimply basses and tenors. The director was Mr. Sidwick, a man with a flop of brown hair over one eye and a penchant for circus-colored ties and baggy pants. Eva nearly refused his offer to take the job, but she thought that watching him flail in front of the chorus three periods a week might be a welcome change from study hall, where she was seated in front of horrible Robert Hathaway, who enjoyed poking his pencil into the small of her back. She was tired of swatting him away, annoyed that the teacher in charge refused to change her seat, and optimistic enough to think that she might learn something about conducting. Which she soon realized she wouldn't.

The music Mr. Sidwick chose was stupid. The piano accompaniments were punctuated with fake bells in the treble clef and thunderous bass notes for storms at sea. The chorus was preparing for a Christmas concert, only weeks away. They practiced Monday, Wednesday, and Friday, fifth period. Mr. Sidwick's main concern was the soprano section. Eva pounded out their notes, trying to keep them on pitch, but the higher they went, the flatter they got. As the days went by and nothing improved, Mr. Sidwick began yelling at them. "Breathe!

Use your diaphragm! Support, support! You sound like scared rabbits. How will you feel, standing up in front of your parents and classmates sounding like that?" He looked at one soprano with particular distaste. "It's you, isn't it, Sandy, bringing everyone down. Let me hear you sing those four measures by yourself."

Sandy began to cry.

The bell rang.

One Friday, Mr. Sidwick asked Eva to stay after school and go over a few sections of the music with him. She didn't want to, but after the last period, she got her books and coat out of her locker and headed toward the music room. The school had emptied out fast for the weekend, and the halls were littered with gum wrappers, rumpled math homework, a stray sneaker. Somewhere in the building, a vacuum cleaner whined and a metal locker opened and banged shut, but otherwise the blue walls echoed with the quiet desolation of a hard-used building.

The music room looked similarly godforsaken, with chairs strewn here and there, instrument cases bulging with horns and violins that had been pushed to their limits by students who didn't know how to play them. Eva imagined the instruments in their hard cases, relieved that the weekend had come and they wouldn't have to make horrible noises for the next two days.

In the midst of the wreckage sat Mr. Sidwick on a desk by the piano, writing something in his spiral-bound notebook. He looked up and beamed when he saw her.

He handed her the piano accompaniments and indicated the piano bench. She sat down, and he sat beside her. He smelled of . . . what? Misery of some sort. Cabbage. Some gaseous vegetable. And meat around the edges. Pork. He wasn't a fat man but fleshy, with plump earlobes.

She stood back up.

"No, no, sit down, I want to go over these pieces with you. First, do you have any questions about any of them?"

She shook her head and sat back down again.

"I'm thinking of dropping 'How I Love Mistletoe.' What do you think?"

"Yeah, it sounds pretty bad."

"They'd never get it in time, anyway. Let's look at 'All Through the Night.'" He turned to the last page. "When you play this page, bang out the bass notes. The boys haven't got a clue about their notes."

"Okay."

"And let me hear you play the beginning of 'Angels Spread Your Wings.'"

She played the first two pages.

"Yes," he said, "a bit more volume just before the chorus comes in . . . This music is pretty easy for you, isn't it?"

"I guess."

"Before we go on to the other number, would you mind humoring me and playing something you're working on? I'd just like to hear you play."

She didn't know why she needed to do that. But she began the Bach Fugue in D Major from *The Well-Tempered Clavier*, which she'd finished memorizing last week. She loved the quick, light running notes, the decisiveness of the dotted notes, and she felt the music taking her away from Mr. Sidwick, from this shabby room. But then she smelled him near her and stopped. "That's all I remember," she said. She inched away on the piano bench.

"Bach, right?"

"Yes."

"You like Bach?"

She nodded. There was a lump forming in her throat, something indigestible.

"Lovely," he said. "Just beautiful. You're the best accompanist I've ever had. I want you to know that. A good accompanist anticipates the needs of the conductor, and I feel you understand everything I'm trying to do. I admire your musicianship, but it's more than musicianship." He paused to collect his thoughts. "I don't know if anyone has ever told you this, but you're a lovely girl." She looked away, out toward the room and its litter of tubas and trombones. She was wearing a white cotton blouse. She felt something pulling at it and then his hands underneath. He undid a button, two buttons to give his hand more room, examining the buttons in a curious way before undoing them. Little white pearl buttons.

He pinched her nipple through her bra. And then her other nipple, and his hand came upward toward her throat. She looked down, she couldn't help herself, and she saw the dark hair on each finger up near her chin where there shouldn't be a hand. She tried to twist away. With his free hand, he laid her hand against his crotch, to a damp lump there. She got up quickly, ripping the other buttons from her blouse as she freed herself, and stood at a distance from him.

"You made me forget myself," he said, chuckling good-naturedly. He said it as though she should be honored. "What's happened will just be between the two of us. Yes? Our own little secret?"

She gathered her books and coat and walked out of the room. Like a thief, she closed the door quietly behind her as she left, then ran from the building. She stood outside in the cold air, gasping, feeling the bile rise in her throat. Her hands shook, then her knees. It was quarter past four, twilight. She gulped up the darkness, glad of it, and fled under the cover of some low-hanging spruce trees, dropped her bag of books on the ground, and hugged her arms around her chest where he'd touched her. Her breath came in spasms.

It was two miles home, and she ran until she could run no more, then walked, ripping off her hat with the heat of her running.

At home, she went straight to her room. She turned on her transistor radio and tried to blot it out, but the evidence was there. She took off the blouse with its pearl buttons and rolled it up and stuffed it in a paper bag. And stuffed in her bra and underwear, her skirt and her socks. She would never wear any of these things again. And the clip holding her hair back. She wanted to throw away her shoes, her coat, her winter hat, her gloves—everything—but there would be questions.

She stood in the shower with the water pouring over her. She closed her eyes, to not see herself. She fumbled for the soap blindly, began with her feet and worked her way up and then worked her way back down again, scrubbing, retching, her eyes tightly closed all the way up, all the way down. Then her hair, scouring and scrubbing some more. He'd touched it. She stuck her face right inside the shower, tried to breathe through the water.

What she'd done to make it happen:

1. She met him after school when she didn't want to.
2. She ignored how strange the room felt.
3. She ignored how his smile didn't feel right.
4. She sat on the piano bench. She stood up when he got too close. She sat down again when he told her to.
5. She played Bach when he asked her to.
6. She was agreeable. She was polite.
7. She switched herself off, switched herself off the way you turn out a light. Somehow it felt important not to hurt his feelings, because he was excited, there was something urgent in him and his earlobes were pink and it was like the tide rising over the sand and the pebbles and the rocks, a tide that can't be denied, the way it flows onto the land with a mind of its own, then pours forward with no containment, the water a force, insisting, insinuating its fingers around and over and through. It felt important not to offend, to pretend it was all still normal, even the pinch of his fingers through her bra, even that hand with its hairy fingers coming obscenely out the top of her blouse and appearing at her throat. But then suddenly nothing was normal. The damp bulge in his pants, his hand over hers, pinning her to that revolting lump.
8. She didn't yell.
9. She was polite. She was agreeable.
10. She picked up her things and closed the door quietly behind her.

She turned off the shower and rubbed her hair with a towel and hurried back to her room and dressed in sweatpants and a sweatshirt.

She didn't want Bernie or her mother or father seeing her. She wouldn't talk about this afternoon. Not ever. Not ever not ever not ever not ever ever ever. So disgusting. *It.*

She crept out of her room and called Fred from the top of the stairs. He was old now and didn't like climbing to the second floor. He came to the bottom of the steps and looked up at her. "Come, Fred." She was crying now. "Come on, Fred." She patted the side of her knee. He put one foot on the bottom step. "Come on, you can do it." And another foot on the next step and hoisted himself up, one step at a time. She coaxed him into her room. She shut the door, and he groaned when his old joints settled down onto the floor. He didn't smell sweet the way he once had as a puppy, when he was fresh with the outdoors. His fur was matted now, his breath was the breath of a bony old man, and she loved him heart and soul. She laid her head on his old, smelly self and put her arm around his neck.

She was sick on Monday, went to school Tuesday, and was sick again on Wednesday. That night, she told her mother she was not going to play in the school concert.

"What do you mean?"

"I don't want to."

"What sort of reason is that?"

"I don't like the teacher."

"Was he mean to you?"

"I just don't like him."

Her mother was sitting at the kitchen table, writing out a shopping list. She put down her pencil and looked at Eva. "What's the real reason?"

Not even her mother. She would never. *Not ever ever ever.* "I told you, I don't like him."

"There are many times when I've played in an orchestra without liking the conductor. You've made a commitment. The concert is a week away. It's not fair to Mr. Sidwick. Not fair to the chorus."

"I don't care."

"You need to honor your commitment."

"I'm not doing it."

"Did something happen with one of the kids?"

She shook her head. *Not ever not ever not ever not ever ever ever.* "Mom, can you call him and tell him I'm not going to do it? Please, Mommy. Tell him I can't. I've sprained my wrist."

"I'm not going to lie for you."

"Can't you just call and tell him?"

"That's your job."

"Please."

"You already know the music. Just play the concert and drop out afterward. Then there'll be no bad feelings."

"There will be. Mine."

"Sometimes other people's feelings also matter."

"I think I know that."

"You'd tell me if there was something else?"

"I just don't like him, that's all."

Back upstairs, she lay on her bed. She'd go to school tomorrow and ask Sandy, the soprano who brought the whole section down, to tell Mr. Sidwick she wasn't the accompanist anymore. She'd tell her to say, *Eva quit and she's not coming back.*

And next time she'd listen to Bernie. When he first found out she was going to be the accompanist for the chorus, he said, "Mr. Sidwick? That guy's a weirdo."

Eva never knew when Margreete would come. Sometimes she drifted in and right out again, and sometimes she climbed into bed, took up all the space, and left halfway through the night.

She heard the scuffling sound of her grandmother's slippers, the uneven steps from her sore knee, saw the outline of her white night-gown moving into the room, heard her palms feeling her way along the wall and patting her way up toward the pillow. Eva pulled back the covers and moved over to make room for her. The bed sagged when her grandmother got in, and she sighed a deep sigh, like someone arriving home after a long day.

"Are you okay, Grandma?"

"Why wouldn't I be?"

Eva held her grandmother's hand and stroked it. Her hand was light, her breath shallow as though her tank of air had shrunk.

"What's your name?" Margreete asked.

"Eva."

"What's your name?"

"Eva."

"What's your name?"

"Grandma, stop."

There was a long silence, which Eva broke. "Something bad happened at school, Grandma. You won't tell anyone, will you?"

"You go to school?"

"I'm fourteen years old."

"I'm seventeen."

Eva laughed. "No, you're not."

"I'm not good with math."

"Grandma," Eva whispered, "something bad happened to me at school. Don't tell anyone, okay?"

"Why not?"

"It would make too big a ruckus. . . . My music teacher put his hands up under my blouse and pinched my nipples and then he made me put my hand between his legs."

"You don't want to do that."

"I didn't. I didn't want to."

"No, you don't want to do that. . . . What did he do again?"

"I don't want to say it again. I quit the chorus."

"Well, you're a good girl."

"Did anything like that ever happen to you?"

"All the time."

"Did it? I'm asking."

"Yes, it happens all the time."

"I wish you could talk."

"I am."

"It's getting worse, your brain, isn't it?"

"I guess it is. I ruined everything."

"You didn't, Grandma."

"I put all the food in my purse when she isn't looking."

"Don't do that."

Margreete pushed back the covers and started to get out of bed.

"Wait. You didn't ruin everything. Do you understand?" Eva kissed her cheek.

Margreete settled back down in bed. "You're my best friend," she said.

"What's my name?" Eva asked.

"Silly, you're my best friend. Your name is . . . wait, it's Frances. Tonight we're going on a trip together, remember? Just the two of us."

"Where are we going?"

"The animal place."

"Which animal place?"

"Where you get the animals."

"Like a new cat?"

"To get a new husband. The old ones died."

"Grandma? I've got a test tomorrow. I have to go to sleep now. Can you go sleep in your own bed?"

"This is my bed."

"I can take you to your bed."

"I know where my bed is," she said. "I can find it myself." She pulled back the covers once more and got out.

"Sweet dreams, okay?"

She shuffled out of the room and headed toward her own room. Eva heard her sigh when she lowered her body onto her mattress, as though she'd come home.

Afterward, they pieced it together.

52

Margreete made her way down the stairs, turned on all the lights in the kitchen. She was wearing her bed socks. Scratchy wool. Her grandmother Crowe came into her head. Her grandmother wore scratchy things. And black, everything black after her husband died. A black glossy dress so old it turned dark purple like a crow's feathers. Every Christmas, Grandmother Crowe stuffed dates with nuts and rolled them in sugar. Little babies in blankets. Her grandmother had rough hands. A fierce chin. Long white hairs coming out of a mole next to her nose.

She turned the doorknob in the kitchen, and the door didn't open. She rattled and pulled at it. She knew that people went in and out of this door. She herself had been known to do so.

She couldn't grab hold of what . . . It was time. She pulled back her sleeve to find the, the, the hand clock.

She turned on more lights, wandering here and there. The black pocketbook was on a chair beside the piano. She picked up the purse and brought it to the kitchen and set it down on the floor. The handles stuck up like rabbit ears.

She tried to open the door. She rattled and pulled at it. She had seen people go in and out of this door. She herself had been known to do so. There was a puzzle to it. A puzzle to it.

She turned the purse upside down, and the contents spilled out across the floor. She bent down and opened the thing for holding money. Inside was a picture of an unsmiling woman. It wasn't

Grandmother Crowe, but it was someone familiar enough. Not herself but like her own breath.

Over by the woodstove, she found the keys.

Grandfather Crowe had his keys on a big iron ring. He used them to open the door of his printing shop. Inside his oak desk, in a secret drawer, he had a key for the safe where he kept his money. The desk had two sides to it, one where he sat and the other where his partner sat. They sat all day looking at each other. You'd think that would have driven them crazy. He had a time thing on a chain, and every now and then he took it out and looked at it and put it back in his pocket again. When he stood and talked to his workers, his toes pointed out and he rocked from his toes to his heels as though he was important.

She tried to fit the key in the keyhole, but it didn't go in. There was a puzzle to it. She rattled and pulled at the door. She knew that people went in and out of this door. She herself had been known to do so. She tried another key, and this one went into the hole. She turned it and the door opened.

The dog was beside her now. He was old, and he wanted to go outside. She put on Irving's lumberman jacket with the black-and-red plaid and the sleeves that were too long for her. In the pocket, she found her hat, and she put that on her head. And her rubber boots.

She stepped out onto the porch and smelled the air. It smelled cold, of dry leaves and the sea. A sliver of a moon hung in the sky like the edge of a coin.

She remembered one night in early spring, swinging on the swing that Irving had hung in the elm tree for the children. The children were in bed, and the two of them went outside and she sat on the swing and he pushed her and she tipped back to pump herself into the high air and she saw a sliver of starry sun like this one and she thought she had never been so happy as she was when his broad hands were on her back, pushing her into the sweet night air.

She took a step down off the porch, slowly, until her eyes grew used to the darkness, then another step until she was on bare ground. The dog was beside her. His face white with age. He whined a little, as though he was asking a question. She patted his head. It was bony, with a point at the top. In the dark, she could see his white fur but not the dark spots on his body, so he looked like a dog made of lace, part of him there and part of him not there. Her mother used to make lace doilies that she put on the back of the chair where her father rested his head at night.

When she was still young, she went with her mother to Washington, D.C. They wore white. White for suffragettes. There was a big march. Women couldn't vote. "A fine state of affairs," her mother said. She wasn't going to have it. President Woodrow Wilson was going to be inaugurated the next day. They'd show him they weren't quiet little ladies without a brain in their heads. She and her mother ate bread and butter sandwiches and slept in a seat on the train, leaning against one another, drooling on each other's shoulders.

She set off down the field, smelling her way toward the sea, feeling her way with her boots. They were cumbersome, clumping through the grass, and she took off one and dropped it, walked a little farther and took off the other one. She could feel the ground through her socks. The sliver of moon was hanging over the place where there was no land, only water. And there was one star next to the moon and one light out in the ocean, shining far out in the darkness. Lola's. She took off the wool hat to feel the coldness on her head. After she dropped it, the dog picked it up and carried it in his mouth, and then he dropped it, too.

The wind was cold in the trees, blowing up the field from the sea. A good cold. She smelled the dog next to her, like old boiled rags. Like cooked carrots, some sweetness mixed with the old-dog smell.

She wanted to feel the fresh air on her, and she took off Irving's lumberman jacket and dropped it at her feet. She stood a minute on the wool, warming her feet. She remembered Irving wearing the jacket in the winter, with his large, chapped hands falling out of the sleeves. He never could remember to put anything on his hands. He was a city boy, not a lumberjack kind of man, but he liked thinking he was an outdoorsy man once he moved to Maine. She remembered once in a boat with him. This was after the children were gone. It was a night like this, with the sound of the water under them, lapping gently against the canoe and the sound of their paddles dipping into the black water. They talked about whether they would ever see each other again once they left the earth. He said no. Once they were gone, they were gone. She said, yes, they would. She couldn't remember where the canoe was floating. Maybe in a pond. Maybe in the harbor.

She continued down the hill with the dog in front of her, and now she couldn't remember where she was or where she was going or where she had come from or how to get back. For a moment she was frightened, but the dog knew where he was going, and she followed him down the hill, just keeping an eye on the white tip of his tail. The elastic was going on her underpants, and they slid down from her waist and down her hips, and she stopped and stepped out of each leg hole and left them there on the grass and continued on, keeping an eye on the bobbing white tail.

When they reached the shore, the water lapped at the rocks. Where the waves broke, the land turned to ragged white lace. The rocks were cold and the seaweed slippery under her wool socks. It was either heading toward high tide or heading toward low tide, in the middle. She squatted down, looked out and up, and felt the large sky and ocean and the icy cold on her feet. She tried to pull her nightgown down and wrap up her feet the way she'd wrapped them in her nightgown as a girl when she'd sat at the top of the stairs, listening to her parents talking. Her heart thumped then, and it thumped now. Some fear went through her, and she crouched inside it. She didn't know how she'd gotten here beside the water. The moon was far away, heartless and untouchable, casting only enough light to see the outline of things.

She closed her eyes and smelled the ocean. When she opened them, she saw near her, half hidden in the bushes, an old aluminum rowboat with stubby oars. She pulled it out of the bushes, struggled with it, and managed to turn it over with a bang. She put the oars in the boat and climbed in and sat down on the seat in the bow. It teetered on the rocks. There was a tarpaulin jumbled up behind her, and she wrapped herself in it. The dog climbed in and sat on the seat beside her. The boat listed to one side on the shore rocks.

The thought disappeared every time she tried to pursue it, like a dream running before her. She pulled the tarpaulin closer around herself and the dog. Her shivering stopped, and she looked out on the dark water to the single light in the distance. Lola's.

When she was a girl, the summer nights were alive with fireflies. Through the damp grass, she chased after their cool green lights and captured them in bottles until their light was bright enough to see by. The poor things. The poor things.

The water lapped, cupping under the rocks with a hollow sound, the way a hand cups around a baby's head. She thought of her first baby, the feel of her hand around that head. Her labor began on a night like this; the baby was born at high tide. She thought of the effort of pushing that baby into the world, how there was no turning back once it all started.

She felt her brain clearing, the way it sometimes did. Irving told her that babies know more about the deep secrets than the rest of us. Our life is spent in the great unlearning, he said. She still remembered how he'd said it. The Great Unlearning. The dog bumped his nose under her chin. His nose was wet and smooth, and his breath smelled of dog food and deep sleep.

She got out of the boat and left the old dog sitting in the bow. She hung on to the painter and pulled the boat toward the water. It was not far, but the labor was hard.

Her feet were wet now, and she dragged the boat steadily, inch by inch, away from shore. As she pulled, she felt something change as the bottom left land and became waterborne, like a bird going from earth to air. She climbed back into the boat and shoved the boat free with the oars.

The wind was offshore, and it carried the little boat sloshing out toward that single light. She sat tall in her nightgown next to the dog. She looked into his white face, and his name came to her. "Fred," she said. The tip of his tail moved. She stroked his neck and wrapped the tarpaulin around their shivering. "Two peas in a pod," she said.

She remembered her mother at the march, all in white, breathing determination, with the other women around them in white, and at the head of the march was a woman dressed in white, riding on a white horse. The determination was on them like a great mantle. Most of the people lining the streets were men. Some cried out in support, but more of them jeered and spat and threw bits of street garbage, and her mother was hit by a stone on the back of her head and blood flowed down and she asked her daughter to stanch the wound by pressing her lace handkerchief over it. Her mother kept marching with the blood still seeping down the back of her head. Nothing was going to stop her. A sea of white, and her mother with red streaming down.

A white whale rising from a milky fog. Where had she seen this? She moved to the middle seat and rowed with the oars for a while, heading toward that lone light. The dog whined a little. Her wool socks were wet up to her ankles. She didn't remember her feet standing in water when she got into the boat. She couldn't feel her toes now.

Somewhere over the rainbow . . . Her voice cracked, as though she were singing through icicles. She had once dreamed of singing onstage. There would be rainbow-colored lights playing over her hair and she would belt this song out like nobody's business.

The water was above her ankles now, and she went back to the oars and pulled on them and heard the slop of sea against the bow. It was heavy work with all the water in the boat. She looked over her shoulder, and the light in the distance didn't seem any closer than before. She had an appointment at Lola's. A perm. But then she wondered if it might be the sun peeking over the horizon. She looked again and the light was still in the same place, not rising into the sky. She thought of all the living things waiting for the sun. The grasshoppers and rabbits, the woodpeckers with their crazy hammering, the running things and flying things, the people that wrecked things on earth, the people who didn't wreck things, the kids running around the fields, yelling with happiness. The dog climbed off his seat in the bow and sloshed through the water and pushed his nose up hard under her arm, and the oar on that side jumped out of the oarlock and fell into the ocean and floated away.

She pulled on the other oar, and the light in the distance was in front of them, then behind them, in front, behind, around and around.

She remembered the owl that called in the deep night of her childhood; she remembered the shadowy green light of the fireflies. She rowed toward the light on the horizon, round and round. The sliver of moon was far away and beautiful and coldly indifferent.

She turned to the dog. She'd forgotten his name and she forgot what she wanted to say to him. She stopped paddling, but it didn't come to her.

The water was partway up to her knees now. She pulled her nightgown up and sat on it so it wouldn't get wet. She'd always loved the smell of the sea, loved the sound of it sloshing against the boat. It was a calm night, the seabirds sleeping. She stopped rowing and listened to the huge stillness.

When the boat filled and turned over, she fought against the salt water and tried to grab the slippery keel in the dark. She had hold of it and then she lost it, and it was just her and the old dog and the ocean beneath them. She swam a few strokes and stopped. She moved her hands and legs to keep from sinking and saw again that light in the distance, far away. She struggled some more and grew tired. Her teeth chattered and her head felt drowsy. The old dog swam in circles around her. It seemed to her, before she went under, that he had made an effort to keep her afloat.

53

Fred was missing, and no one could find their grandmother. The door was wide open, the keys on the floor. Bernie was allowed to go searching with her parents, but Gretchen was told to stay with Eva. When they returned, her father said they'd found her grandmother's mittens by the back door. One black rubber boot lay on the grass, then another. Her red hat with the white pompom farther on. Then Irving's red-and-black jacket that was too big for her. Her underpants down the hill.

The tide was coming in, and her father said there was a groove in the sand that looked like a boat had been dragged into the water. The old rowboat was missing, the one her mother had always said not to go near.

Her father called the police, and Randall, the policeman, came to investigate. He walked down to the shore and climbed back up the hill with his head bowed. That morning, the school bus came down the hill and stood in front of the house waiting for them and tooting its horn and then went on without them.

They found the purse dumped out on the kitchen floor. It seemed that Fred had gone with her grandmother. Gretchen could picture him on the rowboat seat, looking out, his paws together in front of him. He'd always liked boats.

Gretchen went upstairs with her brother and sister. Bernie said when fishermen drown in cold water, sometimes it takes three weeks for their bodies to come to the surface. Sometimes their bodies are never found. They get eaten by sea creatures. Eva told him to shut up. And, besides, no one knew for sure that Grandma had drowned. Bernie said where else would she be if the rowboat was missing, and Eva went into her room, bending over her feet, she was crying so hard.

Gretchen asked Bernie if she could come sit next to him and he said yes, the first time he'd said yes in a long time, and they went up the next set of stairs to his room and Gretchen sat on his rumpled bed and he talked about all the good things about their grandmother, about how she sang funny songs and how she was mixed up about everything except things that happened long ago. He told Gretchen he thought Grandma and Fred might be okay, maybe a lobsterman had rescued them. But Gretchen knew that wasn't true. The boat was too small. The ocean was too big. Her grandmother was too old, and Fred was just a dog who wouldn't know what to do.

That afternoon, Gretchen took her flashlight and crept into her grandmother's room. She opened the door to the closet and stood among the clothes and sniffed. She gathered a skirt toward her, and it came off the hanger into her hands. She balled it up like a baby, carried it into her grandmother's bed and held it tight, and lay her head down on the hollow place on the pillow where her grandmother's head had been.

54

Liddie's grief broke and gathered like waves: She never knew when the next would come and overtake her. She'd known her mother would die someday, but she was unprepared for the suddenness and the savagery of her grief. Like a beast from a black forest. She felt utterly alone, dimly aware of each of them in the house grieving separately, like cocoons welded to scattered twigs. She drank water but could not make anything else pass her lips, neither words nor food.

"Please, honey," said Harry, holding out a bowl of cereal. She closed her eyes.

On the fourth day, she woke. She ate a banana and climbed the stairs to her mother's room. Gretchen's shoes lay on the rug, and an odd smell came from the chair, where her mother's purse stood. She took it downstairs, opened it, and found part of a pork chop and something that looked like creamed corn. She dropped the whole thing in a trash bag, tied it closed, set it in the shed, and closed the door. She nearly threw up. She went back upstairs, made her mother's bed, and closed the closet door. She couldn't bear to see her mother's clothes.

That night, she went to say good night to Eva and found her all the way under the covers. She tried to pull the blankets away, but Eva held on tight.

"You'll feel better if you come out."

"No," came a muffled voice.

Liddie stroked the lump under the sheet and waited. Finally, she yanked the covers away. She took a corner of the sheet and dried

Eva's tears, gathered her into her arms. "Talk to me, honey." Finally, Eva told Liddie that her grandmother had come to her room the night she died and that she didn't want to sleep with her because she had a history test the next day. "If I hadn't asked her to leave, if I'd made her welcome, she wouldn't have died. . . . Don't shake your head. It's true." She cried as though her heart would break.

"It was nobody's fault, honey. And if it was, it was my fault for leaving the keys where she could find them. And someone else's fault for leaving oars near that leaky boat. But I'm telling you, it's nobody's fault."

"I could have prevented it."

"Don't you dare carry that around with you for the rest of your life. Do you hear me?" She held her by the shoulders and shook her gently. "Look at me."

Eva cried harder.

"In some part of her, your grandmother knew what she was doing. Did you hear what I just said?"

"But she didn't really."

"Yes, she did. If she hadn't taken the boat, she would have found another way. She'd been throwing away food. She wanted to go."

Eva was quiet a moment. "What do you think drowning is like?"

"There are better ways to die."

"I feel really bad for Fred, too."

"He was an old dog."

"That doesn't make it any better."

"No. No, it doesn't. In some ways it makes it worse."

They were quiet.

"When we were in the car driving to that recital, do you remember Grandma singing? And when I was messing up, she sang again in front of everyone? She didn't care."

"No, she didn't care what anybody thought. That was one of the great things about her." She rose to go. The wave was coming—she felt it gathering in her chest and throat. Liddie choked out a few words. "You loved her very much. And Fred, too." She kissed Eva good night, left the room quickly, and started down the stairs. Halfway down she leaned against the wall, bunched her sweater up, and stuffed part of it into her mouth while she bawled.

After a time she stopped, dropped her sweater on the stairs, and thought of the way she'd left Eva. She went back, knocked on her daughter's door, and sat down on her bed. "I left because I didn't want to upset you with my crying."

"It's okay, Mom."

"But if we cry alone and pretend everything's okay . . ." Her voice caught.

Eva smelled Pond's cold cream on her mother. She picked up her hand and rubbed her thumb over the back of it, turned it over and felt the calluses on her fingertips where the cello strings had toughened them.

"You asked me what drowning was like, and I didn't answer you," her mother said. "I can tell you.

"When I was about your age—I don't know where your grandmother was that day—we were on vacation on Lake Erie. I remember my father sitting on the shore with a friend. There was a high wind. I met a girl on the shore I'd never seen before. She asked me if I knew how to swim. I said yes, and we waded in.

"She swam out and I followed. I wasn't a strong swimmer, and the water was rough. I suddenly realized I couldn't touch bottom and panicked. My feet touched a rock, and a wave ripped me off and carried me out farther. The waves kept breaking over my head. I kept being pushed farther from shore. I was swallowing water; I couldn't breathe.

"I must have managed to call *help*. The girl pulled me back toward shore a few feet at a time until I could touch bottom. If she hadn't been there, I would have drowned.

"I don't believe it's a good way to die. But I think and hope and believe that Fred would have stayed with Grandma until the end."

They held each other and cried a little more, and then Liddie went downstairs. Harry was reading in the living room, and she sat near him and opened a book without looking at the pages.

"Are you okay?" he asked.

She squeezed his hand. "How could I be?" What more was there to say? She remembered the thick, wet air that day she'd nearly drowned, the way her bathing suit had clung to her body, how that stranger-girl had appeared out of nowhere, asking if she knew how to swim. The water lapped against her knees, then her hips and waist and chest. It was cold, and farther out, whitecaps roughed up the surface. She was so frightened, she gasped in water, and the waves broke over her again and again.

Her mother would not have slid under the surface without a fight. She didn't want to think about the choking and blind terror. But she made herself hope the struggle was brief and that Fred had stayed beside her.

They never found her mother.

Up near the point of land a week later, a lobsterwoman read the phone number off Fred's dog tag and called. It was still attached to his collar, which was still attached to him, and the woman was kind enough not to say what he looked like. Because of Fred, no one needed to be in any doubt about what had become of her mother. Not that there'd been any doubt.

You go on, you just go on, her mother's voice said in her ear.

For most of her life, her mother had hooked rugs. The last rug she made turned out to be a map of her disheveled mind, with its spattered random colors. Every morning, Liddie stepped out of bed onto that final rug, worn and faded like the other rugs, one in each of the kids' bedrooms. They'd been vacuumed so many times over the years, they were slick with wear.

Margreete always put on a recording of bagpipe music when she vacuumed. That unholy, bladdery racket followed her as she moved the hose around her yellow kitchen table and banged its brushy forehead into walls. After she finished cleaning, she'd sit perfectly still in a chair and listen to Marian Anderson. Once Liddie asked her why she was crying over the music. She waved her daughter away. "I'm not crying."

Most people were sympathetic. But a busybody who worked at the elder day care ran into Liddie in the grocery store and asked how Margreete had gotten out.

"The door was locked," Liddie said. "She found the key."

"Where was it?"

"She found it, that's all."

"She'd be alive if you'd put her in a home where she belonged."

"She belonged where people loved her." She steered around the woman and careened down the aisle. Under her breath, she whispered, "How dare you? You old bag." She turned the corner into the next aisle, grabbed a box of Rice Krispies, and there was that woman again, coming the other way.

"I'm sorry I ever let you near my mother," Liddie said. "She never liked you." In a spasm of fury, she rammed the woman's cart, shoving it against a shelf of dog food. By the time she got to dairy, she was weeping so hard, she abandoned the cart, got into the car, and started home.

She nearly made it before she broke down again and had to pull over. Back home, she went upstairs without thinking, opened the door to her mother's room, took off her shoes, and climbed into the bed. She pulled the covers up to her chin, then over the top of her head, and lay in the semi-dark, enveloped in her mother's frowsy, familiar smell. She pulled the covers away from her nose and could almost hear her mother snort at her: *What, you thought I'd live forever?*

One of Margreete's favorite skirts, full of swirling, vivid colors, was balled up in the bed. She remembered lying here as a girl, between her parents, her mother's hands rough on her skin, looking up at the four mahogany posters. Three lives began in this bed, and after she and her brothers were born, the bed continued its raptures: those mysterious, animal cries behind the closed door.

That night in bed, she told Harry about the grocery store and what she'd said to that woman. "Good for you," he said. They were propped up against the headboard, leaning against two flat pillows. Outside, a chilly rain was falling, which made the indoors feel companionable. He held her hand lightly.

"It's strange how we remember certain things," she said, "out of the great trash pile of things we could remember."

"What are you thinking?"

"A day with my mother—she let me outside in bare feet, wearing just a T-shirt and underpants. There was a mist over the fields. The grass under my feet was brown and cold and crunchy. While my mother hung up the laundry, I ran a figure eight around the two poles holding up the clothesline. Our dog, Charlie, was after me—he had a limb of a fallen tree hanging out one side of his mouth."

"I can see you there."

"A big flatbed truck rumbled down the road, carrying two shiny square stones standing upright, with straps around them. Donny Fortuna, who was driving, slowed down and waved when he saw us.

"My mother looked up, holding a few clothespins in her mouth. When she laughed, the clothespins fell onto the grass, and Charlie leapt up on her with his paws on her chest, and she shouted to him to get down. 'What?' I said to her, pulling at her skirt. 'They're not even dead yet,' she said. 'Who's not dead?' 'The people who are going to have those tombstones. They're not even dead,' my mother said, 'and there go their tombstones down the road. Some people like to get good and ready.' She flung a wet sheet over the clothesline. She always slapped the sheets around when she was hanging out the clothes."

Liddie cried a bit in Harry's arms. "There was a song sparrow that day, too," she said. "I remember its song."

PART III

55

WINTER 1967

One of the last times Harry had sat with Margreete, they were in the kitchen and she was talking about her childhood in Saskatchewan, picking at the yellow paint on the wooden table with her thumbnail. Her eyes were lit up like a girl's. Her whole face had a touch of youth in it and more than a touch of age: leathery, simian, wrinkles like parentheses bracketing her eyebrows on either side. It was twilight, the shadows deepening on her face and on the field through the window beyond her head. Looking at her, he'd thought of their almost-human relatives, the great apes living in the forests of Central Africa, their wise, vacant, tender, sorrowful eyes. He and Margreete let a comfortable silence engulf them, and then Bernie crashed into the kitchen and the moment was gone.

Those small flashes came unbidden. Dozens of them. Margreete rocking on the stoop and wailing over her dead cat. Howling in the car because he was kidnapping her. Asking for lobster thermidor while he was cooking freezer-burned fish sticks. Calling him Harry the Lemon-Hearted at one of his low points. She saw right through him. Now, after her death, he saw the limits of his own soul: He had no words for what had happened and no useful words for Liddie. He missed Margreete more than he had his own mother. More than his father. He knew that it wasn't right for him to be locked inside himself, that he should be able to cry and to tell Liddie how sad he was, but in the disobedience of grief, the only useful map he could find in his mental filing cabinet was to resist the Vietnam War to the limits of his courage.

He asked for three days off from Bowdoin and signed up to travel to Washington, D.C., with three vets who were planning to meet up with others for a direct action in front of the White House. Liddie didn't want him to go. On the eve of his departure, he told her there was nothing useful he could do at home. Margreete was dead, and he was lousy at grief.

"If you didn't run away," she said, "you might be better at it."

"I'm not running away."

"Oh, really."

"I'm not."

"Yes, you are."

"I'm doing something I have to do."

"Why can't it wait?"

"I can't stand to live with myself if I do nothing."

At supper, he told the kids what he was doing and why. It might have been his imagination, but he thought he saw a flicker of respect in Bernie. Eva and Gretchen, no.

A guy named Jerry picked him up early the next morning, and then they picked up two other men, one in Portland and one in York. Harry had not known them previously, but the four of them talked all the way down the coast, breaking up the journey for pit stops along the way. By the time they reached D.C., he would have trusted any one of them with his life. Jerry was a shy man, loose-limbed, long-faced, with large ears that reddened easily. He'd done time for selling marijuana. Gus, a former Marine in the Korean War, sat in the backseat, big square shaved head, holes in his tennis shoes, watchful eyes, his long knees up to his chin. ("Fuck Lyndon Baines Johnson. Fuck his generals. They're not the ones dying.") Johnny was a large, bearish man with deep worry lines in his forehead. Six kids. Large extended Catholic family, all of them for the war except him.

In Washington, they slept on the floor of an apartment belonging to another veteran of the Korean War, an older soft-spoken man named Marvin, who gave them lasagna when they arrived and told them how things would be going down in the morning. They'd get to the White House early, five A.M., when it was still dark, chain themselves to the fence, and wait. Others would be on hand with placards, hot coffee, bullhorns. The press would be called in time for them to film the action before arrests took place.

After dinner, some of Marvin's friends stopped by. Marvin made them all coffee, and they sat around his living room, a couple of them on a brown Naugahyde couch, others on straight-backed chairs they'd brought in from the kitchen. It was close to midnight, and Harry was feeling his age. Oscar, one of Marvin's friends, looked at him and asked, "What war did you serve in?"

"World War II. I was a conscientious objector."

"You mean, conscientiously saving your white ass?"

"Sit down," said Gus, "and stop shooting off your fucking mouth when you don't know anything." He pointed a beer can at Harry. "I never met this guy before today, but I found out he volunteered for this experiment to starve himself. There were thirty-six men. They turned into fucking skeletons by the end. Over in Minnesota."

"What for?"

"People were starving all over Europe," said Harry. "The researchers wanted to see how to bring people back from starvation. I didn't want to carry a gun, but I risked my life in another way." He suddenly felt vulnerable, as though he could try to explain himself for a hundred years and this guy would still think he was a white bozo.

They gave him the couch to sleep on, because he was the oldest. Quiet descended, and he closed his eyes. How could you describe to someone what it felt like to be starving to death? At first he'd craved hamburgers and his mother's scalloped potatoes. Then he'd craved cake and ice cream. He'd thought of food constantly; he'd dreamed of food. He would have knocked someone down for a bag of potato chips. The researchers said it would get better, that as their stomachs atrophied, the symptoms of hunger would recede. It was a kindness that the body held for them, the way a mouse feels no pain in the jaws of a cat. That did happen. But when his muscles broke down, he was in pain every time he moved. The world dropped away from him.

Even Liddie. He lost interest in the people in Minnesota who'd become his friends. He no longer cared about what would happen to anyone, including himself.

What does it mean to be alive? To be curious. The opposite was dead. Margreete, for all her confusion, was never dead until she was dead.

It took the police a day and a half to arrest them. Harry thought maybe the authorities waited awhile to let them suffer in the cold, chained to the fence in sight of the White House, warm lights blazing like a palace in the distance, a cold fog settling into their bones at two in the morning. They slept sitting up. Or didn't sleep. Besides the men Harry had come with, there were seven other men, plus three women. Harry ended up chained to the fence near the women. Hazel, tall, with straight Joan Baez–type hair down her back, and her two sisters by the same mother but different fathers: Bee, in an ironic pink bunny hat, and Josie, short, hair dyed blond, clipped speech, high boots, don't-mess-with-me mouth. The sisters had sung ardently during the day, but as the darkness and cold deepened, fell silent.

The police shone flashlights into their faces every hour that night. Someone distributed torn-up cardboard boxes to help insulate them from the cold rising from the ground. Harry rested the back of his head against the iron fence and thought of Lyndon Baines Johnson asleep inside the great house across the North Lawn, Lady Bird at his side. But maybe not by his side. Maybe they had separate bedrooms. Who'd want to sleep next to that beagle-faced galoot? No, that was too kind. That murderous, lying son of a bitch.

Harry slapped his mittened hands together. *What am I doing here? Suffering so others won't suffer? Only Christ did that. Punishing myself for Margreete's death?*

The moon was nearly full but fuzzy. A tune went through his head, and at first he couldn't place it and then he remembered his mother singing it. *Turn off your light, Mr. Moon Man. Go and hide your face behind the clouds. Can't you see we wanna spoon, man? Two is company and three's a crowd.* A song meant for a more innocent time.

Around four, a cold drizzle began to fall.

His head felt bright-frozen.

He felt a sharp pang for leaving Liddie the way he had. The other night, after a Portland Symphony Orchestra concert, she'd walked through the door like a half-feral cat coming in from the cold, a cat with its fur smelling of snow, wanting to warm to a human touch but suffering that touch only on its own terms. She kept her distance, angry with him because he was coming here. He'd come anyway. He could justify himself halfway to the moon and back, but he didn't feel like it.

Never in his life had he been this cold to the bone. His mind floated free, like a tide coming in, semi-hallucinating. Stone-church cold, cold as a witch's tit, gunmetal cold, rowboat cold . . .

It wouldn't have taken long for hypothermia to set in that night Margreete died. He didn't know whether he felt worse about her or Fred. He hadn't said this to Liddie, but he thought that it wasn't really an accident. In some part of her, Margreete had decided. Not Fred. He was as blind to his choices as the faithful horses in World War I, shipped over on boats and sent into battle. He pictured the two of them as if from a great height, two tiny beings on the vast ocean. Margreete with the oars. Fred, his forehead wrinkled with worry in the bow. Orion above them with belt and scabbard.

The fence felt icy against the back of his head; he thought of a nail driven into a wooden fence, the way the cold point is surrounded by the relative warmth of wood. But there was no point of warmth now. Just cold through and through flesh and sinew and bone and groan. He made out the outlines of the others, locked in their own freezers, getting through the darkness. The night was quiet now, only a few cars going by. He was surprised to find himself crying. Until Margreete died, he hadn't known how much he'd loved her. He remembered her, at summer's end, flailing wildly after the silky seed helicopters of a milkweed plant that grew by the back door of the house. The gossamer filaments carrying their brown seeds higher and higher into the air, Margreete stumbling after them.

The rain drizzled on, and they were all soaked through by

morning. Thermoses of coffee appeared again, and donuts, and people holding placards, and more police and police dogs. Behind them loomed the White House, gray in the early-morning light.

The police brought wire cutters and hacksaws in the middle of the second day, cut through the chains, and loaded the protestors into several paddy wagons. Jerry, Gus, Johnny, Harry, and the seven other men went to one prison. Hazel, Bee, and Josie were taken to a women's prison; he was sorry he'd never see them again.

The prison staff strip-searched the men, told them to put their wet clothes back on, assigned two to a cell. Harry ended up with Oscar, the guy who'd asked him if he'd been conscientiously saving his white ass. Because they weren't provided with prison garb, Harry assumed they wouldn't be here long. The bail officer came by, studied each man, assigned one hundred dollars bail to each of them, and left.

Harry and Oscar sat on the lower bunk side by side. "So, what's your story, Oscar?" Harry asked.

"What do you mean?"

"You already know my story, some of it."

"They sent me to Korea. Never been on a plane before. Never been more than twenty miles from home. I was good with machines. They put me in charge of maintaining the jeeps. Halfway through I thought, *This war ain't right.* They put me in a stockade over there and then they put me in prison over here. Dishonorable discharge. When I walked out those prison doors three years later, my family said they didn't know me. Only my sister said she knew me, but she got killed. Her boyfriend did it, said she was cheating on him, but she wasn't. The guy never served a day for killing my sister."

Harry sat with his hands folded. Church hands, sorry hands.

Oscar asked Harry if he had a family.

"A wife and three kids. My mother-in-law just died a couple weeks ago. She drowned. My family lived with her."

"How'd she drown?"

"She was senile, got out one night, found a rowboat, and took it out in the ocean. Her body never turned up."

"How you know she drowned, then?"

"Our dog washed up. He was with her."

"Sorry, man."

"Thanks. I'm sorry about your sister."

"Why don't you go ahead and take this bottom bunk? You're the old man."

During the night, Harry dreamed of a painted desert. The sand ranged in color from rose to turtle green to gray blue. There were two suns—one overhead, and one setting like a sliver of moon. The sky was lit up with the streaky sunset. He walked to a place he'd seen from far away, where the sand was boiling. Out of the center rose a horse, first its head, then its chest breasting the waves, then the broad back, and finally the legs flailing up through the sand. Harry ran, fell, finally rolled over waves of sand.

He woke to the sound of a cell door opening and clanging shut. And then all went quiet again. He'd always been afraid of horses, and the dream unsettled him. He lay with his hands behind his head, listening for Oscar's breath, but couldn't hear a sound. He had no idea what time it was. They'd taken his watch, and there were no windows, only the ugly fluorescent glare from the hallway, shining into the cell.

Harry's clothes were still damp from the rain, and he felt clammy all over, on the verge of feverish. He thought about the calamity of the past years of war; Robert McNamara and his cold, fishy-eyed kill ratios. The way language had been twisted and distorted. *Pacification*, which meant killing every living, breathing being in a village. *Collateral damage*, which meant the bad feeling a soldier gets when he finds a baby crawling over its dead mother.

Oscar stirred, and Harry saw his arms sticking over the edge as he stretched and finally the rest of him as he climbed down off the upper bunk.

"How'd you sleep?" asked Harry.

"Pretty good."

"I wonder what time it is."

"Hard to say . . ." He looked at Harry. "You know something? I didn't like you at first. I thought you was a phony."

"I didn't like you, either."

"Just goes to show."

A couple of Vietnam Veterans Against the War bailed them out that morning and brought muffins and coffee. Harry paid them back the bail fee, plus some, and most of the others did the same. Harry turned to Oscar and shook his hand. "Thanks for being a good roommate."

"Yup. See you sometime." Oscar went one direction and he went another.

Before they set out, Harry found a pay phone and tried to leave a message for Liddie. He couldn't reach her, called Terry Leroux, Margreete's friend, and asked him whether he could let Liddie know he was on his way. By noon, the four of them were on the road. At first, no one was in the mood to talk. Jerry drove out of the city with Gus beside him, giving directions. Johnny sat in the backseat on the driver's side, his mouth drawing in air in a thick adenoidal sleep. Harry sat on the other side, ruminating. It wasn't the thought of his newly achieved criminal record that depressed him. And it wasn't his still-damp blue jeans or the baseball cap he'd lost. It was the futility. What had been achieved, beyond pissing off Liddie, missing work, and squandering a hundred twenty-five bucks?

During his first year of college, he'd argued with Ernest Blumenthal, an upperclassman, about whether human beings as a species were fated to keep slaughtering one another. Ernest said yes. Harry said no: It was impossible for human beings not to wake up at some point in their evolution. He couldn't believe we'd be that stupid. But it turned out he was wrong. We *were* that stupid. Ernest Blumenthal dropped out of college that semester and was killed volunteering in the Spanish Civil War, trying to be a hero.

The snow was falling gently, and the windshield wipers made a rhythmic, weary sound as they drove north. Harry remembered a passage in Homer's *Iliad* when glorious Hektor, on the eve of battle, went home to say goodbye to his wife and infant son. He took his son and kissed him and tossed him in his arms. He urged his wife not to cry and said that it was his duty to fight. There it was, all laid out, the forces that pulled a man toward war, that still pulled men: shame, honor, camaraderie, glory.

Over the slop of tires against wet pavement, he asked the others, "Do you think we've made any progress in three thousand years?"

"Nope," said Jerry, staring at the road.

Johnny slept on.

Gus said, "I don't know. Cannibalism has pretty much gone out of fashion. And human sacrifice. The Church stopped burning people at the stake. But in some places, don't they still fucking mutilate people for fun? All in all, I guess there's some progress."

"But war?"

"There's always going to be war," said Jerry.

The windshield wipers went back and forth. No one else spoke. A semi-trailer passed them, kicking up a slushy mess that slapped against the window. "Christ," said Gus. "The guy could have given you a little more room."

When Harry got home, close to midnight, the house was dark and quiet. More than a foot of snow had fallen, and someone had made a feeble attempt to brush off the front steps. It was strange not to hear the clank of Fred's dog tag or to wonder what bed Margreete had settled into.

He turned on a light and wanted to call out, *I'm home!* Wanted, stupidly, to have his family run down the stairs and welcome him. Like some great warrior.

He got a drink of water at the kitchen sink, leaned on the edge of the porcelain with both hands, and looked out the dark window at the snow thrown up against it by the wind. He could just about make out the old apple tree and, beyond it, the place where he'd buried Romeo. He imagined the moment before his own final breath, when a thousand images and memories might sprint across his brain before all was still: a boy weeping at the dining room table, told to sit there until he finished his onions; an older boy racing down a hill with his brother on a sled; his grandfather on a horse cart; an ironic bunny hat within sight of the White House; a man named Oscar. He climbed the stairs.

56

She felt the bed sag as he got in on his side. Cold entered under the quilt. Harry sighed with what sounded like relief. Or perhaps it was a sigh inviting her to notice him. She didn't want to notice him. He'd abandoned her two weeks after her mother died, and her heart felt as flinty as the ice she'd tried to chop off the front steps this afternoon before the snow fell. Under that ice, though, was a hurt too large to release. Like a wild animal, it was. If she started crying, she might not stop.

The next morning, he reached across to her in bed.

She opened her eyes, turned to him, and said something that shocked her. "If we didn't have kids, I'd say I don't want to live with you anymore."

He withdrew his hand.

"Did you think it wouldn't matter to me whether you were here or not? If I can't count on you now, two weeks after my mother dies, when could I ever count on you? If I broke my leg? If I got cancer? If something happened to one of the kids?"

"There wasn't anything I could have done if I'd stayed."

"That has got to be one of the lamest things I've ever heard."

"What?"

"You could have made a few meals. Chopped the ice off the front steps. Comforted Gretchen. Driven Eva to her piano lesson. Helped Bernie with his college essays for a start. You could have asked me how I was doing. Told me how sorry you felt. Or maybe you didn't feel sorry."

"Of course I felt sorry. Of course I did."

"How was I supposed to know that? When you just took off?"

"We have different ways of showing things."

"Yeah? How do you show things?"

"Inside."

"And how am I supposed to know what's going on inside your mysterious depths?"

"You're not supposed to know. I'm a selfish bastard."

"If you're trying to be winsome and appealing, I don't think you are."

"You're not very appealing yourself right now."

"Shut up," she said. "I don't give a damn if I'm appealing. Why would I want to be appealing right now?" They stared at each other. "Why don't you get yourself a motel room for a few nights? Or if you'd prefer another jail cell, go make yourself into a martyr somewhere else. Just don't come back for a few days. And by the way, you could have found a pay phone and told me what was happening."

"I did try to call you. And left a message with Terry Leroux."

"After you'd spent a night chained to a fence and another night in jail and you were already on the way home. Didn't you think I'd be wondering what was going on? Maybe even worried?"

"I didn't have a chance to call. And you just said you were mad that I left, and now you want me to leave again."

"Christ, Harry, don't you be clever with me. I'm tired of the meetings you go to, tired of your cohorts engaged in their holy struggles. Isn't it just as important to be here for your kids? Isn't it important to be sad with your wife?"

"Vietnamese children are running down the road with their skin burned off. Lyndon Johnson has completely distorted—"

"I'm not talking about Vietnam. I'm not talking about the President. I'm talking about you, Harry. You go too far. Can't you see? You didn't need to go to Washington right now and chain yourself to a fence."

"Are you going to throw that at me for the rest of our lives?"

"Who says we'll be together for the rest of our lives?"

His face broke. "Do you think we won't?"

"I'm just telling you, Harry, I'm tired." She got out of bed and left him there.

He admitted that righteous indignation was his drug of choice. When he gave in to it, he couldn't stop. Like what happened in the classroom with Randy. But he was no longer twenty years old, completely at the mercy of his demons, when no one could rightly expect him to control himself. His old friend from Michigan, Sam, had recently started seeing a shrink. The last time Harry talked to him on the phone, Sam said he reckoned it was time to dispel some of his lifelong demons—well, to be accurate, Sherry, Sam's wife, had said it was time, and Sam had agreed. Harry couldn't imagine lying down on a couch and blathering away for an hour about himself. What could he possibly dredge up that would be of interest? He got out of bed and put on his socks.

But Liddie was serious, like Sam's wife. Have a sense of proportion. He couldn't blame her. He'd still chain himself to the White House fence if he had it to do over again. Just pick a better time for it. And there were other sorts of shrinks. The garden with its worms and dirt, the sky and sea, the seagulls overhead telling him he wasn't the center of the whole damn universe. He got up and packed a few items of clothing into a paper bag. He left after hugging the kids goodbye and telling them he would probably be away for another few days. He tried to be calm and matter-of-fact, but by the time he got out to the car, his hands were shaking so badly, he had trouble getting the key in the ignition.

At dinner that night, Eva asked where their father was.

Liddie said, "I suggested that he find a motel room. I don't want to be with him right now."

Through a mouthful of spaghetti, Bernie asked, "What did he do? Is it because he went to Washington?"

"The timing was very poor."

"Because of Grandma?"

"Of course because of Grandma."

"I still think it's good he went," said Bernie. "It's important to act on your principles."

"Principles are fine and dandy, but your grandmother just died, and there's more to life than principles."

Gretchen took a swallow of her milk. "Are you getting a divorce?"

"For heaven's sakes, Gretchen. Why must you always jump to the worst possible conclusions?"

"Because I want to know."

"We're not getting a divorce."

"When is he coming back?" asked Eva.

"I don't know."

"What if he doesn't come back?" asked Gretchen.

"He'll be coming back."

"Do you remember when we had worms for dinner?" asked Gretchen.

"What made you think of that?"

"Because you were mad like you are now."

"Well, anyway, we're not eating worms tonight." Her voice faltered.

"But we're still not feeling good," said Gretchen. "It's like eating worms."

Something rose up in Liddie, and she began to laugh. Tears streamed down her face. Her kids watched her until she was exhausted and finally stopped.

"We'll clean up, Mom," said Eva. "You better go play your cello."

Liddie stood and left the table. She went and opened her cello case and stared at her instrument. It didn't want to play. She'd spoken the truth to Harry, but tonight she felt frightened that she'd broken something irretrievably. Gretchen had sensed it.

On the wall was the mother orangutan and her baby. The mother's face was gentle, and the baby was nestled against the long auburn fur that hung from her mother's shoulders. She wanted someone to hold her like that. She couldn't remember why she'd put the picture there, but it reminded her of a moment in the kitchen this fall when her mother had said suddenly, "Take me home, I want to go home."

She'd put her arms around her. "You *are* home, Mom."

"This is not my home."

She'd brushed the toast crumbs from her mother's chin, and her mother scowled and went to the phone hanging on the wall. "I ought to know my own home after all these years. What's the number?"

Liddie told her.

Margreete dialed their number and waited. "It's busy," she said, and hung up the phone.

"You can try again later," Liddie said.

Margreete dialed again and waited. "It's busy."

"How about some more toast?"

"What's the number?"

"Mom, sit down."

"I want to go home. Where are the car keys?"

"You're not allowed to drive anymore, Mom."

"What?"

"You're not allowed to drive."

"What?"

"They took your license away."

"Shoot me," she said. "Just shoot me."

Liddie looked at the picture of the mother and baby orangutan once more. She'd read that orangutans have a habit of sitting quietly above the canopy of a great forest, staring into the trees. People who study them believe that this behavior has been developed over millions of years—bringing each part of the forest into focus in order to find edible fruits in distant trees. Primatologists called it "the fruit stare." The behavior, she thought, sounded so calm and effective and wise, and the cello, for her, was the equivalent—sitting in a canopy above the clamor and hoo-ha, searching out her soul's food.

She lifted her cello from its case and tuned it, scraped a few tentative notes out, and then began a prelude from a Bach suite. Every note made sense. The movement began with a low E flat and reached

two octaves above to a second E flat, then progressed through a series of broken chords, changing subtly with each iteration, always
reaching for a high note before descending. There was a sense of maj-
esty and a sighing downward—reaching and falling, reaching and
falling.

57

The house was cold at six the next morning. Unless he was sick or exhausted, Harry generally rose first in the morning. He started the woodstove, made himself a cup of coffee, and sat quietly in his favorite chair for half an hour or so.

Liddie crumpled newspaper into the woodstove, then kindling and a few small sticks of firewood, until she got the fire going. She added a couple of larger logs, watched them catch hold, made herself coffee, and sat in the chair Harry normally sat in. Her elbow touched a small notebook that he kept in the crack between the arm of the chair and the cushion. She'd never known what was inside, but she opened it now, guiltily.

In his careful printing, Harry had greeted each day with a description of the sky and the wind and the sea. The sky and sea from observation, the wind speed from an anemometer she'd given him for his birthday.

Tuesday, November 15, 1966. Gray skies. Wind 18 mph, NNW, steady. Choppy seas, pewter-colored.

Wednesday, November 16, 1966. Pink sky, giving way to light blue. No wind. Sea glassy.

Thursday, November 17, 1966. Altocumulus clouds. Wind 12 mph, NW, gusting to 18 mph. Sea disturbed, greenish cast.

The pages moved her: the economy of words, how carefully he observed the sky and distant water.

He was a decent man, although she was pretty sure he'd cheated on her once. With that nurse at the hospital. It was the surprise in that woman's face when she figured out who Liddie was, the way she said, "Oh, I've met your husband," with a fervency beyond any ordinary knowing and a quick attempt to cover it. And the way Harry pretended he'd forgotten all about her when Bernie said they'd met the same nurse again. She didn't really want to know how it had come about or what it was or how long it had gone on. She thought she'd know if it was still happening. Harry was the worst liar in the world.

She was surprised that she didn't want to know the particulars. In a way, she understood completely. He'd been lonely in those years after Gretchen was born, when she'd been beyond exhaustion, half out of her mind. She'd been lonely, too. Did it bother her? Yes, it did. It was hard to know that she hadn't been enough for him. And probably still wasn't, just as he wasn't enough for her. But who is ever completely enough for someone else? It's a crazy idea that you could be, that you should be.

She'd been unfaithful to Harry only once. She'd known Jack in college before she knew Harry. They'd both married, lost touch, but Jack somehow found her, and he and his wife spent the weekend with Liddie and Harry in Michigan. The last night, the four of them were talking in the living room and drinking martinis. Liddie came into the kitchen to check on the roast, and she heard the swing of the door behind her and thought it was Harry. She was leaning over the open oven, the heat pouring into her face, lifting her hair. As she bent for the roast, Jack touched her shoulder. She stood up, her back still toward him, and his arms went around her waist and his knee between her legs. She turned. He didn't try to hold her in his arms. If he had, she would have wrestled her way out, but he stood away from her a little, his palms up. She whispered, "Yes." Even though that was all, she still counted it as unfaithfulness: If there had been a chance, she would have taken it. Later, after they'd moved to Maine, she woke up out of a feverish flu one night and thought, *Gretchen is Jack's,* but when she was back in her right mind, she realized, no, she couldn't be. Nothing had happened except the wanting.

She thought of a story Harry had once told her about his time as a conscientious objector, before he'd volunteered for the starvation experiment. He'd worked in Terry, Montana, in a Civilian Public Service camp operated by the Mennonite Central Committee. It was located near the railway line, where the COs were building an irrigation facility and pumping station. Harry and one of his buddies walked down the railroad track into town. When they reached the depot, there were some men hanging around, shooting the breeze. Harry and his friend heard one of the men say, "There go a coupla them Conchies." They weren't friendly voices.

One of them called out, "How much money they pay you?" Other men gathered.

"Who?" asked Harry.

"The Germans."

"We don't know any Germans."

"Like hell."

"Grab 'em," someone else yelled.

"We're not what you think," his friend said. "We're conscientious objectors because we believe there are better ways to resolve conflicts in the world."

"Well, ain't we all high and mighty."

"What's in your pockets?" one of the men said. "Empty 'em out."

"I don't see why we should do that," said Harry's friend.

"Do it."

Harry emptied his pockets onto the ground. Out fell a penknife his father had given him, a radish he'd grown in the camp garden, a ball of string, and some agates he'd collected along the banks of the Yellowstone River.

Liddie pictured them standing and staring at the small, benign pile. Then one of the men asked what the stones were.

"Agates," said Harry. "The riverbank is full of them. I'm polishing one of these and making a brooch for my mother. If I live to see her again."

Two men ordered a brooch, and Harry became the unofficial ambassador between the camp and the townies. They could see he meant no harm. All you had to do was look at him, at his sticking-up cowlick, his hopeful, earnest self.

When she thought about ordinary times, she saw that his small acts of decency followed her all the days of her life. Wasn't that worth holding dear, the way he cherished the sky, the wind, the sea every morning? The way he'd cherished her mother? Because he had.

If she was tired of Harry's meetings, there was something in herself that she was just as tired of: a lifelong habit of self-protection. When she was hurt, what came out of her was anger—a hard carapace of bitchiness safeguarding a soft underbelly. Like now. She'd read that in some cultures you become an adult only after both your parents are dead. She was an adult now. So, damn it, stop trying to pretend to be bulletproof. How often had her kids seen her cry? Maybe once. That time with Eva. Or when was the last time she'd told Harry she loved him?

She taught students at home that afternoon while the snow fell quietly. At first it blanketed every twig, every tip of the picket fence that leaned drunkenly toward the road, settled over the red flag on the mailbox, the peaked roof of the bird feeder, over the windowsills, laying itself down on the larger boughs of the maple trees along the driveway. It fell and kept falling, over the dark limbs of the apple tree, which turned white against the gray and darkening sky. Her last student canceled.

That night, the wind rose to 30 mph, hollow-sounding and lonesome. It shook the windows, blew open the kitchen door. Eva jumped up and slammed the door shut, wedged a chair against it, and the four of them huddled inside like peasants in the Middle Ages. They ate dinner soberly, in their own separate selves, until from outside they heard the *r-r-r-r-r-r r-r-r-* sound of a car stuck in the snow.

Bernie exploded out of his chair. He loved pushing cars. He put on his boots and coat and mittens, and Eva followed.

"Wait! Be careful!" said Liddie.

"I know, I know," said Bernie, banging out the door.

"Wait for me!" yelled Gretchen, running after Eva.

"No," said Liddie, grabbing her.

Bernie and Eva came back five minutes later, cheeks on fire, hair white, and pushed the chair back in front of the door. "It was Mr. Ufford," said Eva. "We got him out."

"He drives that boat of a car and gets stuck every damn winter," Liddie said. They draped snowy clothing all over the place, then she asked them to sit down a minute, she wanted to talk to them. They looked suddenly serious.

"Don't worry. It's good news. I called your father, and he's coming home tomorrow."

"Where has he been?" asked Gretchen.

"At a motel in Bath."

"Are you still mad?"

"No. I want to tell you something."

"Is this a lecture?" asked Bernie.

"Can you do me a favor—just be quiet for once?" She looked at Bernie, tears in her eyes. "What I want to say is this: Try not to do what I've done most of my life. Which is this. Keeping hurt places hidden. And then those places turn into anger, and I don't know where the anger comes from half the time. And that anger pushes everyone away, and I'm left feeling all alone.

"I need your father, and I need you." She took a deep breath. "It's not safe to love. There's no way to make love safe. Every time you love someone, you risk losing them. But living in safety is no way to live.

"I pushed your father away. I was hurt when he went to Washington, but I didn't tell him that. I only spoke in anger. Do you understand?

"We need each other right now. I'm sad, really sad. And I don't know how to talk about it. Grandma is never coming back, and I miss her every day. Our family will never be the same again."

"And we miss Fred, too," said Gretchen.

"Yes. Fred, too."

". . . Are you finished?" asked Bernie.

"I'm finished."

He got up, came around to where she was sitting, grabbed her hand awkwardly, and kissed her on the top of her head. There had never been a time, not since he was born, that she loved him more than she loved him in that moment.

58

When Harry first heard her voice on the phone, he thought of saying, *I'll come home when I damn well feel like it,* then hanging up. But he pictured her tumbled hair and heard her dishevelment. She wasn't pleading. She just said she missed him and had spoken precipitously. Would he come home?

He'd been staying in the Bath Motor Court, in a room with a double bed, a brown carpet, and a peculiar smell. He'd thought of asking to change rooms but figured the next room might be worse. After saying goodbye to the kids on Friday morning, he'd gone to work, too upset to get much done. He bought a sandwich and a Coke for lunch, a hamburger for dinner, and returned to the motel that evening. He thought he'd cheer himself up watching *Star Trek*, but the episode featured an eerie parallel universe, too close to what was happening: one of him home where he belonged and one of him here in this strange dingy room. He turned it off.

He spent a good part of Saturday working at Bowdoin, trying to make up for the time he'd missed while he was in D.C. Snow fell all day, so heavily that he left the college at two in the afternoon. He stopped briefly at the Brunswick Diner for fried haddock, french fries, and coleslaw. The diner was nearly deserted, and he made his way back to the motel, his car laboring through the half-plowed roads.

Liddie called him at four that day. They didn't discuss what had happened, but it was clear that neither of them wanted to go on like this. Harry, hanging on to a shred of dignity and trying to return home on his own terms, told her he'd be back early after-noon Sunday.

He checked out of the motel the next morning, feeling buoyant, worked at Bowdoin that morning, and was about to start home when he had a thought and detoured into Bath. It was Gretchen he had in mind, who'd told him that Grandma and all their animals were dead and it made her feel bad. Snow was piled everywhere, and the plows were out in full force. Most stores were closed on Sundays, but some of the small ones ducked the blue laws and opened at random times. He stopped for gas and was pleased and surprised to find Happy Paws open just around the corner. The owner was a gaunt, lank-haired man sucking on a toothpick, who said the wife had wanted him out of the house. He'd had to close early on Saturday because of the snow.

Harry went straight to a pair of puppies—malamute and hus-kie mix—with soft fur and fat tummies, rolling over each other in their sawdust bedding. But a new dog required a summit meeting. He thought, *Turtle. Easy to care for, uncontroversial.* But the pet-store guy told him they could be difficult to keep alive. Parrot? No, they lived too long and were bad-tempered. Parakeet? Who wants to keep something in a cage? And they died too easily, stiff feet stretched to the sky.

He turned to the kittens—three long-haired gray ones sleeping in a cage. In another cage, a scrawny black-and-white kitten stood wobbling on its skinny legs. Harry crouched down. The little guy was a mess, unkempt, smudgy, with small white feet. "Where'd you get this one?"

"I don't know," said the pet-store guy. "A goat farmer brought him in. Said he already had enough cats in the barn, thought about drowning him, but it always made him feel bad."

"Does he have fleas?"

"Probably."

"How much do you want for him?"

"A dollar. He's nothing special."

"That's not a good way to get rid of him."

"Well, does he look special to you?"

"He'll turn out special. I'll take a bag of kitten food. And two bags of litter. And some flea powder."

Harry walked through the door of the house, set down a cardboard box, and Liddie put both her arms around his neck and drew his head toward her. He kissed her, then stooped and kissed Gretchen and told her he had a surprise for her. He opened the box and held up the tiny yowler with its short, crisp tail.

"Aww, awww!" She picked him up. "What's his name?"

"What do you think? How about Liberace? For his tuxedo?"

"No."

"How about Yo-Yo Meow?" said Liddie. "Remember that seven-year-old kid who played the cello for Eisenhower and Kennedy?"

"His name was Yo-Yo Meow?" asked Gretchen.

Liddie laughed. "No."

"You get to choose his name," said Harry. "You know why? Don't tell your brother and sister, but I got him because of you."

"Me?"

"You said you felt bad because Grandma and all our animals died."

Gretchen thought a moment. "How about Meatball? Fred liked meatballs. I bet this kitty does, too."

He looked at Liddie. "Sure, great."

"Where have you been, Daddy?"

"At a dump."

"Where we throw our trash?"

"Not quite that bad."

"Mom's not mad anymore."

"She told me." Then he asked Liddie, "Want some coffee?" There was gladness in her; he saw it.

It was a relief to see the mess on the kitchen counters, the yellow table, the mismatched chairs, the view out to the garden. He filled the coffeepot with water and set it on the stove. Life was simpler in the motel room with the brown carpet, the Coke machine in the hall, and the proprietress who had the small white dog with the squashed-in face. But it wouldn't have been simple for long—he'd learn the history of the woman who ran the place, find out, maybe, that her former boyfriend had run off with all her money and now she had to manage that hole in the wall. Or he'd discover that she had a brother with polio who lived upstairs, a man forty-two years old who never got outside except if someone carried him, and Harry would be the one every day who'd lift the man with shriveled legs out into the fresh air for fifteen minutes and struggle back up the concrete stairs with him. And the man's name would be Jimmy, and there'd be such sweetness in his heart, and maybe he'd turn out to be the world's expert on Matchbox cars. And Jimmy would tell him that he'd fallen in love in high school with a girl named BettyAnne and they planned to be married and have three children, and once he got polio, BettyAnne had left him for someone else.

He waited for the water to boil. Unless you live in a cave by yourself and speak only to the chickadees, life is messy, because humans are messy. Life isn't simple, no matter where you are.

He and Liddie sat at the table with their mugs, and she grabbed his hand. She was quiet for a moment. "I needed you, Harry. That was all."

"I don't think I ever heard you say that."

"I probably never said it."

He moved his chair forward, closer to the table. "Well, I did a little thinking in that dump. Nothing earthshaking. But I was thinking, we're not tied to Maine anymore. We could go anywhere. I don't want to move, but we could. If you're not happy here, we can talk about it."

"We're settled here. But we need to get away more without the kids. We haven't been away since New York." She stirred sugar into her mug and passed the bowl to Harry.

"I have news," she said. "The day after you left for Washington, the Agora Quartet called and asked me to play a concert with them in the fall. I haven't definitely said yes. They'll be looking for a permanent cellist. Liu Wei, their cellist now, is taking a position with the L.A. Philharmonic. The concert would be a kind of job interview. I'm sure I'm not the only one they're considering."

"That's great news, honey."

She didn't say anything.

"It *is* great news, isn't it?"

Her eyes welled up. "Yes. But the concert is all Beethoven, three of the late quartets."

"Why didn't you say yes right away?"

"Can I even call myself a cellist these days?"

"Come on, honey. That's crazy."

"It's not. I've never played the Opus 132. I studied the Opus 127 and the Große Fuge a long time ago when I was in school. But I never played them in a concert."

"You can play anything."

He had no idea what it was like. She'd seen a violist weeping with relief and emotional exhaustion after the final bars of the fugue.

"Call them tomorrow and say you'll do it."

"Maybe."

"Call them."

She gazed at him. "I'm glad you're home."

"Me, too . . . The kitten was an okay idea?"

"Inspired. He'll be a great cat."

59

SPRING 1967

That spring, Martin Luther King Jr. gave a speech at Riverside Church in Manhattan, linking poverty, racism, and militarism. Bernie listened on the radio and the next day bought a copy of *The New York Times*, which printed a full copy of it. It was radical and prophetic and made sense of, well, everything. King spoke about the way the United States was poisoning Vietnam: killing crops, setting children on fire with napalm, murdering grandmothers and grandfathers, raining down thousands of tons of bombs. Once a soldier found himself there, King said, he would realize he was fighting a deeply disgraceful war and return brutalized. And it was African Americans and the poor who would serve, out of all proportion, because they lacked other reasonable choices.

This was the road the country was on. Some of Bernie's own classmates were eager to sign up. He could name them, one by one, drunk on patriotism, excited. Noah wasn't excited, and he wasn't drunk. He just saw few alternatives.

You can't take bad things back. Not as a person. Not as a country. It becomes part of who you are. Did he even want to be an American anymore? If he wasn't an American, who was he?

His mother's younger brother, Uncle Peter, came for a visit, and he and Bernie sat on the porch together, drinking wine his parents didn't know he was drinking and watching the ocean below turn coral-colored as the sun went down. "So I hear you're going to Yale," said his uncle.

"They gave me a four-year scholarship, and I told them I was coming. At least I think I am."

"You don't sound thrilled."

"My best friend is going to Vietnam. He doesn't have any money, and he thinks this is the best he can do."

"I get it."

"The truth is, I don't really know what I'm doing."

"Who knows anything at your age? That's nothing to be ashamed of."

Uncle Peter told him that on the bus from Boston, he'd sat next to a Marine returning from Vietnam. The guy told him that he'd been a gunner in a Huey helicopter outfitted with an M60 machine gun. One day, they flew over an old man tending his water buffalo. He was wearing those black pajamas everybody wears, the gunner said. He decided to shoot the buffalo, just for the hell of it. The buffalo staggered, got up, and finally fell, and the old man ran to him and knelt beside him; from above, he looked as though he was crying. Or maybe praying. And then the gunner decided to shoot the old man, too, who ran zigzag across the field before he fell down. "That man was haunted by what he did."

After Bernie and Uncle Peter finished talking and his uncle went into the house, Bernie threw up in the bushes, partly from the wine but more from the thought of that buffalo going down like an ancient tree and the old man zigzagging across the rice paddy.

He remembered watching war footage on TV with his family, and his grandmother asking, over and over, "Why are they doing that?"

He went downstairs and got on his bike, a bit wobbly from the wine, his brain buzzing. He hadn't planned to head toward Noah's house, but his bike was like a horse that led him there. It turned out that no one was home except Noah's sister, Sarah, who was bent over a bunch of photographs. She said Noah was talking to a man in Brunswick.

"A recruiter?"

"I don't know."

"What are you looking at?"

"Some pictures of my family from a long time ago."

She held out a tiny photo mounted on light cardboard. "This one is my grandmother—my father's mother—when she was a little girl." The lighting in the picture was dark, with just the girl's face and hands illuminated, looking at something just out of range of the camera.

He picked up another picture. "Who's this?"

"My father when he was only five years old."

"Do you remember much about him?"

"Lots of things."

"Like what?"

"The way he brushed his teeth. He was very vigorous. And the way he came home from work. He always put his car keys in the same place and took off his jacket, and then he was ready for anything."

"I'm really sorry he died."

"Me, too."

Bernie shrugged into his jacket, which he'd hung over a chair. "I remember he looked straight at you when he was talking to you. He was tall like Noah. He was a good man and he loved you, you know that?"

"How do you know?"

"I just do."

"Are you going?"

"Yeah, I have to go."

As he pedaled home, Bernie knew that this was the afternoon Noah had signed up. It made him sadder than sad.

He ticked off his own choices. College? He could picture it now: Maybe a roommate named James Wetherby III. Untouchable privilege everywhere. One black face out of two hundred.

Canada? It was harder and harder to love his own country.

Prison? People died in prison, particularly people like him.

He couldn't talk to his parents. He already knew what they'd say.

Go to college, get a degree, then you can give something back. He wished that he had a god. If he had a god, he would pray and wait for the answer. If he still had a grandmother, he'd ask her. She knew things even when she didn't know them. She'd say, *Don't go to jail. What are you, nuts?*

60

LATE SUMMER 1967

Meatball was in bed, purring and pummeling Liddie's pillow with his white paws. She patted him absently. She was wearing one of Margreete's nightgowns, which was in better repair than any of hers. She'd asked Harry last night if he minded. He said no, the nightgown smelled like her now. It wasn't the only thing of her mother's she wore. There was a blouse from Mexico, a gypsy skirt, a sweater she'd wrap herself in this coming winter. And she'd keep Irving's lumberman jacket for bringing in wood from the woodpile, even though it made her want to cry.

The clock beside her was ticking to itself in its quiet little frenzy of timekeeping. She'd picked up this clock, with its red face, in a yard sale over on the open Atlantic side of the peninsula. She'd held it up to her ear to make sure it didn't have an annoying tick, and all she could hear was the sound of the waves. She paid fifty cents for it, brought it home, and here it was. *Tick. Tick.*

Noah had already left for the Air Force, and in a few weeks Bernie would be gone. These days she found herself following him everywhere with her eyes. She figured it bugged him, but she couldn't stop. And she thought about Noah every day. He was at Lackland Air Force Base in Bexar County, Texas. During "zero week," he'd get a bunch of shots, he'd receive his clothes and boots, and they'd shave his head. *No, SIR! Yes, SIR!* He was allowed to receive letters, but he couldn't send any for a month. Liddie had sent a letter to Squadron 3702, and she thought Bernie wrote often, although she didn't ask.

Noah had trained the whole summer—running ten miles three times a week, push-ups, sit-ups, pull-ups. There wasn't an ounce of fat on him when he slung his duffel bag over his shoulder and got on the bus from Portland. She pictured him running with his squadron down a dusty road before dawn and imagined a staff sergeant yelling and saw Airman Eagling slithering facedown over sand, rifle in one hand, inching forward in the desert heat. Where he was going, he could be killed, could be killed, could be killed.

Harry wouldn't talk about it. Neither would Bernie.

This country, *her* country, would never recover from Vietnam. She knew this in her heart. It was impossible to argue anymore that we were the good guys, not that we ever really were. She thought of the history books she'd grown up reading in school: the Puritans happy to make friends with the Indians, the Indians eager to share their food. The United States, the world's greatest-ever experiment in democracy. A pure, classless society. Slavery? Well, yes, that happened, but that was all behind us now, thank goodness. Yes, there were a few Indians who had to be removed to reservations, but it was for their own good, and they were contented on their new lands.

Millions of schoolchildren had been fed these lies over generations, but now the lies were so toxic, not even Lyndon Baines Johnson could believe them. You could see it in his haggard face. He knew this war was not winnable, yet every day he sent young men and women over there to kill and to die.

Were you for or against? If she met people on the opposite side, she could hardly bear to speak to them. And now Bernie was reading pamphlets about war resistance. She'd tried again only yesterday to get him to register as a conscientious objector. "You need to think ahead to the time you'll be out of school."

"I'm not going to be a CO," he said. "They'd give it to me because I'm good at arguing, but how about the thousands of people who can't get it?"

"And you'd go to Vietnam, just to be fair?"

"No. I'd go to Canada, or I'd go to prison."

They were in the kitchen. She was scrubbing potatoes, he sitting backward in a chair. The sun in its golden hour shone through the window over the sink. Bernie had trained with Noah for much of the summer. His body had grown strong and his boyishly round head, framed now with dark hair, had lengthened.

"Not prison, Bernie, please. If you can't keep out of jail for yourself, do it for me."

"Muhammad Ali is probably going to end up there."

"You admire his courage. I admire him, too, but there's a difference between you and him. Who's going to beat up Muhammad Ali in jail? Or try to rape him? I don't think the average war resister fares all that well behind bars."

He didn't answer.

61

Liddie said she couldn't go with them to New Haven, there wasn't room in the car with all of Bernie's stuff, but there was room, and everyone knew it. If Fred, with his radar for emotional distress, had been alive, he would have leaned on her and nosed her hand. Before Bernie loaded his last box of books into the car, his mother stood with him in his room, holding the tops of his arms. "Try not to be like Uncle Willard, who knows the answer to everything." Her voice cracked and she began to cry. "Be your very own dear self. And think of us every so often. I love you, baby."

Bernie kissed her cheek. "It's not as though I won't be back," he said, then mumbled, "I love you, too, Mom."

As he and his father drove away, he looked behind him at the house. His mother and Eva and Gretchen were all standing on the porch, waving. He imagined his mother slowly climbing the stairs to his room, sitting on his bed, and smelling one of his T-shirts or something. He didn't want to feel what he was feeling right now. College students were meant to be ironic.

They drove down the road, that familiar road he knew every inch of. He thought for a moment of telling his father to turn the car around. *I'm not going.* He ought to be fighting this filthy war with everything he had in him. But he didn't have the guts that Muhammad Ali did. Anyway, college had already been sort of decided for him. Well, no. He'd decided. At least for now. Take responsibility for it.

He was going to college. And he hoped it would be better than high school, which had sucked something out of him. There were so many things he couldn't say, or do, or even think. You had to pretend you'd rather read comic books than Tolstoy, you couldn't say you thought football was a stupid, violent sport, and if you were in love with your friend, this secret was buried deeper than the Mariana Trench. You never let on that you liked to bake chocolate cakes with vanilla cream frosting; you pretended that you were too shy to ask anyone out, or, if that failed, you pretended that you liked driving a car, your arm like a dead fish around a girl with a beehive hairdo, every hair on her head lacquered like a bug in amber. All around you, conversations flew: Lorelei's stand-up tits, Kendra's wet lips, born to be sucked. You envied the ease of others' longings, but you wouldn't have given up your own for anything in the world, as complicated and untouchable as they were. He imagined things would be different where he was going, but maybe not all that different.

Lawrence Kingsley Jr. turned out to be his new roommate, and he'd already claimed the best bed and staked out the better closet. Bernie disliked him on sight. After Harry left for home, Lawrence's first question was, "What does your daddy do?" Placing him in the social order, a hint of disparagement in the word *daddy*.

Bernie told him and asked where he was from.

"New York. My family summers in Malta."

Bernie couldn't recall where Malta was, but anyone who used *summer* as a verb was rich, very rich. "Nice stereo," he said, trying to be decent.

"I brought a bunch of records. I left the good stereo at home, but this one should work. You're welcome to use it. Do you like Joan Baez?"

"Not really."

His roommate looked at him. "How come?"

"I don't know. I guess because when she sings, *Not a shirt on my back, not a penny to my name*, she looks as though she's thinking about how good she looks rather than what it's like not to have a shirt on your back. She's got a good voice, but everything sounds the same."

"I like her body."

"Huh. Okay." Bernie grabbed his pile of clothes and hung them in the closet. ". . . Do you know anyone here?"

"Yeah. A bunch of us are going downtown tonight. Maybe pick up some townie girls." It was already clear Bernie wasn't invited. "My father went here, and my grandfather and my great-grandfather. It was expected that I follow suit. My older brother's a senior."

"Quite a family tree." He meant *tradition*. Which would have been a stupid thing to say, even without the tree. He'd hardly been here an hour, and he already sounded like a hick.

Lawrence asked if he had a girlfriend.

"Not anymore," said Bernie. A moment passed. "We broke up this summer. We both thought it was better to start college unattached."

"What was her name?"

"Melinda."

He thought his roommate knew he was lying. He didn't ask about Lawrence's love life, because he didn't want to.

By the end of the conversation, they knew just about everything they needed to know: Bernie was a Democrat verging on Socialist, Lawrence was a Republican verging on rabid. Bernie was against the war; Lawrence's uncle was a general.

A couple of weeks into the semester, Lawrence squashed a ladybug on the windowsill and looked at Bernie. "You're a fag, aren't you."

"Don't do that," said Bernie, not answering. "Leave them alone. They're just looking for a warm place before winter comes. That's what they do."

Lawrence squashed another one.

Through the closed window, Bernie faintly heard wild geese crying high in the sky, urging one another on, reminding him that we are nothing without each other, that there was still wildness in the world. He left the room and walked to Long Wharf, but the ocean didn't smell right; it was tamed, like a gorilla in a zoo, and weighed down with industrial waste. Back home, the ocean was everywhere and everything. You breathed it; you were it, and it was you. When the wind blew, you tasted it on your lips. It made you feel like a human: small and incidental, the right order of things. The ocean here was small, whittled down.

He wrote Noah every week and heard back every so often. Noah told him he was training to be a para-rescueman, which meant medical as well as flight training. Bernie imagined him being lowered to the ground from a helicopter into an inferno, picking up a wounded soldier in his arms. *Just don't die. Please don't die.*

When Noah had left from the bus station, Bernie thought of telling him he still had the duck feather from fourth grade. Instead, he hugged him hard and tried not to cry, but he did cry as Noah mounted the steps of the bus and turned for a moment to wave to everyone. Bernie thought he would never in his life love anyone the way he loved Noah. Now he kept seeing his friend starting up the three steps, his feet pausing. When he swung around and took off his hat, his face was soft with the goodbyes he'd said. A look—loss, fear—reminiscent of how he'd been years before, following his father's coffin up the aisle of the church.

The second letter Noah wrote to Bernie after saying goodbye ended with the words *You're the best friend I ever had.* He'd never said anything close to that in person, and he probably never would. But still, he'd said it, and that letter and the duck feather were part of the Noah reliquary—a small wooden box that he had with him at school. He'd thought about picking up some of Noah's hair once when Noah's mother was cutting it. He could have done it surreptitiously, but that was too weird.

He still thought of his grandmother most days, her face lit by candles, singing in the dark: *Happy Birthday, dear Margreete, Happy Birthday, dear Margreete, Happy Birthday, dear Margreete.* It was always her birthday, no matter whose birthday it was.

62

Liddie stopped practicing and leaned her cello against her shoulder. She didn't know how Bernie would find himself at Yale, or anywhere else. From what Harry had said when he returned from New Haven, his roommate did not seem promising. She knew that the loss of Noah had nearly shattered him—as important as the loss of his grandmother. She felt she ought to visit him, but there was the Beethoven concert, and a day later the whole family would be traveling to Washington for the October 21 march on the Pentagon. Bernie said he'd be going too, but there'd be thousands of people there, and meeting up would be impossible. She felt these days like a mother bear, wanting to draw her son close and sniff him to make sure he was all right. When Bernie was a tiny baby, just home from the hospital, she'd looked at him and spoken to him out loud: "I would give my life for you." It shocked her at the time. Some of that was still in her, but he definitely would not want to hear it now.

She was working like crazy for the concert. Beethoven's Opus 132 was so lovely it made her breath catch, the way its center was filled with deep quiet, punctuated with sudden cathedral-like shafts of light.

She was honored to be playing with this group, and she also had never in her life been so jittery before a concert. Five days a week, from early September on, they rehearsed. Because they'd never had a woman in the group before, two out of three of them hadn't yet figured out that she wasn't interested in chivalry or deference. In one way, their behavior was sweet, but she wanted them to think of her as a musician first and a woman second (or not at all). For now their courtliness was both goofy and a drag. She didn't want help getting her coat on, and she certainly didn't want help carrying her cello. If she hadn't figured out a way to carry her own instrument by now, she had no business playing it. But speaking up would just make her sound like someone who'd been to one too many consciousness-raising groups. If she ever became a permanent member of the group, they'd work it out.

Playing each of these late quartets was like being in the presence of an elder who was gradually receding from this world, the music emanating from somewhere in the great beyond.

The Große Fuge still scared her silly. The beginning was double forte in unison. Then a whisper of the double fugue to come, followed by a ferocious explosion that continued forte or double forte for 128 measures.

The sudden silence was like a death. All that life and urgency and then—stillness. She loved it all: its strange, harrowing, near-demonic energy, its ridiculous challenges, and the fact that it would take everything she had.

Eva had heard her mother say that half the proceeds of the concert would go to an organization that brought badly wounded Vietnamese children to the United States for medical care. She entered the concert hall with her father and Gretchen, and her father put an extra twenty dollars in the coffer. To the person taking tickets, he said, "It's a good cause, but it's ironic, don't you think, that Vietnamese kids are being brought to the United States for medical care, the very same country that's responsible for them needing a hospital in the first place?"

"Dad," said Eva. "Not now." She glanced at the ticket taker, a nice-looking guy she'd once met at an all-state musical event, and shrugged.

They were early and had their pick of seats, and her father headed for the front row. She knew he'd bob his head or tap his foot to the music, and her mother would see him out of the corner of her eye.

"I don't want to sit so far forward," she said, moving back. "You can hear better from the middle."

The room filled little by little, and the sound of voices rose and fell like the call of tree frogs. Since they'd lived in Maine, Eva had been to a number of orchestra concerts with her mother playing, but only one chamber music concert. This, she knew, was her mom's favorite sort of music, and she felt happy and nervous for her. The hall finally hushed, the head of the charity organization came out and thanked the audience, and the manager of the quartet said a few words. Eva gripped her chair. The door opened, and her mother appeared with the other members of the quartet, smiling.

When they began to play, it was hard to remember that the cellist was her own mother. The sound of the four instruments was huge and otherworldly, almost like wolf howls echoing off a canyon, the harmonics binding them close. Eva's breath went shallow, and her hands clutching the chair became numb and tingly.

Following the Große Fuge at the end of the concert, the audience stood up and clapped for a long time. Eva's mother bowed so deep her forehead nearly touched her long black skirt.

Afterward, they all hugged her and met the other members of the quartet, then went to a restaurant. Her mother had a glass of wine and a bowl of cream of mushroom soup. Eva had a chicken pot pie, and Gretchen had macaroni and cheese because she was experimenting with being a vegetarian. Her father ordered a big, strange sausage and ate the whole thing. And he kissed her mother and kissed her again and said how could she do such a marvelous thing, he just couldn't understand how it was possible, and her mother shook her head and said she didn't know, and Gretchen said, "Do you know, Mommy, your ears get red when you play, like Bernie's ears," and her mother said, "No, I didn't know that. That was the last thing I was thinking about."

The next day, Eva peeled eggs for sandwiches they'd take to the march in Washington. Her mother cut up carrots and said, "They're expecting up to a hundred thousand people. They'll be coming in busload after busload from every corner of the country. Some mystics are planning to surround the Pentagon, levitate it so all the bad energy will fall out." She smiled. "Good luck with that." Eva wanted to talk about the concert, but her mother continued on about who was going to speak.

"Mom, be quiet a minute." Her mother stopped, and all at once Eva felt shy. "The concert last night was the best concert I ever went to in my whole life."

"You're exaggerating."

"No, I'm not. I mean it."

Her mother put down the carrot in her hand and pulled Eva close. She looked at her daughter and pushed her hair behind one ear for her. "That means the world to me, coming from you. I've sometimes thought that when the three of you were all grown up, I'd be too worn out to play the way I used to. I'm not saying there would have been anything wrong with that. It just would have made me sad." She touched Eva's cheek with her palm and let her hand linger there. "Whether I end up being the cellist in the Agora Quartet or not, I was happy with last night. Not the applause, not the good review in the paper. I was happy with the feeling of something passing through me that wasn't mine, that belonged to everyone. . . . Well, you know what I mean, because I know you've felt it, too."

63

Bernie took a bus to the march on the Pentagon, hoping to see his family, but the crowd was so enormous he knew he'd never find them. He loved so many things here: the signs, the jugglers in bright colors, people sitting high on light poles, and especially the five gigantic papier-mâché puppets being carried over the bridge to the Pentagon: sorrowing Vietnamese faces with an enormous banner saying, TO SHINE UPON THEM THAT SIT IN DARKNESS AND THE SHADOW OF DEATH. Later, Eva told him she'd seen those same huge faces, and right after, thought she'd seen Bernie and pushed her way toward him through the crowd, but it wasn't him, and by then she'd lost her parents but finally found them again when she saw her father's tall sign bobbing in the distance.

That fall, Bernie exchanged letters with his family every week. His mother told him she'd been asked to join the quartet as their new cellist. His father liked his job and was still writing screeds in his spare time and hammering away against the war. Gretchen had a new interest in herpetology: *Did you know, Bernie, that the only states without poisonous snakes are Maine and Alaska and Hawaii? In Maine we have the northern black racer, the milk snake, the northern water snake. I don't know why people are scared of snakes.*

It was odd and sad being home at Christmas. No Noah. No Grandma. And no Fred to greet him. He'd loved the way Fred didn't expect anything. He just *was*, just a dog wagging his tail and being crazy-happy when anyone in his little kingdom came home. It was just scrawny Meatball now.

The biggest neighborhood news had to do with the Beasley family, who lived down the road in the two trailers. Mr. Beasley had finally landed a steady job driving a cement mixer—until he forgot one day to keep the cylinder rotating. The cement inside stiffened and the truck was ruined. After that, the family went on welfare and Mr. Beasley went into a state of depression. Mrs. Beasley took in laundry and began hunting with a shotgun in the woods for food. On New Year's Day, just before Bernie returned to school, Mrs. Beasley had the not-so-great idea to blast the accumulated ice off the roof of one trailer with her shotgun. She was arrested, and the Department of Human Services distributed the seven kids to relatives up in Aroostook County, leaving just Mr. Beasley with the two trailers and the unfinished bomb shelter he'd tried to build at the height of Russian–American hostilities.

After Christmas break, Lawrence told Bernie he no longer wanted to share a room with him. "Fine," said Bernie. "I don't want to share a room with you, either." He ended up with a guy named Joe Baginski: large ears, smudgy shirt cuffs, out-of-date glasses, white tube socks that sank down his ankles. They liked each other right away. "Don't you hate it," said Joe, "when people who don't know what funny is say, 'Oh, that's hilarious!' and laugh?"

Joe was a bright spot, but waves of homesickness still washed over Bernie. In one of her weekly letters, his mother wrote that she'd be playing in a concert in February with her quartet. He wanted to be there.

He signed up to tutor at Hillhouse, an inner-city high school: something real after the bullshit jacket and tie he had to wear in Commons. Ms. Dunn, the volunteer supervisor, pulled out the file of the kid he'd be tutoring. "He's a senior, but he ought to be in third grade. His mom came and pleaded with me to let him graduate."

"Do you have anything good to say about him?"

"He's failing every subject." She looked at him suspiciously. "You have to understand that these people don't really want to be helped."

The kid slouched into the room, and Ms. Dunn left and closed the door.

"Nice to meet you, Daniel," he said.

"Danny."

"So, Ms. Dunn told me you wanted some tutoring help?"

"She's a bitch. She disrespected my mom."

He looked at Danny Aranjo's wide face, the long square jaw. "What do you want help with?"

"I don't know. History?" He was supposed to write down the causes of World War I, but he couldn't come up with anything.

"Do you know how many people died in that war?" Bernie asked.

"Two thousand?"

"Forty million."

"Fuck."

"Exactly." Someone outside threw a baseball and it hit the window with a dull thud. "You play baseball?"

"Nah."

"Basketball?"

"Yup."

"Are you any good?"

"I guess."

"A starter?"

"They don't let me play. My grades suck."

"Sorry."

"It's not your fault."

They came up with something about World War I and called it good for the day. Bernie would come three times a week.

He quit the track team—he was the slowest half-miler by a long shot, and even if he'd been the fastest, it seemed pointless. And he quit Students for a Democratic Society because the leaders, all male, thought the women around the edges were only good for two things: fucking and making the coffee while the men ran their important meetings.

The war was everywhere, and nothing he was doing made sense, except for the tutoring. And except for the burning of his draft card with Joe on the New Haven green one afternoon with a group of eighteen other young men who wanted nothing to do with the draft or the war. That night, he wrote a letter to his draft board telling them what he'd done.

64

SPRING 1968

February turned to March, ice turned to running water, water turned to green grass, and cows bent to green. Gretchen had paid off her debt to Mr. Wootton and was now a regular helper at milking time. You could hear her young voice across the fields at dusk, helping to bring the cows in.

Eva was sitting by the open window with her math book open, listening, thinking about what had happened that afternoon. A girl named Norma had her piano lessons just before her. Each Tuesday, week after week, Eva had to wait for her lesson while listening to Norma thunder brilliantly through Rachmaninoff, Liszt, Tchaikovsky, never missing a note. When Norma emerged, she tossed her long, thick hair like a colt.

It was worse today because Mr. Zukauskas had asked Eva whether she was going to be a professional musician. With all her heart, she'd wanted to say, *Yes. I've never wanted anything else.*

But she said, "I don't know."

"Because if that's where you are going," he continued, "I notice you are not practicing so much these days."

Her vision blurred. "I'm sorry," she said. "I've had a lot of homework." She hadn't had a lot of homework. She'd been avoiding the piano. At first she hadn't connected the dots, but she knew now that something had changed after that hideous man . . . Music had become something else, tangled up with things gone wrong.

The previous week, her mother had driven them down to Boston to listen to a rehearsal of the Boston Symphony Orchestra playing Stravinsky, and that feeling of danger was reinforced. At one point, a timpani player came in a beat too early. The whole orchestra stopped, and the conductor said, "Again," and once more, the timpani player got it wrong. The man's brain was like a clock set on the wrong cuckoo, and the only way to fix it was to stop the ticktock and set it again. But you can't do that when a whole orchestra is looking at you with disgust and impatience, waiting, just waiting, for your brain to unfreeze. Things like that could happen with music. Bad moments. Very bad moments.

Mr. Zukauskas said, "Maybe you will be interested in this. There is a contest coming up that I thought you might apply for. You and Norma."

"I don't like things with winners and losers," Eva said. Norma would win.

"You and Norma would play together as a duo, four hands, one piano. I am thinking of the Schubert Fantasie in F Minor. Do you know it? You would take the top part and Norma the bottom."

She froze.

"Come, we will try it. You will sight-read a little."

He sat down and touched a few notes. "The tempo is like this. And your part"—he sang a couple of bars—"has one of the most beautiful melodies ever written. Gaby and Robert Casadesus made a recording. I will loan you the record if you like. Sit, sit. Don't be scared. Leave out the grace notes for now."

Four flats. She had never sat so close to him. The room was warm, and she felt the heat in her cheeks. She stumbled over the keys, thinking about how she'd just told him, *I don't know.* All her life, she was going to play the piano. She tried to hold back her grief, but she began to sob over the keys.

"Oh, no, no, what's the matter?"

"Norma is a real musician. Like you." She cried harder.

"And you think you're not?" He put his arm around her. "I'm

going to say just one thing about Norma. She never wonders whether she's good enough. But sometimes doubt is a good thing."

He lifted her chin. "Look at me. You must never compare yourself. You are a dreamer. Many dreamers are like clouds blowing here and there. But you are fierce and determined. It will be harder for you. Everything will be harder. But stop crying now. It's all right."

He dried her eyes with his fingertips. "What's special in you . . . You want to hear? Stop crying now. When you play, you don't ever leave yourself behind. You don't leave your *soul* behind. Do you understand? This is a rare thing, not something I can teach. One day, you will surprise yourself. You will wonder where all the fire came from, but it is already there, even now, waiting." He seemed to be almost crying himself. He bent toward her, as though to take her in his arms, and stopped.

He stood abruptly, picked up the Schubert from the music rack. "Here, please take this now, and go. I am very sorry. We will make up the time another week."

She collected her coat and the rest of her music, her legs wobbly. She couldn't find her voice. "It's all right," she whispered. She'd never seen him agitated like this and felt strangely honored. Her feet stumbled out of the room and down the wooden stairs.

On the way home in the car, Eva was quiet. Her mother asked her about her lesson, and she didn't know what to say. She mentioned the Schubert.

"Do you want to do it?"

"It would be with Norma," Eva said. "For a contest."

"Do I know Norma?"

"She plays loud."

"So do you sometimes."

"And she never makes mistakes."

"You're intimidated?"

"I don't know. Yes."

They were driving along Route 1, past a junk store selling old metal bed springs, lawn ornaments, rusty bicycles, when her mother braked suddenly and threw her arm out protectively across Eva. A dog had run in front of the car—a rakish-looking dog, who took off across a field, nose to the ground.

Eva had never known her mother not to throw out her arm like that when she braked. It was sweet and also insulting, as though she thought Eva was three years old. But she did it with Eva's father, too. It was her reflex; she couldn't help it. They turned down Burnt Harbor Road, and the surface grew rutted and pocked with holes.

Her mother stopped at the side of the road and turned to her. "I just have to say that you have no reason, no reason whatever, to be intimidated by anyone."

"Do you think I should be a musician?"

"If that's what you want, then yes, yes, of course. But you need to want it with everything in you, because it's not easy."

"I don't know whether I do."

"You'll know if you do."

"Did you?"

"Yes."

"I used to know," Eva said, "but I'm not sure now."

"Has something changed?"

"No. Yes. I don't know."

Her mother leaned over and put her arms around her. "Do you remember way back when, how you refused to start with 'Twinkle, Twinkle'?"

"Yes."

"You knew from the beginning what you wanted and what you didn't want," she said.

It was true. She'd known.

They started down the road again, pulled into the driveway of their house, and sat in the car awhile longer together, then went in.

Now Eva sat looking out the window at Venus, shining bright near the half-moon. She would know, her mother said. She would know.

She believed that her father hoped she would grow up to do

something about the injustice in the world, but she didn't believe she had the heart for it. Just tonight, *The Huntley–Brinkley Report* showed a segment about a group of hunters in Oregon who'd figured out that they could sneak up and shoot bears while they were hibernating. A bear woke up after being shot and ran crazily down the hill with her blood pouring into the snow. It was so wrong that Eva wanted to scream and scream. How could you stand to get close enough to what was awful so you could help fix it?

She remembered when Kennedy was shot and Katie Farnsworth grabbed her hand in gym class and squeezed so hard it dug her ring into her hand and Miss McCann told Mariah Littlefield to "shut the hell up, you little fool." That was the first time she'd felt that kind of horror. Now there was napalm. And it was worse than the bear running down the hillside. She couldn't think about it, but she did think about it. And what could she do, anyway? She didn't want to work on hopeless things for the rest of her life.

"You're a good girl," her grandmother had told her the night she died. Which meant . . . well, it meant that she'd make something of her life. She didn't know what, but in her heart she still thought music.

It was after eleven now, and everyone was in bed. She crept downstairs, threw on a jacket, and went out the door. The night felt alive with spring, with all the peeping, growing new things. She hopped on Bernie's bike and rode out of the driveway. Several miles later, she came to Noah's house. The house was asleep, and the stalls for the dogs were empty and still. She thought of the last time she'd seen Noah, the day he was boarding the bus. He'd hugged her goodbye, stooped, and kissed her on her cheek. Out of kindness.

The night was so soft, it felt as though she could hear the grass growing, the birds turning in their nests. She got off the bike and listened for a while, watched the clouds play with the moon, and finally threw her leg over the bar of her brother's bike and pedaled home as fast as she could, feeling the strength in her legs, the strength in her lungs and wildly pumping heart.

The following week, Eva waited outside the door of Mr. Zukauskas's studio for her lesson. Norma was in there as usual, sailing over the keys. Eva touched her lips to the back of her hand, nervous.

The door opened earlier than usual. Mr. Z. stood and said, "You have decided you will play the Schubert?"

"Yes," she said.

"I want you to meet Norma. She has said yes, also."

They shook hands.

"Next week we will use the last quarter hour of Norma's lesson and the first quarter hour of Eva's and you will work on the Schubert together for half an hour. You will only need to prepare the first movement for next week. Yes?"

They both nodded, and Norma glanced in her direction. The look was friendly.

Norma left and Eva entered. Her hands were cold. She took off her coat and busied herself with getting her music out.

"A moment," he said, stopping her. His face was serious. "You are all right?"

Her stomach turned over. "Yes, I've been practicing." The truth was she'd practiced like a demon all week. The first movement of the Schubert. And the last fugue in the first book of Bach's *Well-Tempered Clavier*. A Debussy Arabesque.

"But I'm asking about you, not the practicing. You are all right?"

Her voice caught in her throat a little. "Yes."

"Then we will begin again?"

"Yes," she said.

She sat down at the piano she called the racehorse, with its black high gloss. She stilled herself and took her time, breathed in, and started. The Bach fugue with its sighing motif and weird tonalities moved strangely in and out of consonance and dissonance. She felt her teacher listening, standing a little farther away than usual, but that was all the difference. He was there and she was here, her whole self and soul.

65

When Bernie heard the news of Martin Luther King's assassination, he went and wailed in the woods, leaning his forehead against the smooth bark of a tulip tree. He slipped down the tree and knelt in the dirt, crying hard. He didn't see the yellow trout lilies, the purple violets scattered near his feet, or hear the strident call of a blue jay before deep night fell.

He finally stopped and scrubbed the back of his hand over his eyes, found the limb of a tree, and bashed it as hard as he could against a granite rock until it splintered.

When he returned to his room, his hands were cut and his face covered in moss and mud. Joe was there. "The fuckers," Bernie said. "Who killed him? Everyone. We all killed him."

"You okay?" asked Joe.

"No. Nothing is okay."

The next day, a kid in his biology lab said, "It's not like he was Kennedy."

"Are you kidding me?" Bernie thought of punching him out, but he'd never punched anyone in the face before, and he felt too bad.

People were rioting in the streets, looting stores, burning everything down. Washington, Detroit, New York, Chicago, Boston, Cleveland. Skies red with anger. Good. Burn the whole fucking country down. But then Bernie saw a clip on the news of King speaking to a crowd in Mississippi back in 1966, an angry, impassioned King, blazing with everything in him. *I'm disturbed about a strange theory that's circulating, saying to me that I ought to imitate the worst in the white man . . . killing and lynching people and throwing them in rivers. . . . And now people are telling me to stoop down to that level—Oh NO! . . . I'm not going to allow anybody to pull me so low as to use the very methods that perpetuated evil throughout our civilization. I'm sick and tired of violence. I'm tired of the war in Vietnam. I'm tired of war and conflict in the world. I'm tired of shooting. I'm tired of hate. I'm tired of selfishness. I'm tired of evil. I'm not going to use violence, no matter who says it.*

So, no, don't burn the whole country down.

At Hillhouse High School, Danny Aranjo said, "You knew they'd get him."

"I didn't think they would."

Danny looked at Bernie. "Because you never had nobody gunning for you."

That afternoon, Bernie came home from tutoring and told Joe he was finished. He'd said goodbye to Danny. He was leaving Yale; he was hitchhiking to Canada.

"What? Come on. Don't do that, man. When's your last exam?"

"May eighth."

"Take your exams."

"I'm not going to. I'm leaving. This stopped being my country when that bullet hit. You said you'd go to jail, but I haven't got the guts to go to jail." He was standing over the built-in set of drawers, unloading clothes. He wanted to go home, but he thought his parents might get arrested for harboring a criminal.

"I didn't think it all the way through. I might not have burned my draft card if I had, but it was the right thing to do." He cleaned out both drawers and put everything on the bed and sat down on the mess he'd made.

Joe went down the hall to the bathroom.

He hadn't explained it right. It hit him when he listened to that clip of Martin Luther King saying he was tired of violence, tired of shooting, tired of the war in Vietnam, tired of hate, tired of selfishness. How could you not be tired of it? Guns blasting away on our streets.

The leaders we needed most assassinated. The rockets' red glare, the bombs bursting in air, billions of dollars squandered in Vietnam?

He remembered a TV program he'd once watched with his father, taken from inside the Lascaux Caves. The silence stretched farther back than you could ever imagine. He had to live from where that silence began, from that true place. Like his mother's music, true all the way down.

When Joe returned, Bernie told him he was thinking he'd go to the Canadian Maritimes. It was the same ocean there that he was used to. He had one hundred fifty dollars left in his bank account from the previous summer.

He packed one pair of jeans into a knapsack, two pairs of black socks, a toothbrush, a razor, his good shoes, two flannel shirts, four T-shirts, and the picture Gretchen had given him after she'd fallen at the water's edge. Tucked safely inside his wallet was his driver's license, which he'd need at the border, the wood-duck feather Noah had given him in fourth grade, and Noah's letter when he said, *You're the best friend I ever had.*

Joe turned to him. "How are you going to get there?"

"Take a bus to Bangor and hitch from there. It's about two hours to Calais, and then you go to Saint Stephen and Saint John and take a ferry to Digby. If I can't find a job, I'll go to Montreal. But my French is horrible."

"You could learn," said Joe.

"Maybe. So, you're going home to work at that cerebral palsy camp?"

"If they don't catch up with me first."

"And next year you'll come back to school?"

"I have to see what happens. You're going to need a car up there. Look, why don't you just take mine? I mean it. Take it. I'm going home, and my folks have two cars, and I'll just tell them that I sold the old VW. It's not worth much. You can give me a dollar."

"I'm not going to take your car."

"Yes, you are. After all this is over, you can give me a car. That way, you can take more than just a backpack. And you'll have a way to find a job."

"Are you serious?"

Joe fished in his pocket and tossed him the key. "You're doing me a favor. Really. It's one less thing to worry about."

"Listen . . ." said Bernie, his voice breaking a little.

"You'd do the same for me."

The next morning, Bernie went to the dean's office and told them, then he and Joe carried his stuff to the VW. The car was navy blue, with one fender dented in and the other fender black. Joe said, "My father's mechanic told me it's got rust underneath and someday the engine will just fall through to the ground." He brightened. "But it probably won't happen right off. Its name is Deep Blue."

They stood out on the sidewalk together. Bernie tried to thank him again, but Joe cut him off. "I put the title in the glove compartment and signed it over to you. The insurance is good until the end of the month. You'll have to find insurance in Canada. There's no gas gauge, so if it begins to sputter like it's running out of gas, you move that lever, and it puts you into the reserve tank. You have another thirty miles then." Joe put his arms around him. "So, I'll see you. Good luck, man." He adjusted his baseball cap and turned it backward. "You can write me through my parents. They'll know where I am." He dug a scrap of paper out of his pocket and handed Bernie the address.

Bernie hugged him tight. "I'll miss you, Joe."

"Shut up now. I love you, too."

Bernie started up the car and shuddered down the street until he got the hang of the clutch and gearshift, drove to the bank, emptied out his account, and watched the teller watching him. *I'm not a thief,* he wanted to say. *I earned this money.* He closed the account, stuffed what he had into his pocket, went out the door, and headed to the interstate.

When he reached Bangor, three hundred fifty miles north, the skies were gray and a murder of crows was wheeling over the Penobscot River. Their black wings made shadows on the road and over the water like a prophecy. He thought about turning back, finding his way to Route 1, wending his way down to Bath and out the peninsula to Burnt Harbor and finally to the door of his family's farmhouse. For a long while, he watched the river flow by and the crows disperse. He drank water and ate a banana and got back into the car, stopping at a gas station, where an old man filled the tank and asked where he was headed.

"Canada," Bernie said.

The man looked him up and down and said, "You one of those?"

"I guess I am," said Bernie.

"Well, I don't blame you, not one bit. I served, but this ain't a war to be proud of." He stopped and wiped his hands on a rag sticking out of his back pocket. "My sister's boy come home a cripple."

"I'm sorry."

"You going over the Airline?"

Bernie nodded.

"Ever been on it?"

"No."

"You just want to keep going. It's a lonesome road. You won't find nothing along the way. They say there's unexploded ordnance. Dow Air Force Base used it for target practice back in the day. When you get to Calais, take the middle border crossing. Milltown. They won't hassle you there. But if it's closed, you go to the one in Calais with the sign pointing to Saint Stephen."

"Okay, thanks."

"You shouldn't have any trouble."

Bernie paid him. "You don't happen to have a pay phone, do you?"

The man pointed to a greasy phone in the corner, and Bernie put a dime in the slot and dialed, thinking about that pay phone in Connecticut when his grandmother answered.

66

Gretchen ran for the phone, picked it up, and heard a voice say, "Will you accept charges?" She didn't know what to do. She said yes. The operator said, "Go ahead please," and Bernie came on.

"Hey, Gretchen. How's it going? Is Mom there?"

"She's teaching."

"Dad?"

"He's at work."

"Eva?"

"She's in the bathroom."

"Well, listen carefully. Can you listen carefully?"

"I'm almost twelve years old."

"Okay, I know." Bernie told her he wouldn't be coming home this summer and probably not for quite a while after that. His voice sounded tired and sad and strange.

"My roommate and I burned our draft cards. What we did was illegal, and I need to leave the country or I'll be sent to jail. I'm not going to jail."

"So, wait, you're leaving America?"

"Yep."

"You could hide in the shed. We could clean it out and no one would know you're there."

"I'm sorry, Gretchen. I don't want to live in the shed. The draft board already knows. My roommate, Joe, is probably going to prison, but I'm going to Canada, where they won't find me."

"Where are you?"

"If the FBI comes to the house and asks where I am, it's better for you guys not to know where I am."

She told him it was not better.

"I brought the picture you drew for me a long while ago—remember?—and I'll write to you all when I get settled. Someday, when the war is over, I'll come home again."

"But they can still put you in jail then, right?"

"I don't know. Tell Mom and Dad I'm safe. That's all they need to know."

"How would you feel if I disappeared?"

"I'm not disappearing forever. One d—"

The phone went dead. His voice stopped like someone had chopped his head off. Gretchen waited by the phone in case he called back, thinking of all the things she should have said that might have changed his mind. She dialed the operator to see if they could call him back, wherever he was, but then she didn't think that was possible and hung up. She waited for Eva outside the bathroom and told her when she came out, and Eva asked a lot of questions and went to the piano. Gretchen sat down in the kitchen and peeled paint off the yellow table.

After her mother's last lesson, Gretchen told her. It seemed for a moment that her mother had stopped breathing. "He could have let us know before he did it," she said at last. "He didn't have to martyr himself. Lose everything. He didn't even take his exams." Her father came home, and Gretchen saw the two of them out the window, hugging quickly and then walking up and down the driveway, up and down. Her father looked at his feet. Her mother looked at the sky.

Gretchen went upstairs to her grandmother's bed with a pad of paper and her drawing pencils. The mattress was stuffed with horsehair and crunched when she climbed in. Her parents had wanted to buy her grandmother a new mattress, but she'd said she liked sleeping where she could smell the horses. Gretchen remembered her grandmother sitting on the small stool in the corner over by the window and her mother combing her hair. Sometimes she could see her grandmother's face in her mother's face, like some part of her got left behind. She was glad that her grandmother didn't know that Bernie wasn't coming home. Her eyes always lit up when she saw him. He was her special boy.

She tried to draw Bernie's face, but it wasn't right, and she ripped the paper off the pad, crumpled it up, and threw it on the floor. She drew his face again and crumpled it up.

The piano stopped, and a few minutes later Eva stood in the doorway of the room, then climbed into the bed next to her. "What did he say when he called?"

"I already told you."

"Tell me again."

"I don't want to."

"He's going where it's safer. It's maybe even a good thing."

Eva tried to hug her, but Gretchen shrugged out of her arms. "Don't try to make me feel better."

Their mother's voice came up from the kitchen, through a floor grate. "Where are you?"

"Here," said Eva. "We're here, Mom."

They heard her footsteps on the stairs and then saw her face in the doorway.

"What are you doing? . . . Move over."

She was talking fast. "He has no money. And he's wrong about what you said, Gretchen. He can't get us into trouble. They can't do anything to us here, and they can't arrest him in Canada."

"Is that true?" asked Gretchen.

"Yes, it's true." She grabbed Eva's hand next to her and reached over for Gretchen's. "I love you both so much. You know that, don't you?"

Her words were borderline alarming—their mother didn't usually talk like this.

"Where *is* everyone?" yelled Harry from the bottom of the stairs. They heard his footsteps climbing, one by one, and then he stood at the threshold of the room. The bed rocked like a boat as he squeezed in on the other side next to Gretchen. "This has got to be the worst mattress in the world," he said. "No wonder she spent her nights all over the house. . . ."

"Bernie said Joe is going to prison," said Gretchen.

"If I were his age, I'd probably do the same," said Harry. "Fifty years from now, history will vindicate every single man, woman, and child who protested this war." Harry started to get out of the bed, and Liddie said, "Please come back."

"What for?"

"Just come back, won't you? I want to look for him. Right now, I mean." She looked at Gretchen. "He was still in Maine when he talked to you—right?"

Gretchen said she thought so.

"I bet you anything he's hitching straight north through Sherman and up to Houlton. We could drive up the highway to Bangor, watch for him—"

"If he's made up his mind," Harry said, "we should let him do what he's decided to do."

"I just want to say goodbye." There was a hitch in her voice. "He left without saying goodbye. . . . And he's got this idea that he's going to get us into trouble."

"He said that?"

"He said he didn't want to tell us where he was in case the FBI came here," said Gretchen.

Harry stood up. "That's nuts."

Eva piled pillows and blankets into the backseat of the car. Gretchen fed Meatball, and Harry and Liddie grabbed water and snacks, checked the stove, shut windows. Fifteen minutes later, they were on the road heading up the peninsula, Liddie driving and trusting in some crazy way that they'd find him.

67

The light was beginning to fade when Bernie set out from Bangor. He pictured himself from the air, a small blue car traveling a long, lonesome road. Deep Blue had no get-up-and-go, and oversize trucks thundered by, one by one, like dinosaurs running over a plain. He'd never been frightened of semi-trailers before, but these felt unearthly and terrifying, especially the logging trucks with their giant tree trunks, like fallen warriors. He remembered the free-floating dread from a long time ago when he'd practiced basketball in the twilight. It was there in him now. *Le temps entre le chien et le loup.*

He should have used the bathroom at the gas station, but he wasn't thinking while the old man was talking. He pulled the car over to the shoulder and stopped as another behemoth roared past. He felt better as soon as he got out. The sun was slanted low and having its last moments of the day as it slipped from under a thick cloud. The smell of sweet fern rose to meet him. He stooped and picked a sprig and rubbed it between his hands, then climbed a small incline of gray granite spotted with lichen. He turned his back to the road and peed into a low evergreen, then ran down the hill and folded himself into the VW. Two more trucks blasted by. He got back on the road, couldn't get up any speed, and turned on the hazard lights as the car vibrated and shook sideways on rough patches of pavement.

He thought of Gretchen's voice. He'd lost a couple of dimes trying to reconnect with her and was left with her voice: *How would you feel if I disappeared?*

He felt he'd disappeared from his own life, too. He had no idea what he'd end up doing. Maybe get a job as a sternman on a lobster boat, heading out at four in the morning in the sea smoke, smelling the ocean every day, pulling up traps hand over hand, bringing salt home on his dungarees. Or become a war correspondent, get himself sent to Vietnam, find Noah. Someday his friend would be ready to flee that hell. He knew this was crazy thinking. . . .

He remembered one afternoon when Noah had left to go home and his grandmother asked, "What makes you afraid of him?"

"Who?"

"Afraid of that boy."

"Which boy?"

"The one that just left."

"I'm not afraid of him. His name is Noah." He picked up her hand. "I'm afraid of what I feel for him."

She looked at him hard. "Irving was Jewish. Back then I wasn't supposed to love a Jew." He was surprised she understood.

"I'm not supposed to love a guy."

"Who cares? You're a good boy. Now stop bothering me."

When he crossed the border into Canada, it would be the end of him and Noah. They'd be on different planets, maybe forever. He slowed down, pulled back over to the side of the road, and stopped. He thought a moment, looked both ways, did a U-turn, and headed back toward Bangor. By the time he'd asked directions to the airport, he was only a few miles away. He found the long-term parking lot, grabbed his knapsack, and went inside. He already knew that San Antonio was the nearest airport to Lackland Air Force Base; he'd looked it up when Noah left. He went up to the ticket agent, asked the cost of the flight, and was told it was $138. She said half that if he flew standby. The next flight to Philly would be at ten-thirty the following morning. There was a three-hour layover in Philly before the flight to San Antonio. "Can I stay here tonight?" he asked.

"No law against it," she said.

He spread out his flannel shirt on the linoleum floor in a corner near Gate 12 and closed his eyes. Sleep came quickly, but he woke at four in the morning, muddled and half crazy, squinting into the glare of fluorescent lights. Noah did not love Bernie the way Bernie loved him. He wasn't built that way, and whatever friendship there was, there never would be anything more. It had always been true and, here in this place, Bernie understood it, curled into a ball, and sobbed, driving his fist into his mouth like a child.

His throat and belly ached with the crying he couldn't stop.

He heard a soft voice. "You okay, buddy?" He looked up to see an older man holding a push broom. One blue eye, one brown eye, as though he'd started out as two people.

Bernie scrambled to his feet and wiped his face on his sleeve.

"You lose someone?"

"Yes, sir, I did."

"May he find peace in the hereafter."

"Thank you, sir. You, too. Thank you."

"Was it someone your age?"

"Yes, sir."

The man bowed his head, like someone in church. "God had a plan. You just don't know what it was."

"I guess so."

"You know, young feller, there's not a person on earth can get through life without losing someone. Sometimes you think you can't live anymore." He moved his broom a little, like it was softly pawing the ground. "I lost my wife eight years ago. And then I got fired from my job."

"Was she sick?"

"Died in a car accident. Ran right off the road into the frozen river. They think it was a heart attack."

"That's terrible."

"People tell me to move on. 'Move on, Chester,' they tell me at church, like they're in line behind me and I'm holding them up. Well, I don't believe in that kind of thing. You lose someone you love and you go ahead into the next day and they come right along with you. Wherever they are, they don't forget you, neither."

"Thank you." Tears trickled down Bernie's cheeks, and he lifted his shirt and wiped them away. That feather Noah gave him so many years ago. He'd cared, too. Probably still did, somewhere in his airman heart.

The push broom carried along a pile of old cigarette wrappers, bits of chewing gum, dirt, and the man followed it. Bernie stuffed his flannel shirt back in his knapsack and stumbled out into the predawn darkness, back to Joe's car.

Halfway to Calais, a logging truck came up from behind with its devouring headlights and blatted its air horn. Bernie was so scared he nearly drove off the road. And then came a relatively smooth patch with trees overhanging the road, creating a tunnel of deep green. After two hours, it was turning into day, and he began to see signs to the border. He stopped by the side of the road and looked at the directions he'd written down. Catching sight of his face in the rearview mirror, he stared into eyes like craters of the moon, eyes like orphans, filled with apprehension and spiced with lunacy. Out the tiny windshield, he saw small scuddings of clouds passing over a setting half-moon. *Blink went the moon and black went the sky.*

He drove into Calais, ignored the first border crossing, as he'd been told, and followed the road to the Milltown crossing but found it closed. As the old man at the gas station had said to do, he went on to the next stop and found a sign pointing him toward the downtown Calais crossing to Saint Stephen. It was still early and there were only a few signs of life on the street: two teenage boys on bicycles with a pile of rolled-up newspapers, a dog running free, a pizza parlor, closed but its lights still blazing like something out of an Edward Hopper painting. He turned toward Saint Stephen, clicked off the hazard lights, and the car stuttered up to the border gates. A border guard dressed in a Canadian uniform stepped out of a low concrete building. Deep fatigue shadowed her eyes, but she stood ramrod straight, asked for his license, and studied it for a moment.

"When will you be returning to the United States?"

"I don't know exactly."

She looked him up and down, not entirely friendly. "When will you know?"

"It depends on what happens with the war."

"You're not the first." She made a cursory look toward the back-seat of the car. "Do you have anything to declare?"

"Like what?"

"Drugs, firearms." She paused and smiled a little. "Dead bodies in the trunk."

He laughed. "No. The trunk is too small."

She gave Bernie back his driver's license. "If you're looking for a job, I happen to know that the new fish plant up in Pubnico is hiring. You might want to check it out. Good luck to you. *Bienvenue.* Welcome to Canada. Oh, and if you're hungry, Pat's down the road has decent food."

He thanked her, the gate opened, and he drove through, half-expecting that someone could still stop him.

Eva looked out the car window and thought of Bernie a hundred ways. His excitement over Burma-Shave. His big feet. His laughter. The things he noticed: A tiny brown dog in a car, with its ears blowing back in the wind. The way his leg flew over the seat of his bicycle onto the opposite pedal, all in one motion, with the wheels already turning. His attempts to become a jock, shooting at the basketball hoop, coming in the back door in April with sticky brown mud on his boots, caked so high up his ankles he could hardly walk. She thought of his footprints on the sand at Dyer's Cove, indentations that might still remain in a few grains of sand. She realized she was thinking about him as though he'd died.

He was not dead.

She remembered Bernie once telling her that if you looked out to sea long enough, you'd see a ship passing on the horizon that returned once every thousand years. People fell down on the ground and worshipped it when it appeared. When she was small, she believed this was true. Once upon a time, she'd believed everything he said. Even now it seemed that she'd seen the ship with its strange oxblood-colored sails. Huge square sails like a Spanish galleon, a big-bellied hull.

She pictured the back of his large head and his hair sticking up from behind like surprise and imagined him slowly making his way across a wide field, a bit like the one they were just passing: the grass wheat-colored and brittle with just a suggestion of green. He was moving steadily away from her. When he first started walking, it was still Bernie, but as he receded into the distance, it could have been anyone, except for his walk, a kind of lumbering. It was so vivid in her mind, she nearly asked her mother to stop the car.

She thought of their squabbles, how he once pretended that their mother was gone forever, how he told her that a tidal wave would engulf the house. His tenderness toward the crazy little ant people. She thought of the way he'd once bandaged her knee after she'd fallen off her bike onto gravel, how his fingers smoothed out the Band-Aid so gently it made the hair stand up on the back of her neck. His unreliable love. Love, even so.

Come back.

They passed through Bangor and kept on north. Harry was driving now, with Gretchen and Eva sleeping on piles of pillows, nestled half in and half out of the blankets they'd brought. The roadside was dimly lit. Liddie looked back at their two girls, heads in opposite directions, feet entangled. Eva's cheeks were rosy from the heat of the car, and Gretchen's dark hair had fallen into her face, with her hands balled up under her chin, clutched together. Liddie imagined Bernie abandoning the idea of hitching tonight, stumbling into a dark wood under coniferous trees, lying down, pine needles and cobwebs in his hair, a knapsack beside him. A bear sniffing him in the night. It wasn't wild animals that worried her. Not bears or coyotes or bobcats or moose in rut. It was wild men.

Her first thought after she learned what Bernie had done was to blame Harry for pumping their son full of hopeless idealism. But she was proud of herself: She saw the way the blame concealed her grief, and she stopped. It was no one's fault.

She turned to Harry. "What are you thinking?"

"That we'll never find him. That I love you for wanting to look."

Her eyes smarted. On either side of the road were the dark woods where she imagined Bernie to be. Surrounded by tiny, unseen creatures, wide awake in the dark.

"I was thinking," he said, "that at Bernie's age, I would have been totally unequipped to go to Canada and start over. Bernie hasn't got much more going for him, and it scares me. What did I know back then?"

"I think he'll be all right. You were all right." A half-moon had risen high in the sky, floating above the dark conifers. "I have a confession to make."

"What?"

"When Gretchen told me what Bernie did, I thought it was your fault—following in your crazy footsteps."

"Huh." She heard the defensiveness in his voice.

"I don't think that now. What did you once call it, what I do? Habits of discontent. You don't believe me, do you—that habit might be dying."

"I sort of do and sort of don't."

"Well, it is. I hope it is." She put her feet up on the dashboard. "You know our neighbors? The Beasleys? It's horrible to feel that I've gained some kind of solace from their misfortune, but that's what I've done."

"Why the hell would she shoot ice off the roof?"

"She just lost it, poor thing. I get that. What I mean is, looking at them, I see what they've lost and what we have."

"I see it, too." He reached for her hand.

The lights of the dashboard lit Harry's face. His beard had grown all day and shadowed his chin and cheeks. From the side, she saw how the gravity of years had grabbed hold of him—a slight sag under the chin, his eyes a little less bright with hope. She imagined him a decade from now: a small paunch, a sag in the shoulders, time having its way.

The cars on the road had thinned out to one every couple of miles. The trees looked dark as dwellings, the night clear and full of stars in this north country. Lonesome, too.

"What do you say we turn around?" she said.

He got off at the next exit and pulled over on a scrubby shoulder with a muddy trench beside it. They crept out of the car, and the girls stirred in the backseat but didn't wake. In the light of the headlights she spied a group of skunk cabbages. Harry leaned over and peered at them, said they smelled bad, and when he straightened out, she grabbed him up in her arms. There were many reasons to cry there beside the road, but what she didn't expect was this joy, its flood of tears.

She took over the driving, heading south. "Need coffee?" he asked, turning on the heater.

She shook her head and glanced over at him. "It's nice like this. Like a boat. The stars. The girls asleep."

"Mmmm," he went.

She made a sound in her throat, too, a kind of love-making sound.

The car seemed to speed up the nearer it came to Bath, then down the peninsula onto Burnt Harbor Road. In the darkness of midnight, they'd see the three old apple trees blooming in the field just before their driveway, a pink-white blush in the headlights. The house would be a dark shadow, friendly enough with its wide, welcoming porch, and beyond, down the meadow, the smell and suggestion of the infinite—a booming, fitful, roaming sea. As they climbed the steps with their sleepy children, they'd glimpse the light of a ship moored far out on the horizon, imagine perhaps the people on board, and would never know from what direction it had come or where it was going.

Acknowledgments

Thank you to cherished comrades in writing, Kate Kennedy, Nicole d'Entremont, Robin Lippincott, Sena Naslund, Neela Vaswani, and Alisa Wolf. Your courage for your own work and honesty in relation to mine is a huge gift. I am deeply thankful to other friends who read early drafts of the manuscript with care and insight: Rhonda Berg, Thomas Bohan, Jane Gelfman, David Moltz, and Elizabeth Young.

Heartfelt gratefulness to Deborah Schneider, my agent, who pointed the way to an elusive structure and title, and persisted beyond an ordinary mortal in finding a good home for this book.

Deep thanks to George Witte, editor in chief at St. Martin's, who saw something here to believe in. Your acuity, kindness, and wisdom made the journey of *Margreete's Harbor* into the world a true pleasure.

Thank you to Kevin Reilly, assistant editor, for your patience and hard work; and to Kathleen Murphy Lord, whose copyediting was wondrously thorough. To artist and designer Young Jin Lim, many thanks for your stunning jacket design.

To Tim Cowles, and to my family: Alan Seager, Catherine Seager, Xavier Simcock, Namdol Kalsang, and Lodoe Gyaltsen, you make each day so full of life and love.

In addition, I am grateful to Spalding University's School of Creative and Professional Writing, where fellow faculty members and students have nourished me as a writer and human. To the community of Peaks Island, thank you for the bountiful daily sustenance for heart and soul. And to Miranda and David Vinograd, I am indebted to you for three invaluable August writing retreats in Richmond, England.

Finally, I am thankful to you, my readers. This isn't my book alone. It needed you to complete a circle. And it needed the inspiration of many beloved writers who came before me, whose generous words still hover in the air and feed us all.